continued . . .

"The Dickensian detail and characters bring life to the sordid streets and alleys around London's Covent Garden . . . Highly recommended, especially for lovers of historical mysteries who like to see another time and place blaze into life as they read."

—*Washington Post Book World*

Watery Grave

"Wonderful . . . The high-minded and always astute Sir John is as companionable as ever in *Watery Grave,* and young Jeremy, wide-eyed but maturing fast, makes for a winning narrator . . . Packed with history and lore."

—*Washington Post*

"Enthralling . . . It's a joy to watch the great magistrate apply his formidable intellect to this sordid business."

—*New York Times Book Review*

Murder in Grub Street
A *New York Times* Notable Book of the Year

"A fine tale . . . Historical fiction done this entertainingly is as close to time travel as we're likely to get."

—*Newsday*

"First-rate, original, and persuasive."   —*Boston Globe*

"Alexander has a fine feel for this earthy period, with its interplay of serene reason and irrational cruelty and violence. A bewildering time, to be sure, but Sir John's judicious insight and Jeremy's naïve fascination supply a novel perspective on it."

—*New York Times Book Review*

"Noteworthy . . . A stunning double climax."

—*Publishers Weekly*

Blind Justice

"*Blind Justice* is as much fun to read as it must have been to write. Bruce Alexander has done a fine job of depicting mid-eighteenth-century London."

—*Washington Post Book World*

"A shocking solution . . . Lively characters, vivid incidents, clever plotting, and a colorful setting . . . A robust series kickoff." —*Publishers Weekly*

"A marvel . . . a good read with great historical detail."

—*Chicago Tribune*

"Alexander works in a vigorous style that captures with gusto the lusty spirit of the era. Sir John and young Jeremy are an irresistible team in what promises to be a lively series." —*New York Times Book Review*

continued . . .

MORE MYSTERIES FROM THE
BERKLEY PUBLISHING GROUP...

CHINA BAYLES MYSTERIES: She left the big city to run an herb shop in Pecan Springs, Texas. But murder can happen anywhere . . . "A wonderful character!"
—*Mostly Murder*

by Susan Wittig Albert

THYME OF DEATH
HANGMAN'S ROOT
RUEFUL DEATH
WITCHES' BANE
ROSEMARY REMEMBERED

CHILE DEATH
LAVENDER LIES
MISTLETOE MAN
(new to hardcover from Berkley Prime Crime)

KATE JASPER MYSTERIES: Even in sunny California, there are cold-blooded killers . . . "This series is a treasure!"   —Carolyn G. Hart

by Jaqueline Girdner

ADJUSTED TO DEATH
THE LAST RESORT
TEA-TOTALLY DEAD
MOST LIKELY TO DIE
MURDER MOST MELLOW

FAT-FREE AND FATAL
A STIFF CRITIQUE
A CRY FOR SELF-HELP
DEATH HITS THE FAN
MURDER ON THE ASTRAL PLANE
MURDER, MY DEER

LIZ WAREHAM MYSTERIES: In the world of public relations, crime can be a real career-killer . . . "Readers will enjoy feisty Liz!"
—*Publishers Weekly*

by Carol Brennan

HEADHUNT

FULL COMMISSION

Also by the author

IN THE DARK

CHILL OF SUMMER

BONNIE INDERMILL MYSTERIES: Temp work can be murder, but solving crime is a full-time job . . . "One of detective fiction's most appealing protagonists!"
—*Publishers Weekly*

by Carole Berry

THE DEATH OF A DIFFICULT WOMAN
THE LETTER OF THE LAW
THE YEAR OF THE MONKEY

GOOD NIGHT, SWEET PRINCE
THE DEATH OF A DANCING FOOL
THE DEATH OF A DIMPLED DARLING

MARGO SIMON MYSTERIES: She's a reporter for San Diego's public radio station. But her penchant for crime solving means she has to dig up the most private of secrets . . .

by Janice Steinberg

DEATH OF A POSTMODERNIST
DEATH-FIRES DANCE
DEATH CROSSES THE BORDER

THE DEAD MAN AND THE SEA
DEATH IN A CITY OF MYSTICS

DEATH OF A
COLONIAL

Bruce Alexander

BERKLEY PRIME CRIME, NEW YORK

This is a work of fiction. Names, characters, places, and incidents are either the product of the author's imagination or are used fictitiously, and any resemblance to actual persons, living or dead, business establishments, events, or locales is entirely coincidental.

DEATH OF A COLONIAL

A Berkley Prime Crime Book / published by arrangement with the author

PRINTING HISTORY
G. P. Putnam's Sons hardcover edition / 1999
Berkley Prime Crime mass-market edition / October 2000

The Penguin Putnam Inc. World Wide Web site address is
http://www.penguinputnam.com

ISBN: 0-425-17702-5

Berkley Prime Crime Books are published
by The Berkley Publishing Group,
a division of Penguin Putnam Inc.,
375 Hudson Street, New York, New York 10014.
The name BERKLEY PRIME CRIME and the
BERKLEY PRIME CRIME design are trademarks
belonging to Penguin Putnam Inc.

PRINTED IN THE UNITED STATES OF AMERICA

10 9 8 7 6 5 4 3 2 1

For Judith, again

ONE

*In which Sir John
reveals to me
his failures*

At the age of sixteen, in the year of 1771, I, Jeremy Proctor, could at last say that my education in the law had properly begun. Having read twice through Sir Edward Coke's *Institutes of the Law of England* and made copious notes, I had been judged by Sir John Fielding to be ready to begin the study and discussion of it with him. This, Sir John confided, was more or less the same process he himself had followed when he had read law with his brother, Henry. He was of the opinion that what it lacked in formality, it more than made up for in providing the scholar with a proper grasp of the principles of law. "It is essential," said he to me on more than one occasion, "that in learning to be a lawyer you must first learn to think like a lawyer."

Nor was Sir John my only teacher at the time of which I write (now some twenty-five years past). In an even more informal way I learned something, as well, from young Mr. Archibald Talley. He, though two years my senior, was only a bit further on in his reading of the law, and so we were no doubt well matched in the discussions which took place between us nearly every week. It was commonest for us to share a pew at Old Bailey and then adjourn to a coffee house nearby that we might examine together the trial or trials we had that day witnessed. In this way, each learned from the other, though what we learned was as often false as true—usually the product of mere speculation.

Of course Sir John knew of these visits to the law courts and of their aftermath spent in discussion, and in general he approved of them. He thought it well that I should have a companion in study, though from time to time as we studied Coke, he would chide some of my more bizarre interpretations, saying, "Is that your idea, or something suggested to you by your young colleague?" Invariably this was said with a chuckle, so that I could take no offense at it. (Indeed I could take no offense at anything said to me by Sir John.)

It was inevitable that the two should meet—if only, for no other reason, because young Mr. Talley had asked so often that they might. He admitted that his eagerness stemmed from a chance remark made by his uncle, Judge Benjamin Talley, to the effect that he thought Sir John the most skilled interrogator of any member of the London bar.

The nephew, Archibald, had then told me that he had asked his uncle why, if this were so, Sir John was but a magistrate.

His uncle had replied to that, "Because, you see, he has offended too many of the rich and powerful." Then did he add, shaking a finger at Archibald: "And let that be a lesson to you, young sir!"

But having knocked so often, Archibald Talley at last had the door opened to him. I first sought Sir John's permission to bring my fellow scholar to a session at Number 4 Bow Street. Then, having secured it, I invited young Talley round a week later. Together we sat through an early afternoon of pickpocketing, public drunkenness, and putative breach of contract. Thus it was, one might say, a typical sort of day in the magistrate's court of Sir John Fielding.

Young Talley was visibly unimpressed: he yawned; he dozed; he came fully awake only when Mr. Marsden, the clerk, called before Sir John one Nancy Hawken, who was charged with prostitution and who pled not guilty. And though it was she who stood accused, it was her accuser, a Mr. Pyle, who was made to answer most of the magistrate's questions. It became evident through Sir John's questioning that the situation between the two was this: Pyle had been her client—or had, in any case, accepted Mistress Hawken's invitation to her room in Bedford Street with the intention of committing what he called "the act of prostitution." His contention was that because she had accepted his money—it was but three shillings—she was a prostitute. Her contention was that even though she had first taken his money—"as any sane woman would do"—nothing more had taken place, "due to the fact as he was incapable, owing to his drunken state, Sir John." Therefore, said she, no "act of prostitution" had taken place. If that were the case, declared Mr. Pyle to the magistrate, then she should pay him back his three shillings. Not so, said she. "A customer pays for my time and my consent, and he got both."

There was a loud roar of laughter at that from the crowd that filled the little courtroom. Young Mr. Talley joined in with all the rest. I, having mastered my natural tendency to guffaw with the crowd, waited as, predictably, Sir John beat hard upon the table at which he sat and demanded order from those present.

"And so," said the magistrate when all was quiet again, "it was when you refused to return Mr. Pyle's three shillings that he accused you of prostitution?"

"That's as it seemed to me, Sir John."

"Then let me ask you, Mr. Pyle, would you have run forth and fetched a constable if you had been given back the amount you had freely given Mistress Hawken?"

"That ain't the point," declared the accuser. "What she done was against the law, and I'm for the law, I am."

"Admirable," said the magistrate, "and let me assure you, sir, I, too, am for the law. Yet it seems to me that the validity of your accusation turns upon the definition of what you call 'the act of prostitution.' According to you, it took place when she accepted your three shillings. According to her, it would have taken place only if some manner of sexual congress had taken place between you. Since, according to her, it did not, she maintains that she owes you nothing, since you were given ample opportunity to do what you had paid for. And so, Mr. Pyle, I am inclined to find in her favor. Mistress Hawken's understanding of what constitutes prostitution is much closer to what is generally accepted. And so your accusation is denied by me. Further, the three shillings in question are hers to keep."

At that, Mr. Pyle set to grumbling loudly, complaining at the unfairness of the decision—until the magistrate silenced him with a single stroke of his gavel. Then did Sir John call out to the accused: "Mistress Hawken!"

"I am here, sir."

"And a good thing, too," said he, "since I have not yet dismissed you. I wish to congratulate you on your defense. I must remind you, however, that as Mr. Pyle has said, prostitution is against the law. You are perhaps luckier than you know that in this instance you did naught that confirmed you as engaging in prostitution—but by your own admission you would have done if circumstances had been otherwise. In short, Mistress Hawken, if you come before me again, you may not be so fortunate. My advice to you is to find some other line of work for yourself."

She stood silent before him until, sure at last that he had finished, she raised her voice timidly in response. "I'll certain'y give that some thought, sir," said she to him.

"See that you do. You are now dismissed. And you, Mr. Pyle, if you are still about, you, too, may go."

Then, assured by Mr. Marsden that they had completed their work for the day, Sir John ended the session with another loud clap of his gavel. He rose quickly from his seat, and in a trice, he had disappeared through the door behind him which led indirectly to his chambers.

"Would you now like to meet him?" I asked young Mr. Talley beside me.

"Oh, indeed I would," said he. But then, as we moved

against the crowd toward the door, he made a rather curious comment: "Had it not been for that last case he tried," said Talley, "I should probably have begged off the introduction. To tell the truth, I was quite bored by all those that preceded it. And, I must say, I was a bit disappointed in your man, Sir John. All I could do to keep awake, I fear."

I'd suspected as much, of course, for I'd seen him yawn and doze. But to speak of his "disappointment" in Sir John? Even if he had indeed experienced such, it was hardly the sort of thing one would discuss, was it? "I thought," said I in a manner rather cool, "that you had been quite eager to meet him."

"Oh, I was, and I am," said he. "I thought him quite marvelous in that last matter, the one to do with the whore. He quite took her accuser apart, did he not?"

"As you say," said I, stepping ahead to lead the way through the door to the court's "backstage" area—the strongroom, the armory, Mr. Marsden's alcove with its files and boxes of court records, et cetera. To all of this my young colleague gave close attention. I ushered him swiftly to the room at the end of the hall. The door stood open to us. I knocked upon it, identifying myself and my companion, and Sir John bade us enter.

"Sir," said I, "may I present Archibald Talley?"

"You may, Jeremy, and pleased I am to meet your young friend." Sir John rose and offered his hand, which was taken and shaken politely by young Talley. We were then invited to seat ourselves, and the two of them began to talk.

Theirs was a pleasant conversation rather than one of true substance. The visitor praised to excess the magistrate's handling of the Nancy Hawken case. Sir John, for his part, made little of the matter, insisting that all credit was due to her. "I daresay," said he, "that formula she stated— how did it go?—she offers her time and consent and nothing more—that should prove worth remembering, don't you think?" He mused silently for a moment, then added: "I think it interesting how many matters, even criminal cases, turn on questions of contract—just as this one did." Being blind, Sir John could not then see the look of near baffle-ment that appeared on Talley's face. Yet correctly interpret-ing the lack of response from him as signifying lack of understanding, he tactfully changed the subject of their dis-cussion.

"Benjamin Talley is your uncle, is he not?" asked Sir John. "You have begun reading law with him, have you?"

"I have, sir."

"By all reports, he is a good Chancery judge. I have heard naught against him. And there are few—perhaps none—of whom that can be said."

"He also has a high opinion of you, sir."

"That is always good to hear," said Sir John in a manner somewhat complacent. (He was a man who knew his own worth.) "But tell me, what is your object in reading the law—that is to say, what plan have you for your future? Your uncle might be of assistance in procuring a judgeship for you, but that can be only much in the future. You will need courtroom experience—as a barrister, I assume?"

"Oh, I suppose so, yes." This was said with a singular lack of enthusiasm. "But neither, really, fits into my plans as a course I wish to follow."

"Well, what, then?"

I, too, wanted to know, reader, for I had ever assumed that Archibald Talley's interest in the law was like unto my own, and to me the law had always meant the courtroom—the drama of it, the combat. I was naturally curious regarding his plans and wondered why I myself had not before heard of them.

"I've my eye set on Parliament," said Talley in a manner most confident.

"Ah, you have, have you?" Was there something chal-lenging in Sir John's tone? Yes, indeed there was.

"In general, my father is behind me in this, yet he insists I have some means of supporting myself in the event that I'm not successful. Oh, I quite agree that what he insists upon is the prudent course—but reading law is, you must admit, rather a dreary business."

"Oh, it has its rewards for those of a certain turn of mind," said Sir John. "But do tell me how you plan to make your beginning in politics. Will you simply announce your interest to the world?"

"Well, the beginning should not be so terribly difficult, for Papa has promised to buy me a good, safe Tory seat just as soon as one becomes available following my majority. But after that, says he, I shall be on my own. It will be my responsibility to hold on to it ever after."

"And if you fail in that, you have always the law to fall back upon. A judgeship, perhaps? In a pinch, I suppose you might even accept an appointment as magistrate."

"Oh, I doubt that should be necessary," said Talley with a smile. "Once I've made my entry into politics, I intend to remain."

"Well, then," said Sir John, rising of a sudden from his chair, "I applaud your sense of purpose but offer a word of caution. Be not too certain of the future, for fate has a way of offering us willy-nilly that which we least expect. So was it in my life, and so it may be in your own." Then, with a nod, he added, "Pleasant as this has been, young Mr. Talley, I fear I must put an end to our chat. I have letters to dictate, and Jeremy is, as you may know, my chief scribe. In my blindness I depend upon him greatly."

"Ah, yes, of course," said Archibald Talley, fairly jumping to his feet. "You must forgive me for overstaying my leave somewhat. I was quite fascinated by our conversation. And I do thank you for allowing me to attend your magistrate's court. I found it"—he hesitated—"most entertaining."

"Hmm, well, thank you, I suppose. Jeremy, will you see your young friend out?"

As I did so, I found myself brooding upon that word "friend" with which Sir John had described Talley and his relation to me. My young friend? Was he truly? I was sore embarrassed by what he had said in the course of their conversation, and indeed before. He had not only denigrated Sir John's position as magistrate, he had also spoken dismissively of the law as a profession. I certainly believed and had heard from others that Sir John deserved better than what he had gotten—yet he was no ordinary magistrate: He had made the heart of London safe, and, with the help of the constables who made up the Bow Street Runners, had kept it so; he had been knighted; his powers of investigation and interrogation were such that even Judge Benjamin Talley was made aware of them. And, well, as for belittling the law, that seemed to me pure folly, and I must tell Mr. Talley so sometime. In fact, I determined that I must discuss a good many things with him. But I knew that this was not the time. I felt it best to get him out the door as quickly as ever I could.

It was easily done. Though he blattered on as I led him to the door which led to Bow Street, he seemed to expect no response from me to anything he said, so content was he to listen to the sound of his own voice. As it happened, when we parted at the door, he wished me a simple "good day" and made his way quickly out into the street. I then hastened back to Sir John.

Tapping on the door I had left open, I called out to him that I had returned and asked if he wished now to dictate the letters. I confess that I was somewhat taken aback at the vehemence of his reply.

"Jeremy, I give neither a farthing nor a fart whether we write the letters now or later. What I want from you, lad—and want most immediate—is a promise from you that you will not ever again bring that . . . that puffed-up, self-satisfied child of privilege into my presence again."

"Why, sir, you have it," said I. "In truth, I believe I was as pained by him as you were annoyed."

"Mind you," said he, "I do not forbid you to see the fellow. That is your affair—though why or how you should expect to learn anything in the company of such a blockhead I cannot suppose."

"Blockhead, sir?"

"Indeed! He had no understanding of my remark regarding contracts. Surely you, Jeremy, saw what I was getting at."

"Yes, Sir John. The two of them—Mr. Pyle and Mistress Hawken—had entered into a contract of sorts, yet each had differing notions of the terms of the contract."

"Bravo! Put right to the point. I daresay that fellow Talley has given no thought to contracts whatever. Perhaps his uncle has not yet mentioned them to him." At which point he loosed an abrupt laugh before continuing: "Then was I unwise enough to ask about his ambitions and plans in the law—and what did I learn? That the law is not sufficiently entertaining to hold his interest. It's politics. Ah, wouldn't it be so?"

"Who is his father that he may buy for him a seat in Parliament? I didn't know they were for sale."

"Oh, they are, right enough, and his father can pay any price. He is Lord Lammermoor. Your fellow Archibald had the bad luck to be born a second son. He will inherit nothing. His elder brother takes it all. And so Papa feels it incumbent upon him to set Archibald up in business, and the business his son has chosen is politics, which can indeed be quite lucrative. However, it is of them all one of the most insecure, and so Lord Lammermoor has insisted that his second son be educated in a profession so that he may have something to fall back upon."

"So Archibald Talley is the second son of a great lord," said I, musing.

"Yes, and that means he will be granted favor and helped along his whole life through. It is a great advantage to be even the second son of a nobleman—as you will, I'm sure, discover in your career to come."

(Ah, reader, how I liked the sound of that!)

"But let us put such matters aside," he resumed. "Now, as I recall, I began to rant in this unholy manner when you asked politely if I wished to dictate some letters. Let us indeed do that. There is one that demands special attention."

"And what is it, sir?"

"I received an invitation from the Lord Chief Justice to serve on a commission of some sort. Since I am in his debt in the matter of Constable Cowley, I think it prudent to accept."

"Then," said I, pulling a chair up to his desk that I might sit opposite him, "let us pen it at once, and I shall deliver it this very afternoon to the manse in Bloomsbury Square."

Thus the letter was written and, as I promised, brought that day to the residence of William Murray, Earl of Mansfield, Lord Chief Justice of the King's Bench. Neither Sir John nor I could reckon then what an important part that missive would play in our lives, nor that it would greatly, even fatally, affect the lives of others.

It was perhaps a week later that I came to learn a bit more of this commission of which Sir John had spoken so lightly. As it happened, it was a day that started badly for me. No sooner had I returned from a morning buying trip to Covent Garden than Mr. Marsden called to me that Sir John wished to see me as soon as I had done with the groceries I had bought us. And so I hauled the packages up the stairs and put them away in those places which our young cook, Annie, had designated as proper for storage. What I had done for her upon occasion I now did as a matter of routine—all this since her schooling had begun. Yet withal, I begrudged her naught.

Then at last to Sir John, who awaited me in his chambers. Somewhat abstracted was he, evidently deep in thought, so that he failed at first to perceive my polite tapping upon his open door. There was indeed nothing wrong with his hearing, but there were times when he did concentrate so upon his thoughts that he became quite oblivious of all else. And so I knocked loud upon the door, knuckle against wood, and called his name.

"Ah, Jeremy," said he, "come in, lad, come in. I've an idea—oh, call it an exercise—that may interest you."

"Oh? And what is that, sir?"

"To make it quite clear, I shall need you to locate a particular file of cases for me."

"And where might it be?"

"Well, in truth, lad, I've no idea at all. I simply tell Mr. Marsden to put the files away, and he does it. If you ask him where he has it stored, I'm sure he can tell you."

"Certainly, Sir John, but what shall I look for? What title has been put to it?"

He put two fingers to his chin and rubbed it reflectively as he considered the matter I had put before him. At last he declared, "Now, that is a good question. We can't very well find it if we know not what title he has put to it, can we?" Frowning, he lapsed once more into silence. Then said he, "I have it! Just tell him we are looking for the red file. That should be all he needs to know. There was a very good reason for calling it the red file, which I shall reveal to you when you have found it."

"Very good, sir. I'll be back with it as quick as ever I can."

So saying, I left in quest of Mr. Marsden, curious what might be in this mysterious file, and eager to know to what use Sir John would put it. I found the court clerk not in his alcove, where I first looked, but standing on the doorstep to Number 4 Bow Street, puffing away at his morning pipe. When I told him my purpose in seeking him out, he began to shake his head slowly, a look of deep concentration upon his face.

"The red file, is it?" said he.

"Yes," said I, "do you remember it, sir?"

"Oh, I recalls it right well. It's just I can't bring to mind when it was I put it away. Y'see, the *when* of it would tell me the *where* of it."

I nodded my understanding as he knocked ash and a wad of spent tobacco into the palm of his hand and allowed it to drop down onto the walkway. "Let's go along inside," said he. "P'rhaps I can advise you what boxes to look in."

"Well, if you would not mind, sir, I'm sure it would be a great help."

But it was not. We returned together to his alcove—a scrivener's table surrounded on three sides by sturdy boxes filled with files—where he stood looking at each one thoughtfully. He designated three that I might try, each marked with dates many years before.

I had bare begun on the first of them, when a thought occurred to me. "Mr. Marsden," said I, "is the file truly red, or has it simply a mark upon it?"

"Oh, well, I'm not quite sure. But it seems to me, now that I think back upon it, that I had an artist's brush for makin' signs and some red ink, and I just painted a great red stripe across the top of the file. Sir John asked me to mark it in some such way."

"Did he say why he wished it so?"

"Oh, he did, but his reason now escapes me."

"And the title of the file?"

"That also."

So there was naught to do but look for a great stripe of red along the top. That indeed should have made it easy to locate, and might have were it not for the disorder of the individual files. Papers—notes and foolscap pages—seemed to have burst higgledy-piggledy from each one, obscuring those behind it. It would take a great effort and much time to put them all in order. Mr. Marsden's court session notes were accurate and complete, yet he was rather careless of how he disposed of them when done. Now, I thought, if *I* were Sir John's clerk . . . (I often had such exaggerated notions of how I could set the world to right.)

The red file was not to be found in the first three boxes designated by Mr. Marsden, nor in the next three, nor in any of them piled round in his alcove. When I had been through them all, he shook his head sympathetically and suggested that since it was near noon, and the day's session of his magistrate's court would soon begin, I might wish to carry my search to the file boxes kept in Sir John's chambers; in that way, I would cause no bother and make no disturbance.

That is what I did, yet with no greater success than I had earlier had. These files seemed to be in better order, yet in contrast the boxes were dustier and more numerous. As a result, it took at least as long to examine these as the rest in the clerk's alcove. Indeed, it must have taken well over an hour, for just as I opened the last box, Sir John entered the room and halted just inside the door.

"Jeremy?" he said. "Is that you?"

"It is, Sir John, and I've still not found the red file."

"Hmmm . . . well . . . it must be somewhere about."

As he took his customary position in the chair behind his desk, I continued my search. I saw no red stripe. There was no such file. I came to doubt its very existence. Had I been sent upon a fool's errand? I could not believe that Sir John would intentionally put me on the track of an object he knew could not be found. Yet perhaps it had long ago disappeared without his knowledge. It might have been borrowed by the Lord Chief Justice. Not knowing its contents, I could not say who else might have taken it away, but of course there might be a great many.

"There," said I to Sir John, "I've been through every box in Mr. Marsden's alcove, and every file here in this room, and I can tell you in all truth, Sir John, the red file simply is nowhere to be found."

"Hmm . . . looked both places, have you? All those files?"

"Yes, sir, and the last I examined in this box was dated 1764."

"Well, if they go back so far in time as all that, you may as well look in the cellar."

"In the cellar, sir?" My heart was sinking.

"Ah, indeed," said he. "The records of the Bow Street Court back to its beginnings are kept below. If it's not here, then it must be there. It stands to reason, don't you think?"

"As you say, Sir John." (With a sigh, reader, with a sigh.)

"Ask Mr. Marsden to take you down there. He'll acquaint you with the order in which the records have been stored. Surely you'll find it there."

With that, I turned smartly and started from the room.

"And Jeremy?"

"Yes, Sir John?"

"Do be sure to bring with you a sufficiency of candles. There are many files stored there, and Mr. Marsden tells me that it is as dark as pitch in the cellar, even in the day-time."

I sighed. "Yes, sir."

It was, as described, dark as pitch. As Mr. Marsden led the way down the stairs, candle in hand, he seemed to move through the surrounding blackness with some slight diffi-culty, as if it were a substance so heavy, so thick, as to be almost palpable. And so it was as I followed him: The dark-ness pressed in upon me.

"Mind your step here at the bottom," said he. "There's a bit of a bump down where the brick floor leaves off and the dirt bottom begins."

I did as he admonished, feeling my way carefully with my toe, discovering a drop that I reckoned at no more than an inch or so. Still, it would have been sufficient to send me sprawling had I come upon it unwarned and lost my balance.

"Give me two of that handful of candles you've got, and I'll stick 'em up here in the holders on the wall and light them," said he.

We managed the exchange without difficulty, and he did as he said he would do. The light of three candles pushed back the darkness somewhat and made the cellar seem more commonplace and far less threatening. There were, it is true, boxes piled upon boxes all along the wall, indeed more than I had examined thus far up above. It looked to be a daunting piece of work.

"These go back to the beginning of the Bow Street Court, do they not?" I asked. "Back to the time when Henry Field-ing was magistrate."

"That'd be right, Jeremy."

"Were you his clerk, as well?"

"Not I," said he. "I followed a fellow named Brogden. He'd been clerk as long as anyone could remember—back to Henry Fielding's time, anyways." He stood silent for a moment, hesitating. Then he added: "Well, I'll leave you, Jeremy. I must write my accounts of today's session. As you can see, the boxes are marked by year—usually about two boxes per calendar year. The farther you go back in time, the deeper into the cellar you go."

"I understand."

He then left me with a nod and a good-luck wish and, ascending the stairs, he deprived me of a fraction of the light by which I had viewed the cellar. Should I light another candle? Probably unnecessary. Even as a child I had had no fear of the dark. Yet this place, dank and a bit mysterious, was not merely dark; it seemed somehow threatening, more like a dungeon than a cellar. From deep within it came the sound of water dripping, and from somewhere nearer I heard the scurrying of little feet. Rats, they were, and I quite disliked the filthy little creatures then as much as I do now. I wondered if they had ever kept prisoners down here. Perhaps a discreet inquiry to Mr. Marsden . . . Ah, well, I had put matters off quite long enough. I must resume my search for that ever-elusive red file. I dragged down the first box, which was marked with the year 1764, and began my way through it.

I found the red file in the next box, one that bore the date 1763.

"What title did Mr. Marsden put upon the file?" Sir John asked of me.

In responding, I held up the file, which as I had been told was marked with a wide stripe across the top, then read to him the legend printed in bold black letters upon the red. "It says, 'Unresolved,' sir. I confess I looked inside and found three separate cases, one from 1756, another from 1759, and the last from 1763, the year under which it was filed."

"Yes, I had Mr. Marsden gather the three together in a single file. He generously called these cases 'unresolved,' whereas I referred to them as my 'failures.' "

" 'Failures,' Sir John?"

"Aye, Jeremy, failures. And that was why I encouraged our worthy clerk to decorate the file in some manner with red, which is universally recognized as the hue of embar-

rassment. In other words, lad, these were the cases that left
me red-faced and full of shame."

This was altogether a surprise to me. I knew not what to
make of this confession of failure—or more, failure in tripli-
cate. Among the magistrate's many virtues, neither I nor
others would have rated humility high. Though never arro-
gant or excessively proud, he nevertheless felt himself the
equal of any man, aristocrat or noble, and superior to most.
Yet as I gazed at him across the desk there in the simple
room he called his chambers, it seemed to me that for him
now to call attention to his mistakes, his "failures," was but
final proof of his great confidence in himself. Only a man
who believes profoundly in his own worth will undertake to
criticize himself.

"I thought, Jeremy, you might benefit from my mistakes."

"Oh? In what way, sir?"

"I should think it reasonably evident, if not obvious," said
he in a somewhat peevish manner. "If you were to read
through them one by one, I believe you might put your finger, so to speak, upon the place—or perhaps places—where
I went wrong in my investigation. In each case, I believe,
my failure can be attributed to mistakes in
interrogation—though in the earliest instance bad medical
advice certainly played a part."

"But," said I, "would I be able to grasp the background,
the circumstances, of these cases from these notes?" I
glanced through them and saw, as I suspected, that there
were oddments of every sort mixed together—scraps of
paper, letters, interrogation records, and in two instances full
accounts of coroners' inquests. What was I to make of such
a hodgepodge?

"Well . . . I had thought so," said he, "though perhaps not.
Perhaps I should give you something on the order of a
sketch of each one . . . the details . . . the context." And that,
reader, he then proceeded to do.

The first case taken up by Sir John in this manner was the
earliest. In 1756 (only a year after my birth) a chemist of
Tavistock Street fell ill. His wife summoned a physician,

who diagnosed his difficulty as acute indigestion and pre-
scribed a common powder to ease his upset. Yet the problem
continued into the next day and the next. He did then rally
somewhat and throw off the symptoms of this lingering dis-
comfort. On the fourth day he was back behind the counter
of his shop, serving his customers; whereas earlier he had
been forced to remain behind a curtain, whispering instructions to his wife. That night he fell ill again in the same way;
the doctor was summoned again and was present when the
chemist expired. Sir John—then simply John Fielding—
suspected poisoning, but the attending physician assured
him this was quite unlikely: Though there were many poisons in the chemist's stock, the wife (now widow) was a
simple country girl, recently married, who could not even
read labels on the bottles, much less know the power of the
potions they contained. Thomas Cox, then coroner, held an
inquest into the death of the chemist, and his jury found
"death by natural causes." The widow sold the shop and
returned to her home, a village in Hampshire. For a time,
and a brief time it was, she lived with her mother; but then
she remarried, taking as her new spouse one near her age
with whom she had grown up. There were rumors in the village.

"And so," said I to Sir John, "you suspected her still."

"I did indeed."

"Why, then?"

"Because she was young, pretty, and half the age of her
husband, the chemist. As I later discovered, though it was
true she had no letters and no knowledge of chemistry, it
was also true that her mother was a midwife and an herb
healer with a great store of knowledge regarding natural
medicines and natural poisons."

"How did you learn this?"

"From the magistrate who served her part of Hampshire. I
at last took it upon myself to write a letter to him inquiring
what had become of her, something we would not hesitate to
do today. Yet then I had simply delayed too long to make a
proper case against her. I attribute my ill-handling to my

inexperience. And inexperience was to blame for my next failure, as well."

The next tale told by Sir John concerned the death of a young maidservant from one of London's great houses. Notification had come to him from another of the servants that she had been buried in a most irregular manner—at night, it was, and outside the gates of any churchyard or cemetery. The master of the house, a duke, had had an eye for the girl, and the duchess had been called out of London to her parents on the night in question. So it was that about midnight or sometime thereafter the servants were wakened by a great bellow from the master. He had, he said, just discovered the body of the serving girl at the foot of the stairs. She was dead, her neck broken, fully clothed but disheveled. It was obvious, said he, that she had lost her balance and tumbled head over heels down the stairs and broken her neck as she went. What was she doing upstairs, after all? Up to no good, you can be sure, declared her employer and proceeded to "find" a gold ring belonging to the duchess in the apron pocket of the corpse. He ordered that she be prepared for burial that very night, for a thief who had died in the course of her crime did not deserve Christian burial. It was done as he had told them: She was buried in a winding sheet in the garden at the rear of the mansion. When Sir John heard of this sad event, it was two days after it had taken place. Nevertheless he insisted, over the strong objections of the duke, that the body be disinterred. There could be no disputing the cause of death: Her spine was truly broken at the base of her skull. Still and all, the circumstances were sufficiently questionable that the magistrate interrogated the duke closely and repeatedly. The duke's friends visited Sir John and suggested that he was not showing proper respect for the fellow. Pressure was brought to bear. In the end, when the coroner's jury returned a verdict of "death by misadventure," Sir John pushed the matter no further. He did, however, insist that the maidservant be given a proper Christian burial and that the duke pay the cost.

"And you believe," said I when Sir John had finished

relating the facts of the case, "that this nobleman . . . this duke . . . had pushed the woman down the stairs?"

"Nothing as specific as that," said Sir John. "I believed, let us say, that the master of the house was in some way responsible for her death. Whether in forcing his will upon her he snapped her neck, or, in pursuing her, he made her run for the stairs, where she took her fatal tumble, or just what the precise circumstances were, well, I cannot say. Yet I was certain then, just as I am now, that directly or indirectly he was responsible."

"And the gold ring in her apron pocket?"

"Oh, *that*!" Sir John said with a deprecating shrug. "There was not sufficient reason to believe that she herself had put it in her pocket. All the servants gave her a good character, and even the duchess was puzzled and said that the maidservant had many opportunities to steal far more valuable pieces."

"But I take it there was no way to prove your case. No physical evidence? No testimony against him?"

He sighed. "No, nothing at all. I might have broken him down had I kept at him long enough. On the other hand, I might not have. In any case, after the coroner's inquest there seemed little to do but accept 'death by misadventure' as the final word on the matter. But I believe, Jeremy, that if you will read through the notes on the interrogation taken by the former clerk, Mr. Brogden, you will find one, and perhaps two places in which I was provided with an opening which I failed to use. In other words, I made a mistake—perhaps two."

I nodded soberly at that. "Yes, sir," said I, "if it is there, I shall find it."

"I'm confident that you will." He paused then, as if organizing matters in his head or summoning up some important detail. It was only after a few moments spent thus that he did resume. "The last of these failures of mine offers no such specific mistake or oversight—at least I, in repeated reconsiderations, have been able to find none. However, there remains with me a certain unease about the resolution of the case. But let me tell you of it—"

Two men from the North American colonies registered at the Globe and Anchor, the largest and most respectable hostelry in the Strand. Though they arrived together and clearly knew each other, they asked for separate rooms and neither voiced any objection or disappointment when the hostelry was unable to provide them on the same floor. They sometimes took their dinners together at the hostelry's chop-house and seemed to get on well enough—except for their last meal together there. At that one they quarreled, the larger and rougher of the two raising his voice often in anger, and the younger and more refined of them hissing his responses in vexed whispers. Sometime during the night that followed, the second of them evidently committed suicide, for he was found next morning by the maid, hanged by the neck. Except for the quarrel, there was naught to cast suspicion upon the surviving colonial—and he even denied that a quarrel had taken place. Though there was no note left, the suicide seemed genuine; there were no marks upon the body, nothing to indicate that he had been knocked unconscious before being hanged. Perhaps more important, the porter on that floor, who had a good view of the hanged man's room, gave testimony that he had polished boots and shoes all night and would surely have noticed if there had been a visitor to the room in question; he swore there had been none. There was thus nothing to be proven against the survivor, though Sir John was extremely suspicious of the man. The colonial gentleman claimed to know the other fellow hardly at all, having met him only on shipboard. His story held up through Sir John's repeated interrogations and, as well, against the milder questioning of the coroner, Sir Thomas Cox. The coroner's jury returned a verdict of "death by suicide" shortly afterward.

"You are free, Jeremy, to find my mistakes in this case, and I shall accept them with head bowed low. In my opinion, however, mine are sins of omission here. Should I have been more aggressive with my questions? What question did I not ask that I should have asked? That sort of thing."

I was about to make some suitably humble reply to the effect that I thought it extremely unlikely that I should find any sort of fault with him, when of a sudden he rose swiftly from his chair and announced his fear that as we talked it had grown late. "Have you some idea of the time, lad?"

I gave it a moment's thought. "I should think it about three by the clock, or perhaps a little earlier."

"If you're correct," said he, "then we've no time to spare. In any case, you must go quickly and do a wash-up and then change into your best. We ought not be late."

"But where are we going, sir?"

"Why, to the Lord Chief Justice's residence. Did I not tell you?"

Hesitating, I said, "No, sir, I think not."

"You'll recall taking a letter in which I accepted a position on the Laningham commission? Well, I received word in return inviting me to the first meeting of said commission today at four."

By this time I was near out the door. "I'll not be long, sir."

"Very good, Jeremy, but take with you the red file. I think it will prove a diversion from Sir Edward Coke—a bit of real life, something of the here and now."

"As you say, Sir John."

TWO

*In which the commission
meets and discusses
the claimant*

I t must have been strange for one new to our part of London to view Sir John Fielding out a-walking of a day. Seeing him thus for the first time, the passerby might well wonder if the blind man he saw was indeed blind. True enough, there was a band of black silk tightly covering Sir John's eyes—I for one seldom saw him without it—and out on the street he was never without his walking stick. Yet he moved at such a brisk pace as no blind man ever moved before, not timidly tapping before him with his stick but flailing out with it in bold half-circles—and let those within its range beware!

So did he make his way through those streets that bordered Covent Garden. At most hours of the day the Garden itself was far too well filled with buyers of fruits and vegetables to permit him passage in his usual reckless manner. Yet he knew the surrounding streets well from years of tromping them up and down, and those he made his own. He often went alone, even sometimes after dark, with no more than his reputation to protect him; indeed, it must have sufficed, for he had never been accosted upon his home ground. If he had enemies there—and he had a few among the denizens of Bedford Street, Half Moon Passage, and Angel Court—there were far more about at any time of the day or night who would, at risk to themselves, defend his person most vigorously. It was not Sir John's constables kept him safe, but, rather, the ruffians and villains of the district who would have him as magistrate rather than another who would be less fair and less generous.

To see him make his way through our streets, a stout figure often in a greatcoat which served as protection against our foul London weather, caused little comment or excitement among his fellow pedestrians, for he was indeed a familiar figure in the district. Venturing beyond it, however, was quite another matter. He seemed to attract a good deal of attention on his longer rambles, and though much of it was of the favorable sort—respectful glances of recognition from some and polite greetings from others—not all of it was near so friendly: A lieutenant of horse took offense and became insulting when dealt a blow upon the ankle by Sir John's wide-swinging stick; on another occasion, walking alone in the dock area on the other side of London Bridge, the magistrate was set upon by a gang of wild boys who knocked him down and stole whatever they found in his pockets. As a result of these and other incidents, he fell into the practice of enlisting my aid whenever he walked beyond the precinct where he was well known and that he well knew.

Thus it came about that I was to be his companion on the journey to the residence of the Lord Chief Justice in Bloomsbury Square. Sir John was well aware, of course, that I knew the way. He must have sent me there with messages and letters well over a hundred times since that day when, just turned thirteen, I was saved by him from a term in Newgate, made a ward of the court, and taken into his household. Ah, yes, how well I knew the path to Bloomsbury! So well, in fact, that I was able to listen, quite captivated, as he explained to me the reason for his visit, and at the same time steer him along my route with a touch at the elbow here and a slight tug at the forearm there—which was all he ever needed or wanted in the way of guidance.

It was my ever-insatiable curiosity that drew from him the purpose of the commission. Imagine my surprise when I discovered that an august company had been assembled to deal with a matter with which I myself had more than a passing acquaintance.

We were, as I recall, marching up Drury Lane, always packed with pedestrians at any time of the day or night, when I was informed by him. My astonished response was such that the moment I had made it, all heads on Drury Lane seemed to turn in our direction. "The Laningham fortune?" said I—and, reader, I fear I fairly shouted it out.

Sir John grasped me by the arm and jerked me to a halt.

"Jeremy, have you gone quite mad? These are confidential matters. They're not to be blattered out so that the whole street may hear!" He, by contrast, whispered, yet did so with such urgency and so dramatically that he managed to attract even greater attention from those nearby.

"I beg your pardon, sir," said I, quite contrite. "I simply did not give proper thought to it."

"That much is obvious."

Then did he hold me where we stood for near two minutes, forcing those who had stopped to move on around us up Drury Lane.

"Have the eavesdroppers passed us by?" he asked at last. When I responded in the positive, he nodded, and we moved on.

You may well wonder, reader, how the mention of a mere name would cause such notice in a crowd of ordinary Londoners. But only a few months past, that very name, Laningham, had been bruited all about the city. Our dear cook, Annie, who seemed to know every ballad sold and sung in Covent Garden, reported that one had been written to commemorate Lord Laningham's demise, but it was such a poor piece she'd had no wish to learn it. Yet for a time the spectacular death of the elder Paltrow and the public passing of the younger did much concern the mob; and though the memory of the mob be short, the name Laningham, possessed by one and coveted by the other, was sufficiently well lodged that these months later it could halt traffic in Drury Lane.

Sir John stormed silently onward until, having ignored my warning at High Holbourn, he stepped boldly into the street and would have been trampled and run over by a coach and four had I not jerked him back to safety. The team rushed by near simultaneous with our sudden retreat.

"That was rather close, was it not?" He seemed a bit abashed.

"It was, Sir John."

"Well, I thank you for saving my life on this occasion, as you have no doubt on others."

"Think nothing of it, sir."

"I shall think whatever I like of it, Jeremy. If I choose to be grateful, then that is my affair."

"Yes, Sir John."

As we made our way across High Holbourn when at last it was safe to do so, I wondered what it was had put him in such a foul mood. Surely not my little offense in Drury Lane. I had often carelessly done worse and not been punished with such a long period of silence. Surely it was something greater. It took but a moment until I had my answer.

"I do not look forward with any enthusiasm to this meeting I must now attend," said he without preamble.

"Oh?" said I. "And why is that, sir?"

"I have been warned that the nature, the very existence of this commission, is to be kept secret. I was gruff with you a short time ago, as I should not have been, for in truth I do not much like lending my presence and therefore my support to causes that dare not be named to the public. You saw the reaction of those in Drury Lane to that name, and I sensed it. To mention it in conjunction with the word 'fortune' is to set racing the mind of the common man, awakening fantasies of wealth and feelings of greed in him that are better left dormant. Or that, in any case, seems to be the feeling shared by those who have brought this commission into existence. They wish to keep it hid in what ample pocket the fortune—and it is a great fortune—will come to rest."

"Why, it will all go to the King, will it not?"

"You know that because I told you so, but most do not. It is a custom which has the strength of law. There is no wish to call attention to it, because to do so could promote unrest among the people—and well it might, for it is a bad custom."

"But if not to the King," said I after no more than a moment's consideration, "to whom should the wealth of a condemned criminal go?"

"Well, to the poor, to the church," said Sir John. "I can think of a dozen institutions and charities more deserving than the royal pocket. Do you not see the pernicious danger in it, the possibility of encouraging corruption and tyranny, lad? With the power and influence that a King has, it might be possible for him thus to rob his nobles of all their lands and wealth."

Naive lad that I was, I could scarce believe my ears. "You mean, by arranging their conviction?" said I, holding my voice down as my indignation rose. "Why, sir, King George would never do such a thing! He is as good and just a monarch as could be."

"I agree," said Sir John. "*He* would not, but that does not mean that another would be equally restrained by a sense of what is good and just. We need not look too far back in history to find kings of Britain who were capable of great misdeeds."

"Oh," said I after a long pause, "I see your point."

"At long last," said he. "As I have told you before, Jeremy, to be a lawyer, you must learn to think as a lawyer."

"Yes, Sir John."

"I myself think as a lawyer, and being of that habit of mind, I greatly fear that the sole purpose of this commission is to ensure that the King gets his fair share of the fortune—which is to say, all of it."

Thus did we come to Bloomsbury Square and the residence of the Lord Chief Justice. By the time we had arrived, the magistrate had made it clear that he wished me with him at this initial meeting, if for no other reason than there would be a few present whom he had never met and he wished me to give him physical sketches to match his voice impressions. He instructed me to take a place directly behind his chair, close enough that all I need do was bend to him to hear his instructions or answer his requests.

The butler, my old adversary, threw open the great door in response to my persistent knock. Seeing my face first, he prepared to make his usual effort to send me swiftly away; but then did he perceive Sir John's face and figure behind me, altered his expression, and bowed us in.

"Right this way, Sir John," said he. "The gentlemen will gather in the library."

"Are we the first?" asked Sir John.

"Among the first. Lord Mansfield awaits you there, with Sir Patrick Spenser."

"Ah!" said Sir John. "The Solicitor-General, no less."

"Yes, sir," said the butler, "and another gentleman, a certain Mr. Trezavant, who, I believe, holds the office of coroner of Westminster."

This exchange had taken us as far as the library door, which was closed to us. Rather than open it directly, the butler poised to knock. Yet just then the door swung open, and the Lord Chief Justice appeared in company with one who was decidedly not Mr. Trezavant. The unrecognized gentleman framed in the doorway was tall, slender, and was dressed, as one might say, at the very peak of style. Him I took rightly to be Sir Patrick Spenser, a baronet and, as Sir John had observed, Solicitor-General to the King.

As the butler retired from the door, Lord Mansfield—that is to say, the Lord Chief Justice—stepped forward and introduced the two. Sir Patrick, who looked to be a rather prideful man, bobbed his head politely and extended his hand to grasp Sir John's; the two wiggled hands in a more or less cordial manner. The younger man murmured something which I for one was unable to hear properly. Yet Sir John evidently had no difficulty, for he gave emphatic agreement.

"Oh, indeed," said he. "I should think that most important." Then, frowning, he added, "But you are not remaining?"

"I think not," said Sir Patrick. "My part in this was simply to see that a commission was formed. That, Lord Mansfield has attended to admirably. I shall leave matters in his hands—and your own—with confidence that all will be handled effectively *and* discreetly."

"But what—" said Sir John. (Though he never got further, it seemed to me he had begun a protest of some sort.)

"I do hope, Lord Mansfield," said Sir Patrick, addressing the Lord Chief Justice though staring straight at me, "that it will be made clear to *all* of those in attendance today that the purpose, even the existence of this commission, is to be kept in strictest confidence."

It was almost as if he had been witness to my blunder in Drury Lane. There was no question in my mind but that his caution was meant for me in particular. But was it what he had said, or how he had said it, that led me to such an unlikely suspicion? His soft voice did little to hide his insinuating and slightly threatening manner.

"But I must be off," said Sir Patrick. "I shall perhaps look in on you again sometime in the future, when there are some developments in the matters at hand." With one quick look, he surveyed all present. "Goodbye, then."

"Joseph," said Lord Mansfield to his butler, "show Sir Patrick out."

And the two were gone in a trice.

"Come in, Sir John," said the host. "It should not be long until all are present."

Nor was it. The prompt arrival of two more members of the commission excused Sir John from the onerous task of making talk with Mr. Trezavant, the coroner, for whom he had little respect. Mr. George Hemmings, a prosperous solicitor specializing in matters of property, and Mr. Hubert Dalrymple, a barrister known to be a close friend of Sir Patrick Spenser's, evidently fulfilled the commission's roster. Perhaps only Lord Mansfield knew that (Sir John did not), and he signaled his satisfaction that their number was complete by stepping smartly before them, calling them to order, and asking if anyone present might wish to serve informally as secretary and take notes on the proceedings. It was a task none seemed to wish. As Lord Mansfield surveyed the room, his glance fell upon me, who stood as I had been instructed, immediately behind the chair occupied by Sir John in an attitude of attention.

"What about the lad here?" said Lord Mansfield, pointing in my direction. "Your lad, Sir John. Can he write? Has he letters?"

"He is well read, and I'm told writes a very handsome hand. Nevertheless, I believe you would be ill advised to use him—or any other, for that matter—to keep a record of this meeting."

"If I understand you aright, you think it wrong to keep minutes of this meeting?"

"Just so," said Sir John. "Sir Patrick Spenser has dinned into us the need for confidentiality, even secrecy, regarding whatever is done or discussed here, and I think it would be acting against his instructions if a record of our meetings were to be kept."

"I don't quite follow you," said Lord Mansfield.

"Well, simply put, if there is a written record, then there is always a chance that it may fall into the hands of those from whom Sir Patrick would keep it. If we rely upon our memories, there is no such chance."

"Ah, yes, I understand now. But I'm afraid I must disappoint you."

"Oh? In what way?"

"It was Sir Patrick himself who particularly requested that a record of this and future meetings be kept so that he may pass a copy on up to other interested parties."

"The King, no doubt," said Sir John rather sourly, "and perhaps the rest of his family, as well."

"Be that as it may, Sir John, I believe you've been bested, so if you, young man, will come over here and sit down at this secretaire, you will find paper in the drawer and pen and ink in the usual place. So come now, lad, hop to it, if you will, and we'll begin."

In just such a way, then, did I become recording secretary for this mysterious commission with neither name nor, to my knowledge, a purpose made public. Looking upon the members of the commission from my new vantage point, I must say I found them a motley group, as different one from the other as January from July. Sir John had withdrawn into himself following the friendly dispute with the Lord Chief Justice; eyes covered by the familiar black silk band, features at rest, he looked to be as one asleep. Mr. Trezavant, on the other hand, seemed wakeful indeed, yet he seemed solely concerned with ingratiating himself with the others—flashing little smiles here and there and even at me, looking round the room in such a way that he seemed to be taking stock of it, tallying the worth of this piece of furniture and that set of books. Of the two later arrivals, I fear that I liked Mr. Dalrymple the better of the two, for no good reason except that he was the better dressed, handsome in the blue-eyed way of Dutchmen and Swedes, and was the more commanding presence. Mr. Hemmings, sharp-eyed and intelligent-looking, also had that manner of viewing things in the room as if assessing their value, yet there seemed no element of envy or greed involved in this habit of his; one had the feeling that his was simply a practiced professional eye which never rested. And as for William Murray, Earl of Mansfield, the Lord Chief Justice, I had come to know him fairly well during his flying visits to Sir John; and him I judged to be proud (often excessively so), and one who bore the traits of many proud men: a choleric disposition and an overweening certainty of the rightness of his own causes and opinions; these led him often to a certain callousness in the dispensation of justice; he was by reputation, inclination, and practice a hanging judge.

Yet say what you would of Lord Mansfield, he matched Sir John in the quality of his directness. In fact, the two men were in that way and others a bit alike. So it was that I was not in the least surprised when, echoing Sir John, the chairman of the commission (Lord Mansfield, of course) began by announcing to the little group that the purpose of the commission was to save the Laningham fortune for the King.

"Save it?" echoed Mr. Trezavant. "Why should that be necessary? It is his by law, is it not? That fellow Paltrow was condemned to hang, and, by God, thanks to Sir John here, he was hanged."

At the mention of his name, I noticed Sir John wince slightly. He said nothing, however.

"I fear I must correct you on that, sir," said Mr. Dalrymple. "The possessions of a condemned man go to the King by custom."

"It is, however, a very old custom," said Lord Mansfield.

"And a very *bad* one," said Sir John.

"Now, none of that," said Lord Mansfield, mildly reproving as one might correct a child. "We are not here to judge the custom but, rather, to see that it is followed."

"But again I ask, why should it not be?" This, most insistently, from Mr. Trezavant. "It is doubly the King's, is it not? I understood that this Paltrow who was hanged was last in the line. Unless some distant cousin step forward and prove his claim to the Laningham title, the fortune would, under those circumstances, also go to the King."

There was silence for a moment.

"Would it not?" repeated Mr. Trezavant. He looked about uneasily.

Again silence—until Lord Mansfield at last spoke up: "Well, that, you see, is the problem. A claimant to the Laningham title has, in fact, appeared—and he is no distant cousin but a younger brother. His name is Lawrence Paltrow."

"Where has he been all this time?" asked Sir John.

"In the North American colonies. In fact, he quite disappeared eight years ago and was presumed to be dead. Not a word was heard from him all that time—until he read of his brother's death and realized that he was next in line. Or that, in any case, is what is told by this supposed younger brother."

"You are doubtful, then, Lord Mansfield?"

"Indeed I am."

"Well, that is good," said Sir John, "for much as I dislike being the bearer of bad tidings, I think it only fair to tell you that the King has not a chance of claiming the Laningham fortune under the first set of circumstances you discussed—that is, seizing the property of a man condemned."

There was a moment's quiet, followed by a flurry of talk—exclamations of surprise, challenges, demands to know on what he based this strange conclusion.

"Yes, Sir John," said Lord Mansfield in his most sarcastic manner, "whence comes this sudden revelation?"

"Why, it came unbidden and but a moment ago. I had felt that there was something false in accepting Arthur Paltrow as *Lord* Laningham—that is, for purposes of royal seizure—and then, of a sudden, did the reason occur to me. It had meant so much to Arthur Paltrow that he properly be considered Lord Laningham that he wrote demanding to be tried before the House of Lords. Do you recall that, Lord Chief Justice?"

"Hmmm. Something about it, yes."

"Then you may also recall the reason for which he was denied such a trial. He was advised that though he had, immediately following the death of his uncle, submitted his Letter of Patent, claiming a seat in the House of Lords, the Writ of Summons to Parliament had not yet been issued. The fact that he was now bound for trial at Old Bailey on a charge of homicide made it highly unlikely that the Writ would ever be issued—except in the unlikely event that he be found not guilty. Now, gentlemen, as we all know, he was found guilty and suffered death by the rope. He died as a commoner and not as a noble. The King cannot lay claim to the Laningham fortune through the death of Arthur Paltrow, for it was never Paltrow's. According to the House of Lords, he was never one of them. He cannot be posthumously granted what he was once denied solely for purposes of seizure. Such a tactic would be beneath the King. It would also, I hope, be beneath the King's lawyers."

Let me interject here that as I listened to the short discourse quoted above, taking notes upon Sir John's words as he spoke them, I was so delighted by the strength of his reasoning and the felicity of his expression that I felt the impulse to applaud him when he had done. I resisted it, of course, and a good thing, too, for I looked up from my notes to find the faces of the other four commission members wearing expressions of the deepest consternation. It was certain that none would have joined me in paying tribute to him.

When at last he and the rest had recovered from the blow dealt them, Lord Mansfield spoke up most soberly. "You would advise, then," said he, "that we take the matter of the claimant most seriously and concentrate upon defeating his efforts."

"That would seem to me a reasonable conclusion," said Sir John. "Perhaps you could tell us more of this Lawrence Paltrow. How does he account for his silence during the eight years he was presumed to be dead?"

"Oddly enough, he can give no explanation for his silence, nor does he apparently feel the need to do so."

"How can that be?" asked Mr. Dalrymple. "The fellow has simply appeared and made his claim, has he? Does he refuse to answer questions? How is he now occupied?"

"What occupies him chiefly since his appearance here in England is the business of collecting signed statements attesting to his identity as Lawrence Paltrow."

"Is it then so doubtful?"

"Well . . . let me say only what I have heard: to wit, that he does not perfectly resemble the young man who left for the colonies eight years ago."

"Do be more specific, Lord Mansfield," said Mr. Trezavant.

"He has, so they say, grown a bit—not merely filled out but acquired an inch or two in height, as well. Not impossible for one in his twenties, yet not likely, either. His manner of speech is also questionable. There are, in sum, any number of discrepancies—matters that might seem . . . oh, not quite right to the interested observer."

"Ah, well," said Mr. Trezavant, "perhaps he may not prove so difficult an obstacle, after all."

Ignoring him rather pointedly, Lord Mansfield continued: "One might say he is so little like his old self that his claim to be Lawrence Paltrow would probably not be taken at all seriously were it not for the fact that Margaret Paltrow, the mother, has recognized him as her son and herself signed an affidavit to that effect in the presence of a solicitor."

"The mother?" echoed Mr. Trezavant, quite crestfallen. "Oh, my, oh, dear."

"What, then?" put in Mr. Dalrymple. "How will he proceed? Who passes judgment on his claim? I'm quite ignorant of these matters."

Rather tellingly, all turned then to Sir John, who, blind, was ignorant of this tribute to his greater knowledge. Yet as silence reigned, and thinking no doubt that the answer could come only from him, Sir John cleared his throat and spoke up at last: "I believe it would go again to the House of Lords. A Letter of Patent would be written, accompanied in this case by affidavits, statements, and whatever other documentation he may have collected. If disputed by the claimant or any other interested party, the decision of the House of Lords would be brought to Chancery Court."

At that, there were groans in chorus.

But somewhat in the manner of a teacher calling the class to order, Lord Mansfield chided them. "Gentlemen, please," said he. "Chancery Court is operating much more efficiently these days—though I admit it is in our own best interest— and the King's—to keep the case out of Chancery. But tell me, Mr. Hemmings, you, who are most experienced in these matters, have not spoken at all. What have you to say? Give us some benefit of your wisdom and experience."

Mr. Hemmings returned the gaze of the Lord Chief Justice as one perfectly sure of himself would do. He was a canny sort, well into his sixth decade of life, yet more lively than many a younger man.

"You flatter me, m'lord—and to no good purpose, I fear,"

said Mr. Hemmings quite bluntly. "As you well know, I am not one for making plans and theories and such. It's true I have had some experience in these matters, enough to know a few things about this one. What I know, first of all, is that Sir John Fielding is quite right: There is no chance of the King's entitlement to the Laningham fortune through Arthur Paltrow; our only hope is to discredit the claim of his younger brother—if indeed the claimant be truly his brother. And if possible, that must be done swiftly—even before it reaches the House of Lords. I have a good notion of why I was recruited for this group, and it is because of my known expertise in surveying and estimating wealth. I can only assume that you want a price put upon the Laningham fortune—and quickly. I suspect it will be sold off within the year."

"Perhaps not all of it," said Lord Mansfield with a sly smile and a bit of a wink.

"What do you know that we do not?" asked Mr. Dalrymple.

"Oh, do tell us, m'lord," said Mr. Trezavant.

"Well, as I understand it," said Lord Mansfield, "the King has his regal heart set upon the Laningham country house and estate as a palace for the Prince."

"For the Prince of Wales?" blurted out Trezavant. "He is but nine years old."

"To be given him when he reaches his majority, of course."

"Ah, well, that makes better sense."

"It seems that the King visited there of a night some years back and was immediately taken by the place."

"And now the place will be taken by *him*!" Mr. Trezavant crowed in jolly fashion at his own witticism; none joined with him.

"Yes, well, what the King does with it is of no consequence to us," said Lord Mansfield. "But Mr. Hemmings has brought up an interesting point. In fact, he is correct. My intention is to request him to survey the wealth and holdings that the Laningham fortune comprises. He will be compensated for his work quite generously, as indeed you all will be—for, yes, I have tasks for one and all."

"Sir John?"

"Yes, Jeremy, what is it, lad?"

"The Lord Chief Justice gave you no task, did he? He did simply skip over you, did he not?"

"Oh, he may have done, but then again he may not."

There, for certain, was a puzzler. What had he meant by that? "I . . . do not quite understand, sir."

"Simple enough," said he. "It's true that Lord Mansfield announced nothing for me, which disappointed me not in the least. But then—I thought you surely would have noticed—as the meeting ended and we filed out, he slipped something into my coat pocket, a letter. Quite surprised me, he did. I suspect that the letter has in it some special and specific duty he wishes me to perform."

"You have it with you now?"

"Why, yes, of course."

"Then, would you like me to read it to you?"

"Here? Now?"

In truth, this hardly seemed the time or place, for we were making our way back to Number 4 Bow Street, once again surrounded by the great multitude in Drury Lane, stepping along at a brisk pace.

"Well, perhaps not," said I, "but there is a coffee house just ahead that might serve the purpose."

Sir John gave that some lengthy consideration. "No," said he, having weighed the matter sufficiently, "I think not. I believe I am less curious about the matter than you. Having so little enjoyed the last hour, or half-hour, or whatever the length of the meeting may have been, I simply wish to put it out of my mind for as long as possible. I agree, Jeremy, that the letter must eventually be read, but grant me please something of a recess from that band of pettifoggers and spies."

"Spies, Sir John? All of them, sir?"

"Oh, perhaps not the Lord Chief Justice. He is what he is,

and far worse and less able men have held his position. He owes nothing to any man. I suppose I would also except George Hemmings, a mean man, perhaps, but unafraid to speak his own mind. But the other two? I daresay Trezavant has run off already to tell the Prime Minister what transpired. And Dalrymple, who is well known as Sir Patrick Spenser's great friend, will now have put his head together with the Solicitor-General."

"But Sir Patrick will receive my minutes of the meeting, will he not?"

"Oh, yes, and I'm sure that after they have been improved upon, they will make interesting reading for the King."

"But I kept a good record of the meeting, sir—quite accurate as to content. Mr. Marsden taught me how. Why should it be necessary to improve upon it?"

"So that it be made to say what Sir Patrick wishes it to say."

"But that is unfair—and no doubt illegal, too."

"No, not illegal," said Sir John, "simply immoral."

We went past the Drury Lane Theatre, swept along by the crowd as evening was coming on. The sun, declining in the west, gave light of a distinctly muted character. In little more than an hour, dim twilight would cover all London. I vowed to say no more to Sir John about the letter which, even then, protruded from his coat pocket. Though curious, I had my dignity to maintain. If he wanted it read to him, he would have to ask me.

I thought surely at our dinner in the kitchen that he would make his request to me. But no. As we five sat at table, enjoying the flow of talk from one to the next, not a word was said by Sir John of the meeting which we had attended that afternoon. Annie had fixed a fine dinner of mutton and dumplings. That, Lady Fielding's tales of happenings at the Magdalene Home, and Clarissa's commentary upon them were quite enough to keep us entertained for the better part of the meal. Annie, in answer to a query from Sir John, reported upon the progress she had made in her reading lessons with Mr. Burnham. When he heard that she had not long before read through *The Governess* by Sarah Fielding, he became quite animated.

"Why, the author is my sister," cried he in delight. "Or was, for she is dead now, God rest her soul. Did you know that, Annie?"

"Sir, I did," said she, "for Jeremy told me of her when he fetched the book down for me to read."

"And did you enjoy it?"

"Oh, I did! It was all about a class of girls and their teacher. Since I am myself now a scholar, I was pleased to read of them—even though I am older than they in the story are."

"Well, I am pleased to hear it," said Sir John. "I'm glad you read the book and gladder still that you liked it. But I confess to you now, Annie, that I myself have never read *The Governess*. Years ago my wife, Kitty, God rest her soul, read *David Simple* and its successors to me. That, alas, is all that I know of my sister Sarah's writing."

"Well, then, sir, let me put to you the same question: Did you enjoy it?"

"Ah, well, that's a difficult question," said he.

"Why should it be, sir?"

"Because I have no wish to speak ill of my sister—half sister, actually—but the fact remains that there was far too much of sentiment in that book of hers, to the point that it lacked any sort of verisimilitude. Now, this I attribute to the influence of that fellow Richardson, whose romances she openly esteemed more highly than our brother, Henry's. And that I thought both daft and disloyal."

With that, Clarissa leapt in with a defense of Samuel Richardson as author and man of sentiment; in the course of it she revealed what I had always assumed—that her bookish mother had named her after Richardson's heroine, Clarissa Harlowe. Lady Fielding stood solidly with Clarissa, praising both Sarah Fielding and Samuel Richardson and defending sentiment. I, quite naturally, took the side of Sir John. Thus begun, we must have argued round the table for the better part of an hour, at the end of which neither side was declared winner, nor (to be honest) was any conclusion reached. Yet in this way we often passed our time at table—in argument and heated discussion with never a word of gossip, tittle-tattle, or the like. We three—Annie, Clarissa, and myself— were not to know until years later just how fortunate we were to spend our time in such a household.

As a result of that night's spontaneous debate, I quite forgot the matter of the Lord Chief Justice's letter until much later in the evening. I might not have remembered it at all had it not been for the fact that I found that very letter beneath Sir John's chair as I was washing up. It had fallen, no doubt, when he dipped his hand in his coat pocket to pull out his kerchief, or some such thing. No matter how it came to be there, however, it would have to be returned to him.

So it came about that directly I had finished in the kitchen, I visited Sir John in that small room down the hall from his bedroom which he called his study. There was room in it for a desk and two chairs—and not much more. I had brought with me a lighted candle in a holder, because I knew from my countless earlier visits there that he would doubtless be sitting in the dark. The candle I carried would save me the trouble of fumbling with flint and tinder—for, of course, I would be asked to read the letter to him when I returned it.

Sir John sat silhouetted against the window. The moonlit sky behind him was like a sheet upon which the darker figure of a man appeared as in a magic lantern show.

I rapped lightly upon the open door.

"Who is there?" said he. "Is it you, Jeremy?"

"It is, Sir John. I have here something of yours."

"Oh? What is that?"

"A letter—the one given you by the Lord Chief Justice."

"Where did you find it?" He seemed a bit disturbed, patted his pocket, and found indeed that it was missing—at which he let out a sigh.

"I found it beneath your chair in the kitchen, sir," said I. "It must have dropped out while you were at table."

Again a sigh; this one was much deeper than the last. "I

fear," said he, "that I am not altogether as careful with such things as I should be. Lately, in fact, I seem to have become downright careless."

"Oh, you seem to manage well enough, sir," said I in a manner rather grandiose, I fear, as if it were within my power to forgive him his faults. My words rang hollow to my listening ears. "In any case," I added, "here it is." Then did I lean over and place the letter on the desk before him.

He smiled and nodded. "Thank you, lad," said he. Then did he wait a space of time, as if in expectation. And finally: "Was there something more, Jeremy?"

In spite of my intention to say nothing, and in contradiction to my vow to maintain my childish dignity at all cost, I then offered to read the letter to him.

"Oh, certainly," said he with a shrug of his great shoulders. "I suppose I must face what they have in store for me. Waiting will not make it vanish away. But do light a candle and sit down. Let us hear what the Lord Chief Justice has to say to me."

And so, retrieving the letter from his desk, I settled down in the chair opposite him and placed candle and candle holder on the desk between us. I broke the seal on the letter; though by that time its design was quite familiar, it never failed to awaken within me a sense of awe—the very scales of justice were upon it, after all!

I bent near the desk and candle that I might better read the contents of the letter. Surveying it quickly, I remarked to Sir John that it was writ in Lord Mansfield's own hand. (The Lord Chief Justice usually dictated his communications to his clerk.)

"No doubt he was forced to serve as his own scrivener by Sir Patrick's demands for secrecy," Sir John suggested.

Glancing ahead, I added: "He is also a bit more informal, a bit more himself here." Glancing up, I noticed fidgeting a bit. "But here," said I, "let me begin."

And so I read:

"*My dear Sir John:*

"*By the time this is read to you, my assignment of tasks will have been done, and you must have noticed I had none to offer you. Think not for a moment, however, that you will get off quite so easily. I have saved for you the only real work likely to come from the first meeting of this nonsensical body which I am obliged to call a commission.*

"*I would like you to interrogate Margaret Paltrow, the putative mother of the claimant to the Laningham title and fortune, he who says he is Lawrence Paltrow. Actually, her word that he is her son is the only impressive bona-fides that he can offer. Examine her. Question her closely. Perhaps you can persuade her to reconsider her relationship to the claimant.*

"*As it happens, Margaret Paltrow resides in rather humble circumstances in the City of Bath, and so it will be necessary to travel there to meet her. Yet because we are forced to respect the confidential nature of this mission, I wish you to go there as if on holiday. Take Lady Fielding with you and two servants—no more should be necessary—and stay the better part of a week, or more if you've a mind to. I am, in effect, ordering you off on a holiday which, by the bye, you ought to have taken long ago.*

"*Because I fear you will argue against this, I have taken steps to ensure that any resistance you make to this plan of mine will be quite futile. First of all, your week in Bath will cost you nothing; any commission of the King's is sure to be well financed, and one whose purpose is secret is just as sure to be better financed than most. Secondly, I can offer you my own coach and four to travel to Bath. Lady Mansfield will be returning in it the day after you arrive. (I wish I could offer you our little house there for your stay, but my good wife leaves our two wards and their aunt behind, and believe me when I tell you that you would not wish to share a house of modest size with them.) Thirdly, to make your time in Bath your own, I have written Mr. Saunders Welch, who styles himself 'Magistrate of Outer London,' and charged him to take over your duties, as well, for the length of your stay. He may complain, but he will do what I tell him.*

"Finally, two details should prove important. The widow Paltrow lives in three rooms in the upper floor of Number 6 Kingsmead Square; she was not well provided for by her late husband, but prefers to live in Bath rather than in some village in the Laningham district—for obvious reasons. Lastly, then, word has come to me that the claimant and another who assists him are presently in Bath and look in on Margaret Paltrow from time to time. If you happen to meet them, use discretion; it would not do for them to suspect that we are moving against them.

"My coach leaves for Bath the day past tomorrow. I hope you will be able to avail yourself of the use of it, for it should be far more comfortable than the stage-coach which plies between here and there."

At last I came to a halt. All that remained of the letter was a most polite and dignified farewell and an illegible signature which sprawled near the width of the page.

"He signs it in the usual way," said I to Sir John.

The magistrate said nothing in reply but sat slumped at his desk, an expression of dismay upon his face.

"Uh, sir?" said I.

He maintained his silence until at last: "Jeremy, do you realize what he has asked me to do?"

"Well, to go to Bath, sir."

"And do what? To seek out the mother, not only of Lawrence Paltrow but of Arthur Paltrow, as well. He wishes me—nay, *expects* me—to visit her and persuade her to retract her recognition of the claimant as her son."

I decided to be encouraging. "Well," said I, "if anyone can do that, it's you."

"But, Jeremy, the situation reeks of cheap drama. I caught her elder son in murder! I doubt, when I present myself, that she will even consent to speak to me."

I said nothing, did not dare to speak for a considerable while, yet managed to point out to him that though a great deal was asked of him, something was offered in return. "A holiday in Bath, sir—Lady Fielding would greatly benefit from it, would she not?"

Again he sighed, though not quite so deep as before. "I suppose so," said he. "Perhaps the thing to do is to bring the matter before them all for discussion. Jeremy, summon them back to the kitchen table."

THREE

*In which Sir John
converses with
Margaret Paltrow*

The loan of Lord Mansfield's coach and four for the trip to Bath seemed to us perhaps less a boon than he had hoped it would be. The driver, in his eagerness to abbreviate the traveling time from London, pressed the horses so mercilessly that one might have supposed that the devil himself were in pursuit of us. Rest periods were cut short. Meals were taken, as it were, on the run. There was but a single stop made at an inn along the way, of a duration which permitted us a few hours' sleep—then it was up and out on the road again, gray-faced to meet the gray dawn.

In this manner, a few hours were, in fact, saved. Yet so great was the expense in sore backsides and general exhaustion that indeed it seemed to matter little when at last the four tired horses pulled the dusty coach up to the portico entrance of the Bear Tavern. It was a hostelry of some considerable size, where the Lord Chief Justice had advised us to stay.

Annie, who by right of service was entitled to a place in the coach, had chosen to remain in London. As she said, she had no interest in any part of the world beyond Clerkenwell or Kennington, nor did she wish to interrupt her tuition with Mr. Burnham. And so Clarissa Roundtree went to Bath in Annie's place, thus relieving Lady Fielding of the anxiety she felt at the possibility of leaving the twelve-year-old Clarissa alone in London—even though she be left alone in a house full of constables.

She, then, the fourth in our party, was the first to climb down from the coach, and as she did so, she was transformed in what seemed to me quite a remarkable manner. I, who had been seated next to her all that long way from London, had felt her bounced right, left, and up and down (just as I was), and had listened to her continual complaints freely given sotto voce. She had, in sum, survived the trip no better than the rest of us. Yet the moment her feet touched the cobblestones, they began to dance to some sprightly rhythm in her head. She whirled round to view her surroundings better. Then did she cry out in the manner of Mr. Garrick's grandest heroines:

"Bath! Bath! I've waited so long to come. Now I must see it all!"

I turned away in embarrassment from her display.

"Clarissa, please!" wailed Lady Fielding indulgently as Sir John simply laughed loud, as if greatly amused.

But the porter, who had come forth to take charge of our baggage, laughed loudest and longest, causing Clarissa herself some degree of mortification. "Well, mistress, the old town's been here since the time of King Bladud, which is to say even before the Romans was here. So I reckon it'll stay put for the day or two it'll take for you to walk around it." Then did he remove his hat and turn to Sir John: "You'll be stayin' with us, sir?"

"For about a week, if you've room."

"A few days past, we were full up—height of the season, y'know—but the town's startin' to clear out a bit, which makes it a good time to be here. Plenty to see, plenty to do, and the waters bubble up the same, no matter what the time of year—but ain't so many here to fight you for a place in line." Then did he replace his hat atop his head and begin gathering up portmanteaus, boxes, and bags where they had been unceremoniously dropped by Lord Mansfield's footman. A small man the porter was, but wiry and strong, and before I quite realized it, he had all our baggage in hand and was leading the way into the Bear. "This way, all," he called over his shoulder. "We'll have you in your rooms in no time!"

The porter's promise was kept. It could not have been more than half an hour until I found myself in bed in one of the small servants' rooms next to that larger one in which Sir John and Lady Fielding then slept. The moment they had arrived, she had declared it absolutely necessary that she take a nap to restore herself after the rigors of our journey from London. Sir John said he thought that a grand idea for himself as well as for Clarissa and me. Thus we two were sent off to bed at sometime after noon, an unusual situation at best. Through the thin wall that separated me from them, I heard Sir John and Lady Fielding deep in sleep, snoring, as was their wont. And I? Well, I had dutifully followed Sir John's suggestion, thinking myself quite exhausted, yet as I lay in the narrow little bed I experienced a phenomenon that every traveler must know from time to time: It sometimes happens that following a particularly demanding trip, such as the one we had just made in that fast-moving coach, true rest is somehow impossible. The motion of the road continues within one, when you have been jostled about like some sack of meal for hours and hours, then it often happens that sleep will not come.

In any case, it would not come to me that day in Bath. The curtains were drawn; my eyes were closed; yet no matter how attentively and expectantly I waited, that which was most desired never happened. I was about to climb out of bed and search for the book I had brought in my bag, when upon the door came a tap-tap-tapping.

I jumped to my clothes and pulled on a shirt as I went to the door. I listened and waited. Again came the light tapping.

"Who is there?" I whispered cautiously.

"It is I, Clarissa."

"What do you want?"

"Open the door, and I will tell."

Reluctantly, I drew back the bolt and eased the door open. I noted she was dressed for the street—a cap upon her head and a light cape over her shoulders.

"I cannot sleep," said she, "as I see you cannot neither. So why do we not go out and take our first look at Bath, just the two of us?"

"But what if they should wake while we are gone? They would doubtless fret, not knowing where we had gone, what we were doing."

She gave that a moment's serious consideration, then brightened quite sudden as a thought occurred to her. "I know! I shall write a note for them explaining our absence and promising our swift return. Then I shall slip it under the door."

"That should do nicely," said I. "Go write it, and I shall dress myself."

Thus a few minutes later, Clarissa and I stepped out the door of the hostelry, sought directions from the porter to the center of town, and set off on our bold exploration of Bath. Though I had made no grand show of it as she had, I was near as curious about the place as Mistress Clarissa Roundtree was. Sir John had made two previous journeys to Bath in 1768, the first year of my association with him. He had attended the funeral of his sister, Sarah, in the spring, in this place; and then, in early fall, returned with Lady Fielding on their wedding trip. On those occasions I had, as a thirteen-year-old, imagined Bath to be a great and shining city, near as large as London yet somehow grander and more beautiful—and, above all, cleaner. (How could it not be with such a name?)

As I walked through it with Clarissa, I discovered that I was both wrong and right in my earlier vision of the place. Certainly, I saw that it was no city but more or less what the porter had called it: a town. Nevertheless, it was by any standard a beautiful town, one in a most inspiring natural setting—green fields, rolling hills, et cetera—to which had been added structures of the most graceful design. London, which could be called beautiful only in parts, had with those parts clearly inspired the whole of construction in Bath. There were squares composed of handsome façades; a crescent of vast planning, not yet fully built; and a grand circus of inspiring size and beauty. And so much of it was clean in the way that only that which has been newly built can be clean.

There was no great difficulty in following the directions we had been given. We proceeded along the broad streets and across the wide squares, inspecting and observing as we went. I believe it was Clarissa who pointed out how greatly the sedan chairs outnumbered coaches and hackney coaches.

"I wonder why that should be," said I. "You do not see so many of them in London."

"Which counts greatly in London's favor," she declared. "I hold them to be quite the most disgusting means of travel available to man or woman."

"Sedan chairs? Disgusting? Why indeed would you think that?"

"Why, I think it because that is what they are. They make beasts of burden out of human beings. Is that not disgusting?"

"Well, those who haul them about," said I, "seem to do so willingly enough."

"Simply because a slave accepts his slavery does not make him any less a slave."

At that I laughed in spite of myself. "Clarissa," said I to her, "where do you get such ideas?"

"Well," she said with a proud smile—and there she left her response suspended for a moment as she leapt from a pair of snarling, ill-tempered sedan-chair bearers who cursed her for straying in their path. Quite automatically, she stuck her tongue out at them. "Where was I?" said she once they had passed. "Oh, yes! As to where I get such ideas, I got that one from my mother. I only wish she were here with me that she might agree with me now, as you clearly do not. I'm sure she would feel exactly as I do about sedan chairs."

"You're sure of that, are you?" (Perhaps I was carrying on a *bit* pompously.)

"As sure as I can be about anything. She was an intelligent woman, and intelligent people tend to agree with me."

Though Clarissa Roundtree had put on a few needed pounds since joining Sir John's household, and had proved herself helpful in many ways, this recalcitrant, overconfident female had in no wise acquired any of the social virtues which I then thought so essential to womanly maturity; particularly, it seemed to me, she was lacking in intellectual modesty. Or perhaps it was willfulness plain and simple that made her behave as she did. Whatever her essential fault, I found her most annoying in argument, though (I was forced to admit) occasionally rather stimulating, as well. All would be well between us, I thought, if she simply did not take on such airs.

Perhaps equally disconcerting was her habit of suddenly descending into childishness when she apparently most wished to be taken in earnest—as indeed she did when sticking out her tongue at the two surly sedan-chair bearers. And just see her now, thought I. Having made what she thinks a telling point against me with her last remark, she skips on ahead like some five-year-old at play, chuckling to herself. I watched her move thus down the broad walkway, a promenade upon which only strollers and ramblers were allowed. Fearing that she might collide with one of these grand gentlemen or elegant ladies, I was about to call after her in caution, when of a sudden she stopped; her attention had been completely captured by the contents of a shop window. It was not till I had come close that I saw that it was a bookshop of some grand size.

I took a place beside Clarissa and stared silently at the crowded display. Though I was an habitué of the Grub Street shops and well known in the few along the Strand, I had never seen quite such profusion in a window before—the stacks of books, the handsome bindings, the buckram and leather, the gilt. Who could tell what treasures were inside?

"Isn't it all beautiful? Did you ever see the like?" asked Clarissa in a voice quite hushed with awe.

"No, I never did," said I.

We continued to stand before the big window and stare. From time to time we would call out the title or the author of a book and point out its location. It had become a kind of game we played between us—and indeed I knew of no one else with whom I could have played it. Trying as Clarissa could be, exasperating as she was in argument, self-conceited as she often seemed—nevertheless she was the only one I had ever known who shared my passionate but unspoken wish to read every book ever written. My few years' seniority and her two years in the poorhouse had given me something of an advantage over her in this regard, yet at the rate she was devouring libraries whole, she would catch me up in no time at all.

"Would you like to go inside?" I asked. But, receiving no answer, I turned to her, prepared to pose the question again. What I then saw quite surprised me: There was a tear coursing its way slowly down her cheek; another which had just escaped her eye was about to follow the first.

Aware of my gaze, she glanced in my direction and dabbed at her tears with her sleeve. Then, after snuffling once or twice and clearing her throat, she said: "I do truly wish my mother were here. She talked so often of this place—of Beau Nash and the Pump Room and . . ." There was more to be said, I was sure, but there she ended her brief reminiscence and turned back to the window.

"But she herself never came here to Bath?" I asked.

"She never did."

"Then your mother, of all people, would want you to enjoy yourself here. You must see it all with her eyes as well as your own. You must enjoy it for two. And so I shall put the question to you once more: Would you like to go inside this grandest of all possible bookshops?"

Clarissa smiled then, having overcome her tears, and shook her head in the negative. "No," said she, "I think not. I fear that once inside, I should lose all sense of time."

"It does look a bit like one of those enchanted castles inside, does it not? Where one grows old without ever knowing?" I pointed to a well-dressed man in one corner who must have been well into his sixth decade. "Do you see that old fellow there? When he entered, he was no older than I, but ever since then he's had his nose in first one book and then another, poor man."

She laughed at that, as I'd intended she should. "We can come back another time," said she. "I've some money to spend. Lady Fielding gave me a bit." Then did a look come over her, which said clear enough she had quite forgotten those we had left back at the Bear Tavern. "And I do suppose we should be getting back to them," she blurted out.

"I suppose we should."

"But could we not first visit the Pump Room? I believe it is quite nearby—just around the next corner, I think."

And so we walked on, and Clarissa's estimate of the location of that landmark proved quite correct. The Pump Room did indeed lie just around the corner to the left. We stood before it just at the steps which led to one of the open entrances. Though in no wise crowded within, the ladies and gentlemen we saw through the latticed windows were the most grandly dressed we had viewed anywhere in Bath.

"I had hoped to taste the famous waters," said Clarissa, "but I'm dressed in such plain style, I dare not go in amongst those so wonderfully adorned."

"Oh, come along," said I. "There are those inside dressed no better than we." On that point I sounded to myself more confident than I in fact was.

"But you look fine in your green coat. You really do cut quite a dashing figure, Jeremy," said she. "I tell you, why don't you go up to the well and get glasses for the two of us. When I see you coming, I shall step up the stairs and just into the room. None will notice me if we do it so."

I attempted to persuade Clarissa to accompany me, yet

she refused quite absolutely. In the end, with a shrug, I surrendered: I marched up the five steps and through the open portal to the fountain. Of a sudden I became aware of the sounds of music about me—and quite beautiful they were. Beyond the fountain was a group of musicians, about four or five, playing stringed instruments of the ordinary orchestral sort. Yet none there—neither man nor woman—seemed to pay the musicians even polite attention, so busy were they talking and laughing amongst themselves.

I went to the fountain and asked the pumper the price of the different glasses, for there were three separate sizes.

"The water is free, young sir, no matter what the size of the glass."

"Ah, well," said I, "if that be the case, then give me two of that size there." And with that, I pointed to the middle-sized glass, neither the largest nor the smallest.

"Two of the pint-size—yes, indeed, young sir." And with that, he filled them and set them before me. "The water is free, as I said, but if you care to donate something to my health and that of my family—but that is strictly your affair, young sir."

I gave it a moment's thought and set down a shilling before taking up the two glasses.

"A bob, sir? More than generous, half that would do. Take this with my thanks." And so saying, he counted out eight pence and pushed them toward me. "The remainder for me and mine is still generous."

Unused to such fair treatment in London, I thanked him profusely before taking up the coins and leaving with the warm glasses. Clarissa was where she had promised she would be—just inside the large portal doorway, awaiting my return. Handing her a glass, I told her of my experience with the pumper as she sipped and listened. When I had done with the telling, she gave me a serious smile and a firm nod.

"Well, then," said she, "it seems I owe you tuppence."

"You've misunderstood completely," said I. "That was *not* my point in telling you the story. You owe me nothing."

"All right, then, what was your point in telling it?"

"Simply that . . . that . . . well, people seem a bit more decent here in Bath than in London."

"That's nonsense," said she with a quick wave of her hand. "You would not call the behavior of those two brutes hauling that sedan chair decent, would you?"

"What two brutes?"

"Those who cursed me for not jumping from their path quite quickly enough to suit them."

"Well . . . I . . ."

"No," said she, as if settling the matter for good and for all, "I believe the proportion of good people to bad is roughly the same no matter where one may go. I discussed this question once not long ago with Sir John, and that was the conclusion which we reached."

How well she knew that I was unlikely to take any position in an argument opposed to Sir John! Yet was this even an argument? Did I not hold with the principle she had stated? Had I not also heard it from Sir John and nodded in agreement? How had she the knack of defeating me by turning that which I believed upon its head? I had no desire to explain, nor even in any way to carry the matter on further. I thought it best if we returned to the hostelry.

"Have you finished with the glass?" I asked her. Though half full, it seemed to interest her no longer.

"Oh, indeed. It's frightful stuff, worse than ever I'd supposed." She surrendered the glass quite willingly. "But you've had none of yours. See what you think of it."

"No need," said I. "I accept your opinion. But I do think that now we must go back."

With that, I left her and carried the glasses to the bar. Before depositing my own, I drank a deep draft from it and found it quite refreshing though not exactly pleasant to the palate. Warm still, it had an astringent, slightly sour taste which I rather liked. I could not but reflect that even in such fundamental matters as that, Clarissa and I differed greatly.

Whether because we took a wrong turning as we left the Pump Room, or whether I compounded the difficulty by failing to note the difference in the route we took, I simply cannot say. It did not help matters, of course, that neither she nor I had much to say to the other. We simply marched on, side by side, in the wrong direction. Or perhaps better said, in a number of wrong directions, for once we had noticed our error, we altered our way no less than four times (and perhaps more) in hopes of finding the correct one.

Our last turn took us into a rather dismal part of Bath, out near the edge of town, where the river runs by. There was a constant flow of wagon traffic along Avon Street, yet we saw barely a single pedestrian along the walkway. We noticed few shops, and half of them, darkened and empty, looked to be shut. Adding to the general dreariness of the scene, the sun had quite disappeared and was now obscured behind a heavy layer of gray clouds.

"Could this also be Bath?" said I. "This hardly looks like the same place at all."

"True," Clarissa replied. "It seems to be haunted."

"Ghosts?" That seemed a rather fanciful notion.

"Not of the threatening kind, but the sad and pathetic sort." I understood a little better what she meant. There was that feeling all about us of wasted lives and dwindling fortunes.

We came out upon a square of no great size. It was dominated by a large building of a design as graceful and handsome as any in Bath, yet different from all or most in ways that eluded me. Facing it were rows of houses of no beauty or distinction.

"What square is this?" I asked (as if Clarissa knew the answer). "We cannot be far from the Bear Tavern. The town is not so large, after all, and it was from this general compass point we came."

She sighed. "Well," said she, "there is a tablet upon that great building just ahead. Perhaps that will tell us where we are."

We went to it and read. "Kingsmead Square," it said, and that sounded a note in my memory. Was that not the location of Margaret Paltrow's residence?

"Jeremy, look! Two men have just come out of one of

those houses across the way. Perhaps they can tell us the way back to the Bear."

Together we ran to them and managed to capture their attention before they turned off down Avon Street, whence we had come. They stopped and turned. When they did, it became apparent immediately how different the two men were. The elder of the two, rawboned, bearded, and hard-faced, gave a tug at the sleeve of the other, making it clear he thought Clarissa and I not of sufficient importance to detain them. He stalked away. But the younger would stay a bit and find out more; he smiled at our approach, even took a step or two back in our direction; there was, above all, an openness in his expression, a welcome in his manner, which invited our inquiry.

"What may we do for you?" he asked in a manner that suggested that we had only to make our request, and it would be granted.

"Why, sir," said I, "if you would be so good as to tell us the way to the Bear Tavern, we would be greatly obliged."

"Easily done," said the younger, "for we came from there not long ago." He pointed behind us to a street leading out of the square. "Now, that," said he, "is Bristol Road. You have but to walk it past two more streets, and you will be there." He smiled an altogether winning smile. "You'll find it is quite nearby."

I thanked him quite sincerely; Clarissa not only thanked him but also curtsied deep in a way that I for one had never seen her manage before.

"Now," said he, "if you will excuse me, I will wish you a good day, and be on my way."

Thus, tipping his hat, he left us, jog-trotting to catch his companion up. Once he had done so, the two walked off in close step. I could not help but notice how closely they resembled one another from the rear. Both were big men—broad-shouldered, tall, and stronglooking; both were dressed as gentlemen, yet only he who had spoken to us wore his clothes well and gave forth the impression that he might actually *be* a gentleman.

"He made it sound simple enough," said Clarissa, ending my observations for the moment.

I nodded my agreement and we set off in the direction of Bristol Road as it had been pointed out to us. Again we lapsed into silence. As for myself, there was a maggot gnawing away at the back of my brain, a question that demanded answer, a mystery that called for solution.

"Clarissa," said I, "did you happen to notice which of these houses those two men came from?"

We were at that moment passing by the block of dwellings where I had first glimpsed them. They were a rather sad-looking collection, not at all well matched.

"Oh, I don't know," said she. "Is it important?" But then, not waiting for my response, she stopped and pointed. "It was this one, I think—or perhaps the one next to it." Her first choice had been Number 6, and her second, Number 8.

I looked back as we resumed our pace and studied Number 6 Kingsmead Square, which was the address, according to the Lord Chief Justice, of the mother to the Laningham claimant. The best that could be said for it was that it was quite undistinguished in appearance. Brown brick with an upper story, it looked to have been built well back into the last century. But it was said that the mother, Margaret Paltrow, had been reduced to rather humble circumstances. Could not the two who had emerged from the house wherein she kept her residence be the claimant himself and his traveling companion? Was I putting too much faith in coincidence, or was there perhaps truly a likelihood that I had seen them here? I wrestled with that as we left the square and started up Bristol Road. In the end, I decided that there was less a probability of it than a possibility. And as Sir John often said, "All things are possible, so it is best to deal in probabilities when there are no certainties."

I might have put it out of my mind altogether had it not been for Clarissa. About the time I had settled the matter with myself, she turned to me and said, "They were a strange pair, were they not?"

There was no need to ask which pair she meant. "I think I

know what you mean," said I. "They didn't fit together well, did they?"

"Not well at all. The person who spoke to us seemed of noble character—well spoken, generous—yet the other . . . Jeremy, I know not what sort of impression he made upon you, but to me he seemed quite sinister, with that beard of his and all. I did not care for him in the least."

"Sinister, you say? Truly so?"

"Yes, indeed."

"Hmmm . . . well, now," said I, perhaps in unconscious imitation of Sir John. "I must give that some thought."

There had been no need to hurry so. Once Clarissa and I arrived at the Bear and viewed the clock in the corridor, we saw that not near so much time had elapsed since our departure as we had supposed. We had tramped Bath clear across and returned in less than two hours. It was indeed a town and no city.

We stood at the door behind which Sir John and Lady Fielding slept and listened to the sound of rhythmic breathing inside.

"Still asleep," said Clarissa. "What do you suppose we ought to do?"

"Come along," said I. "We shall repair to the lobby, where I shall have coffee, and you will have whatever pleases you, so long as it is not coffee or other strong drink."

It was there that Sir John and Lady Fielding found us sometime later. They seemed refreshed and were, they announced, ready to tour Bath properly. Thus it was that Clarissa and I repeated the journey we had made to the Pump Room; yet it did not hold near so much interest for us as before. What is viewed for the first time shines bright to our eyes; each time it is viewed thereafter, it loses a bit of its luster.

People visit Bath from all over England, Scotland, and Ireland. Do all attend because of the salutary effect of the waters? I doubt it. Having observed them on the occasion of which I now write and a few others since then, I know that many who come to the town would rather do any number of things than splash about in that substance for which the place is so famed. Among those things they would rather do, gaming at cards ranks high, as does gossiping, and the drinking of spirits. Because of his affliction or by personal disinclination, Sir John had little interest in such pastimes. He did, however, diligently pursue an activity quite as popular as the rest, and that was strolling. Now, it must be understood that in Sir John's estimation, as indeed in my own, there was a considerable difference between walking and strolling. Walking was what one did to reach a specific destination; it was usually done in a great hurry, particularly in London, where one had to move swiftly simply to keep up with the crowds in the streets. Strolling, however, was quite another matter. Not only was it done at a more leisurely pace, it was even more—the very expression of leisure. It allowed the stroller to greet his fellows and be greeted; to converse at length on a variety of matters with other strollers only recently met; it was, for a number of reasons, the sort of pursuit that fitted well such a place as Bath.

And so, on those mornings on which Lady Katherine Fielding left, with Clarissa in tow, to take the waters, Sir John and I would wait about the dining room in the Bear, drinking our morning tea until at last he would turn to me and ask, "What would you say, Jeremy, to a bit of a stroll? I believe it might aid digestion." Then off we would go, trying one route and then another, sometimes altering the one we had chosen to the north or south, even occasionally doubling back again; yet no matter how devious our route, we would eventually arrive at the Pump Room, where we would drink each a glass of water (like me, Sir John liked the stuff rather well) then set off once again to continue our stroll.

A good two hours or more might be thus consumed—not so much in strolling here and there as in talking with first one and then another along the way. It all began the day after we arrived as Sir John and I crossed that vast round open area which was known as the grand circus. Though not crowded, the place had a good many people milling about in all directions, so I cannot say that I was completely surprised when Sir John was recognized by one of them, a London merchant named Henry Harley, who approached him in a most friendly (not to say presumptuous) manner and offered enthusiastic congratulations on the way that criminal activity had been reduced in his corner of Westminster. He was so generous and *loud* in his praise that he attracted a small group of listeners, most of them evidently Londoners like himself. At the end of Mr. Harley's fulsome tribute there was a smattering of applause. Then it seemed that each who had attended the little scene must have a word or two with Sir John. We must have spent well over an hour there before at last we were allowed to move on. The next day, there on the promenade, we were hailed by a man whom we had never met, yet one who proved to be well known to us: He was Matthew Tiverton, Magistrate of Warwick. It was his letter which told in detail of the last days of George Bradbury in the city of his birth. He wished to know all there was to know of the trial of Mary Bradbury. At his invitation, we went with him to a coffee house nearby, where the matter was discussed at great length.

Each day seemed to bring a new encounter, or often more than one. In truth, Sir John seemed to enjoy the attention, the sudden celebrity which he gained once away from London—and I, of course, was glad for that. Nevertheless, I began to wonder just when he would carry out the task which he had been assigned by the Lord Chief Justice. Perhaps to remind him of that task, or perhaps only to relieve the monotony of our usual trip back to the Bear, I took him along the route upon which Clarissa and I had blundered on our trip back from the Pump Room. Nothing was said about it until we reached Avon Street and the river. And when we did, he began inhaling deeply, taking in the deep damp of its grassy banks. He seemed greatly interested in what he smelled.

"We have not come this way before, have we, Jeremy?"

"Not together, sir, no, we haven't."

"But you have been here without me?"

"Yes, Sir John. Just ahead is Kingsmead Square. You'll

recall, I'm sure, that Margaret Paltrow resides on one side of the square."

"Ah, yes, the mother of the claimant." We ambled on in silence for a short distance. "Do you feel that I have shirked my duty here in Bath?"

"Beg pardon, sir?"

"Please, lad, do not falsely assume an attitude of innocence with me. You know very well what I refer to."

"To your meeting with the claimant's mother?"

"Exactly. Do you feel that I am delaying that meeting unnecessarily?"

"That is not a matter that I am fit to comment upon," said I in a manner most forthright. "I will confess, however, that I am wearying somewhat of walking about Bath, and perhaps I thought that if I were to take you back to our hostelry by way of Kingsmead Square, you might be inspired to interrogate the lady in question. And I should like to be present when indeed you do."

"Why? For your entertainment?"

"No sir, for my instruction. It is sure to be a difficult interrogation, and while I learn every time you question a witness, I learn most of all when you question a difficult one."

"Jeremy," said he, "I do not think that you quite grasp how difficult it will be for me to confront Mrs. Paltrow. Good God, lad, it was I who sent her son to the gallows!"

"So you said before, sir—or something quite like it. It does seem to me, however, that it was Arthur Paltrow himself who brought it upon himself—with some assistance from the judge, of course. All you did was make public what he had kept private. The deeds were his; the discovery was yours."

"Hmmm . . . well . . . perhaps," said Sir John. "You may be right, Jeremy, and I may accept what you say, yet that does not mean that *she* will."

We had by then reached Kingsmead Square and were, in fact, passing through it on a path that would lead us past the modest edifice in which Mrs. Paltrow made her home. That must indeed have been her door from which the odd pair—the young man of good character and his sinister friend—had emerged four days past. Could that indeed have been Lawrence Paltrow and his companion? I had pondered that often in the time that had elapsed since our meeting, and I had drawn two conclusions. Firstly, I had decided that I was not sufficiently sure of the young man's identity to tell Sir John of my suspicions. But secondly, if he whom I had met were indeed the claimant, then his claim to the Laningham title was no doubt a just one, for no matter what had been said against him, the man to whom Clarissa and I had talked had certainly about him the air of nobility.

"Well, if you must know, Jeremy," said Sir John after an uneasy silence, "you are quite right."

"Sir? Do you mean in the matter of the deeds being his, and their discovery yours?"

"No, no, of course not. I mean in the matter of shirking my duty."

"But, Sir John, I never said that you—"

"No, it's true! I have put off, postponed, done all I could to avoid performing the task I was sent here to do—and for one reason only." He had come to a halt there in Kingsmead Square and was shaking a finger—one finger—at me. "And that reason, plain and simple, is that I simply cannot suppose what I would say to the woman. I have thought upon it for days now, and I can't begin to imagine what might be done to persuade her to change her mind regarding the claimant."

I felt myself in a rather awkward state. While what I had told him was true, I did wish to watch and listen to the interrogation of Mrs. Paltrow, for I was certain he would rise to the occasion and provide an exemplar from which I might learn much. Yet, on the other hand, now believing it possible that the claimant was indeed who he said he was, I had come to doubt the justice of the entire enterprise. I was for the moment quite confounded and knew not what to say.

"So," said Sir John, "I've surprised you with that, have I? It's not often I admit defeat, is it? Quite at a loss for words, I'll wager."

"Well, yes," I admitted, "but I'm not entirely—"

"If you're not entirely certain that I'm giving up now, then you're correct, Jeremy. By God, I'll not let mere embarrassment stop me. It's not shame that I feel. I am in no wise ashamed of my part in punishing that murderous son of hers. And I would have you know, too, lad, that I am no less tired than you of rambling about Bath and conversing with strangers."

"What, then, do you plan to do, Sir John?"

"Why, we are here in Kingsmead Square, are we not?"

"We are, sir."

"And I've no doubt that the woman's place of residence is quite nearby?"

"Oh, quite, sir. I can spy it now from where we stand."

"Then take me there, Jeremy, for I would exchange a few words with Margaret Paltrow."

While there was no difficulty conducting Sir John to Number 6 Kingsmead Square, it proved a bit harder to locate the resident herself. We found, upon making inquiries to a Mrs. Eakins on the ground floor, that she lived at the top of a stairway so steep that it would have kept most women prisoner there on the upper floor.

Climbing those stairs, I understood how one of advanced years might indeed feel marooned if one like her was faced with the prospect of ascending them each time she went out. For that matter, the descent might also be dangerous. Nevertheless, once above, there was a further problem in discovering the correct door. There were three to choose from; hers was the last upon which we knocked.

Margaret Paltrow was a small woman, a bit over seventy years of age as I judged her. When she opened the door, she stood for a moment blinking from behind thick, square-framed glasses, unable quite to focus upon us, so short-sighted was she. When at last she had us properly in sight, she seemed to me perhaps a bit disappointed. It could be, I told myself, that she awaited the arrival of that same odd pair.

"Hello," said she, wasting few words in greeting. "And who might you two be?"

"I am Sir John Fielding, Magistrate of the Bow Street Court in London," said he, summoning all the considerable dignity that he possessed. "And this"—placing a hand upon my shoulder—"is my young assistant, Jeremy Proctor."

She took a step back—for a better look at us, I supposed; it seemed sure to me that she had not invited us to step inside. Yet I was wrong. She gestured inward with a nod of her head, and I moved Sir John forward, touching him lightly at the elbow. Thus I took him to the very middle of the room, where we stood awkwardly, awaiting some further word from her.

She frowned as she pressed the door shut behind her. "I know your name," said she to Sir John. "Yet I cannot think at the moment how it is that I know it. I'm a woman growing old, you see, and my memory seems to grow worse each day. But do sit down, both of you, please do."

As if to provide encouragement, she seated herself in a chair just opposite us.

I eased down on the sofa beside Sir John, looking over at him as I did. Never, I think, had he seemed quite so much at a loss for words. His mouth opened and shut, then opened again—yet no words escaped it. He turned to me, an expression upon his face that could be read only as a mute call for help.

Indeed, he had been put in a bad position. She evidently expected him to inform her of why it was his name was familiar to her. What was he to say?

"Have I had dealings with you in the past?" she asked quite innocently. (Poor soul, she did seem a bit addled.)

"No, madam," said he, "I am sure you have not."

"Then my son, Lawrence," she suggested, "perhaps you, as magistrate, have come to inform him of some matter to do with his claim. I can direct you to him if that is what you wish."

"No, I fear not. The matter does pertain to the claim, right enough, but it is indeed with you I wish to speak and not with him, even if he were here with us now." He paused but a moment, then added. "And by the bye, is he here in Bath?"

"Yes, of course he is. You know . . ." She did not complete that sentence—and probably never would—for in an instant she was upon her feet, advancing across the short space that separated her chair from us on the sofa.

I jumped to my feet also, for I liked not the look in her eyes, nor the sudden set of her jaw. I would protect Sir John if need be, yet would there be need? She seemed quite incapable of doing him physical harm. A verbal assault, however, was well within her power.

"*Now* I know who you are!" She fairly growled it out; anger seemed to have deepened her voice. "I was deceived by your blindness. I thought, 'This poor blind man means me no harm,' and so I let you into my humble rooms. How wrong I was! You had already done me the greatest harm ever a mother could have. You are the one who sent my elder son to be hanged."

She hovered over him in what I deemed a threatening posture. I was about to move her back, forcibly if necessary, but then did Sir John rise, and in doing so sent her three or four steps into retreat.

"Madam," rumbled Sir John, using a voice he usually saved for the courtroom, "your son committed the crime of homicide. In point of fact, he murdered three people. That much was proven in the course of a just trial. Would you have such a one, were he not your son, go unpunished?"

"But he *was* my son," said she. "And now if I understand you aright, your interest in the claim of my son, Lawrence, upon the Laningham title bodes no good for him—or for me. I believe you would now take my younger son from me."

Sir John put his weight upon his walking stick and leaned toward her rather aggressively. "*Is* he your son, Lawrence? This young man who presents himself as such?"

"Why, yes, he is," she declared. "Of course he is."

"How can you be sure?"

"A mother knows."

"Does a mother also know how it was he managed to reappear after eight years hidden away in the American colonies but only after the Laningham title came vacant?"

"We have discussed that."

"With what result? Did he tell you what it was he did all that time he was away?"

"He has told me a few things." Having said that, her eyes shifted away from Sir John and to the floor. It was evident that she grew less sure of herself—and of the claimant—with each question put to her by the magistrate.

"Among those few things that he has told you, madam, has he given you a satisfactory reason for not writing, or in any way communicating with you during those years he was away?"

She faltered perceptibly, beginning to say one thing and then another, and finally, after a pause, no more than this: "Not perhaps to my complete satisfaction."

"I should think not," said he with great certainty. "One guilty as he of such neglect can hardly call himself your son. You show great generosity in calling yourself his mother."

With that, the woman gave in to the tears which had been threatening for moments past. She covered her face with her apron and wept most bitterly and unashamedly. I could scarce believe what next I saw, for Sir John then opened his arms to her, and she stepped inside them, allowing herself to be comforted by him who had, so to speak, brought on her tears. He patted her shoulder, muttering words of consolation as one might to a child; thus the two remained for a considerable while.

At last, Sir John said to her, "Mrs. Paltrow, I shall leave you now, having planted a seed of doubt in your mind. Let us see if it takes root overnight. We shall return to you tomorrow morn and talk about this once more. Doubt can be a healthy thing. It is faith misplaced that so often betrays one." He inclined his head in my direction. "Jeremy?"

And together we left, I guiding him through the door, and he descending those steep stairs with his hand upon my shoulder.

FOUR

*In which Sir John
receives an unpleasant
surprise upon his return*

A change came over Sir John as I described to him certain details of Mrs. Paltrow's appearance—her manner of dress, her shortsightedness, her spectacles—as well as the general look of her small apartment. We had not gone far from Kingsmead Square, when I noted that he had picked up the pace a bit. He no longer strolled, but forged ahead at something close to his London speed. And, surprising me further, it was not long until he began whistling a tune—a lively jig it was, perhaps "The Rakes of Fallow." I could not resist commenting upon it.

"You seem now to be in good spirits," said I, "certainly better than before our visit to Mrs. Paltrow."

"Yes, well, it does no good to put off such matters," said he.

"As, no doubt, you have always said."

"It is a rule I practice with some regularity," said he, stiffening a little, "though perhaps not with the religious devotion that you might prefer." Then did he add: "May I ask,

Jeremy, since you were eager to learn from this interrogation, what bit of instruction did you come away with?"

It was of a sudden no longer a game. I thought hard upon how I might answer the question truthfully, for I knew that indeed I had learned from him that day. Yet how to isolate it? How to distill the lesson to its essence? I glanced at him. He seemed to be enjoying this more than I.

At last a phrase came to me. "I would say, sir, that what I learned from what transpired there in Kingsmead Square was that the questioner can learn a great deal if he will *be sympathetic*."

"Could you elaborate upon that a bit?"

"I can try." After a moment's concentration, I began as follows: "In the beginning, you were more harsh with Mrs. Paltrow than I would have expected, reminding her that Arthur Paltrow was indeed a murderer and that he had been justly punished. Your tone remained harsh when you took up the matter of the claimant, yet it was all directed at him on her behalf. You feigned anger at him for his callous treatment of her. You found her sore spot, perhaps made her more keenly aware of the hurt she had tried to hide from herself."

"Very good, Jeremy," said Sir John. "I would also call attention to the fact that I did not try to accomplish all in a single visit. When she began to weep, I thought it best to leave her to ponder her doubts. Not that I enjoy making widows weep, but when the tears began to flow, I could not but take it as a happy sign."

We walked on. The Bear Tavern was by then within sight, as large and imposing a structure as any at this end of Bath, save perhaps for that rather large church near the grand circus. We would, I know, be arriving a bit later than was our usual. No doubt Lady Fielding and Clarissa would now be returned from the baths. There seemed to me little to do but stroll about or take the waters. But Sir John was about to prove me wrong in that.

"Jeremy, you will not guess what this town of Bath offers that none other its size does!"

"No, perhaps not, but what is it, sir? Could it be a zoological garden?" Though I had seen nothing of the kind in my rambles, I thought it possible such a collection might exist in Bath.

Yet at that, Sir John smiled. "No, lad, I know of none such, except for the menagerie in Windsor Castle. And perhaps one day we shall be able to visit there. But until then, what would you say to a trip to the theater tonight?"

"Here in Bath, sir?"

"Indeed! I heard about it only this noontime when I sent you off to search for Lady Fielding. It was that boring fellow from Bristol told me. You remember him? He was still talking when you returned. At any rate, he told me of the theater, said where we might look for it, and informed me that a new actor named Courtney will play *Hamlet* tonight. What think you of that, Jeremy?"

What I thought of it was precisely what the rest did: that a trip to the theater would be a welcome break in the routine into which we had settled after only a few days' time. In the event, it proved to be far more worthwhile than that. Though our seats were not the best, that mattered nothing to Sir John and little to the rest of us, for Mr. Courtney was the kind of actor who made the most of his vocal presentation. He had little else to work with. Not a tall man, he tended toward corpulence and in no wise possessed a commanding presence— except when he spoke. Then did he become a greater man altogether: His resonant voice filled the theater; he found the music in the words of the poet by making good use of the pauses, so that the great soliloquies were delivered in a stately rhythm as one might indeed expect from a prince. At the recess, Sir John sang Mr. Courtney's praises and would hear no criticism of the actor's physical limitations, his occasional awkwardness in movement, et cetera. All that, he swept aside and did insist, as he had upon other occasions, that in playing Shakespeare, all was in the music of the words. "And Mr. Courtney," he added, "has learned all the songs."

Whether in spite of or because of our disagreement on this matter, we judged our theater outing to be a great success; we talked of the play and Mr. Courtney's portrayal of the Danish prince all the way back to the Bear, and even took the matter up next morning at breakfast.

Of that evening there remains only one more thing to be said, and that had naught to do with any of the players but, rather, with one of the audience. It so happened that as the curtain descended a final time, the applause died away, and the small auditorium began to empty, Clarissa caught sight of one known to both of us moving parallel to us in the far aisle. She tugged at my sleeve and, having caught my attention, nodded in the direction in which she wished me to look. It was the young man who had spoken to us two in Kingsmead Square, showing us the way from there to the Bear Tavern; it was him I thought to be the claimant. He smiled and nodded politely in recognition. I saw that he was quite alone and without companion. Neither the bearded older man whom Clarissa had branded "sinister," nor Mrs. Paltrow accompanied him as he made his way to the door. Somehow I felt glad because of that.

"I saw him earlier," said Clarissa, whispering in my ear, "during the recess."

"Why did you not tell me?"

She looked at me queerly. "But why? Was there something you wanted to say to him?"

I thought about that for a moment and shook my head in the negative. It occurred to me that if indeed I were to speak to him, I should probably ask him why he had spent eight years in the North American colonies and failed all through that time to communicate with his mother. That was what puzzled me most.

Yet I had not the chance to ask him anything at all, for as it happened, those in the far aisle moved along much faster than we were able to do, and he had quite vanished by the time our party had reached the door. It was probably just as well. If there were introductions to be made, it would surely have been awkward.

•   •   •

Next morning, at Lady Fielding's insistence, we sallied forth to Spring Gardens for breakfast. While taking the waters, she had heard from one of the ladies that the breakfast rolls served there—fresh, hot, and dripping with butter—were among the great treats that the town had to offer. As we discovered, her informant was quite correct. To me, they seemed especially satisfying, for one was given the choice of having them with tea or coffee. Naturally, being something of an addict, I asked for coffee. And when the server came round again, I accepted another cup and received with it a frown from Lady Fielding.

"Jeremy," said she, "is it good to drink so much coffee? Surely it will keep you from sleeping sound."

"I've not had trouble in the past," said I. "Besides, I don't really have the opportunity to drink it often." Which was indeed a gross misstatement, for it was not opportunity I lacked, but, rather, money. Had I more of it, I should have had coffee two or three times a day—and what heaven that would be!

"Even so," said she, "you drink a great deal of it."

"Ah, Kate," said Sir John, "leave the lad be. We ought to be happy that it's coffee he craves and not gin."

"Jack! At his age? What a thought!"

"Look in the faces of some of those who sleep in the gutters, and you'll see that many are younger than Jeremy."

Lady Fielding shuddered at that. Yet I knew, having walked Bedford Street of an early Sunday morning, that he was quite right. I had seen children of ten in the condition he described.

"But tell me, Kate," resumed Sir John, "what will you and Clarissa be doing during the rest of the morning? I take it you'll not be going off to the baths this particular morning?"

"No, I believe I have got all the benefit I can from them. In fact," said she, "they've done me a world of good. That little tic I had in my back is gone, and I've a spring in my step once again."

"I'm happy to hear it, my dear."

"Clarissa has told me of a large and quite marvelous bookshop not far from here. I believe we shall go and make a visit. There is surely no pleasanter place to pass the time than a bookshop."

Having heard this, I glanced over at Clarissa and gave her a proper grin. She in return winked broadly at me, contorting her features most comically. At that, quite unable to help myself, I burst out laughing. Naturally, neither Sir John nor Lady Fielding saw Clarissa's part in this.

The magistrate's forehead knit into a frown. "Jeremy lad, what has got into you? Is this some bizarre effect of your coffee drinking?"

"Uh, no, sir, naught but silliness, I fear."

"Well, show a little restraint if you will, for we must make a return visit to Kingsmead Square, and I wish you to behave in a proper manner. We want no more difficulty with the Widow Paltrow."

"Yes, sir."

"Indeed, we should be on our way. Does anyone see the server about? Wave him over, and I shall pay. Wonderful breakfast rolls, were they not?"

There was no difficulty in finding our way once again to Kingsmead Square. And while the area seemed no less dismal than before, it was not near so deserted. I was rather surprised to see that a group of people had gathered before one of the structures in the middle of the square. They seemed to be variously occupied: Two stood on either side of the door to the house as if guarding against intruders; two more appeared to be deep in discussion—gesticulating, nodding—before the open door. And looking on, also talking amongst themselves, were a goodly number of neighbors, men and women, and a child or two. All this, it seemed to me, could mean only no good, for such groupings (as I knew quite well from life in London) usually meant that misfortune of some sort had been visited upon the house where all had gathered. Since, as we drew closer, I saw that the house in question was

Number 6 Kingsmead Square, where we had visited the Widow Paltrow the afternoon before, I became alarmed and told Sir John of the scene just ahead.

"Perhaps we should hurry," I suggested.

"No need," said he with a sigh. "If the gawkers have gathered, then what has happened cannot be undone by our haste." And as if to prove his point, he slowed from a stroll to an amble; and then, as I led the way into the crowd, he followed at no more than a shuffle.

"Get me to those two who were talking at the door, Jeremy, if you can."

"Certainly, sir—if I can." I pushed on through the assembly, solemnly repeating, "Make way, make way, please, for the magistrate." It was a chant that worked well in London; in Bath, however, its use had a rather unexpected result.

"What do you mean, make way for the magistrate?" came a petulant voice from just beyond. "*I'm* the magistrate in the City of Bath."

At that, Sir John let forth a great booming laugh, and all those before us did turn and regard us with great curiosity. "Now, see what you've done, lad," said he, chiding me in sport. "You've got me in a jurisdictional dispute with your 'Make way, make way!' "

What remained of the crowd melted away ahead of us. I believe Sir John's laugh intimidated far more than my demand to be let through. At last, none stood between us and the men at the door. One of them stepped forward and looked intently upon us. He was a plump man, red-faced and possessed of an officious manner.

"I would hazard," said he, "that you are Sir John Fielding." He, it was, as I suspected, who claimed respect as the Magistrate of Bath: The voice was certainly the same.

"That I am," said Sir John. He took a fixed position, leaning upon his stick.

"I had heard you were in Bath. Are you on holiday?"

"You might say so. I do, however, have some business with the Widow Paltrow, who lives in this house." He paused but an instant. "Whom, by the bye, do I have the pleasure of addressing? You have the advantage of me."

The Magistrate of Bath came forward a step or two and extended his hand, grasping Sir John's and giving it the requisite squeeze. "Forgive me. The name," he grunted, "is Thaddeus Bester, and I am, as I said, the magistrate of our little city. As for your business with the Missus Paltrow, I fear you will be unable to complete it, for it is her death is the cause for us to be here."

"Her death, you say? To what do you attribute it?"

"It's not me does the attributing. This gentleman with me is Dr. Thomas Diggs, who has just been appointed city coroner by the Corporation."

"Well, if that be an introduction . . . ," said Sir John, and thrust his hand forward, exploring the air around him for the medico's hand; at last, he found it, and the two men muttered their salutations as they did barely touch hands. "Then, tell me, Doctor, to what do *you* attribute her death?"

"Misadventure, plain and simple."

"You say that with great assurance. Could you describe the nature of her misadventure? Supply a few details?"

"Of course. First of all, you must keep in mind her age. She was well over seventy—nearer eighty, I would say."

"Perhaps. Over seventy I'll grant you, and no more."

"Had you been earlier to visit her?" asked Dr. Diggs.

"Jeremy and I looked in on her just yesterday."

"Very well, then you know how steep are the stairs that lead to her door."

"That I would also grant."

"Then, of course, it follows, does it not?"

"What follows?" growled Sir John. "Be more specific."

"She was an old woman," said the coroner, his voice rising steadily, "and none too sure on her feet. She made a misstep on the stairs, took a tumble, and broke her neck."

Magistrate Bester nodded in vigorous agreement with his townsman. "It happens just so with such ancient parties as her," said he. "It's a sad end for them, but really quite a common one—and not a bad way to go, all in all. Beats some terrible wasting disease, if you ask me."

"Oh, perhaps, perhaps," said Sir John, "but have you considered the possibility that perhaps she did not fall, that indeed she may have been pushed?"

"How could one tell, after all?" queried the coroner.

"Well, you might examine the carpet on the stairs and see if there was a place loose enough to cause such a fall. I recall no such place, but that proves nothing. But was she really so clumsy that she would simply lose her footing on a flight of stairs which she had traveled up and down hundreds of times in the past? Tell me, did either one of you gentlemen know the deceased?"

"Well," said Mr. Bester, "I can't say as I had the pleasure."

Dr. Diggs shook his head, then muttered a simple no.

"Then, it seems," said Sir John, "that of the four of us, only one is in a position to comment upon the likelihood of Mrs. Paltrow making such a fatal misstep. What would you say, Jeremy? Would the widow have been clumsy to such a degree?"

I thought about it for a moment or two, then answered quite honestly, "No, sir, on the contrary. As I recall, she was quite surefooted."

Neither the Coroner nor the Magistrate of Bath was eager to accept the word of Sir John's sixteen-year-old helper as definitive in this matter. That much was evident from the expressions—doubt on the first and anger on the second—which they wore upon their faces. Yet only the second gave voice to his feelings.

"This is all very well, Sir John," said Mr. Bester, "but what you're suggesting is murder . . . homicide. That sort of thing isn't done here in Bath. You come out expecting to find the same sort of lawlessness here that you meet every day in London. That just isn't the way of it. We have lords and ladies, nobles and gentlemen, the very best of society, and these just ain't the kind to commit murder. Occasionally, we'll have a duel that ends fatally for one of the two involved, which is against the law, of course, but you can't call it murder."

"Nor could I call Margaret Paltrow's death the result of a duel." Sir John paused and resumed in a different tone, not in the least aggressive, nor sarcastic. He sounded, for all the world, like the voice of pure reason: "See here, gentlemen, since you are so certain that the poor widow died as the result of a mishap, you should not mind if my helper and I were to view the premises of the widow and perhaps make a cursory inspection of her corpus. I promise to say no more to you of murder."

The two seemed surprised by the request. They looked at one another and frowned.

"I take it she has not yet been moved? I was told that there are constables guarding the door."

"No," said Mr. Bester, "she's not been moved. Seeing it's you, Sir John Fielding, we'll allow you and your young friend inside. You may look at whatever you like, but you may not remove anything. Her son has claimed the body."

"I suppose that all her belongings should go to him, too," said Dr. Diggs.

"Just one more thing," said Sir John. "When was the body found?"

"This morning, fairly early, about eight o'clock," said the Magistrate of Bath. "That was her son, as well. Said he'd come by to take his mother to breakfast, but when he found her at the bottom of the stairs, her body was cold to the touch. He came right to me, however, and reported the death. I can find no fault with him there."

"What time did you arrive, Doctor?"

"About an hour ago. By that time, the rigor of death had already taken hold of her body."

"So that she would have been dead a good many hours."

"I suppose so, yes."

"As long ago as last evening?"

"All right, as long ago as that, perhaps."

"Thank you, Doctor. Come along, Jeremy. Let's take a look inside."

I led the way, with Sir John following, his hand grasping my shoulder. The two constables, who stood one at each side of the double door, gave us sober-faced nods as we approached, though not a word passed from their lips. One did politely bend and pull open the door that we might make entry. It so happened, however, that in the space thus presented to view, the top of the victim's head was revealed. There was not much to be seen—a cotton dust cap with a few gray curls beneath, nothing more. But the crowd in the street, seeing no more than this, did suddenly stir and begin a general murmur. I informed Sir John of the cause and cautioned him where best to plant his foot so as not to disturb the body. In this way, we made it safely inside. I pulled the street door shut behind us, and we did both breathe a bit easier.

"What a pair they are!" exclaimed Sir John. "I believe they are competing for some prize to be awarded to the greatest booby. What twaddle they talked! Did you ever hear such, Jeremy?"

"No, I never did," I whispered. "But if you continue to talk in that tone and at such volume, I fear they will hear you, sir."

"Oh, I care not. Better they should know." His jaw was set, and he thrust his lower lip out quite pugnaciously. "Well, let us get to it. The poor old thing deserves an investigation of some sort into her death. All she is likely to get, she must get from us." He paused but a moment. "Describe the body to me."

That I did in detail and with no little degree of care. I gave particular attention to the position of the body there at the bottom of the stairway, the dishevelment of her clothing, and the unnatural angle of the head upon its broken support. Sir John listened carefully and nodded at each new bit of information. When at last I had done, he stood quiet for what seemed a good long while, leaning upon his stick, bowed in concentration. Then, of a sudden, his head bobbed up, and he turned in my direction.

"What about her spectacles?" he asked.

"Uh, I don't know," said I. "What about them?"

"Has she them on?"

Her face was turned to the floor. It was necessary for me

to feel round the head to be certain as to whether or not she wore them. Cold to the touch she indeed was, rigid and unyielding in every joint. So shocked was I by this that I forgot for a moment why it was I had begun feeling about her face. But only for a moment.

"She is not wearing her spectacles, sir."

"Well . . . ," said he, "then perhaps they fell off in the course of her tumble down the stairs."

"That seems reasonable, sir."

"Look into that, will you, lad? Check the stairway for her spectacles, and while you're about it, give a tug to the carpet at each step along the way."

He waited patiently as I did what he had told me. It took a bit of time to accomplish the task, there being a full twenty steps from one floor to the next; nevertheless, when I had done, I could make my report with certainty: "There are no spectacles anywhere about, and the carpet on the stairs fits just as tight as Mr. Trezavant's breeches."

"Careful with your similes there, Jeremy. You may get us both into trouble. But stay right where you are. I'm coming up."

Grasping the banister firmly, he did not let it go until he had reached the top of the stairs. He knew his limitation. While armed with his walking stick, he might blaze through the streets of Westminster as fast as any man with two good eyes, but when challenged by rough ground, or a steep incline or decline, he sought and accepted whatever help might be available—if not my shoulder, then a good, solid oaken banister did quite well.

"Try the door to her apartment," said he. "See if it is unlocked."

"No need," said I. "It stands half open."

"Then, let's inside. I should like you to continue your search for the spectacles. This is no maggot of mine, lad. I feel sure that you will find them in her apartment and probably not far from the door."

And so I did. As Sir John took a place to one side, I searched that part of the floor without result. I was about to report this to him, when a beam of the morning sun glinted sharply upon an object near the window.

"I believe I see them," I called out in triumph, leaping to the window. And there it was indeed that her spectacles lay. They rested upon the carpet, one lens cracked and the other quite shattered. I picked them up quite carefully, cupping them in one hand so as not to allow any bits or pieces to be lost.

"I have them, sir," said I, "but they are all cracked and broke. I've a clean wipe in my pocket. I'll wrap them in it for you."

"Cracked and broke, is it? Do you realize the significance of this discovery, Jeremy? You yourself said you were sure the Widow Paltrow could in no wise survive without her spectacles."

"Oh, no, sir. She was most dreadfully shortsighted. She would not have dared to venture beyond her door if she were not wearing them."

"Unless?"

I considered the question carefully. "Unless she were so frighted that she thought only of escape. And without her spectacles, fleeing in fear, she might easily have tripped, fallen, and begun that awful tumble that sent her to the bottom of the stairs with a broken neck."

"Certainly, a more reasonable theory than that put forward by the coroner. But what do you make of the broken lenses of the spectacles?"

"Why, that only supports what I have said, for she likely lost her spectacles in a struggle. That the lenses were broken suggests that they were trod upon. That they were found in a far corner near the window says that they were likely kicked there."

"Very good indeed. You've done so well that I must now impose another task upon you."

"Anything at all, sir. Just tell me what you wish."

He rubbed his chin in thought for a moment, then said he: "Perhaps I had best leave that to you. I may as well confess to you that I intend to ignore their caution that we take nothing with us. We shall take whatever aids our investigation. So let that be your measure. If you see anything—old letters, pertinent papers of any sort—then by all means take it and tuck it away. We shall make our evaluation later."

I roamed the apartment through. A sitting room, a small bedroom, and a tiny kitchen were all that required my attention, and there were not a great many places within these three rooms where matter of the kind described by Sir John might be stored—or hidden. I began my search in the bedroom. At the foot of her old canopy bed there was a chest; digging into it hopefully, I found it contained no more than bedclothes. Though there were drawers at the bottom of the wardrobe in the corner, they yielded no more than undergarments and stockings. The kitchen shelves contained only what one might expect to find on kitchen shelves. Then finally into the sitting room, where Sir John awaited me, and where I saw only a bureau of modest size as a likely repository for that which I sought. There were drawers and compartments aplenty in it, and each one seemed to be overburdened with papers of one kind or another. I went through them as quickly as I could, retained a few old letters from her son Lawrence, and disposed of the rest by stuffing them higgledy-piggledy into the places whence they had come.

I looked about and sighed, thinking that I had spent a good deal of time and had little to show for it. Then did my eye come to rest upon a bookcase which was well filled and seemed to invite examination. Well I knew from discoveries made among the books left in my attic room that papers of all kinds (some of them of interest, though most quite valueless) are often tucked between the pages only to fall out quite unexpectedly. I saw that a thorough search would mean a search of the Widow Paltrow's books, as well. I fell upon them without much sense of purpose but with the feeling that when at last I had done with them, the onus would be lifted. I had grown weary of the search. I gave each book a shake. Every now and again I was rewarded when a bit of paper would come fluttering out of the book in hand and onto the floor. What I had harvested in this way could not be said to amount to a pile but, rather, at best to a slender sheaf. But in this way, quite unexpectedly, I came across Lawrence Paltrow's diary.

I call it that, though he did not. It was a sort of notebook cum sketchbook bound in rough durable leather; across its cover was lettered in bold style, "Journal of Exploration and Discovery" and the name, Lawrence Paltrow. It was on the bottom shelf that I found it, secluded behind three larger books. It was evident the Widow Paltrow had attempted to hide it—but why? and from whom? I glanced through it and found myself fascinated by the drawings of birds, leaves, and flowers on nearly every page; the text was, for the most part, descriptive of various phenomena of nature, though there were personal notes, as well. Gratified that I had come across what seemed a substantial finding, I tucked it away into one of the capacious pockets of my bottle-green coat. With that, I counted my search complete.

"I am ready, Sir John," said I.

"Have you found anything of interest?"

"A few things, perhaps—one of almost certain significance."

"Let us, then, be gone from here."

Outside her door, a downward glance told me that Mrs. Paltrow's body had been removed. To what place I knew not, yet it seemed to me that anywhere would be better than that patch of floor she had occupied at the bottom of the stairway.

As we two descended in tandem, Sir John remarked to me that he wished to revisit Mrs. Eakins.

The name was familiar, but . . . "And who is she, sir?"

From him came a deep sigh of disappointment. "The short-ness of your memory does sometimes astound me, Jeremy. You should attempt exercises to increase and lengthen it. However"—again that dreadful sigh—"to answer your question, Mrs. Eakins is the woman who dwells on the ground floor. It was she who directed us to the Widow Paltrow yester-day afternoon."

"Ah, so she was!"

"Indeed, she was."

No word more was spoken until we stood before her door, at which time he said in a manner rather severe: "I have noted that you have taken to knocking in a timorous, tentative style. A good knock should be done with strength and authority. Let me demonstrate."

And so saying, he measured the distance to the door, then gave four or five solid thwacks to it with his doubled fist.

Indeed, I was impressed, and so, reader, was Mrs. Eakins. We heard footsteps, and then through the door, her voice: "Who is it pounding on my door so rude? There's constables about. I'll stick my head out the window and holler one here, I shall. Now, away with you!"

"Madam, I assure you I meant no harm with my knock upon your door. I have but a few questions for you regarding the death of the Widow Paltrow."

She made no move to open the door. "And who are you?"

"Sir John Fielding, Magistrate of the Bow Street Court in London. You gave me directions to your tenant yesterday afternoon."

Then at last we were relieved to hear a bolt slip and a key turn. Slowly—and one might even say *suspiciously*—the door came open, and the gray-haired woman peered out at us.

"Now I remembers you," said she, "the blind man. Why didn't you say so?"

Her question seemed to confound Sir John quite properly. He sputtered, then made what I thought was an odd declaration. "Because . . . because, madam, I do not particularly think of myself as a blind man. I am simply who I am."

"Hmmm," said she, unwilling, at least for the moment, to examine the implications of what he had just said. "Well, what do you wish to know?"

"I fear that what I have to ask you were asked earlier by Mr. Bester or Dr. Diggs."

"Who are they?"

"Why, they are, respectively, the Magistrate and Coroner of Bath."

"That's as may be, but none came to ask me a question, save a constable name of Merryman I knew from before."

"And what did he ask you?"

"He asked who lived up above besides old Mrs. Paltrow. I told him what I'd tell you, that as of this week none lived there but her. We had some flooding, chased everyone out but her. I don't know why those two had to leave. 'Twas me got the worst of it. All they had to do was get their feet wet before they climbed up the stairs. I had to—"

"I regret that, madam. I do, truly. But that is not the question I wished to ask you. I wish to know when it was you heard poor Mrs. Paltrow fall down. Could you give an estimate as to the time of the day or evening?"

She looked at Sir John oddly. "I never did hear her."

"You mean you heard no fall, no tumble, no cry for help?"

"Course I never heard her. You think I wouldn't have run out to help? Peg and I, we go back a ways. She wasn't just a tenant. She was my friend."

"Then I am sorry for your loss," said Sir John. "But surely you must have slept through it all. Such a fall would have caused a great deal of noise."

"And more, sir," said she, "my bedroom is below the stairs. If she had fallen so, I would have heard. Of that I'm sure, for I'm a terrible light sleeper."

For a moment or two, Sir John appeared utterly baffled. He rubbed his chin and shook his head, then did he turn to her at last and asked: "How many visitors had she after we left yesterday?"

"Well, now, I'm not sure. Let me think about that," said she. And that she proceeded to do. "One thing I want you to understand, though. I am not the sort of landlady who spies on her tenants."

"Oh, certainly not! That is understood—perfectly understood."

"Well, all right, then—just so you know. First of all, there was you and this lad here. You know better than I when you came by, but as I remembers, it was sometime after four but well before six, because it was right after six, though maybe half past, that those two came by."

"What two? Madam, you credit us for knowing more than we do."

"Oh. Well, I suppose I do. But the two I meant was her son and that other one he travels with, the wild-looking older fellow with the beard, the one I don't like. Now you must know something more about me."

"And what is that?" He seemed to be wearying of this woman, but had not (as yet) grown cross with her.

"Just as I do not go peeking at my tenants' visitors through the curtains, I do not go about listening at their doors to learn their private affairs. Nevertheless, I did hear a deal of shouting and foot stomping whilst those two were here. Yet Peg held her own with them. She was shouting right back. Oh, I was proud of her."

"Did you happen to hear what was said?"

"No, like I said, I'm not the sort to listen."

"Naturally not, but—"

"Well, I will say there was one word come up often at one time," she said, interrupting, "and that word was 'affidavit.' I'm not even sure myself what it means, though I've heard it said a time or two. But then, after the shouting stopped, the two of them left."

She stopped then, folded her arms, and nodded her head, as if to say, "There, you have it." Sir John, assuming he had gotten from Mrs. Eakins all she had to give, seemed ready to end their interview. He shuffled his feet. He juggled his hat in his hand. He opened his mouth to speak. Yet before ever a word came out, she had resumed:

"Then one of them came back," said she.

"What's that you say?" Sir John asked, obviously taken off guard.

"One of them came back."

"Well, which of them was it?"

"I couldn't say. The fact of it is, I can't even be sure it was one of them two. I just assumed that it was. His step on the stair was heavy, and so it was with both of them. She seemed to know whoever it was, for she opened the door to him."

"When was this?"

"Ah, well, that's difficult to say. It was after dark—of that I'm sure. The two of them left just as night was coming on. It couldn't have been much more than a quarter of an hour after that one of them came back—half-hour at most. It gets dark this time of year round seven, so you can figure it for yourself."

"And when did her visitor leave?"

"That I couldn't even guess, for I never heard him depart."

"Never heard him leave, you say? And in the ordinary course of things you would have done so?"

"Oh, yes, I suppose I would, for as I said, my bedroom's beneath the stairs." Then did she add, as if it had just occurred to her, "But do you know, I woke up during the night, and I don't know why. Could it have been Mr. Who-ever taking his leave?"

"It might have been the sound of the front door shutting," suggested Sir John.

"Why, indeed, it might have been," said she. "But why would he stay so late?"

"No doubt he was waiting for you to fall asleep."

Once out in the street, Sir John at first showed little inclination to discuss the substance of Mrs. Eakins's interview. He made a few remarks about the woman herself, none of them of a slighting nature, and praised her willingness to give information to a visiting magistrate. "I believe," said he, "that she truly meant what she said in claiming the Widow Paltrow as her friend."

"She shed a few tears whilst giving her responses," I volunteered.

"That surprises me not at all. I detected a thickness in her voice on a number of occasions that suggested as much."

We proceeded along Bristol Road in the direction of the

Bear Tavern, saying nothing at all for what seemed a long while. Sir John seemed to be considering the information given him by Mrs. Eakins in the light of our earlier discoveries in the widow's small apartment. It seemed to me that we had learned a great deal.

"Will you go to the Bath magistrate with what we have found out thus far?" I asked him. "All this certainly indicates murder."

"No," said he, "I think not. That fellow Bester and the coroner will not be convinced, for they do not wish to be. You heard what he said? 'Murder is simply not the sort of thing that is done here in Bath'—or words to that effect. What nonsense! Would he have us think that this is some sort of earthly paradise where such violent actions for base motives simply do not and will not take place? People are no better whilst visiting here than they are at home."

He continued: "I shall take what we have learned here to London and present it to the Lord Chief Justice. If nothing more, this puts a much darker complexion upon this business. Before, it seemed no more than a conspiracy to gain a title and a fortune. In fact, I half hoped that the claim would be valid, so little was I in sympathy with the true purpose of this commission upon which I foolishly agreed to serve. But . . . no more. Now murder has been committed in furtherance of that conspiracy. Now the situation is altogether different."

I was, of course, rather troubled by the direction these events had taken. For no matter what the evidence I had myself discovered, and in spite of the testimony given by Mrs. Eakins, I had my doubts still. For I could scarce believe that he whom Clarissa and I had encountered in Kingsmead Square would be capable of murder of any sort—much less that of an old woman whom he had called "Mother." But then, it was also true that I could in no wise be certain that the man we had met and seen again at the theater was indeed the claimant. There was thus no point in mentioning him to Sir John.

"You may be interested to know," said he to me, "that I have revised your conception of the crime somewhat, based upon what we learned from Mrs. Eakins."

"In what way, sir?"

"In a manner that reveals him as the cold-blooded murderer that he certainly was. As you suggested, and Mrs. Eakins confirmed, he was admitted to the apartment. There was a struggle, in the course of which the Widow Paltrow lost her spectacles, a struggle so violent that her spectacles were broken and kicked halfway cross the room. Am I correct so far?"

"Well . . . yes, sir, I suppose you are."

"Then it is here that my conception deviates from your own. You suggested, as I recall, that she had managed to break away from her assailant, sought escape down the stairway, and unable to see well because she was without her spectacles, she lost her footing and fell the full flight, thus breaking her neck by the time she reached the bottom." He paused but a moment. "Does that do justice to your theory of the crime?"

"Yes, Sir John, and as I recall, you were in agreement with me."

"I was indeed. But what we heard from Mrs. Eakins makes me believe that during that struggle the Widow Paltrow's assailant quite purposefully broke her neck—killed her by means of his superior strength. And then—what seems to me most monstrous of all—he simply sat down and waited, in fact waited for hours until he was sure that Mrs. Eakins was asleep, then carried down the corpus of her tenant and arranged it at the foot of the stairs so that it would look as if she had fallen into that position. And then he simply left."

"Yet he forgot her spectacles," said I.

"Indeed he did, and having forgotten them, he left an opening for us."

I thought a moment upon the picture that Sir John had just presented. I saw the figure of a man sitting in the dark, the body of an old woman at his feet. Had he simply waited so on into the night? Sir John, I decided, was quite right. There was something monstrous about one who could share hours in a room with the corpus of one he had just murdered.

"What a strange one he must be," said I. "The normal thing would be to flee the scene of the crime as quickly as possible. Yet he, apparently, simply sat and waited. There seems something quite inhuman about it."

"Indeed," said Sir John. "He seems to have murdered altogether without emotion—without anger and without fear. It is said, that is how the animals of the jungle kill."

Our entrance into the Bear Tavern was abetted by the ever-friendly porter. Holding open the door, he spoke his greeting and called our attention to the fact that, as he put it, the ladies had preceded us by a good quarter of an hour.

Looking about, I found them in the Orangerie (so it was called), wherein meals were served at mealtimes and drinks of every sort were offered at all others. I brought Sir John round and, seated at the table, I ordered coffee for him and me. Lady Fielding told us of their morning: at length of their visit to the grand bookshop the first time with Clarissa, and then of their chance meeting with Mr. Bilbo.

"With Black Jack, you say?" exclaimed Sir John. "And what might he be doing here?"

"Well," said she uncertainly, "he was a bit vague about that. However, he did say that he would be here the better part of a week and would expect us as his guests at dinner this very night."

At that, Sir John pursed his lips and grunted unhappily.

"What is it, Jack? Not feeling well? Perhaps it's that strong coffee." She looked at me a bit crossly and all but shook her finger as she said: "Jeremy, you ought not order such for Sir John, nor should you drink it yourself. Tea would suit you both better."

"No, no, Kate, nothing of the kind. The coffee suits me well enough. I was merely exclaiming in disappointment."

"Oh?"

"Indeed. There is no one I should rather spend some hours

with than Mr. Bilbo, yet I fear we should return to London—this very day, if possible."

"But, Jack," she wailed, "it seems we've only just arrived."

"Oh, I know, I know, but in truth I've lost my reason for being here in Bath."

"How do you mean? I don't quite follow."

"Well, you do recall, don't you, that I had come to interview a woman, a Mrs. Paltrow?"

"Yes, of course I do."

"Well, she is no longer with us."

"You mean she has departed Bath?"

"For good, I fear," said he. "She is dead."

"Oh, Jack, what a shame! An accident of some sort? Or was she taken ill of a sudden?"

"Neither, Kate. It appears certain that she was murdered."

Lady Fielding gave an uneasy look about the near-empty room. Apparently relieved that none had heard, she leaned forward across the table and whispered earnestly in remonstrance. "Jack, dear Jack, I do understand that crime is your occupation, so to speak, but you really ought not to be quite so loose with talk of murder. This is a very respectable hostelry. There are gentlefolk hereabouts, even nobility, who would be shocked to hear the word 'murder' bruited about."

"I fear," said he, "that it is one of the gentlefolk, or better put one who aspires to nobility, who is responsible."

Lady Fielding heaved a troubled sigh. "Then you might at least think of the children."

"The children?" Sir John seemed honestly perplexed. "If you mean to include Jeremy, it was he who first postulated the details of the homicide. He, it appears, can no longer be shocked. It would seem that he is quite beyond redemption."

"Perhaps so, but in truth, it was Clarissa whom I hoped you might spare. She is but twelve, Jack."

Through all the above, I had been exchanging glances with Clarissa. At the mention of murder, I had noted that her eyes had begun to glisten with interest and excitement. Yet with Lady Fielding's last remark, a look of dismay suddenly clouded her face. Clearly, she had no wish to be spared.

Nevertheless, Sir John seemed to be affected by this appeal. "Perhaps you're right, Kate," said he, "though it is sometimes as difficult to keep in mind Clarissa's chronological age as it is to remember Jeremy's. But we have, I daresay, drifted far from my original point. I see little justification in remaining, since the reason for my coming has, if you prefer, ceased to exist."

"But could we not stay one more night?"

He weighed the matter silently as we waited for his answer. "Perhaps. After all, no decision may be necessary. Jeremy, would you go now and inquire as to the immediate availability of coach space back to London for the four of us?"

I hopped to the task and went direct to the porter, purveyor of such essential intelligence. He listened sympathetically to my query, nodding in the manner of some village sage as he stroked his chin.

"Well," said he, "you've come to the right man."

"Ah," said I, quite reassured.

"But, I fear, you've come a bit late." He went on to explain that the midday coach had just departed, and the only space available on the evening coach was up on top of it. "And that," said he, "would not do for folk like yourselves."

"Oh, right! Right you are."

"But I can offer you four places in the morning coach," said he. "Leaves at eight, which is a better time to travel, after all."

"Excellent," said I. "Is the post coach house nearby? I'll run over and book places for us."

"No need. I'll send the errand boy in your stead. I'm sure you've better things to do, lad. Enjoy your last night here."

Thus it came about that some hours later, we four sat at table with Mr. Bilbo. Now, it must be admitted that he was an unusual sort of friend for one such as Sir John Fielding. Not enough that he was proprietor of London's grandest gaming establishment, he had also come to the city pursued by rumors that he had acquired his fortune by piracy in the Americas. There were indeed those who would say that Mr. Bilbo was not merely an unusual friend for an eminent magistrate, but an unsuitable one, as well. That bothered Sir John very little. He had said often to me, "Perhaps I should not like the fellow, but I do, and I also trust him. He is, in short, my friend, and there's an end to it. Let them say what they will."

Mr. Bilbo was known for his physical strength (he personally ejected dukes and earls from his premises when they misbehaved); for his dark, thick beard (which had won him the nickname Black Jack, by which he was universally known); and for his great, booming laugh (which sounded often through the Orangerie on that memorable evening).

I would not pretend to remember in any great detail what was said in conversation over dinner. Nevertheless, I recall in truth two significant instances, one of which gives a suggestion of the flavor of the table talk, and the other which proved of no little importance to this tale I have here undertaken to tell.

We sat at a round table, Clarissa and I farthest from Mr. Bilbo, listening to our elders chatting and laughing in a most easy manner. Eventually—and no doubt inevitably—they touched upon a question that had certainly occurred to me.

"What brings you to Bath?" asked Lady Fielding. "You are indeed the last person I expected to find here."

"Ah, well, that may be, m'lady," said he. "Yet I make an effort to visit this place at least a couple of times a year—more if I can manage it."

"Not, surely, to take the benefit of the waters?"

"No, though in truth I have heard marvelous reports as to their power to heal various and sundry ills, I have yet to test them myself, either internally or externally."

"Well, when you do, you will find them extremely beneficial," she assured him.

"Oh, I've no doubt of it," said he, and simply left it at that.

"Jack," said she to Sir John, "do make him tell what he does here."

"I cannot force it from him, Kate," he replied. "He's not in my court."

"No," said Mr. Bilbo, "and I hope never to be again." He burst out laughing at that, no doubt remembering, with some embarrassment, his only previous visit to the Bow Street Court. "But I'll not make it a secret. I've come, as many do, for the gaming."

"Games, is it?" said Sir John with a chuckle. "Did you have bowls in mind? Or perhaps cricket?"

"Neither," said he. "They seem to favor whist hereabouts."

"Playing at cards?" said Lady Fielding, making a great show of disapproval. "Goodness gracious!"

"It's what I do best, m'lady."

"Oh, I doubt that," said Sir John. "I seem to recall stories of your skills in seamanship . . ."

"As I've often said, all that's behind me now."

"Yes, as you've often said." This was delivered with an amused smile. Sir John then did add: "But after all, what hurt can there be in an innocent game of cards?" A pause. "If that's what you had in mind."

"Well . . ."

"Surely, Mr. Bilbo, you would not cheat!"

"Well, sir, there's cheating and there's cheating."

"Meaning . . . precisely what?"

"Meaning, Sir John, that while you would no doubt condemn me for cheating to win at the game, you would look perhaps a bit more favorably on cheating to lose."

"Well, I might if I could suppose why in the world anyone would wish to lose at a game of cards."

"It's simple enough," said Black Jack Bilbo with a wink. "When I sit down at a table of gentleman players, I make no secret of who I be. I present myself to one and all as John Bilbo—and let him who knows the name make the proper association. Then the game starts, and I begin to lose, and I continue to lose through hand after hand. I won't say I do much cheating—only as a last resort—but I make every mistake a man can make with cards in his hand. Whatever it takes, I lose. Then, finally, when things slow down and come to a stop, as eventually they must, the game breaks up, and I pass out the cards for my gaming establishment. I have them always on my person in great number. They look at them, look at me, and they say to themselves, 'If this cod runs a gaming house, then I shall visit it next time I'm in London, for he is the worst gambler ever I played with. It should not be hard to beat his tables.' In just such a way, I keep them coming."

He told his tale with such a sense of childish conspiracy that we could not but laugh when he had done with his performance. Yet, as we did, Sir John suddenly fell silent and, with an expression of mock concern, asked him: "Your tables are run fair, surely?"

"Well, of course they are, sir—and I'll take an oath on that."

"Someday you may have to."

And we all did laugh again together at the jesting look of consternation on Mr. Bilbo's face.

Thus went near three hours of the evening. The food was good. The drink was plentiful. But they were somehow the least of it. Rather, it was the companionship at table, the warmth and good cheer, which held us so long. This was, as it happened, Black Jack Bilbo's first meeting with Clarissa Roundtree. While he had heard something of her from Annie and me, he pretended to know naught of her troubled past—her term in the Lichfield poorhouse, her escape from it, et cetera. He asked her but a few questions (it was never necessary to ask her many) and she answered them, as she always did, quite volubly. Ultimately, he made what I judged to be a mistake by seeking amplification from her on that career in letters she would follow.

"And what sort of books will you write?" Mr. Bilbo asked quite innocently.

Whereupon, as Lady Fielding smiled indulgently and Sir John set his jaw, Clarissa proceeded to tell Mr. Bilbo the plot she had devised for her first romance. She later told me that she was sure he would wish to hear it, for the hero of her tale was a dashing pirate captain. Had I known that, I would have headed her off, for Black Jack Bilbo was aware of the rumors surrounding his past and was quite sensitive about them; I had no wish to see him given cause for embarrassment. Yet she told her story in such detail that she had barely penetrated the second chapter (wherein the pirate captain makes his first appearance), when two familiar figures made their entry into the Orangerie. They were the two Clarissa and I had met in Kingsmead Square—the gentlemanly fellow I had supposed to be Lawrence Paltrow and his much rougher bearded companion.

As they were led to a table and passed quite close to us, the bearded man talked quite loudly to the other; his words were meant to be reassuring ("Think nothin' of it—you'll see I'm right in this," et cetera), but they were said in a harsh, hectoring tone which caused those about them to look up in annoyance. Still, the response of Sir John and Black Jack Bilbo went well beyond that. As Clarissa prattled on with her tale, Mr. Bilbo turned his attention away from her completely and focused upon the new arrivals. As for Sir John, the sound of the bearded man's voice seemed to hold him momentarily transfixed. His face wore an expression I had come to know quite well. It was a look of intense concentration; he seemed, when it appeared, to be asking his ears to do the work of his eyes.

"I believe I know that cod," said Black Jack Bilbo.

"I believe I do, too," said Sir John. Then did he add: "But tell me, are we speaking of the same man? Describe him to me, Mr. Bilbo."

The bearded man and the putative Mr. Paltrow were given a table nearby; so close to our own was it that there was but one between us. Yet that loud, dominating voice continued only slightly less in volume than before. It was as if its owner were oblivious of all in the room except him that he addressed.

"The one who's doing all the talking," said Mr. Bilbo, "is

a man well into his forties, near as thick set as me, but taller. He has a beard longer than mine by a couple of inches and has it tied in braids the way it was done in the last century."

"That is how he was described to me some years ago. Do you have a name to put on him?"

"I do. As I remember, it was Bolt—Eli Bolt. I knew him in the colonies before I came here—in Virginia, to be exact. I was sailing out of a little upriver place called Frenchman's Bend in those days, when this man Bolt came into town with his party of about a dozen to collect a shipment of what's marked 'trading goods.' He was then one of them who went out beyond where it was safe to go and traded with the Indians in their own territory. Such pursuit took some nerve, but he'd plenty of that. Now, these 'trading goods,' as they were called, never usually amounted to much—some beads and some mirrors, trinkets and gewgaws. They would generally bring good value in feathers and animal pelts and such. A good, tidy trade could be handled in such a way and no harm done. But as it happened, that did not satisfy Mr. Eli Bolt."

"Oh?" said Sir John. "What then?"

"Well, as it happened, this all took place during the war with the French. Bolt moved in and out of the town then, provisioning and whatnot, as I did with my ship and crew. It was certain that we would meet, and we did on two or three occasions. On each of them I came away not liking the man but forced to respect his pluck in dealing as he did. Then I heard rumors that he had taken to offering firearms—mostly old matchlocks and fowling pieces—in trade to his Indian clients. They wanted them bad and would rob and steal whatever it took to get them. As I say, this was at the time of the war, and as I understand it, Mr. Bolt was not particular to which tribes he sold his wares. Some of them were hand in glove with the French."

"Giving aid and comfort to the enemy, would you say?"

"What I would say is that from what I heard at the time, it is almost certain that some farmers out on the frontier and a few British soldiers were cut down by bullets from guns that came from Eli Bolt."

All of the above discussion was carried on in tones barely above a whisper. There could be no question of Mr. Bilbo having been overheard by the two men at the nearby table, and by the time he had concluded, both were staring across the space that separated them from us. No doubt Bolt had recognized Mr. Bilbo—or was at that moment trying to place him.

"An interesting tale you've told," said Sir John. "Yet I fear the name you've given him is only something like that one I seek now to remember."

"Names can be changed, even invented," said Mr. Bilbo. "You know that as well as I, Sir John."

"Oh, indeed. Faces are more difficult to alter, and voices almost impossible. Still, since you are certain of the fellow's identity, and I have my own suspicions, as well, I would like to know what Mr. Bolt and his companion are doing here in Bath."

After hesitating a moment, I gathered my courage, leaned forward, and then said, "Perhaps I can offer a guess, sir." Wherewith, I told him of the meeting Clarissa and I had had with the two men at the other table.

Of all that occurred thereafter in Bath, I have now only a little to add—and that in summary. First of all, let it be said that Sir John Fielding welcomed what I had offered in hazard, only voicing his desire that we find some way to confirm that the two sitting so near to us were indeed the claimant and the one who was said to be always in his company. Such reassurance came from the innkeeper of the Bear Tavern himself; he showed us that the two were registered as Lawrence Paltrow and Elijah Bolton. The latter prompted Sir John to comment, "When men set about to improve upon the name given them by their parents, more often than not the original may be found signaling to us coyly from the counterfeit. Elijah Bolton is undoubtedly the same man as Eli Bolt, though I cannot be absolutely certain that he is *my* man, for neither is that one the name I have been searching for."

Having learned all he could at this time and in this place,

Sir John surprised us by consenting to accept Mr. Bilbo's invitation that we ride along with him in his coach and four to the center of town; once arrived, he left us immediately and went in search of a proper game of cards. Lady Fielding was determined that since it be Friday, we should all attend one of the balls for which Bath is so justly famed. Clarissa Roundtree thought it a superb way to pass our last evening there. I was, I admit, curious. Sir John was simply obliging: For one afflicted as he was, there was naught to gain, neither in social discourse nor physical exercise. Within the assembly room, however, he found great pleasure in listening to the music. He had me station him near the five musicians that he might hear them better and without interruption as Lady Fielding set off in the company of Clarissa to discuss matters with the ladies she had met while taking the waters.

Thus were we occupied, when Thaddeus Bester, Magistrate of Bath, descended upon Sir John, greeting him as jovially as he might if they were long-acquainted, long-separated friends. He came soon to reveal the reason for his approach when, following that effusive welcome, he puffed his cheeks, pursed his lips, then queried in a manner most innocent: "I take it that you found nothing of significance in the Widow Paltrow's quarters?"

Sir John offered him a rather frigid smile. "Nothing that would interest you."

"I thought not," said he, clearly relieved. "Bath is a peaceful place, and not the sort of setting for one of your London murders."

"Sir, let me assure that I am not in the least possessive in the matter of homicide. And let me also reject the notion, implicit in your statement, that London or any other large city has a monopoly on murder." With that, he put out his hand, groping for my arm. "Come along, Jeremy," said he. "I believe Lady Fielding may require our presence."

I took Sir John's elbow and was about to lead him away, when he signaled to me that he had not done with the Bath magistrate. We halted.

"I said, sir, that I had found naught to interest you upstairs in Mrs. Paltrow's rooms. Probably true. Yet I would carry a bad conscience away with me from Bath if I did not advise you that I learned a great deal from talking below with Mrs. Eakins, the landlady. Since she has not been interviewed, I advise you also to talk to her. There is much to learn from that woman." Then, with a sharp bob of his head to Mr. Bester, he took his leave, wishing him a good evening. And then to me the call to action: *"Jeremy!"*

I guided him through the crowd, round about the large room, looking this way and that for some sign of Lady Fielding and Clarissa. It was a grand hall, well lit, with candles burning from holders set in the wall and a great chandelier hanging above the dance floor in the exact center of the room. Beneath it, the dancers ranged wide across the space in a stately minuet. And while there were many thus engaged, there were even more encircling them, filling the corners, congregating at the doors which opened out into the garden. Male and female, they chattered and laughed so loudly that at certain places about the room it was near impossible to hear the music. How were we to find Lady Fielding in such chaos?

In fact, reader, she found us. Whilst I was anxiously looking left and right, I felt a rapid tap-tap upon my shoulder, turned, and found Clarissa had been beating upon it with her fan. (Ah, yes, her mistress had decked her out in full costume for the occasion, complete with accessories such as fan and gloves.) Lady Fielding had spied us from her place near the door and sent Clarissa to fetch us.

"Jack," said Lady Fielding when he came to her, "it has grown so warm here inside. I wonder, would you take me out into the garden so that I might breathe a bit of that cool night air? I am quite desperate for relief."

"Why, of course, my dear," said he. "Yet if you are, as you say, 'desperate,' why did you not take yourself out for a breath of air?"

"But . . . really . . . a woman unaccompanied out there in the darkness? What would people say?"

"Kate, you go about London at all hours attending to

emergencies at the Magdalene Home, why should you hesitate? I truly don't understand."

"Of course—but that is London, and this is Bath. There are dukes and duchesses, barons and baronesses, present here this evening!"

"Do you honestly believe that such as they would bring with them a *higher* standard of conduct? On the contrary, in my experience the nobility, so-called, tend to propagate *mis*-conduct wherever they go. They are bad masters and poor examples."

"Even William Murray, Earl of Mansfield?"

"There are exceptions, of course, to that rule as to any other." He extended his arm to her. "But let us not bicker over such matters. I should be happy to accompany you into the garden."

She took his arm quite proudly and moved the two of them to the door. "We should not be long," she called back to us.

"Take as much time as you like," Clarissa called back as we watched them disappear into the darkened garden. Then did she turn upon me and fix me with a keen stare. "Jeremy . . . ," said she in a manner most conspiratorial.

"Yes?" I could tell she was up to no good.

"I should like you to do something for me."

"And what is that, pray tell?"

"I should like you to dance with me."

"Ah!" said I. "Then I fear I must disappoint you, for I do not dance. I do not know how."

"Then it is high time you learned."

"Perhaps, but this does not seem the proper place," said I. "And besides, the musicians have stopped playing. Perhaps the ball is ended."

"It is no such thing. The musicians are merely resting. Now— listen!—now comes an announcement."

Indeed it was so. The leader of the musicians had stepped forward, his violin tucked under his arm. He waited a moment for some semblance of quiet, which remarkably enough he was granted. Then did he call forth to all and

sundry: "We shall now play a sampling of country dances."
At that point, his announcement was interrupted by applause
and cheers, which swelled to a considerable commotion as
he shouted out: "Hunt the Squirrel will be followed by Moll
Patley." Then did he turn back to rejoin his fellows, and the
dance floor began to fill with noisy young people, partners
who congregated into larger groups to perform the lively
dances.

"Come along, Jeremy!"

Clarissa grasped my hand and tugged me along, showing
surprising strength. In truth, I did not resist greatly, for
though I had said truly enough that I had not learned to
dance, I meant that I knew nothing of performing such formal steps as those of the minuet. Country dances I had
watched from the time I was a very young child; as partner
to my mother, I had even played often at Hunt the Squirrel,
which I would then call "the chasing dance." And so we
formed up into a square with the other couples, and Clarissa
instructed me simply to keep my eye upon them and do what
they did. Yet when the music began, and I heard that bounc-
ing rhythm once again, all came back to me quite effort-
lessly, and I was soon hopping about to the music as one well
practiced. When it came my turn to chase Clarissa round the
square, I did so with a skipping shuffle I had learned from
my mother, which had been quite admired at the time.

Clarissa, all flushed and happy, called to me as the dance
came to an end: "A fine sort you are, Jeremy. You *lied*!"

"I did *what*?"

"Why, you lied, just as plain as can be. You dance well—
for a boy."

"Ah, well, I do not count this as dancing. I learned it as a
child as a kind of game or sport."

"Just as I did," said she.

We had lined up again for Moll Patley, and were just taking our bows and curtsies when, looking beyond Clarissa, I
spied Lady Fielding hurrying toward us, her face set in an
angry expression. Why should she be so distressed, so
upset? She had never before objected to dancing; it was she,

after all, who had wished to visit the Friday ball. And while she may have been a bit annoyed to find, upon her and Sir John's return, that we were dancing, surely the extent of her displeasure was not such that she would grasp Clarissa by the shoulder and drag her bodily from the floor, as she was doing, and command me to follow. I saw from my partner's face that she was as confused as I.

Only minutes later, our little company, so hastily organized by Lady Fielding, was moving at quick-march down King Street in the general direction of the Bear Tavern. Clarissa and I led the way, since we knew it better than Lady Fielding and Sir John, who knew it not at all. We tramped along no more than a few paces ahead, unwilling for a while to say a word lest we draw the wrath of our mistress upon our heads. What was most puzzling, however, was the fact that in spite of Lady Fielding's anger (perhaps even because of it), Sir John seemed much amused. The truth was that he had hardly ceased chuckling to himself since we had left the ball.

There was a sudden jerk at my sleeve. As was intended, it brought my attention to Clarissa, who, by soundless lip movements and a bit of miming, managed to communicate a question: "Is Lady Fielding angry at you and me?" I gave that some serious thought and at last shook my head, indicating the negative.

Then, shrugging, palms up, in an exaggerated manner, she signaled her own confusion. Thus we could but plunge onward, listening to Lady Fielding clucking in disapproval and to Sir John's barely suppressed sounds of merriment.

"Jack, I do wish you would stop that."

"Stop what, my dear?"

These were the first words we had heard spoken between them since we had departed the ball.

"You know quite well what I refer to—that continual sniggering."

"Kate, I do not snigger. I have never sniggered. I am, however, known to laugh from time to time when things strike me as funny."

"*That* struck you as funny? That indecent display? That scene from the barnyard? At times your sense of humor does truly astonish me."

"Not at all, my dear. What you saw did not amuse me. It was simply that you had seen what you did so soon after our discussion of the level of conduct of the nobility. You must admit that it is no more edifying to see Lord Limerick relieving himself against the garden wall than to see the same thing done in Bedford Street by any common drunkard."

Lady Fielding sighed audibly and deeply. "I suppose I must," said she. "Though I believe I would not have been quite so shocked had he not tipped his hat and wished us a good evening."

"Do you think he may simply have thus attempted to save the situation?"

"Certainly not! I condemn him as brazen and rude! You—" At that point she broke off and exclaimed: "Goodness, Jack, what have we done?"

"What is it, Kate?"

"Why, the children—I had forgotten about them completely!" And then to us: "Clarissa! Jeremy! Have you two been listening?"

"To what, m'lady?" asked Clarissa. "We have been discussing literary questions."

That might have satisfied her, but then Clarissa began giggling and quite ruined matters for us.

FIVE

*In which we return
to London and our
quotidian labors*

Though Lady Fielding's dismaying experience in the garden may have brought us back earlier than intended to the Bear Tavern, it nevertheless returned us at a favorable hour for a proper night's sleep prior to our trip to London. And a good thing that was, too, for after we had been on the road in the post coach but a few hours, each one of us would have gladly admitted the superiority of Lord Mansfield's slightly gentler coach and four in which we had journeyed to Bath. Though we had thought the latter impossibly brutal to our backsides, we found the former far worse. The only relief we experienced from the constant jostling and bumping about were stops at inns along the way, that we might answer the call of nature, or, contrariwise, have a sip or a snack. When at last it came time to dine and rest for the night, none but Sir John was able to sleep, save for a few hours before dawn; the elderly couple with whom we shared the coach swore they had literally passed the entire night without once drifting off. By the time we arrived in London, a full thirty-eight hours had passed since our departure from Bath. This, I was told, was about the average length of time for the journey.

We arrived at the onset of evening and made direct for Number 4 Bow Street. Annie Oakum, our blessed cook, had somehow foreseen our arrival and prepared a glorious meal of roast mutton, with which she greeted us as we climbed the stairs and entered the kitchen. It was a grand welcome—and that Lady Fielding told her over and over again. For her part, Annie, quite overcome, declared quite tearfully that she had missed us, each and every one, more than she could ever tell. Then, without so much as unpacking, we did sit down and eat the feast that Annie put before us; and to my mind, it was better by far than any dinner eaten in Bath. When we had done, we sat silent at table, and warmed by the meal, we reflected upon how thankful we were to be home, and how long it would be before we would wish to journey forth again.

"Bath was lovely," said Clarissa in response to Annie's predictable question, "all that my mother said it would be, and all that I hoped."

"Oh, indeed," agreed Lady Fielding. "I believe that taking the waters did me a world of good, and I met so many charming people."

"Such a beautiful place," said Clarissa.

"Yes, isn't it?" Then did Lady Fielding go silent for the moment as her eyes took on a somewhat abstracted appearance; it was as if she were reconsidering the entire experience. "But, you know," she added as if in summary, "I would not have stayed a day longer in Bath. I believe we got from it all we possibly could have gotten."

"Well said, Kate," declared Sir John. "It is quite beyond me that those who live lives of leisure are pleased to spend whole summers there."

"Some choose to live there the year round."

"Or perhaps better put, choose to die there."

To that there was naught to say. I, at least, could think of no response. I could but wonder why Sir John had said what he had and what he meant by it. Surely not that the Widow Paltrow was responsible for her own death.

Eager though I may have been to give close examination to those items which I had removed from the modest quarters in Kingsmead Square, I found that once I was in my little room atop all the rest, I simply lacked the will to give them more than a cursory perusal. Even though the so-called "Journal of Exploration and Discovery" did greatly interest me, so exhausted was I from our journey that I fell asleep with the candle burning at my bedside and the book upon my chest.

Next day, of course, I found myself thrust back into the routine I knew so well. I was up at six, or shortly thereafter, to build a fire for Annie. Once past breakfast, I shaved Sir John, that he might meet the new week smooth-cheeked and handsome. Before leaving for the Magdalene Home with Clarissa in tow, Lady Fielding urged me to scrub the kitchen floor, "ere potatoes grow in the cracks between the boards." Annie, before leaving for her morning reading classes with Mr. Burnham, left with me a list of victuals of every sort to be bought in Covent Garden for the week ahead.

Thus it was not until the middle of the morning that I was able to present myself to Sir John and ask how I might be of service to him. I was informed that there were letters to be written and a thing or two for discussion. That left me wondering, as I prepared to take his dictation, just what those matters might be.

Among the four or five letters written that morning were two which were pertinent to this narrative. The first was a report to the Lord Chief Justice describing what had transpired during our trip to Bath. Though of necessity long and rather detailed, it was, in a way, more interesting in what it left out than in what it included. Sir John made it clear that the claimant was in Bath, but mentioned only in passing that he was usually in the company of one who was said to be a native, or at least a resident, of the American colony of Virginia. He said nothing of Eli Bolt, made no mention of his evil reputation. This had the effect of focusing blame upon the putative Lawrence Paltrow when the death of Mrs. Paltrow was described. Sir John made it clear that he suspicioned homicide, and he pointed out, as well, that the claimant may have had a good deal to gain by it, since her support for him had seemed to be weakening. Clearly, in spite of what he had heard from Mr. Bilbo regarding Eli Bolt, he held the claimant suspect.

Having had time to think upon it, Clarissa had decided as we talked at one of the rest stops on the journey to London that perhaps we ought to say something of our glimpses of the claimant at the theater on the evening of the murder. "That would surely have made it impossible for him to commit so ghastly a crime as matricide," Clarissa had said, "for he was some distance away at the time." "Difficult," I had then said, "but not impossible," which I was certain would have been Sir John's judgment in the matter. Having once thought so, I had no reason at this later moment to alter my opinion. We may not have felt that the claimant was capable of such a cold-blooded murder, but feelings mattered little to Sir John; he would have facts and unimpeachable testimony.

And so it was that I said nothing as I offered the letter just taken in dictation for his signature. I dipped the quill in the inkwell, put it in his hand, and placed the point where he might make his famous scrawl. He executed it with a proper flourish and returned the quill to me.

"Now," said he, "there is one last letter to be written. Little good it will do, I fear, for it may well be six months or more before we receive an answer. Nevertheless, the information given us by Mr. Bilbo while in Bath is such that it demands that we seek *more* information. Yet before this letter be written, I must ask you to go up and bring to me that file I set you searching for some days ago."

"Ah, yes," said I, "it was before we left for Bath, was it not? I believe the file was marked 'Unresolved.' "

"No doubt something of the sort. I believe I told you that it contained my failures."

I remembered very well and did not hesitate, but left him directly, leaping steps three at a time as I proceeded from ground floor to top in less than a minute. This, I told myself, was what I had hoped for—some attention, surely, would have to be directed at this man Bolt. It was evident that Sir John had no intention to ignore him. I was satisfied, even though, having forgotten the exact contents of the file for which I had been sent, I had little idea which of the cases in that curious file he deemed pertinent (though I did seem to recall that one of them had to do with two gentlemen come from the colonies).

"Ah," said Sir John upon my return, "back so soon? You must simply have flown up and down those stairs. Where do you find the energy?"

"I seem to recall, sir, that when last we walked together in London, I had difficulty keeping up with you."

"Did you? Well, perhaps I am not as old as I feel at this moment. I fear that grueling trip back from Bath sapped from me much of my vitality. A good sleep will help. I lay awake some time last night thinking upon that poor woman and how she died. But . . . that is neither here nor there. Let us get on with that last letter."

"What do you wish me to do with the file, sir?"

"Keep it close by. We shall refer to it anon."

I did as he said and put before me a clean sheet of paper, then I dipped the quill into the inkwell and waited. "I am ready when you are, sir," said I.

"You may address this to the Chief Justice, Crown Colony of Virginia. Mr. Marsden may be able to provide you with a name to go with the office—but then again, he may not, so we may as well address it so. It is certain to reach the right party."

That said, he commenced to dictate. As I, his amanuensis, transmitted his words to paper, I saw clearly that Sir John was keen to know all that could be provided regarding Mr. Eli Bolt. Or, as he put it to the nameless colonial Chief Justice, "Naturally, I wish to know of any convictions for wrongdoing, be it felony or misdemeanor. But I would know more. What other offenses has he been charged with? And if not convicted or charged, what villainous acts has he been suspected of? He has put in an appearance here in England, and I wish to know what sort of individual I must deal with. He is here using the alias, Elijah Bolton, and—" At that point, Sir John halted and turned to me. "Now, Jeremy," said he, "if you will open that file which I sent you to fetch . . ."

"Certainly, Sir John." I did as he directed.

"And look now at the most recent of the cases—the two men from the North American colonies." He paused, waiting, and then: "What was the name of him whom I questioned so long and with so little result?"

I found it with little difficulty. "Here it is," said I, "Elijah Elison."

"Elijah, the son of Eli, or so it would seem."

I remembered what Sir John had said to Mr. Bilbo about such false names. "There does certainly appear to be a relationship among the three," said I. "When did you remember this name from years past, sir?"

"When did I remember? Why, Jeremy, I did not remember—indeed not until you read it off just now."

"Really? What then? Surely not the sound of his voice alone!"

"I fear that is the case." And truly he did say it almost apologetically. "I have always found it easier to remember the sound of a voice than the name that goes with it. Even when I was a boy—that is, before my blindness—it was so."

"Have you some idea, sir, why this should be?"

"I've given it some thought now and again," said he, and with that he halted, held for a moment in a trance of remembering. "When I was a boy, I remembered always how people said my name—whether John, Johnny, or Jack. Then, later, I became aware of the specific differences between voices."

"Differences, sir? What sort of differences?"

"It's difficult to describe. Well . . ." said he, hesitating, "let me put it this way. Most voices, or perhaps about half of the many, have to them some claim to beauty—high or low, there be little difference in that. Yet one listens to the pitch of the voice, the loudness or softness and how specific words are said. Put it so: Every voice of some beauty has its own song. Learn it, and you will always remember that voice. I know not how else to express it."

"But," said I, "what about the rest? Those voices that lack any claim to beauty?"

"Well"—he shrugged—"all have some, I suppose. Yet those that have little are the most distinctive and they say most about their owners. For instance, people who speak always in the same tone, on the same note, come close to having no song at all in their voices. They have lives in one tone and must shout to express emotion of any kind. And then, of course, there are accents—accents of all sorts from every region of these isles, from every foreign land. They fix the speaker as certainly as the color of his skin."

"I have noted, as well," said I, "that I am judged by my speech, as others seem to be, too. Some seem to think the less of me due to my pronunciation of certain words and the like."

"Who does this?"

"Oh, butlers and such."

"Pay them no mind," said Sir John. "You speak as a good lad born in Lichfield should speak. But come, Jeremy, we have strayed far from the subject of our letter. Add that name, Elijah Elison, to Elijah Bolton. Give my profound thanks to the Chief Justice of the colony of Virginia for his attention to this matter. Then end it all with some suitable phrase of insincere groveling, and I shall sign it."

Delivery of the letter to the Lord Chief Justice proved no problem. I made my way to Bloomsbury Square along the route I had traveled so many times before, mounted the steps, and rapped upon the door with the heavy hand-shaped knocker. Indeed, I made such a racket with it that even Sir John would have been satisfied, I'm certain. The door came open directly, and there stood Lord Mansfield's butler, looking down upon me. Strange that a man no more than two or three inches taller could manage always to be regarding me, as it were, from a great height.

"Ah, so it's you," said he.

"So it is," said I.

"What do you wish?"

"Naught that should trouble you overmuch."

"Let me be the judge of that. For I must inform you that Lord Mansfield has left and will not return until evening. To be blunt, I simply will not have you about all day, waiting for the master that he may give an answer to that missive I see peeking from your coat pocket."

Since he had noticed, I whipped it out and offered it to him. Oddly, he seemed to recoil from it; he did not, in any case, immediately lay hold of it. "Here," I urged, "take it. I have no need to wait. Sir John has asked for no reply from the Lord Chief Justice."

Only then did he accept it—yet, nevertheless, rather tentatively. He seemed to weigh it in his hand, and indeed it was heavier by a sheet or two than most of the letters I bore to Bloomsbury Square. "It feels important," said the butler. "With what does the letter deal?"

"With murder, for one thing—and much else."

"Murder? Oh, dear!"

"But it is now in your hands, sir. The onus has been lifted from me and now rests upon you."

And with that I hopped down the steps to the walkway, waved, and, grinning, ran fast as I could in the direction of the coach house. There were letters to be posted—three altogether, one each to magistrates in York, Bardwell, and Salisbury; they were answers to inquiries of the kind that Sir John himself often sent to men of the law situated in parts of the country, both near and far. And so, once arrived at the coach house, all that needed be done was duck inside the postal office and present the three letters to the clerk.

Then it was on to Lloyd's Coffee House, one of my favorite locations in all of London. It was no ordinary coffee house, as you may be sure. Located at a convenient corner in the City of London, it housed a brisk trade in maritime insurance. It was a place wherein there was ever a great buzz of talk, occasional shouts, and bleats of laughter from the "brokers," so-called, who sat at the tables round about the large room. The shouts were directed at the front corner, where a fellow stood before a large slate board, making notations in chalk upon it, which followed the names and destinations of ships that would sail from London that day and the next. Thus were ships and their cargoes insured by the men who sat at the tables, conversing, jesting, and drinking London's finest coffee. Many who came to look upon this scene were shocked that matters so serious should be handled so casually.

None indeed was more casual than Mr. Alfred Humber. For years he had been a friend of Sir John's. He was said to be quite wealthy, but one would never have guessed it, for though he dressed well enough to mix in any company, there was naught of foolish fashion or frippery in his choice of clothes. He was comfortably stout—or perhaps a bit heavier than that suggests—yet at near sixty years of age he carried himself well still, and went by foot all about the town. Though a bachelor, he had two great loves: music, an enthusiasm he shared with Sir John; and coffee, which he shared with me.

"Ah, Jeremy," said he as I presented myself, "come sit down with us and have a cup. George, move over," said he to his young assistant. "Make room for him, if you will."

George, a few years older than myself, accommodated me agreeably enough, moving to another chair and leaving his vacant for me. All this he accomplished without moving his eyes from the ever-changing numbers on the slate board at the front of the room. As I settled myself, Mr. Humber waved down a server, and a moment later I had before me a cup of deep brown, near black liquid, wafting aromatic steam upward to delight my nose.

"What have you, lad?" said Mr. Humber. "A message from Sir John? A letter?"

"No, sir, only a request for your help in the way of information."

"Well, make the request, by all means, and I shall do my best to fulfill it."

I brought from my pocket the letter Sir John had dictated to the Chief Justice of Virginia and put it before Mr. Humber. "This concerns a court matter. Because the post to the American colonies is so uncertain, he would like your advice on which ship would best carry it. We take it that the next to depart is not necessarily the best choice."

"Oh, by no means," said he as he fetched up his spectacles from his waistcoat pocket and fitted them over his ears. "Let me see where it is directed . . . ah, the colony of Virginia, is it?"

"Yes, sir—as you see, Mr. Humber."

"That's another matter entirely."

"Oh? How is that, sir?"

"Most of the ships headed for a port in Virginia are engaged in the triangle trade."

At that I frowned. "I can't say that I'm familiar with the term."

"Well, it simply means that before ever they set sail for Virginia, they will first call at one of the trading ports in West Africa and take on a black cargo."

"A black cargo? Do you mean slaves?"

"Well, of course that's what they *will* be once they reach Virginia." Mr. Humber peered at me for a moment; the lenses of his spectacles did magnify his eyes somewhat, giving to him a rather owlish appearance. "Now, your face is easily read, Jeremy, and I want you to know that I myself approve of such commerce as little as you obviously do. Nevertheless, the trade is quite lucrative, and one should not allow his personal feelings to influence him in such matters." To punctuate that, he gave a nod of his head so emphatic that his spectacles jumped on the bridge of his nose.

"I understand, sir," said I, which was not at all the same thing as to say that I agreed.

"Very well, then, you would be far better off if you sent

your letter on a ship bound for one of the northern ports and made arrangements to have it posted from, say, Boston or New York to Virginia."

"Do they move letters from colony to colony?" I asked. It was a matter I had never before considered.

"Oh, indeed. Things move quite well up and down the ocean coast, though not so well into the interior. From what I hear, they're quite well organized. They like to pretend they could do quite well without our help." He himself chuckled at that. "George?"

"Yes, sir, Mr. Humber, sir?" His eyes left the big slate at last but with obvious reluctance.

"What is the next ship departing for one of the northern colonial ports—Boston? Philadelphia? New York?"

"That would be the *Ocean Rover,* sailing next week from St. Saviour's Dock in Bermondsey for New York." He spoke from memory.

"What is the cargo this trip?"

"Bricks, books, and livestock."

"And the captain is as before . . . ?"

"Uriah Harrison."

"Ah, a good man, Jeremy—experienced, of sound judgment, altogether capable. I should be happy to provide a note to Captain Harrison requesting special handling for Sir John's letter. So you see? If you content yourself with the delay of a week until the *Ocean Rover* sails, you will ultimately save at least a month. Would that not be preferable?"

"Oh, much," said I. "By all means, write the note, sir, and I shall take it with the letter across to Bermondsey."

That indeed is what I did, crossing over the Thames by London Bridge, following the guidance given me by Mr. Humber, continuing along Tooley Street off the bridge, which led into others and brought me at last to the timber yard that stood hard by the dock. I was as unfamiliar as most Londoners who lived north of the river with this rather disreputable district. There may well have been greater crime and villainy in and about Covent Garden, yet the Borough of

Bermondsey had a worse name. This was due, for the most part, to the presence of a number of docks and a great many wharves along the south bank of the Thames. There ships put in, paid off their crews, and sent them out, whoring and drinking late into the night. Seamen ashore are, for some reason, believed to be the greatest sinners of all.

Having arrived at my destination, I made inquiries after the *Ocean Rover* and found it riding at anchor nearby. It was, by any measure, a good-sized merchant vessel, one built close to the dimensions and to my untrained eyes, approximating the shape of a Royal Navy frigate. Only one figure was visible on deck, and he a junior officer who idled above on the poop. I thought it best to hail him.

"HALLOOO, the *Ocean Rover*!"

The figure moved across the poop deck for a better look at me. He cupped his hands round his mouth and let forth a mighty bellow: *"What is it you want?"*

"Captain Harrison!" I yelled back. *"Where is he?"*

He did a most curious thing: He pointed—though not to the left, nor to the right, but apparently directly at me. What did he mean? That *I* was Captain Harrison? Of course not.

"Where is he?" I repeated.

Then came a voice behind me—commanding and sharp, though not unkind. "He stands behind you, lad," said the voice. "If you but turn about, you will see him plain."

I did as directed and found a man of no more than forty years of age who wore a somewhat contradictory expression upon his face. He seemed to frown with his brow, yet had a smile on his lips.

"Oh," said I, "forgive me, sir. Are you Captain Harrison?"

"I am your man. Now, what is it you wish?"

"I have a note for you from Mr. Alfred Humber, sir." I delved into my coat pocket and brought up the note, which I handed over to him, and the letter, which I held back.

His eyes glided swiftly over the lines written in Lloyd's Coffee House and then returned to me. "Let me see the letter," said he.

"Certainly, sir."

And then, accepting it, he checked the address and the addressee and turned it over to the back side on which I had written Sir John's name and, below it, Bow Street Court, City of Westminster. "Mr. Humber has insured ship and cargoes for us for years," said he. "I would take this letter and give it my personal attention as a gesture toward him in any case. But as it happens, I had several years ago a brief acquaintance with Sir John Fielding, and he impressed me greatly, so you may assure the Magistrate of the Bow Street Court that I shall do all I can—short of delivering his letter myself—to see that it reaches the proper party in Williamsburg. You have my word on that."

"Thank you, sir," said I to him. "I shall tell him that."

With a nod, he tucked the letter away, turned, and started toward the warehouse, whence indeed he may have come. Yet, as I watched him go, a maggot nagged away at my brain. I wondered if he would consent to answer a few questions. In hope that he might, I ran after him, covering in a trice the few steps that separated us.

"Sir . . . uh . . . Captain Harrison, I wonder if I might trouble you a bit about that occasion?"

"Occasion? What occasion?"

"When you became acquainted with Sir John."

"Ah, well, that. It was in the course of one of his investigations. I was not, thank God, the subject of the inquiry. I was merely a witness from whom he wished to extract some information."

"When was this, if I may ask?"

"Well, I said it was several years ago. Perhaps I can be more exact." Rubbing his chin, he looked off into the distance in rather a dreamy manner. Then, of a sudden, he turned upon me. "Is this truly relevant, young man?"

"I believe so, sir. And if Sir John were here, I'm convinced that he would agree."

"Hmmm, well, in that case, it was 1763."

Perhaps the best way to persuade him to be forthcoming was to surprise him, I thought. But how to do that? A thought came to me then: "May I ask, Captain, do you know the name Elijah Elison?"

Captain Harrison looked at me oddly, as if perhaps engaged in a reassessment. That took a moment or two, yet I prompted him not, nor did I add to the bait I had put before him. "Elijah Elison was the name of him Sir John pursued in his inquiry," said he at last.

"He is also the subject of this letter Sir John has written to the Chief Justice of Virginia."

"How do you know this?"

"Because I took it in dictation."

"Yes, of course—his blindness. That is easily forgotten. What would you know of this Elison? He was a rough sort, the kind of half-savage that seems to thrive out on the North American frontier."

"What was it you told Sir John about him?"

"Well, you must know that the crime for which Elison was suspicioned was murder. Both he and his victim were passengers on my ship. We had not many on board, so I became acquainted with them. Sir John was chiefly interested in whether the two had met on shipboard, as this fellow Elison maintained, or if they had known one another previously."

"Which was it?" I asked.

"In all truth, I couldn't be certain. I did not see them come aboard. In fact, I don't believe I met either of them until our second or third day out. I did tell Sir John, however, that the two of them spent all their time together on deck. Elison did his tricks, and the other one—I can't for the life of me remember his name—laughed at them and drank his corn liquor. Elison, at least, was drunk through most of the voyage—or so he seemed."

"You said that 'Elison did his tricks,' Captain. What sort were they?"

"Rope tricks, they were. That fellow had a good-sized length of leather rope with which he could do near anything."

"Leather rope? I've never seen such."

"Oh, it's common enough in the colonies, especially out on the frontier, wherever there's aborigines about. His was the best of its kind I'd seen—two long strands of leather braided together. With a loop at the end of it, he could pick up near anything. He could lift a belaying pin, seize a kerchief from a pocket, near anything at all."

As he spoke, his eyes had strayed upward. It was as if he had seen his memories given shape and substance against the sky. But now, of a sudden, his recollections were done. He regarded me almost dubiously.

"Yet why now?" said he. "Why a letter to the Chief Justice of the colony about the fellow at this time?"

"He has returned to England," said I. "You must have known that Sir John allowed him to leave. He felt that the case against him was not strong enough to bind him for trial at felony court."

"Oh, indeed I did," declared the captain. "I said, if you will recall, that Sir John Fielding had impressed me greatly. It was not so much in what he did as what he did not do that he proved himself to me. He was utterly convinced that Elison was guilty of murder—yet had not the proof of it. Even then, as I understood, it was generally accepted at Old Bailey that if Sir John sent a man up for trial, he was guilty. Yet he would not abuse his reputation by relying upon his feelings in the matter. He could have sent a man to the gallows who was almost certainly guilty, yet it was the 'almost' that prevented him."

"Perhaps this time round," said I, "he will satisfy himself as to the strength of the evidence and testimony against Elijah Elison."

Captain Harrison stood, frowning, until he was struck by a most shocking supposition. "Good God," said he, "has Elison murdered again?"

"That, I fear, I cannot answer, for it is, or soon will be, a matter before the court."

I had heard Sir John use those words, or others quite like them, often enough in the years I had been with him, and though I had never before taken it upon myself to repeat them in forestalling further inquiry, I saw no reason why such a formulation should not also be used by me where it applied. Alas, reader, I made no distinction between what was proper and acceptable coming from the lips of a distinguished magistrate, and what was merely pompous coming from his sixteen-year-old helper.

In any case, the captain took umbrage at what I had said. He looked at me sharply and took a step back. "Indeed," said he, "you are a young coxcomb, are you not? I do not mind telling you, young sir, that if you were under my command, I would soon teach you a bit of respect."

Abashed, I stared after him as he strode away. "But, sir," said I, "I did not mean—"

Yet it was too late. Captain Harrison banged loudly through the warehouse door and immediately was lost from sight.

All the long way back to Number 4 Bow Street, I reproached myself for my boldness toward the captain. At one point I recall asking myself if perhaps I had so annoyed him that he would renege upon his promise to see the letter on its way to Virginia. But then I assured myself that the great respect he had announced for Sir John would not permit him to do that. Taking heart in this alone, I hurried on—down Fleet Street, down the Strand, then through the tight little streets that led to the Bow Street Court.

By the time of my arrival, the day's court session was long done. Sir John sat alone in that modest room behind the rest which he called his chambers. It was his habit, when naught stood in the way, to send Mr. Marsden out for beer, which he would drink from a cup, shoes off, his stocking feet propped up high upon the desk before him. And that was how I found him—alone and asleep, snoring away what was left of the afternoon. I was not greatly surprised, for that punishing coach ride, which had quite overwhelmed Clarissa and me, must also have taken its toll upon him and Lady Fielding, as well. I envied him, his chin down upon his chest, his hands folded over his belly; he seemed perfectly at rest—and likely to stay so for many hours to come. In fact, seeing him thus inspired me to turn round and tiptoe out of his chambers that I might myself go up the stairs to my bed and sleep. After all, had I not done the buying for Annie in Covent Garden, washed the kitchen floor, tramped the length and breadth of London? Did I not deserve a rest as much as he? I determined I would have it. But then, arriving as far as the door without making a sound, neither squeak nor creak, I realized I had little chance of bringing off my exit, when behind me there began a noisy chain of snorts and snuffles, and then a dark rumble: "Jeremy? Is that you?"

I halted where I was and turned about. "Yes, sir," said I somewhat guiltily. "I thought to let you sleep a bit longer."

"Longer? Was I asleep?"

"Yes, Sir John."

"Hmmm, strange," he reflected. "I'd no idea of it."

He swung his feet down from his desk, beckoned me to him, and asked if all had gone well. I told him that it had, assuring myself that there was no need to go unbidden into my meeting with Captain Harrison.

Satisfied, he nodded and said, "I have a task for you, one that may keep us both busy until dinnertime."

"And what is that, sir?"

"I believe you left that file regarding . . . what name did he use those several years ago? Elijah Elison, I believe it was."

"Yes, that was it."

"You left it here with me. Is this it . . . here?" Moving his hand over the desk, he allowed it to come to rest upon the file which was positioned at the corner nearest me. I was able to read, upside down, the letters which spelled out its title, "Unresolved."

"It is, sir."

"Then I should like you, Jeremy, to read to me the entire file pertaining to that fellow Elison. It may tell us a thing or two about the death of the Widow Paltrow, perhaps even give some indication why he has turned up in the company of the claimant. For my part, I'm puzzled by the connection of the two deaths—or, let us call them two homicides—at a space of many years."

That was indeed troubling. Had I not further taxed my tired body on that long walk about London, I should have welcomed the opportunity to read through it all with Sir John. As it was, I fear I showed little enthusiasm as I proceeded to separate those pages pertaining to Elison from the rest, take a place opposite the magistrate, and prepare to read to him.

Sir John seemed to sense my reluctance. "Is there something wrong, Jeremy?"

"No, sir," said I. "Just a bit tired."

"Well, perhaps we'll not be about it all the rest of the afternoon if we but put our minds as to the content of these notes. Now," said he, "you may proceed."

And so I did. The sheets in my hand may have been dusty, but Mr. Marsden had put them in good order. He had even contributed a short memorandum of his own devising which summarized the contents of the folder. I read that out first.

"The following," I began, "is a collection of notes taken in the course of the inquiry into the death of Mr. Herbert Mudge, gentleman, of Roanoke in His Majesty's North American colony of Virginia on September 3, 1763. Mr. Mudge was found dead of strangulation, his head in a noose at the end of a leather rope, by employees of the Globe and Anchor, a hostelry in the Strand. The Bow Street Court was notified, and Constable Edward Ballentine answered the call in the company of Mr. John Fielding, Magistrate of the Bow Street Court. Those questioned at the hostelry were Andrew Dubber, night porter; Nicholas Teller, manager, and Mr. Elijah Elison, trader, also of the colony of Virginia. As the inquiry continued during the next three days, Mr. Fielding also interrogated Uriah Harrison, captain of the trading ship *Ocean Rover*, and William Patton, server in the Globe and Anchor. In addition, he re-examined Mr. Dubber and Mr. Elison twice and thrice respectively. Notes from all of these interviews, dictated by Mr. Fielding, follow, as do an account of the finding by the coroner's jury in the inquest conducted by the coroner of the City of Westminster, Mr. Thomas Cox."

Then, with a nod from Sir John, I laid aside Mr. Marsden's summary and, beginning with the first interrogation of Andrew Dubber, the night porter who had discovered the body, began reading aloud through Sir John's summary of each of the interviews. The account of the case he had improvised on the day he sent me in search of the "Unresolved" file proved to be quite accurate. It was only in the details that there was some conflict in that version with what I had before me now. It was not, for instance, the maid who discovered the body of Herbert Mudge, but, rather, the night porter. She had complained to him that a lock had been thrown from the inside, and she had not the key to unlock it; then she had gone on to another room. The night porter had such a key and did not hesitate to use it. Having seen what was inside, he closed the door and went straight to report the matter to Mr. Teller, the manager.

And so on. Most, if not all, such discrepancies were of that niggling sort: mere details. But Sir John made it clear again and again that it was in such details that he was most interested. Once I had hurried through the coroner's report, he challenged me to go back with him, page by page, and see how many pertinent details, no matter how small, we might find to question—or at least discuss.

"There is one on the first page—that is, in Mr. Marsden's memorandum—which I think worthy of discussion."

"And what is that?"

"Why, the date of Mr. Mudge's death—or the discovery of his body. I had little time to examine Lawrence Paltrow's journal before sleep overcame me—yet time enough to note that the last entry was dated sometime in May of that same year, 1763. That would easily have given time, with favorable winds, to reach London by early September or late August. In other words, I believe Eli Bolt's journey was connected in some way to the death of Lawrence Paltrow. After all, I found the Paltrow journal in his mother's bookcase, did I not?"

"Indeed you did," said Sir John. "And I accept your theory as a distinct possibility. I never truly took in his own account—that he had come to London to interest makers of clothing in the beaver pelts he took in trade from the North American Indians. There is no such interest, and I am told that there is never likely to be."

He paused, then plunged ahead: "Something occurred to me during your reading of my comments upon the night porter's interviews. I did not believe him when he said that he had remained awake through the night and would have seen anyone who entered, or attempted to enter, Mr. Mudge's room from midnight to eight in the morning. In fact, I believed him so little that I had him brought back the next day that I might question him again over the same matter. But listening to you read my words back to me, Jeremy, it came to me that he might indeed have been telling the truth. For the intruder—let us say Eli Bolt—may have been in place before the night porter came on duty and the vicious deed committed. Then the murderer, mindful of the night porter's presence, may have simply remained the night and arranged all to look like suicide and hidden himself as the night porter discovered the body. He walked off when the porter ran to give the word to the manager."

"I believe I see what you are getting at," said I.

"Exactly. We have recently seen just such callousness, have we not? Long hours spent beside a recently dead body."

"You mean a recently *murdered* body."

"Indeed. Not many are brave enough—if 'brave' is quite the word—to do that."

"Mrs. Paltrow's murderer, of course."

"Of course."

Thus did we go through all the pages assembled by Mr. Marsden and saved by Sir John as one of his "failures." We found further discrepancies and similarities—and all simply by looking at this matter closely and studying the details. When we had, I supposed, concluded our review, I felt oddly troubled. I could not have said what it was that troubled me,

for my difficulty was unfocused, and I felt something was
amiss, rather than thought it. Perhaps it was only that I
wished for sleep. Or perhaps it was my need for rest that
prevented me from concentrating upon the difficulty at hand
and seeing it plain, rather than as some shapeless, threatening, dark cloud brooding over me. Sir John seemed to sense
my difficulty.

"What have you, lad?" he asked. "Toward the end of our
exercise you seemed to grow dull."

"That, I fear, is how I feel, sir."

"Nothing more?"

"Well, that could be. I sense that there is something amiss,
something overlooked by me in all this, but I cannot, for the
life of me, think what it might be."

"Perhaps if you were to read through it again?"

Unconsciously and certainly unwillingly, I must have let
out a groan at that, yet Sir John's response was not quite
what I would have expected.

"Oh, I did not mean that you need read through it *aloud*,"
said he. "We have accomplished a good deal this afternoon.
There is no need for us to repeat the entire exercise again.
You might take it back upstairs with you and look at it again
after you have had a bit of rest. How far did you go today?
You were gone quite some time."

"All the way across the river to Bermondsey." And
before I quite knew what I was about, I had launched into
the tale of my visit to the *Ocean Rover* and my interview
with Captain Harrison. Yet I omitted details and told not
quite all of it, for I omitted its abrupt and somewhat acrimo-
nious ending.

"Why," said Sir John, "what an extraordinary coincidence! Why did you not tell me of it sooner?"

Then, trapped, I was forced to do just that. I quoted to him
what I had said to the captain and his angry response to it.
Again Sir John surprised me, for he simply laughed at what
I told him.

"Ah, it was that way, was it? The captain took offense, did

he? Well, he had no right to. You were correct in ending discussion when you did. You might, however, have framed your refusal differently—something like this: 'Much as I should like to answer that, Sir John never allows me to discuss such matters.' Put the blame on me."

At that, I started to rise, thinking to take my leave—then, of a sudden, I dropped back in my chair, for what had been vague was now clear, what had been amorphous had assumed a proper shape: I realized that I now had firmly in mind that which had eluded me until that very moment.

"Sir John," said I, "you recall that in Mr. Marsden's memorandum he mentioned that Mr. Mudge was found with his neck in a noose at the end of a *leather* rope?"

"Yes, of course I do. I remember that length of rope very well. It was put in my hand so that I might examine it. Leather, it was for certain but no mere great long thong. It was of two strands, thick and tightly woven. I recall the feel of it very well."

I took a moment to confirm what I suspicioned by looking at Sir John's account of his interview with the captain. Reassured, I spoke up with some measure of confidence.

"Sir, I know to whom that leather rope belonged, and I am quite amazed that nothing of it appears in your summary of your interview with Captain Harrison."

"You do not mean to say it was the captain's!"

"No, sir, nothing of the kind. But the captain, in recalling his two passengers, Mudge and Elison, went on at great length about Elison's rope of woven leather and his skill with it."

"Skill? What sort of skill?"

"He could use it as if it were almost an extension of his hand, according to Captain Harrison—by looping it over objects and giving them a good strong pull. Why, he could pick pockets, pull belaying pins from their places. He did tricks with it there on deck. But he told you nothing of all this when you interrogated him?"

"Nothing at all," said Sir John, and then sat musing for

near a minute without a word spoken. Then this: "In spite of the captain's professed admiration of me, I recall him as a rather reluctant witness. He was within a day or two of setting sail for America and was no doubt busy with details of departure, but he gave me very little of his time. He addressed my main concern, which was whether Bolt—or Elison, or whatever his name—had known Mr. Mudge before the voyage. He had claimed they had met only on shipboard. He could not give me a definitive answer, though he said the two were constantly together on deck. I tried to open the inquiry a bit and have his impressions of them, but he would have none of it. He all but pushed me down the gangway to be rid of me. I confess I was not near as forceful in those days as I have since become."

"That is strange, sir, for he gave to me the impression that he had discussed the matter at length with you, perhaps more than once. He said that you were certain of Elison's guilt, but because you lacked evidence to support your conviction, you allowed Mr. Mudge's death to stand as a suicide. He said he admired you for that."

"Well, what he said was correct, as far as it goes. Nevertheless, I cannot suppose how he could have gotten such—" He stopped then and nodded wisely. "Or perhaps I do know. As you found out, Alfred Humber has been Harrison's insurer for years. It could well be that at some later date the captain discussed the case with my friend, Mr. Humber, who imparted to him my beliefs and feelings in the matter."

"But why would he have done such a thing?"

"Why indeed? All I can suppose is that because less than a year later I was knighted, he may have wished to seem on intimate terms with me and made Mr. Humber's conversation with me his own. I cannot account for it, but some are powerfully impressed by such honors."

"But to tell it so to me, knowing that I might repeat his words to you. Surely—"

"Perhaps," Sir John interrupted, "Captain Harrison has told it this way often enough that he himself believes it. It happened years ago, after all."

"Can one truly delude oneself in such a way?"

"Oh, indeed, Jeremy. A few do it in large matters and do so right often—many such are in Bedlam. All the rest of us are guilty of it from time to time in small ways. And that, my lad, is why a good witness is so hard to come by."

In truth, there was not much of the day left when we completed our reading and discussion of the Mudge-Elison file. And at the end we could but sigh, for we had uncovered no detail, no bit of evidence that absolutely and beyond doubt fixed the man with three names (Bolt-Elison-Bolton) as the murderer of Mudge. Even the matter of the woven leather rope meant little, for if it existed still, which was doubtful, it was wrapped round some trunk in the cellar of the Globe and Anchor hostelry.

That evening at dinner, all four of us who had made the journey from Bath were still somewhat travel-weary. We made a few sorry attempts at table talk, all of which seemed to end in sighs and yawns. I fear we should all four have drifted off to sleep right there in the kitchen were it not for Annie Oakum, our cook. She had earlier that year begun a course of study in reading and writing under the supervision of Robert Burnham, tutor to Jimmie Bunkins, who was my friend and Black Jack Bilbo's ward. Thus were we, from time to time, given reports on her progress, and occasionally proof of it, as well. It was occasioned in this instance by a polite inquiry by Lady Fielding as to whether Annie had managed well with her lessons in our absence.

"Oh, yes, Lady Fielding, rest assured."

"And you continue to do well, do you?"

"Indeed! Mr. Burnham is most encouragin'. He even presented me with a book to mark my graduatin' from the *Public Advertiser* to *The Governess,* which seemed quite fittin'."

"Oh? How do you mean that, Annie?"

"Well, the way Mr. Burnham put it, the only proper reward to give a scholar for reading one book was another book. For after all, said he, his wish is to get us to love books, and when you do, you go from one to the next without so much as takin' a breath."

Clarissa laid knife and fork down upon her plate and applauded Annie. "Well said!" she declared.

"It was Mr. Burnham said it," Annie corrected her gently.

"Then, well repeated!"

"What was the book?" asked Lady Fielding.

"*Poems upon Several Occasions,*" she said, pronouncing the words with great care. "Mr. Burnham said he found it in a bin before one of the shops in Grub Street, and he thought it right for me, for it was poems by a woman."

"By a woman, you say?"

"But he said he would in no wise have given it to me if her poems were inferior."

Clarissa: "Indeed not! And no reason why they should be."

Lady Fielding: "What is the name of this poetess, Annie?"

"Her name is Mary Leapor. Would you like to hear one of her poems?"

Lady Fielding drew back slightly. "Well . . . perhaps when we've finished dinner, you might bring the book to the table, and—"

"Oh, there's no need," said Annie. "I'm putting them to memory. I can say one for you if you like."

Then, before Lady Fielding could say no, Sir John spoke up for the first time and with considerable authority: "I for one would like very much to hear the poem, Annie." And that, of course, was all that she needed in the way of encouragement.

She swallowed the bit of food she had in her mouth, cleared her throat, and began her recitation in a voice and manner somewhat elevated yet not altogether false. What followed was said in a tone of deepest respect—to the words of the text, to the sentiment they expressed, and, lastly, to the poet herself:

" 'Autumn,' " said she, "by Mary Leapor." She cleared her throat once again.

" 'Twas when the Fields had shed their golden Grain,
  And burning Suns had sear'd the russet Plain;

No more the Rose nor Hyacinth were seen,
Nor yellow Cowslip on the tufted Green:
But the rude Thistle rear'd its hoary Crown,
And the ripe Nettle shew'd an irksome Brown.
In mournful Plight the tarnish'd Groves appear,
And Nature weeps for the declining Year.
The Sun too quickly reached the western Sky,
And rising Vapours hid his ev'ning Eye;
Autumnal Threads around the Branches flew,
While the dry Stubble drank the falling Dew . . ."

Through the last words of the last line her voice trailed slightly, and at the end she came to a complete halt. Her jaw set and her lips pursed as she sought vainly to remember the next line. We waited.

"Is there more?" asked Lady Fielding. "It does seem to end rather suddenly."

"Yes, m'lady, there is. It's just that I haven't yet got it by heart."

"Nevertheless," said Clarissa, "what we heard should be enough to prove to us that she is a true poet, don't you think? Annie, what do you know of this Mary Leapor?"

"All that I know is sad to tell."

"Oh, do tell us, please!" said Clarissa. Her eyes seemed of a sudden to shine. Tragedy and pathos seemed ever to inspire her deepest feelings.

"Well, she was dead by the time her book came out."

"Ah, posthumous publication—that is truly sad indeed."

"And she no more than twenty-four years of age."

"Did she die of a broken heart?"

"No, it was measles. Could you believe it? She was a simple cook-maid, as I once was, and her father a gardener at some grand house in Northamptonshire. All this I got from a note at the book's beginning. How sad to die so young!" Annie turned to the head of the house. "And what is your thought on that, Sir John?"

"My thought? I presume you refer to the subject of longevity," said he. "In truth I have not given it much consideration, for I am not yet of an age to do so." He paused a moment and considered. "Yet, having said that, I realize what folly I have spoken, for I am sure your Mary Leapor herself had given little or no consideration to the matter of longevity. If asked, she would, no doubt, have said that at twenty-four she was far too young to think upon such matters. And so I must revise the answer I would have given and say to you that we have no way of knowing our allotted span of years. There are too many ways that death may find us. So I can then only echo what Mr. Bilbo has said so oft to me: 'Life itself is but a gamble.' "

"Oh, goodness!" said Annie. "Mr. Bilbo!"

"What is it, girl?" asked Sir John.

She had delved her hand in her apron pocket, and now she pulled from it a letter, folded, wrinkled, and somewhat the worse for wear. "I had quite forgot," said she to him. "I was given this letter from him to you when I left, following my lesson this noontide. It was with others brought to the house."

"You have it there with you?"

"In my hand, Sir John."

"Then read it to me, by all means."

Annie hesitated. She had never been called upon to perform in such a way. It was apparent that she feared the task might be beyond her limited ability. Still, she broke the seal and unfolded the letter, taking a moment to study it before she began.

"Uh . . . he has a rather queer hand," said she.

"I'm not surprised to hear it," said Sir John. "He has his own way of doing most things. There are those, you know, who claim that much about a man can be read in his manner of writing. And so," he said, "let us allow him that. You may read on now, if you will."

That was what she did. There was, it's true, a bit of hemming and hawing over certain words, yet I myself had seen samples of Mr. Bilbo's hand and would no doubt also have had some difficulty with it. In any case, she read it aloud right to the end, and this, reader, is what the letter said:

"Sir John"—it began bluntly—"Since you and me was
both interested in the sudden appearance of that cod with the
beard, I thought you might be interested to know that him
and his partner have disappeared from Bath just as sudden. I
asked the porter here at the Bear, who seems to know most
of what goes on here, just where those two went off to, and
he didn't have any proper idea. They didn't take the London
coach, nor any other, but rode off on their own horses which
was stabled at the Bear. Tell Jeremy to keep his eyes peeled,
and you keep your ears open, for they may be coming your
way soon." Then, below the text, there was naught but a signature of sorts: "Black Jack."

At last, after dinner and following my washing-up duties, I
was free to do whatsoever I pleased. Annie and Clarissa had
retired to the room they shared to whisper their secrets and
giggle until the candle burned low and they fell asleep. Sir
John sat behind the desk in the small space he called his
study. Lady Fielding lay in bed, reading, awaiting her husband. And I? I went up the stairs, saying my goodnights
along the way, climbing all the way to my eyrie, where I,
too, would light a candle and read.

The night before, I had little chance to do more than look
inside the "Journal of Exploration and Discovery" before
falling asleep. Yet on this night I found strength within me to
remain alert and attentive long enough to read the first fifty
pages of this fascinating document. There were well over
fifty more to be read and a hundred or so blank pages that
followed them; it was, to be sure, a book of some size. Perhaps its most intriguing feature was its binding: Though
plain enough in rough leather, it bore a rich gold-brown
spine of leather upon which "Essays, Francis Bacon" had
been imprinted. I had not seen this when I took it from the
bookshelf. Perhaps when the Journal came into the posses-
sion of Mrs. Paltrow, she had it immediately bound in order
to preserve it. Whether intended or not, however, the letter-
ing on the false spine disguised what was inside.

Yet no matter. Once I was properly into the Journal, I put

such questions behind me and soon found myself reading along out of enjoyment. Not only was I learning details of an expedition into a part of the world in which I had always had a keen interest, it also brought Lawrence Paltrow into focus for the first time. I found him eager, intelligent, likable. In entry after entry—each was dated—I recognized the serious naturalist he might have become; I also sensed within the lines of the Journal the author's talent for narrative: There was a flow in his description of the expedition westward; there were interesting characterizations of the individuals in the party of twelve. (He seemed to respect Eli Bolt as a scout and woodsman, though he seemed not altogether trusting of the man.) And throughout the text there were well-executed sketches of the flora and fauna encountered along the way—leaves of trees, wildflowers, birds, and mammals, small and large. I saw that the Journal might indeed have provided the basis for a proper book on that part of the country through which they traveled—mountainous, thickly wooded, populated with those fierce North American aborigines about whom I had even then read a great deal.

SIX

*In which plans
are made for
another journey*

"Having tromped this verdant country o'er, I do now believe that there is no other place for beauty, neither in the old world, nor in this, the new, like this great land of Virginia. Well do I recall our trip through the A-pa-la-chins which culminated in our passage through what Mr. Bolt has called the Cumberland Gap, a path between the tallest and most forbidding of the mountains that led to a view of the valley below and beyond. What a sight it was! The green of the newly-leafed trees stretched on for tens, perhaps hundreds of miles, to meet at the horizon with the light blue of the sky wherein I could see no sign nor even hint of a cloud. There, what seemed to be directly beneath us (but proved to be some distance removed) the sun blinked and shimmered upon a swift-moving body of water: the Cumberland River, so I was told.

"We struck south upon reaching the river, the six of us marching along its margin as Mr. Bolt and Sa-Ku-Nah searched ahead for the ford which seemed always to be just ahead. It was found twelve miles SSW today. Tomorrow we shall attempt the river-crossing. I, who had always prided myself on my strength and vigor while in school and at Oxford, find myself taxed each new day by the pace set by my companions over this rough, beautiful country. Yet each morning I rise, rested and ready to meet the challenge once more. I doubt that any of my fellows at Balliol could match me in this.

"In my continuing attempt to survey the flora and fauna of these parts, I present on this page a drawing from memory of a bird said to be right common hereabouts—a red-headed woodpecker. While the woodpecker is common enough in England, and well known for its ability to bore holes in trees, we have not one with this coloration. Here it is called a 'sapsucker.' "

That entry from Lawrence Paltrow's "Journal of Exploration and Discovery," which was dated May 11, 1763, was not yet the last in the book. There were a good many additional entries, each filling a page or more. And each represented a day gone by on this mysterious expedition into the backlands of the colony of Virginia—and beyond. Not that there were formal and absolute boundaries in this primitive frontier region (for there were no towns, settlements, or even freeholds to be seen along the way once passage had been made through the Cumberland Gap); nevertheless, he was given to know that at some point in their journey they had passed out of Virginia and into what was known as Kin-Tuh-Kee. By the sound of it, the name clearly had its origin in one of the numberless tongues of the North American Indians. What the word—or words—meant I have no idea, yet in my reading of life in the North American colonies, I had come across reference to it a number of times; so it was that I knew it to be a wild region, one filled with ferocious and dangerous animals, as well as Indians capable of the most ferocious behavior.

Though Lawrence Paltrow gave no firm indication of the purpose of their journey, I found that with the aid of a detailed map of the Virginia colony and its surroundings which I purchased at Bricker's, the cartographer in Grub Street, I was able to follow what Paltrow called their "trail" with fair accuracy quite some distance. It was clear that they had made a long journey southward. Was it truly a journey of exploration? No, the title of Paltrow's Journal notwithstanding, Eli Bolt was not the man to lead a map-making expedition: His sort would do what he could to keep those back trails secret; he carried his map within his head. But a journey of discovery? Now, that was another matter, was it not? The question was, however, what was it they sought to discover? They must be there in search of something. If we knew what that something might be, I would better understand what Lawrence Paltrow was doing in such strange company; and conversely, if we knew what his role had been on this expedition, we might then know its purpose. I could but wonder at such questions as these.

"May 12, 1763
    "On this day we made a ford of the Cumberland River. It was not accomplished without great effort nor without loss. I, who had no experience in such fearsome maneuvers, had little notion of what lay in store—yet that was perhaps just as well. Had I known, I might well have fled at full speed back the way we had come.
    "The fundamental reason for the extreme difficulties at which I have hinted was no more than a simple consequence of nature, to wit: Heavy spring rains that year had lasted late into April. As a result, the river had reached its flood crest only a week or ten days before, and was higher by at least a foot on this day than when Mr. Bolt had made his crossing at approximately the same time the year before. Two of his own men, Coley and the unfortunate Miles, balked and protested the plan, saying that the water ran too high and the current too swift to undertake the fords at this point. When Mr. Bolt asked in his rough way what they proposed, they responded in chorus that it was only sensible to wait until the river be down to a safe level. Their leader said nothing in immediate response to them, but turned away and put the

matter briefly to Sa-Ku-Nah. (At least one assumes that was
what they discussed, yet for all I knew of the latter's guttural
talk, they might just as well have been conversing upon the
price of tea in Williamsburg.) The aborigine let forth a
proper laugh in reply, then stepped out into the river to show
them they had nothing to fear; I noted, however, that he did
not step *far* out into the river. In any case, Mr. Bolt allowed
no more discussion of the matter, but set the party to work
building the raft upon which we would transport packs,
rifles, powder and shot, tools, and my instruments. Since
trees had been cut the evening before, they had only to be
sectioned and lashed together to make a raft, which to all
appearances might be used again when we made our return.

"Thus by mid-morn were we ready to make our assault
upon the river. Near naked, pushing the raft before us, we
ventured cautiously into the water. We soon felt the pull of
the current, but could do no more than keep a grasp on the
lashings and hope for the best. Alas, the best was not to be!
We were not even halfway across—no more than up to our
waists in those chill mountain waters—when we were quite
suddenly hit by the full force of the current. I held tightly to
the braided leather; others could not. I found myself lifted
from my feet. The raft began to whirl in the current, taking
me with it. It knocked one of our number down, which of
them I could not tell, so busy was I trying to plant my feet
firmly upon the river bottom. Then was I grabbed by the
shoulder by one who proved to be Mr. Bolt. He alone, it
seemed, with his remarkable strength, managed to halt the
whirligigging of the raft by grasping the lashings with one
hand and me with the other; as long as I held on as tight as
he, he had control of the situation. So was I able then to find
the river bottom with my feet. Mr. Bolt ordered us all back
to the shore whence we had come. As we hauled and heaved,
I glanced round the raft and saw that one of our number was
gone. The missing man was Timothy Miles; it must have
been Miles, I realized, who was knocked down when the raft
went out of control. He and Coley had insisted the crossing
was unsafe—and so it had proved to be. The proof, however,

was in the loss of Miles himself. I had seen him knocked down, perhaps knocked unconscious; he disappeared beneath the water's surface, never to rise again in my sight; indeed, he might by then be half a mile downstream and most certainly drowned.

"Mr. Bolt made no mention of that. Indeed, he had very little to say. With the help of Sa-Ku-Nah, he fixed hemp rope to the leather lashings of the raft. The two conferred briefly, then he announced that they would let the rope play out across the width of the river. We were to follow with the raft after they had made it across, and only upon their signal.

"So it went. Mr. Bolt and Sa-Ku-Nah, more experienced than the rest of us, made it to the far riverbank without mishap. Yet, as we watched, we noted that the river, at its deepest, covered Mr. Bolt up to his shoulders and Sa-Ku-Nah all the way to his neck. They wound the rope around a birch tree of a reasonable thickness, then signaled us to push the raft into the water and follow them across. Thus, we were in this way able to march along behind the raft, holding it steady and on a straight course. At the deepest part of the ford, young Coley, who was quite the shortest of us, found it necessary to float behind, mouth and nose raised out of the water, that he might not drown.

"In this way we came across without more serious difficulty. Mr. Bolt, with the help of the Indian guide, had managed it with his strength; and with it, too, he had saved the raft. Had he not intervened successfully on our first attempt and the raft had been lost, there would have been no point in continuing the expedition; my scales, my weights and measures, were the very reason for enduring these hardships. Without them I would have been quite unable to do that for which I had come.

"Having reached the farther bank, we could do little more than rest through the remainder of the day. We made an early camp and dried our clothes by the heat of the fire. I took the opportunity to write this long account of the day and draw this picture of the raft which bore our 'possibles.' "

•   •   •

And below the account Lawrence Paltrow had written of the fording of the Cumberland River, he had indeed sketched the raft on which their belongings and necessities ("possibles") had been piled. There was even a detail drawing which showed just how the logs had been bound together. He had a wide-ranging interest in many matters and an unlimited curiosity regarding details of every sort. Reading through the "Journal of Exploration and Discovery" I was struck again and again by the excitement engendered in the reader (in this reader, in any case) by the tale he told. In truth, reader, I believe that I must have reread the passage just quoted three times or more in the preparation of my report to Sir John, so taken was I by the thrill of that dangerous crossing.

He had asked me to read and report to him on all the material I had taken from the Widow Paltrow's rooms. He wished me to treat Journal, letters, and all in the same way we had done the Elison/Mudge papers—questioning, searching for inconsistencies or coincidences, and above all, giving attention to details.

The letters had not much to yield. They did, however, fix the time of Mr. Paltrow's departure from England quite specifically. He made a hellish and frightening voyage from Bristol on the good ship *Hesperian*, which sailed January third and did not put in to Baltimore until the second of April. Though he wrote a good account of it in the letter which he mailed to his mother upon his arrival, there was naught in it that would explain *why* he had made the voyage, nor why it could not have waited until a more convenient and less violent time of the year. And again, the letter written upon his arrival by coach in Frenchman's Bend had little to say about such matters. Only the last of the three gave some hint to her of the purpose of his long journey, when he wrote, "I am confident, Mama, that this great gamble shall prove worthwhile. I could return to England a wealthy man; then would we be poor relations no longer. We deserve better."

Yet all through his "Journal of Exploration and Discovery" were scattered such optimistic musings as that. And each time I read that entry of May twelfth, I found myself wondering what sort of instruments Mr. Paltrow had taken with him. Scales, weights and measures? Only these? For what purpose? And why were they so necessary to the expedition that, had they been lost, all would have been lost with them? Still, no matter how he tempted speculation, he would not say specifically why he had come, nor what it was they sought on this expedition into the "back lands," as he called them. It was as if he had been given specific orders to make no mention of these essential details; and while he might follow these orders to the letter, he was not above dropping hints to whomever might read the Journal.

One more matter caught me as I gathered my material for the report: There were implications in a number of the entries that when their party reached its mysterious destination, he would be unable to write more—whether for lack of time, or because matters would then become so grandly secret that he would have to stop writing altogether for fear that he might divulge some important bit of information quite unawares. Perhaps it might be best to illustrate what I mean by quoting the rather short final entry.

"May 18, 1763

"We have arrived at our destination—or so I am told. There is naught to distinguish this place from any one of a hundred similar places I have seen along the way here, except perhaps for that one oak tree. I recall we had emerged from a deep forest of such darkness that when we at last left it and came out into the natural meadow, it was as if we had gone from night to day in a single step. The open meadow, more or less round in shape and no more than a hundred rods in diameter, was covered by a grass that in most places seemed already to have reached half a foot in height. A stream (called a 'creek' in these parts) twisted its way through the grass and led past the oak tree which stood more or less in the middle of the meadow. It was probably no older than the many oaks in the forest from which we had just emerged; nevertheless, standing alone by the stream, it seemed utterly ancient, its trunk immense and its boughs and branches overhanging a territory of rods and acres—if I may be allowed a bit of poetic exaggeration. Mr. Bolt pointed at the tree and said that we would camp under it that night, and in the morning build a permanent shelter. Mr. Coley says he believes we have entered the colony of Georgia.

"I am pleased that we have arrived at last, though it seems likely that this will mean the end of these comments and descriptions, this record of exploration and discovery. I did, after all, make a solemn vow, and Mr. Bolt is determined to see that I keep that promise. I fear I have deceived him shamefully.

"Work—my true reason for having come this long way—begins on the morrow. And so below, my last drawing no doubt for some time to come. Let it be a sketch of the oak tree which I sought vainly to describe in words."

And there it was at the bottom of the page—the spreading oak, with its trunk a full four feet round, and a suggestion of the stream which ran past it to the line of trees beyond. There was something about the drawing which lent the scene a somewhat mysterious, even a frightening, aspect. Yet I said nothing of this in my report to Sir John, for he would have naught of impressions and vague feelings. Still, each time I returned to the sketch, that slight sense of dread did come once again to me. What was it? Had young Mr. Paltrow died on this spot? Been murdered? What had happened to him?

Just as I left my personal impressions out of the report, I also spared Sir John my speculations on such matters. I had chosen to write out the report on the letters and the Journal. To him it was a matter of indifference, so long as the report was complete and accurate (for he would acquire its contents by ear in any case). For me, however, it was a far easier matter to handle the material with pen in hand than without. I had not then, of course, acquired the barrister's ability to summarize, quote, and organize while I spoke—nor was I to do so for quite some time to come. Recognizing this, Sir John gave me near two full days to do what had to be done.

At the end of that time I descended the flight of stairs from the kitchen (where I had written the report) to the ground floor wherein the magistrate kept his court and his office, and the Bow Street Runners their headquarters and arsenal. Mr. Fuller, the gaoler, had just returned from his routine trip to the Fleet Prison, where he had left the day's harvest of prisoners. In truth, I heard him enter as I came down the stairs. He was waiting for me as I reached the bottom.

He greeted me in his own, somewhat sullen way. Then, before I had a chance to greet him, he added in the manner of an accusation: "Where've you been these past days?"

"Doing work for Sir John," said I, answering him smartly.

"Not down here you weren't."

"No, sir, I wasn't. I'd a report to prepare, and I did that upstairs at the kitchen table."

"Listen to him, would you?" said he, as if to some invisible companion. "He *prepares reports* now. Next thing I hear, Jeremy, you'll be pushin' Sir John aside and takin' over as magistrate."

"I'd say his position is safe," said I in a manner right cool.

"Ah, well, I'm sure he'll be happy to hear that."

With that, I turned sharply away and stalked off down the long hall toward Sir John's chambers. Behind me I heard Mr. Fuller sniggering.

Though he bore the title of constable, he was seldom called upon to venture forth from Number 4 Bow Street to enforce the law or to bring to justice some miscreant. No, Mr. Fuller was the "day man," whose duties consisted chiefly in overseeing the prisoners in the strong room, seeing them into the courtroom, out again, and then off with them to the Fleet Prison, or occasionally to Newgate. He did his job well enough, and I knew of no instances of outright cruelty to those in his charge; yet he loved dearly to inflict little indignities and injustices upon them. I had seen evidence of this and heard mutterings from Mr. Marsden. Insofar as I knew, however, Sir John was ignorant of all. I had in the past managed to get on well enough with Mr. Fuller, yet of late—since he had heard that I was preparing to read law with Sir John, that is—he had baited me often and seemed to belittle me at every opportunity. There are those, it seems, who are ever watchful that others do not rise above themselves.

I had passed the strong room, which now stood empty, and was just getting on to the alcove which served Mr. Marsden as his office, when the man himself popped out his head and beckoned to me.

"Jeremy," said he in a whisper, "I wonder if I might have a word with you."

I nodded and stepped back with him deeper into the alcove.

Then, still whispering, he said: "I take it you was going back to visit Sir John?"

"Yes, sir, I was."

"Well, I just wanted to put you on notice that Cowley's with him now."

"Cowley?" It was but six months past that I had last seen him. Had I forgotten him so soon? "Oh, you mean Constable Cowley, of course. Well, I could come back in a bit."

"No need to do that," said he in a manner most serious. "I just wanted to prepare you, so to speak."

"Why, I know, of course, that he's lost a leg . . ."

"Aye," said Mr. Marsden, "but there's more." He paused, hesitating, as if searching for the right words to express something altogether abstruse. "He's . . . just, well, different—that's all. He even looks different."

"So would we all, I suppose, going about on crutches."

"All right," said he, "I've warned you. Now you've been prepared. You're better with words than I am, Jeremy, I'll admit it. So why don't you come back after you been in there and tell me what it is in him that's changed."

I studied his face and saw only sincerity in it. What he had said conveyed neither irony nor sarcasm. I could do no more nor less than answer him in kind: "Indeed, Mr. Marsden, if I recognize this peculiarity you have seen in Mr. Cowley and can put a name to it, you shall be the first to know."

That seemed to satisfy him, and so I took my leave, setting my course, as I had earlier, for that door at the end of the hall. I noted, as I approached, that it stood half-open.

How well I remembered the action which led to the loss of Constable Cowley's leg! An unhealed, untended leg wound had become infected, gangrenous, though this was unknown to the rest of us. He and I had gone out together in pursuit of one villain and discovered an even greater, whom Cowley dealt with quite mercilessly. Yet the action of that night had proved altogether too much for his wound: It bled; it suppurated; its hideous condition made amputation necessary.

The two were talking in low tones just inside the door. I had just perceived that and was withdrawing, that I might not be thought to be eavesdropping. Yet quiet though I tried to be, Sir John detected my presence.

"Who is there?" said he, asking in a manner not at all unfriendly.

"It is I, Jeremy."

"Come in, lad, and see who has come to visit us. He has been singing your praises to me."

"*My* praises, sir?" I stepped inside the door and had my first glimpse of Constable Cowley. I smiled at him and bowed my head politely, though I did not allow my eyes to dwell upon the tall figure leaning upon crutches. To stare thus at first sight would have been rude, it seemed to me, perhaps even cruel.

"It's true," said Mr. Cowley to me. "I was just tellin' to Sir John of how you stuck by me, you and that girl, once we got out of that stinking firetrap in Half Moon Passage."

"I'd no idea," said Sir John, "that when you were refused by a hackney driver, you threatened to shoot his horse if he did not take you here."

"Uh, well," said I, fumbling for some reasonable response, "Mr. Cowley was in a rather bad way at the time, sir."

"I was indeed," he agreed.

"Do not misunderstand me," said Sir John. "While I might disapprove the act, I certainly have no objection to the threat. Desperate situations call for extreme measures." At that he laughed, and I joined in, as well.

Yet Mr. Cowley did not so much as smile. Mr. Marsden was correct. Young Cowley was indeed different in many ways. Most obviously, he was thinner. Though the youngest of the Bow Street Runners, he was one of the biggest. Yet he had been plump and boyish in his proportions and had none of the mature masculine hardness of, say, Mr. Bailey or Mr. Perkins. There was always something of the overgrown child about Mr. Cowley—and in his manner, too. He was forgetful, inattentive, and somewhat dull, the sort of lazy boy whose parents would wonder whether he might ever be prepared for the rigors of adulthood.

That was what Constable Cowley had been. What he had become was something quite different. Lean and hard he was. His cheeks had lost their chubby roundness, and the bones of his face were visibly prominent as never before. Altered most dramatically of all were his eyes, which before, often as not, seemed rather vacant. Now they moved swiftly about until they found an object to fix upon; when they did, they looked steadily, so steadily indeed that they seemed to bore in as upon a target. There was a powerful sense of concentration about Mr. Cowley now. So fascinated was I by the changes that I perceived in his face that I all but failed to notice the empty space where his right leg had been. He leaned so confidently upon his crutches that I could have sworn that he had been on them for years.

"Mr. Cowley has decided to apprentice himself as a weaver," said Sir John to me. "It seems a good choice, all in all."

"As good as any," said Mr. Cowley. "It has the advantage of bein' the sort of craft can be worked at whilst seated. For me, that's now of considerable importance."

"I'm sure you're right, sir," said I.

"It has another advantage," said Sir John, "and that is that it is a very stable profession. So long as people need shirts and undergarments and bed linen, there will be a need for weavers."

"I hope you're right, Sir John," said Mr. Cowley. "I've come in these last months not to count on anything as sure certain."

"Quite understandable, young man. You may, however, rely upon that pension until such time as you can support yourself and your little family. I have the word of the Lord Chief Justice on that."

"As you say, sir."

Mr. Cowley said a good deal in that reply—not so much in *what* was spoken as *how* it was otherwise expressed. The look in his eyes said, Yes, I believe you have the word of the Lord Chief Justice on that, Sir John, but what is his word worth? And the twist of his mouth seemed to indicate he thought it not worth a great deal.

A pause ensued. Perhaps Sir John was assaying the ambiguity of that response which, though blind, he had perceived by his own mysterious means. In any case, it was Mr. Cowley who spoke up at last.

"Well," said he, "I had best be getting on. You've plenty to do without me taking up more of your time."

"You may take up as much of my time as you like," said the magistrate.

"Perhaps I'll come again."

"Please do. I should be greatly disappointed if you did not."

"Well, then . . . goodbye to you."

Mr. Cowley offered his hand, and Sir John groped for it. This was a rather awkward moment, for neither could quite reach the other. I urged Sir John a step forward, and brought his hand close; Cowley managed to grasp it without shifting the crutch which was tucked into the pit of his right arm. The handshake consummated, they parted.

"Goodbye to you, Jeremy. Thanks for seein' me back that night."

"Goodbye, Mr. Cowley."

He turned nimbly on his crutches and, as I stepped aside to give him passage, went swiftly through the door and down the hall. He called out a farewell to Mr. Marsden as he sped past and received one in return. We waited, and in a few moments more, we heard the door to Bow Street slam closed.

"Tell me, Jeremy, what did you think of him?"

Not knowing quite what to say, I attempted some neutral comment. "He certainly manages well on his crutches," said I.

"No doubt he does. But I wondered what you thought of him in a personal way."

"Ah, well . . . I think him much changed, and so also did Mr. Marsden. He sought to prepare me before I came here to meet him."

"Is Mr. Cowley so different physically?"

"He *is* much changed," I repeated. Then did I proceed to tell him how much and in what manner. Sir John was specially taken by my description of Cowley's eyes, restless and staring by turns.

"I daresay," he declared, "that they mirror what is going on within his head at this time. He has had a great shock from which he is only beginning to recover. I recall that when I lost my sight I went through a period of bitterness like unto Cowley's. I could hear all that in his voice—such asperity, such anger! Yet for me it was but a phase. I was soon on to better things—as I hope he will be, too. While it may be true that while he was with us as Constable Cowley he was sorely in need of maturity, he now has what he then lacked. Ah, but maturity bought at such a price! It is fearsome even to contemplate!"

He remained as he was for some time, head bowed, stroking his chin, lost in thought. I neither said nor did anything to disturb him, for it had occurred to me that, likely as not, he was considering Mr. Cowley in the light of his own experience. I had no wish to trespass on territory so private.

Of a sudden, however, he raised up and turned in my direction. "Well, Jeremy," said he, "what have you for me, eh?"

• • •

I read to him the report I had written. There is no need to quote from it here, for it was in its essentials like unto that which I presented earlier in this chapter; nor could I quote from it, for that matter, for the only copy was filed away long ago at Number 4 Bow Street. Accept it, reader, that I made to Sir John the same points I had done for your benefit. And indeed they intrigued him just as they had me.

"What was the purpose of this expedition?" he asked rhetorically. And after proper consideration, he responded to his question: "Why, it must have been the mining of some ore. Yet what could they hope to remove with only five men to work the mine? And with no pack animals, how could they transport what had been mined back beyond the mountains?

"And what was young Mr. Paltrow's purpose among this gang of evildoers?" Sir John continued. "Was he there as an employee? A partner? It is evident he fully expected to grow rich from this venture. What special knowledge had he to contribute to the enterprise? I believe I can guess—he with his weights and measures, et cetera. But I should like to be certain."

Sir John set me thinking with his questions. Having listened, having given consideration to the matter, I spoke out at last. "Sir," said I, "in writing up my report for you, I took pains to avoid speculation."

"You needn't have," said he. "At this point, your speculations are as worthy as mine."

"Then here is a point you might care to contemplate: It does seem to me, sir, that there is another party here who is not yet accounted for."

"And who is that?"

"I do not know, sir. I can but describe to you his role in all this."

"Then proceed, by all means."

"You questioned earlier just what Lawrence Paltrow might have been doing with this 'gang of evildoers.' It is difficult, after all, to suppose any connection there might earlier have been between him and Eli Bolt. There must have been a third party to put the two together. And it seems to me, too, that this unknown third party would have planned this enterprise and very likely have financed it, as well."

"Oh? Explain."

"Well, frankly, I doubt that Eli Bolt had either the sophistication or the wherewithal to bring an expert over to the colonies—and I believe you will agree that that is the role in which Lawrence Paltrow has been cast?"

"Ah, yes, no question of that."

"According to the picture drawn by Mr. Bilbo, Bolt is a man who possesses a certain cunning—but little else. Whatever he had was not sufficient to organize an expedition of this sort. And as for Paltrow himself, he lacked the necessary knowledge of the North American colonies."

"And so therefore," said Sir John, "this third party you posit becomes not just a possibility but a probability." He nodded, leaning back in his chair. Then he added as if it were a mere afterthought, "He would have been in England. He would have directed matters from here, of course."

"Possibly, well, probably, I suppose."

"That was reluctant agreement if I ever heard such," said he.

"I didn't mean that it should sound so."

"Ah, well . . ." He fluttered his fingers dismissively, as if to say that it was of no importance. Waiting, he thought, and thinking, he waited longer; I said naught to interrupt him. He finally spoke up, so unsuccessfully at first that he must needs clear his throat and begin again. This, then, was the question as at last it was formed: "You do see the significance of this, do you not?"

"Well, I would say that it means there was an individual altogether unknown to us who was involved in this expedition at some distance, and may even have been involved in the murder of Mudge, if indeed a murder there was."

"No, Jeremy, it means more than that. To me it means that if you are correct in what you speculate—and, as I say, I think it likely that you are—then I think it also probable that there is a third party involved in the matter of the Laningham claimant, one who has planned and financed this enterprise, just as he did that one in 1763. In other words, I believe them to be one and the same."

"But, Sir John, are you sure of this?"

"Of course I'm not sure, but it is the sort of theory that one must test in the course of an investigation."

"How do you plan to do that, sir?"

"How indeed! To be truthful, I'm not quite sure. It is a matter that I shall take up tomorrow with Lord Mansfield."

"Tomorrow?"

"Yes, he has called another meeting of that damned commission that they might discuss the news which we brought back from Bath. We shall meet with him a full hour before the rest attend."

"Let me be frank, Sir John," said the Lord Chief Justice. "What I do not understand, have not understood, and I suspect will never be able to understand, is this: If we assume that the Laningham claimant is an impostor, as I believe we must, how could his own mother have been deceived by him? I suspect that she could only have been bribed to acknowledge him as her son."

"Oh," said Sir John, "I think not, and had you met her, as I did, you would know that she could not be bought. The woman may have been foolish, but she was at least honest."

"So you say, but a bribe is not necessarily put forward in quid-pro-quo fashion. It is perhaps more often offered with a wink and a nudge. The briber may say to the potential bribe-taker, 'With your cooperation, this great bounty will be mine, and when it is, I shall set you up in grand style! You will live as royalty!' Now, there, Sir John, you see? No specific action is requested, nor is a price named. I doubt that one who couched his request and offer in terms so general could be convicted—at least not in my court—yet a bribe nevertheless."

"I call that no bribe at all," said Sir John, "and for the reasons you have just stated—and particularly not if such a speech were delivered from one who claimed to be a son to his putative mother. Indeed it would be his duty to improve her state when it was in his power to do so." The magistrate paused, evidently to give greater weight to what he then added: "I do not, however, believe that is why she recognized the claimant as her son."

"You do not?" said the Lord Chief Justice rather gruffly. "What, then, would you say?"

"I would ask you to look upon the situation of the Widow Paltrow. She had been left little on which to end her days, and so she took that little with her to end them in Bath. She knew it to be a place of beauty in which some vestige of the old grace still prevailed. Merely to stroll in Bath for a single morning provided more interest and amusement than she might find during a month in Laningham, which was precisely why she had left what had been her home for so many years. Yet in only a few years she might have become somewhat dissatisfied with her situation. Visitors to the town came and went. They offered opportunities only for conversation. Friends were difficult to find. In fact, during her years in Bath, she made only one—and that was her landlady. Margaret Paltrow was lonely, growing old, and was losing her sight. She had little to look forward to but her death.

"Imagine such a woman in such a state," urged Sir John. "Now try to imagine her feelings when into her life came, quite of a sudden, a young man telling her he was her younger son, the one whom she had not heard from in eight years, the one she had given up for dead. He courted her, gave her attention to a degree which she had never before known in her life. Visiting her every day, he exercised his considerable charm upon her, and all he asked in return was that she acknowledge him as her son. Well, why shouldn't she? How could he not be her son? Though he was perhaps a little taller than she remembered him, he seemed to look like the boy who had set sail so many years ago for America—though it was true she could see him only dimly, due to her failing eyesight. His voice? Well, you know she never was very good at remembering voices, and eight years was a long time to keep one in mind, especially at her age.

"In short, Lord Mansfield," he concluded, "she gladly acknowledged him as her own. If he wished her to sign an affidavit to that effect, then she would do so. She may no longer be able to see as she once could, but she could see well enough to write her name, could she not? All this she did with no payment offered, not even for a wink and a nudge, or a vague promise to do right by her in the future. No, she did it because he was a pleasing young man who lavished attention upon her. She did it, in fine, because she was a lonely old woman who badly wanted diversion."

"Only that?" said the Lord Chief Justice.

"It was what she needed most," said Sir John.

"Then you came along, so you did, and destroyed all her illusions."

"I did what you would have me do."

"It was obviously sufficient. The doubts you planted bestirred her to voice those doubts to the claimant—and that was what led to her death." The Lord Chief Justice paused a moment to ponder. "Yet, I must admit," said he then, "that I do not comprehend why it was necessary to murder the old woman. Surely the claimant, who had charmed her once, could charm her again."

"Certainly it would seem so," said Sir John. "Nevertheless, while it may not have been necessary to remove her permanently, it may have been an option offered them which proved altogether too attractive to decline."

"What do you mean? I don't quite follow."

"Why, with the mother dead, there could be no question of her withdrawing her recognition of the claimant as her son. Yet with her dead, they still held her affidavit. If her death could be made to look accidental . . ."

"As it was."

"Indeed. But perhaps we lay too much blame in this matter upon the claimant himself. He may not have been directly responsible."

"If not he, then who? At times, John Fielding, you seem to—"

Then sounded the heavy, hand-shaped door knocker, which I knew well from my many previous visits to this house in Bloomsbury Square; thrice did it beat upon the oak right solemnly and loud, as if launched by the very hand of fate.

"Oh, damn!" said Lord Mansfield, having thus been interrupted. "It must be one of the commission. Is it an early arrival? Surely it is."

But it was not. The Lord Chief Justice himself had been more than half an hour late. So that we, Sir John and myself, who had come promptly, could do nothing but sit in silence until our host made his appearance. I was annoyed on behalf of my chief. Why must he always wait at the service of the Lord Chief Justice? True enough, Lord Mansfield valued him highly—though not near highly enough, to my way of thinking. He had, at least, the good grace to beg for Sir John's pardon when he came late into the study, and he even offered an excuse, something I had never known him to do before.

In any case, Sir John's opportunity to acquaint the Lord Chief Justice with all we had learned while in Bath and afterward was, alas, much diminished by the latter's late arrival. I could tell he was about to present him with some of the facts, as well as a few of our speculations regarding Mr. Eli Bolt. But then that knock came upon the front door announcing the arrival of Thomas Trezavant, prosperous tradesman, friend of the Prime Minister's, coroner of the City of Westminster, and member of the nameless commission.

So it was that all who had been invited to this meeting assembled within the space of a few minutes. George Hemmings, solicitor and an expert in matters of property, was the next to beat upon the door. And last came Mr. Hubert Dalrymple, a most successful barrister. (Absent in body, though present through the participation of Mr. Dalrymple, was Sir

Patrick Spenser, Solicitor-General, who had called the commission into being.)

As I had done before, I took a more active role than usual by recording the minutes of the meeting. It was a burdensome task, for while I was made keenly aware of what was said in the course of the meeting (since I was obliged to quote or paraphrase every last bit of it), I was unable to study the unspoken reactions of the listeners. Sir John had taught me that what is said with the eyes, face, and body is often more eloquent than that which is spoken.

It began with Lord Mansfield's brief recapitulation of the proceedings of the previous meeting. Then did he call upon Mr. George Hemmings to deliver a report upon his survey of the Laningham estate. He had a way of deprecating his efforts while at the same time persuading his listeners that his "casual estimate" was probably accurate to within 100 pounds. He gave the figure as £ 650,000, but then he added that a truly accurate and detailed figure would take some months to prepare. "I have done as well as time allowed," he concluded, "yet I believe that this figure reached by different methods and from information gleaned from different sources should stand reasonably well."

Then did the Lord Chief Justice read to the group the letter which Sir John had dictated to me upon our return from Bath, and which I had delivered to this house only a few days past. It dealt not only with Sir John's interview with Margaret Paltrow, but also with her subsequent death. It was plain from Sir John's report that he believed that the woman had been murdered. This indeed caused a great stir among members of the commission. They grew rowdy of a sudden, demanding to know more.

"On what do you base this opinion, Sir John?" Mr. Dalrymple demanded. "This seems a rather reckless conclusion."

And Mr. Hemmings wished to know just why she should have been murdered. "I see no sense to it," said he.

Lord Mansfield sought to calm them by explaining that he

intended to bring the matter up personally with the Magistrate of Bath. "Let us put off further questioning on this matter until I have heard from him."

That seemed to suit all present. Nevertheless, it did not ultimately bring calm. Mr. Trezavant declared that he had that very day been in conversation with the Member of Parliament for Laningham, who informed him of "certain irregularities" in the methods employed by the claimant in gathering signed statements. "I propose Sir John go out and look into this matter."

Mr. Dalrymple scoffed at this. "He would be recognized in a trice," said he. "He is probably the best-known blind man in London!"

"But I doubt the claimant would recognize Jeremy here," countered Sir John, pointing in my general direction.

"Are you proposing that we send this lad out alone?"

"By no means," said Sir John. "I propose that he and I journey out together in pursuit of the claimant. Where is he now?"

"He is in Oxford," declared Lord Mansfield. "I happen to know that he is seeking affidavits from Lawrence Paltrow's old teachers."

"Why, m'lord, I do believe you're having the fellow watched," said Sir John.

"You may believe what you like, but depend on it that he is now in Oxford."

"Then Jeremy and I shall make Oxford our destination. I shall seek out those teachers, and Jeremy shall follow the claimant about town, and we shall see if the report Mr. Trezavant has been given is true."

"Yes," said Mr. Trezavant, "I have heard he is a great one for setting up at an inn with that fellow who travels with him. They buy statements with gin and ale—or so it is said."

"And that is where Jeremy may prove to be of help," said Sir John. "If the claimant pays for statements with coin of alcohol, then we shall know it. Such practice would disqualify him as a claimant, surely."

"It would certainly count strongly against him," said Lord Mansfield.

"Then it's agreed?" said Sir John. "Jeremy and I shall take ourselves to Oxford, search out the claimant, and keep him under observation."

"Agreed! agreed!" shouted Lord Mansfield, the Lord Chief Justice.

Whether less enthusiastic, or simply confused by the suddenness of it all, the other members of the commission said nothing.

SEVEN

*In which we bring
the investigation
to Oxford*

O ne of the travelers on the post coach had made an arrangement with the driver to stop before we reached the City of Oxford that he might alight from the coach and make his way to his home nearby. Yet the traveler in question was a rather elderly sort, and since I sat nearest the door, I thought it best to step down myself to give him a hand. Thus it was that I was afoot at the side of the road as the old gentleman's portmanteau was lifted down to him. I stared into the distance, taking in the view of Oxford ahead. It was a place of spires and towers, all of which seemed to gleam in the setting sun; it seemed quite magical in such a light.

"And so, young sir," the driver called down to me, "what think you of this view of the city from Bear's Hill?"

"I think it quite grand," said I.

"Aye, so it is, but you'd best—"

His advice to me was blotted out by the sudden intrusion of a score of bells and clocks as they announced the evening hour. Yet I perceived quite rightly that he wished me to climb back into the coach, which I did right swiftly, settling in beside Sir John. The wheels beneath us began to turn once again. We should soon reach our destination.

We had been on the road from London all through the afternoon. The distance to Oxford was not great, yet there were many stops made to drop off quantities of mail at villages and towns along the way. Because the Lord Chief Justice had insisted Sir John leave the next day, it had been necessary for us to accept bookings upon the afternoon post route, for all the earlier (and swifter) coaches had been filled. If Sir John were displeased by this, he did not show it. He rode, as he always did, so silent and so indifferent to what was said around him, he might well have been sleeping. Yet only I, of the five other passengers within the coach, could be certain he was not.

He had been visited earlier that day by Lord Mansfield. I would not have known had I not discovered that grand coach and four of the Lord Chief Justice awaiting him when I returned from the post coach house with our tickets to Oxford town. As it was, I heard nothing of their conversation, for as I was going in, Lord Mansfield was coming out. I stood aside politely and raised my hat to him as he passed by; he mumbled something, perhaps to me or perhaps to himself, which I failed to understand. But then of a sudden he stopped, turned round, and caught me with his eye, perhaps recognizing me for the first time.

"Here, you, boy, come here."

Indeed I came, hastening to him across the few feet which separated us. "Yes, m'lord. What was it you wished?"

"You're Sir John's lad, are you not?"

"Well, uh, yes, m'lord, I suppose I am."

"*Suppose?* Don't you *know*?"

How could I repair the damage I had done with my slightly ambiguous reply? Obviously, only an emphatic affirmative or negative would do for him. "Oh, I do know, and I certainly am Sir John's lad. I hesitated only because your question seemed to imply that I might be his son. That I am not, though I should be proud to be."

He seemed mildly annoyed by what I had just told him. "Oh? You're sure, are you?" said he with a frown. "I'd always assumed you were his natural child. Why, I believe I heard it so from someone or other."

"Oh, yes, m'lord, I am indeed sure. Though I am but an orphan, I remember my father well. He was a printer and well educated, who taught me—"

Again I was interrupted by the Lord Chief Justice. "Leave off!" he commanded. "I would not hear your entire family history, for I have no interest in it. I asked you only because I wanted to be certain that it was you who would accompany him to Oxford."

"It is, m'lord."

"Very well, I will tell you true, young man, that just now I urged him to bring one of his constables to Oxford for his protection. He refused me, so he did, and said it was quite unnecessary. But still, with what may well be murder to be reckoned as part of this conspiracy, I believe that precautions are necessary. So I charge you, young sir, to look after his safety. If anything should happen to him, I shall hold you responsible."

With that, he bobbed his head in a most decisive manner, turned abruptly, and banged through the door to Bow Street.

I stood, staring after him in rather a confused state. I felt as if I had come off rather badly in this exchange with Lord Mansfield, yet what might I have said different? How rude he had been to ask if I was the natural son of Sir John! That is the sort of thing one might wonder upon, speculate about, but never *ask* about. How could he have done so?

Still somewhat dazed by the encounter, I set off down the hall at a slow pace, turning over in my mind what had just transpired.

He had barely recognized me—that much was plain. Yet just think of the many messages from Sir John I had put into his hands and asked for an immediate reply. Only consider that he had seen me just the day before in Sir John's company. Had I no existence in his eyes? Was I faceless? Voiceless? What sort of judge would that make him?

What was it Lord Mansfield had said? "I would not hear your entire family history, for I have no interest in it." Indeed had he not! At that moment I made a vow to myself—and ever afterward I remembered where it was that I had made it, as well as the circumstances that had led up to it. I stood at the door to Sir John's chambers, my hand poised to knock, and swore to myself that in some way I would force the Lord Chief Justice to take an interest in my family history; I would one day prove to him that I was worthy of notice.

And then I knocked upon Sir John's door.

"Come ahead, Jeremy. Have you found a place for us on the stagecoach?"

"On the post coach," said I as I entered. "Alas, it was the best I could do."

"It will take a while longer, but it will get us there by evening," said he. "Did you ensure places for us by purchasing tickets?"

"I did, sir." I then hemmed and hawed a bit, looking for a way to bring up the matter which troubled me, but in the end I settled for the direct manner: "I noted Lord Mansfield's departure as I arrived . . . ?"

"Ah, yes, well, most of what he had to say was plain foolishness."

"Oh?"

"Yes, well, I'll tell you about it later, perhaps when we are under way on our journey."

Yet, as I have said, reader, he remained silent during the length of our journey to Oxford. As the coach slowed, approaching our destination, Sir John shifted in his seat and adjusted his clothes, as if making ready to climb down from the coach. How could he have known that we were so close?

The driver reined up before the Blue Boar Inn, which was located on High Street. The place had been chosen for us by Lord Mansfield, who had, the day before, sent down a request for a single large room for the two of us. The Blue

Boar was not near as big as the Bear Tavern, where we had stayed in Bath, but I liked it much better. First of all, the room we were given was larger and better appointed. Secondly, the Blue Boar was in the very center of the small city which I had glimpsed from the hill—and not on the outskirts, as was the Bear. And finally, the dining room at the inn was as cozy and comfortable as our own kitchen back in Bow Street, and the meal we ate there was near as good as those fixed for us by our own dear Annie.

A warm fire awaited us. It was yet early when we came down for dinner, but we were travel-weary from our trip from London and quite ready to cheer ourselves with food and drink. As we settled down at a table near the fireplace, I must have let out some deep sound of satisfaction, a hum of appreciation, or something of the sort.

"What a strange noise," said Sir John. "It must signify happiness."

"Yes," said I, "I suppose it does."

"And why, especially?"

"Well, I am not quite sure, but here I am in a city famed as a great seat of learning, a place which I have always wished to visit. And here we sit, about to eat our dinner in the most pleasant surroundings. Certainly, I confess, sir, I am happy."

"Pleasant surroundings, is it?" said Sir John with an amused smile. "Why not describe them to me?"

Why not indeed? "Well, to begin with," said I, "the room where we sit, which is neither too large nor too small, is rather dark. There burns a candle on each table, and a candelabrum hangs behind the bar, but most of the light in the room comes from the fireplace which is directly behind you."

"Ah, I was aware of that fire. Not only does it provide light, as you suggest, it warms my rump rather pleasantly, as well. But tell me, Jeremy, is that all you see?"

"Well, no, there are others at the tables, though not *all* the tables."

"How many tables in all?"

I counted hurriedly. "Nine in all, counting our own. There are four that are occupied."

"Well and good, but tell me, what of the walls? Are there no decorations? No pictures? No—"

"Oh, but of course there are, Sir John. Let me see now, where to begin? First of all, the walls are of wood and of brick—that is, three walls of wood and one of brick. There are four pictures scattered about, though not very good ones to my mind."

"And what do they represent? What sort of pictures are they?"

"Portraits all."

"And is that all you see? Only four portraits? Nothing else hanging upon the wall?"

"No, sir, I think that be all."

"Perhaps not," said Sir John. "Now, I, who have lost my sight, have not lost my reason. And reason dictates that in a place such as this, which is called the Blue Boar Inn, after all, there must somewhere be some representation of a wild boar. Look once again. Do you see no such picture—a hunting scene perhaps? Nothing of the kind? Perhaps if you were to take a look behind the bar . . ."

As my eyes swept the room very slowly, I considered what Sir John had said—"reason dictates"—and then did I realize that I was being given a test. That made me search ever more diligently. I asked for a bit more time—and was granted it. And I was then just rising to leave the table for a look behind the bar, when I happened to glance behind Sir John and above the fireplace—and what did I see? What indeed but the mounted head of a most vicious-looking wild boar! His eyes glistened fearfully. His tusks curled most threateningly. I could not imagine a more dreadful creature.

Nor could I suppose how I had missed it while scouring the room so diligently with my eyes. Nevertheless, I knew I must tell Sir John of it—and tell him I did; he replied with no more than a wise expression of superior amusement. Naturally, I was embarrassed—more than embarrassed: I was altogether abashed by my failure. What must he think of me? Since I was quite unable to imagine what I might say to excuse my oversight, I felt relieved at the appearance of a server come to learn what might be our pleasure for dinner. He presented himself with a smile and offered us a choice of every sort of chop a man could wish for; Sir John wished for beef, and I was pleased to ask for the same. When he called for a good bottle of claret, I knew he intended to make a feast of this, our dinner away from Bow Street.

Once again alone with me, he leaned across the table and said indulgently: "There is obviously a lesson to be learned from this exercise, Jeremy. The lesson is simply that when reason and the information given us by our senses are in conflict, then we must not always and immediately assume that the senses have it right. Give reason its chance, as well."

That seemed no more than common sense to me, though of course I would not say so to him. The lesson *I* had learned—or believed I had—was that I simply must be more observant. What interested me far more than any of this was the earlier visit to Bow Street by the Lord Chief Justice. I must know more of that.

"You—" I hesitated, but then plunged on: "You indicated that there were some things you could tell me about Lord Mansfield's visit."

"I suppose I did, yes."

Had he chosen to be evasive? I hoped not, for when he did so choose, there was simply no possibility of drawing him out. I decided it might be best for me simply to wait. And indeed it proved to be so.

"Ah, well," said he after no little space of time, "perhaps there are a few things we might discuss. Do we sit a safe distance from others here in the dining room? I would not have them listening in."

I assured him that his words were safe from eavesdroppers. He accepted that, gave a thoughtful rub to his chin, and began talking at not much more than a whisper and as one might if talking to himself.

"As I suspected," said he, "Lord Mansfield does have this fellow, Paltrow, watched. And generally speaking, his watchers are among the best at their filthy trade. Nevertheless, they have failed to find where the claimant and Eli Bolt make their home here in the area of Oxford."

"Is that so important?" I asked.

"Yes, because they have evidently spent a great deal of time in Oxfordshire. Lord Mansfield assumes they have, for they are continually appearing and reappearing in the city and in various parts of the shire. It is not as it was when they visited Bath—that is, they are not guests at any inn or hostelry—of that Lord Mansfield's spies are certain. They are here on the invitation of one who lives in Oxford, or, more likely, in the city's environs."

"But Laningham is nearby," I objected. "Could they not be residing somewhere near the border with Oxfordshire?"

"Perhaps," said Sir John, "but in either case—whether in or near Oxford or in or near Laningham—if we knew with whom the two of them were staying, we would very likely also know the third man in this conspiracy."

"And in the earlier one which led to the death of Mr. Mudge."

"Exactly so, yes . . . yes, indeed," he mused. "You realize, do you, that this will make your task far more difficult than my own."

"Oh? How is that, sir?"

"If you will recall, I nominated you to watch our two conspirators while I interview certain of the younger Paltrow's teachers. It will undoubtedly be much easier for me, for I know where to look for the teachers, but you, Jeremy, must go out and search Oxford for the claimant and Eli Bolt. You may find them and you may not. They may be soliciting signed statements, and they may not. Yet if you find them, and that is what they are doing, then you must observe them at some length to see that they are doing it right."

"Yes, of course," said I, "to make certain there be no buying of affidavits with booze or beer."

Sir John chuckled at that. " 'Booze,' is it? Where do you

hear such talk?" Yet not waiting for my reply, he proceeded to instruct me in the proper methods to employ. (No doubt I should have paid him better attention.) "You should observe the two without yourself being observed. Under no circumstances should you call attention to yourself by arguing, accusing them, or otherwise challenging them. Is that clear to you?"

"Oh, quite clear, sir."

"If that be so, Jeremy, then I shall be glad," said he. "You must be careful in this matter, lad, for by being aggressive, you might cause considerable difficulty for all of us."

"I'll remember, sir."

When, just then, the server returned with the bottle of claret which Sir John had ordered, I was glad for the relief thus provided. I had had quite enough of lessons and admonitions. At no other time, it seems, do young men have greater confidence and wisdom than at the age of sixteen.

As I expected, I was up and about the next morning well over an hour before Sir John. That gave me time enough to leave the inn for a brief walk about this small city. There was none to greet me or give me direction on the ground floor, so I made my exit and hallooed the first fellow I saw, to ask him where I might look for the university. Rather than answer me in a forthright manner, he responded with a gesture: Pointing his index finger into the air, he whipped his hand round in a circle. It was only after I had tramped through the city in that early hour for some time that I understood what he meant to say with that odd movement of his hand: The university was all about; colleges seemed to lie in every direction round the Blue Boar Inn.

Thus when, after breakfasting, Sir John and I made our way out into the day, I was able to be of some aid to him in finding Balliol College. It had been, as I correctly assumed, the residence and more of Lawrence Paltrow during his years at the university. There were a number of references to Balliol in his "Journal of Exploration and Discovery," all of them sentimental and backward-looking. I, who had had very little formal schooling but had prospered well under the tuition of my mother and father, felt there was little sense to such feelings. How, I wondered, could one wax nostalgic over a great pile of bricks and stone, no matter how impressive it may appear? Was Balliol grander or better than other colleges I had glimpsed in the course of my morning's ramble? It evidently seemed so to the youthful Paltrow. Or was it his fellow scholars and his teachers who excited such loyalty? That would seem to make better sense, would it not?

So it was that I led Sir John, who tended to silence, across and down from our inn to the college. It was not a great journey by foot, but there were many more pedestrians out on the walks than when I had gone out before. I knew not where all had come from, nor where they were headed. Most were too old to be students, and in any case had not the black robe and distinctive cap which all the undergraduates wore—nor were they teachers. Yet I was certain that they were hurrying off to their various places of employment. It must take a great number working at many different jobs to keep a university such as this one running smoothly day in and day out. I could not otherwise suppose who would employ them all, though I must admit they looked better dressed and fed than the London crowd.

As we approached the college, Sir John at last divulged the name of him we sought there. An interview had been arranged by Lord Mansfield through one of his spies with a Reverend Titus Talmadge.

"A vicar, is he, sir?" I asked. "Or perhaps chaplain to the college."

"The latter seems likely, does it not?" said Sir John. "Nevertheless, I have been instructed that Reverend Talmadge is known officially as 'a Fellow of Balliol College.' "

" 'A fellow'? What is that?"

"Ah, well, of that I'm not quite sure, never having attended university myself. I do have the notion, however, that a fellow is something more than a student, but something less than a professor."

"I see—or in any case, I think I do."

"Perhaps we may learn more definitively."

"I hope so," said I. "But here we are. We shall have a chance to do so."

I announced to the doorkeeper our desire to see the Reverend Titus Talmadge, a Fellow of Balliol. The doorkeeper fixed us with a disapproving gaze and asked our business with the good reverend.

At that point, Sir John took over the task. "I am Sir John Fielding, Magistrate of the Bow Street Court in London," said he. "I have come to see the gentleman in question on official matter. Just what that business may be, I have no intention of revealing to you, for you seem to me to be the sort of self-important, all-knowing wiseacre who would, at the first opportunity, blatter it about for no better reason than to impress your fellow doorkeepers. Now, *where is he*?"

I thought Sir John in good form. Given a proper challenge, he could intimidate a sergeant major of the guards; he could wilt the confidence of a high court judge. Yet the effect of his eloquent recital upon the doorkeeper of Balliol College, Oxford, was remarkable in that it had no apparent effect at all. The man—even his eyes—showed not the slightest response. He listened in an attitude of stony-faced politeness, glancing neither left nor right, simply waiting until Sir John had done. Then, with the magistrate's urgent query still hanging in the air between them, the doorkeeper inclined his head and said most soberly: "Indeed, Sir John, Reverend Talmadge is expecting you. His quarters are located on the floor above, second door on the right." That last was said to me, for he knew that it would fall to me to convey Sir John up the stairs and to the Reverend Talmadge's suite.

For his part, Sir John seemed slightly nonplussed by the doorkeeper's reply, though not so confused that he neglected his manners. "Uh, well, thank you," said he, "thank you very much."

"My pleasure, sir." From the look of him, the doorkeeper appeared not to have taken pleasure in anything for thirty years at the very least.

Together, Sir John and I mounted the stairs. We were halfway to the floor above and well out of earshot, when he whispered to me: "He seemed uncommonly sure of himself, did he not?"

"Indeed he did, sir, and looked it, too."

"I wonder what it is they feed these fellows to give them such confidence."

"Whatever his diet, it must be well steeped in vinegar. You cannot imagine the sour face he wore."

Sir John chuckled at that, but added: "I do hope our Reverend Talmadge will be more easily intimidated."

He was, reader—and then again, he was not. Titus Talmadge seemed at first to be one of the most obliging men I had ever seen. Yes, he had heard of Sir John Fielding—of course he had! He was quite flattered that the appointment for this visit should have been requested by none other than Lord Mansfield, and he assured that he was honored, more than honored, to receive Sir John in his humble rooms. Nevertheless, he had not the slightest notion what such a distinguished personage as the Magistrate of the Bow Street Court should wish to discuss with him. Perhaps he could elucidate?

(Reader, in my attempt to capture the good reverend's mode of speech in this way, I fear I do him no justice, for mere words do not convey the manner in which he fluttered about the room as he spoke, offering a pillow, preparing tea, pouring it—all with surprising swiftness. Surprising, that is, for two reasons: First of all, he was of really quite an advanced age. Mr. Marsden would probably have said that Reverend Talmadge was "older than time." In my judgment, however, he was eighty years of age, no less and perhaps a bit more; but he was remarkably nimble and sure in his movements—this in spite of the fact that, like so many of his years, he was plagued by failing eyesight. It seemed to me that he saw no better than the Widow Paltrow, though, remarkably, he managed without spectacles, squinting so pitifully that I thought it remarkable that he could see anything whatever.)

As requested, Sir John attempted with some success to explain to his host just what it was had brought him to Oxford, and in particular, why he had sought this interview.

"I believe," he began, "that you signed a statement supporting the claim of one who presents himself as Lawrence Paltrow—or so I have heard. Is this correct, Reverend Talmadge?"

"Why, yes," said his host, "the young man came through here only last week—or was it the week before that? In any case, we had a pleasant conversation—reminisced a bit about his varsity days—and he certainly convinced me he was who he said he was. And so I had no hesitation in signing the affidavit when it was presented me."

Through his response, Reverend Talmadge had ceased his tireless, birdlike flights about the room and had come to rest in a chair opposite Sir John. But once he had had his say, he jumped up and continued his circuit. At last, finding nothing more with which to busy himself, he settled down once more in that same chair and forced a smile.

Sir John waited in order to make certain that his host had finally come to rest. When he was certain of it, he spoke up at last: "How could you be certain he was who he claimed to be?"

"How is anyone to be certain? I have known Lawrence Paltrow for over ten years, after all."

"But for the last eight of them, he was absent, was he not? Or so he claims to have been."

"Many of our old boys return after many more years than that."

"And ask you to sign sworn statements?"

"No, I believe this was my first ever. Yet how could I withhold my support from him?"

There was a pause at that. Sir John seemed puzzled by the reply. "I don't quite understand," said he then.

"It should be evident. He was a Balliol man. That much was plain."

Sir John's frown grew deeper and darker. "Why was it plain?"

"He gave me his word as a gentleman he was just who he said he was."

"But how would you know he was a gentleman, unless he—"

"Indeed, he is more than a gentleman," said Reverend Talmadge, interrupting, "for as I understand it, the statements that he is collecting have something to do with his claim upon the Laningham title. He will be the next Lord Laningham. How *could* I deny one of a noble family?"

By that time it was clear to me, as it was patently clear to Sir John, that the fellow was a doddering old fool. We waited. First he, then I, took a sip of the tea that had been given us. I for one was ready to depart. But not yet Sir John.

"What was your relationship to Lawrence Paltrow?" he asked. "You were his teacher, were you?"

"Oh, no, by no means."

"His tutor?"

"Again, no. He had no interest in my field, nor was there any reason he should have had."

"Your field, then, is . . ." Sir John hesitated. "Theology?"

"Ancient languages—Aramaic and Hebrew. So you see, he would have little need for either one in the study of nature."

"Nature?"

"Natural science and natural history were the studies he pursued."

"Ah, yes, of course," said Sir John as if merely reminded of the fact.

"I tutor when there is need—divinity students, for the most part. But as for my dealings with Lawrence Paltrow while he was here at Balliol, well, I am a Fellow of the College, after all."

"Meaning precisely what?" Sir John seemed as eager for the answer as I.

"Why . . ." He raised both hands in such a way as to indicate that surely the answer was self-evident. "I am here. I am a Fellow. I give support . . . advice . . . counsel. In short, I am available to all who need me."

"And did Lawrence Paltrow often need you?"

"I would not say often—no—occasionally, rather."

"And in what way? What sort of advice and counsel would you say he required?"

"Would you not say, Sir John Fielding, that your question is somewhat impertinent, considering that him about whom you inquire is soon to be one of the House of Lords?"

"I take it, then, that the matter was much too personal to discuss here and now?"

"Not a bit of it. His difficulty was quite common among students." Reverend Talmadge said nothing for a moment or two; he seemed to be giving consideration to a course of action. "I believe I shall tell you the matter of it, for it was clear to me at our last meeting that what had once been a problem to him no longer was such."

"Well, then," said Sir John, "let me hear it."

"Lawrence Paltrow was a very bright young man who, alas, lacked confidence."

"That was it? That was his problem?" Sir John's disappointment was all too evident.

"That was his problem. Oh, it manifested itself at many times in a number of different ways. But yes, fundamentally, that was his problem."

"Only that?"

"Only that, I'm happy to say. And now, not even that, for he seems fair bursting with pride in himself."

Sir John emitted quite the deepest of sighs; then did he rise and give a nod in my direction. "I do thank you, Reverend Talmadge," said he. "You've been most generous with your time, and a perfect host, but we really must go now. I've many more to see today."

"Oh, I'm sure you do—though I must confess I'm no wiser as to why you wished to talk to me than I was earlier. Is there some criminal matter involved?"

"There was, of course, that unfortunate matter of his brother."

"Ah, yes, so I suppose you must be very sure with regard to Lawrence."

"Something like that, yes."

"Well, you may rest assured that Lawrence is indeed who he says he is."

"Ah, well, then . . . Jeremy?"

In a trice, I was at his side and had him facing in the direction of the door. But there he remained.

"Reverend Talmadge," said he of a sudden, "I have a question or two more for you. When you were visited by the claimant, was he alone, or did he come in the company of another?"

"Why, he came alone."

"Did he make an appointment prior to his visit, or was one made for him by another?"

"What need had he to make an appointment, or have one made? He was a Balliol man! All he had to do was present himself at the door."

"And the doorkeeper would admit him?"

"Of course."

"Thank you, Reverend. That will be all."

With that, Sir John set off briskly for the door. It was all I could do to have it open for him so that he might pass through. As I caught him up, I heard him mutter, perhaps more to himself than to me: "Must talk to that doorkeeper once more."

And talk to him he did. He approached the fellow in a manner most severe and put the matter to him: How came it about, said he to the doorkeeper, that the man claiming to be Lawrence Paltrow was admitted so readily when he has in no wise established himself before the law as the one rightfully bearing that name? "Have you some special wisdom that gives you the power to divine the truth before England's greatest jurists have determined it?"

If I had hoped to see the doorkeeper thrown into confusion, then I was disappointed. He did not so much as blink as he responded: "No, sir, I have no such power, but what I have is the 'domesday book.' "

"You have what?"

"We call it so. It is a list of all Balliol men from the very beginning."

"Of time?"

"No, sir, the college's beginning in the thirteenth century. Here, let me show you—or show your young man here."

With that, the doorkeeper reached beneath his writing table and hauled up a thick, large, heavy book and placed it before me.

"Show him the entry for Lawrence Paltrow," said Sir John.

The doorkeeper frowned in concentration. "Now, if I may but think what he gave as his year in the college."

"Try 1760 and come forward from there," I suggested.

The doorkeeper looked at me rudely and let out a grunt of affront. Nevertheless, he did as I said and found the entry for Lawrence Paltrow quickly enough.

"It is here," said he to me. "You see it?"

I passed this on to Sir John. But then, just as the doorkeeper was about to shut the book, something there was that caught my eye. I touched his arm and stayed his hand that I might look closer. On the line on which Paltrow's name and last known address were written, I saw that someone had inscribed what looked like an X, though it might have been a cross. I found it puzzling. None of the other entries on the page bore a similar mark.

"What is that?" I asked, pointing. "What does it mean?"

"I've no idea," said he. "Never noticed it before."

I studied his face and gave particular attention to his eyes—and yet I learned nothing. He was no easier to read at that moment than he had been earlier. I removed my hand and allowed him to clap shut the great book. He swept it off the writing table and inserted it into a shelf below. Then I touched Sir John at the elbow to indicate that I was ready to leave.

"Thank you," said Sir John to the doorkeeper. "We shall be going now. Come along, Jeremy."

Away we went—back to High Street, that we might find

our way to All Souls College. I had passed it as well on my early morning ramble and had no difficulty putting us in the right direction. Quite naturally, we fell immediately into a discussion of what had transpired at Balliol. We were barely out the door, when Sir John demanded to know what it was had come to my attention in the so-called "domesday book." I described what I had seen—the X that could have been a cross—and said Lawrence Paltrow's entry was the only one on the page that was followed by such a symbol.

"What do you think is the significance of the mark?" asked Sir John.

"Well, if it indeed be a cross and not simply an X, then it probably means that Paltrow is known to have died."

"And if it be an X?"

"Then I have no idea what it means."

"And that was also what the doorkeeper said, was it not? That he had no idea what the mark meant?"

"Yes, but I believe that he was lying."

"Why do you think that?"

"I believe he lied to protect himself. When I called his attention to the cross that followed the name, he realized that he had failed to note it when the claimant made his visit. He had passed an impostor through the door and given him the opportunity to roam free about the college."

Sir John slowed his pace, giving consideration to what I had just advanced. After a bit of chin-rubbing and tuneless humming, he said: "Hmmm, yes, well, it could have been that way, I suppose."

I felt somewhat stung by his halfhearted endorsement of my theory, and so I said nothing at all for some time. Yet with All Souls in sight, I realized we would soon part, and so if I had any more questions to ask, I must needs ask them now.

"Uh, sir, I was wondering . . ."

"Yes, Jeremy? What were you wondering?"

"I mean no rudeness, sir, but what was your purpose in interviewing Reverend Talmadge?"

"That booby? That nincompoop? He is living proof that a good education benefits some men not at all."

"Truly so," said I, "but why waste time talking to him?"

"Ah, but we did not know how great a fool he was until we had spent some time with him, now, did we?"

"True enough."

"That, you see, was the point of my visit. I had heard from Lord Mansfield that he had signed an affidavit in support of the claimant. First of all, I wanted to know why he had done so. Secondly, because of his association with the university, I thought it quite likely that he would be called as a witness—should the case for the claimant ever reach Chancery Court. And if he were to be called, I wanted to know just what sort of witness he would make."

"Having learned," said I, "you must feel much relieved."

In response, he gave no more than a chuckle.

"Are the rest of your appointments with others here who have signed affidavits in support of the claimant?"

"No, on the contrary. They are with others who were asked to do so—but refused."

"And I suppose you wish to know why they *refused* to sign statements in his favor."

"Indeed! And I would also know what sort of witnesses *they* would make."

Before us loomed the twin towers of All Souls College. There I had agreed to depart from him. Yet I had misgivings aplenty about leaving him to his own devices in Oxford. I voiced them; he dismissed them—as follows:

"All you say is true enough," he declared, "but what do you suppose I did when you were but a boy back in Lich-field? Why, I carried on without you—and that is what I plan to do now. People have always been good about helping me onto my next destination. The citizens of Oxford are no worse than Londoners, I'm sure. In fact, they seem to me a good deal better in the generality. Do not make the mistake of supposing that you are in some way indispensable to me insofar as traveling about from place to place. Your task this day is an important one. Find the claimant and his compan-ion and observe them as they solicit statements. As I said last night, yours is the more difficult task—and in my view, equally important."

These stern words were delivered at the entrance to All Souls College, where Sir John had come to a halt. He held his ground belligerently and smote the bricks of the walkway beneath his feet.

Then said he: "I take it I am near the entrance to All Souls College?"

"You are, yes, sir. Turn around completely. Move four or five steps forward and prepare to mount three stair steps to the door."

"You've given me a greater answer than I required, but I thank you for it, as I will also thank you to leave me now."

I hesitated. We had attracted a small crowd of onlookers who seemed half amused by Sir John's behavior. They looked from him to me, no doubt curious as to what I might do or say next. I hardly knew myself, so embarrassed was I by such attention.

In the end, I could do naught but call weakly as I backed away, "All right, if you wish it so. I will meet you at the inn at day's end."

Then I turned and walked swiftly away from him. I looked back but once and saw him pushing away one of the crowd who had been so bold as to offer him assistance up to the door of All Souls College.

EIGHT

*In which I am lost
and found in
a single night*

I knew not what to do, nor where to go. Set adrift in
Oxford, I could but wander the streets, looking into the
faces of those whom I might pass during that midmorning,
in the vague hope that I might by chance encounter those
whom I sought tramping through the town as I was. Had I
met them thus, what might I have done? Would I have slyly
passed them by, then turned round and followed them wherever they might have gone? That was my imagined fantasy.
But there were matters to be considered. Would I recognize
them? Yes, I was properly certain that I would. But then the
question came, might they not also recognize me? That, I
had to admit, was a distinct possibility. Sir John was aware
of the chance meeting Clarissa and I had had with the
claimant and Eli Bolt in Kingsmead Square, Bath. On the
basis of that and the brief view that they had had of me on
our last night in the dining room of the Bear Tavern, Sir
John had warned me not to call attention to myself and to
observe them as nearly as possible in secret. Thus I knew
that it was doubly important that I escape their notice. To

attempt to trail them, even at a distance, might indeed put an end to my worth as an observer. At least, it seemed so to me at that time.

Mulling these matters for more than an hour, I coursed back and forth between the town and the university, never leaving completely one nor the other. There was an abundance of bookshops there; as I grew less interested in sighting and pursuing claimant and Bolt, I gave more attention to the bookshops and began browsing their windows. Then, tempted inside by a copy of Daniel Defoe's *The True-Born Englishman,* I entered one of the bookshops which was located in George Lane. I emerged an hour later with Mr. Defoe's poetic work under my arm (bought at a good price) and *The Adventures of David Simple,* by Sir John's half sister, Sarah. Two doors down stood a drinking and eating place called the Swan. I repaired to it that I might examine the books I had bought.

Inside, I chose an obscure corner of the bar, safely out of the way of the noisy comings and goings of the crowd from the street. The Swan was much favored by the university people, though not necessarily by the students. Those who entered seemed older and rougher in their manner—college servants they were, doorkeepers and porters and the like. In fact, sometime after I had settled at the bar with a cup of coffee before me, the doorkeeper from Balliol College came into the place and seated himself at a table a distance away with a number of his fellows; he paid me no attention whatever. The purpose of these visits to the Swan, which were none of them very long, was to gulp as much ale as possible and gobble as many oysters as could be kept down. Of great duration they may not have been; they were nevertheless frequent: During the course of my two hours in the Swan, I saw one red-faced, elderly fellow duck into the place three times—and each time he downed a pint of ale. All the while I sat sipping my coffee, turning the pages of the books, and quietly moping.

Yes, reader, I moped. If I had earlier been stung somewhat by Sir John's failure to accept my theory on the doorkeeper's presumed lies, I was really quite hurt by his refusal of the help I offered him in getting about Oxford. What was it he had said to me as we stood before All Souls College? "Do not make the mistake of supposing that you are in some way indispensable to me. . . ." In truth, I had never thought that I was indispensable in helping him through the streets, nor in any other way. I had perhaps grown a bit more contentious than before, and sitting there in the Swan, I vowed that I would remedy that in the future. Nevertheless, it seemed to me that some of the blame must fall upon Sir John himself. He had grown quite tetchy of late, and I could not fathom the reason. Perhaps it was simply a matter of growing older. It occurred to me then that I had no idea whatever of his age. To me he *looked* quite old, though he didn't *seem* so. But, I asked myself, was it merely the encroachments of age that inspired him to send me off on this fool's errand? After all, asking me to locate two men who may or may not be somewhere about the town on this day! They could be a hundred miles from here—or perhaps even in London. Now, there would be a bit of irony for you, would it not? As I searched for them here, they might very well be in London, seeking more signatures on their affidavits.

Having, for a considerable while, become lost in such thoughts and considerations as I have described above, I became only gradually aware of a commotion there within the Swan. It was, after all, only a small commotion—a quickening swell in the usual hum of conversation. At last it had risen to such a level that it could no longer be ignored. I looked up and around me, just as a great voice boomed forth, drowning out all else:

"Hear ye, one and all, I ask kindly for your attention."

Though the voice was new to me, I had no difficulty locating its source: Eli Bolt stood, broad and tall, at the far end of the Swan. Only one man in the room was in any sense more prominently in view—and that was the claimant himself. He, as it happened, had taken a place, standing upon a chair beside Mr. Bolt. He was visible from every corner of the room. I, fearing recognition, shrunk back a bit and hid behind an open book; neither of the two men, however, gave me so much as a glance.

"We ask only that you take a look at Lawrence Paltrow, who is next to me here," continued Mr. Bolt. "If any of yez remembers him from his time at Oxford ten or twelve years past, then we'd like to speak to you in private. Any who wants a closer look, just come forward and take it."

With that, a number rose from their tables and a few pushed away from the bar. They came forward for the sort of clear view that the dim light within the Swan prohibited. The claimant stepped down from the chair that he might meet them and present himself in the best possible manner. He smiled, offering his hand in good, manly fashion to those who approached him. One by one, each who had come forward had a few words with him; after that, one or two fell back, returning to their companions. Those who remained began to move closer to the claimant and talked freely with him. As if by magic, pints of ale appeared and were accepted.

All this I watched with considerable interest. Much as I would have liked to move closer so that I might hear what was discussed among them, I dared not for fear of being recognized. Nevertheless, I could well suppose that a sort of game was being played between them, wherein some hint of the presumed association was given by, say, a porter of Merton College, and was immediately picked up by the claimant with great enthusiasm and much laughter; the porter joins in, supplying more details of some anecdote or adventure; and soon both are joyfully reminiscing, old chums reunited at last. It was indeed a difficult sort of game to play. I could see, too, that it depended greatly upon the claimant's ability to improvise and even more upon his charm. There could be no doubt that with his quick wits, ingratiating manner, and ready smile, the claimant was a very charming fellow.

There was, however, the matter of those pints of ale. Soon after their arrival, while all the rest were quaffing and conversing, Eli Bolt pulled a sheaf of papers from a bag he had rested upon a nearby table. He called out to the innkeeper for pen and ink, and they came forthwith. Then did he beckon to the five who surrounded the claimant, and they came obediently and signed the forms where they were asked. I thought critically of this and decided that one could not honestly say that their signatures had been paid for with pints of ale, for, after all, the drinks had appeared *before* they were asked to sign the affidavits, but it did seem to be pushing the mark a bit. I wondered what Mr. Bolt might have done if those at the Swan had been less responsive. Perhaps then there would have been another round called for, perhaps gin, as well. Would they go so far as to offer payment in coin? That seemed unlikely—and ultimately unnecessary.

Bolt and the claimant made ready to leave. Clearly, they had no wish to remain at the Swan once they had completed their business. Did that mean they would be on to another such tavern or inn, where they might collect more signatures? Now that I had watched them in pursuit of their objective, I wished to see them again. And so, as Bolt called over the server and settled with him, I beckoned the barman to me and paid for the cups of coffee I had drunk and the meat pie I had eaten. I was in no hurry to go and would certainly not leave before the two who held my attention so completely. Nevertheless, I wished to be prepared to leave swiftly once they had departed, for I had decided to do what I had earlier determined not to do: I would follow them to their next destination.

They left with a great swagger and to a loud chorus of goodbyes. Had any of the crowd at the Swan been questioned on the matter, all would have said that both Eli Bolt and the one who presented himself as Lawrence Paltrow were fine fellows indeed; that is certainly how they would be remembered here. I myself watched them go as I hung back in the shadows, hiding from their glance. Once they had disappeared through the door, I forced myself to wait a full minute, counting the seconds, before I left in pursuit of them. Then did I follow quite hastily. Yet, when I came to the door of the Swan and made to pass through it, I found my way blocked by one seeking entrance. He was enormously fat, so large that he quite filled the doorway. I had no choice but to retreat, allowing him passage through the portal and past me; only after he had squeezed by could I then make my exit. When I did, I fairly leapt out into the street and peered left and right—but all to no avail. Neither Mr. Bolt nor the claimant was anywhere to be seen. Both were notably tall men—tall enough so that I was certain I would see their heads and hats bobbing above the crowd that moved along the walkway. In desperation I ran to the nearest corner, which happened to be St. Aldgate's, and looked it up and down—but again I saw nothing or no one worthy of pursuit. How could they have disappeared so completely in little more than a minute's time?

The day was dimming to dusk. Yet the failing light would not conceal two as large as they. What they had done with themselves was, and would, remain a mystery to me.

Where would I now take myself? It was perhaps a bit early to seek Sir John at the Blue Boar Inn, so perhaps it mattered little where I went. But I tucked my two books under my arm and set off down St. Aldgate's in the direction of High Street and the inn. As I approached it, I found myself opposite Christ Church College and was suddenly beset by a great gang of shouting undergraduates. They came running out of the entrance as if they had of a sudden been liberated from some frightful prison. All were dressed in black gowns and wore the distinctive caps that marked them for who they were, what they were, and where they were from. Without quite intending it so, nor on the other hand offering much resistance, I found myself swept along by this noisy crowd of young men in black and into Mother Radford's Ale House, which was round a dark corner and up what looked to be a blind alley.

Though from its shadowed exterior Mother Radford's may have seemed the least inviting of drinking places, inside it was warm, bright, and relatively empty (though filling fast). A team of giggling serving maids was bustling about the tables, and a sour-faced harridan, whom I took to be Mother Radford herself, occupied her station behind the bar.

The sudden arrival of well over thirty young scholars

altered the temper of the place quite radically, for with them they brought their shouting and laughter, and their wild high spirits. They were no more than settled at their places around the tables and at the bar, when a powerful rhythmic chanting went up from them. They beat in time with fists and palms to a kind of savage snarling, which at first eluded me completely. It was, however, repeated again and again, so that I was at least able to divine that what I thought to be simply noise was, after all, Latin noise. They shouted it out. They roared it forth. They ended their chant only when the serving maids reached them with foaming pints of ale.

It occurred to me as I witnessed this curious ceremony that this was the first true experience I had had of the student body. Oxford had until then been no more than a great reputation and a number of very impressive structures. My only glimpse of the university's faculty, in the person of the Reverend Titus Talmadge, had certainly not impressed me favorably. And this view of those who attended the lectures, stood for the university's degrees, and would later enjoy preferment in the professions and in politics seemed to me then even less impressive. In truth, as I looked about me, they seemed little more than a loutish, ale-swilling mob.

"Here, you, town boy, move away, will you?"

The blunt arrogance of that request was voiced, as you might suppose, in a sneering and aggressive tone. There could be no doubt that it was directed at me. I turned to the one who had spoken and found him to be another of that black-robed, noisy crew. No more than two or three years my senior, he was plump in the way that a spoiled child is plump; he gestured me away impatiently from my place at the bar with a stubby hand that had never known a day's hard work.

"I beg your pardon," said I in a manner which made it plain that I had heard him aright but had not the slightest intention of budging from my place.

"You," said he, leaning toward me in a manner meant to be menacing, "*move*! Is that plain enough? We claim this sec-

tion as our own. If you do not obey at once, I shall be forced
to thrash you."

I turned toward him but kept my backside firmly planted
upon the stool. I noted that the aggressor had a friend behind
him, one of about the same size and shape as he was. I
decided to make it plain to them who I was and where I was
from, and thus warn them away:

"My good fellow," said I, "you seem to have the mistaken
notion that I am a town boy—that is, from here in this
benighted, bad-smelling borough they call Oxen-ford, or
some such. That, thank God, is not the case. I am from the
city—specifically Westminster, in what you no doubt think
of as London. I do not fear you, young sir, for where I come
from we roast young capons such as yourself—and eat them
for dinner."

With that, I did for effect what one should ordinarily
never do: I swung round on the stool and turned my back to
him. In this manner, I found myself staring at the scowling
face of Mother Radford. She slammed down the cup of coffee in front of me and looked from me to those at my rear,
and then back to me.

"We'll have none of that here," said she to me in a voice
deeper than that most men could produce. "No fightin', neither here nor outside." I heard deep sighs behind me; the two
were no doubt glad not to be put to the test. "And you, Lord
Dickie," said she to my antagonist, "go find you a place on
that side the bar. This young cod in the green coat was here
first, as you very well knows. There ain't no reserved seats
here, as you also knows quite well."

She had handled the situation with a dispatch and aplomb
that would have made her quite the envy of her colleagues in
Covent Garden. Needless to say, I was rather pleased with
myself, as well. I was, however, a bit uneasy to learn I had
traded harsh words with a young nobleman. Ah, well,
thought I, far better to trade words than blows.

"Hear ye, one and all, I ask kindly for your attention."

I knew that voice, as I knew those words. I looked about,

and in a bare, brief moment I had found him: Eli Bolt had taken a place at Mother Radford's like that he had chosen for himself at the Swan. Up against the far wall he was, with the claimant climbing up on a chair beside him. From there they had a commanding view of their audience, and for a long while indeed they commanded attention from them. A kind of stunned silence fell over the black-gowned scholars at the presumption shown by these interlopers who dared intrude upon the private affairs of the chosen of Christ Church College. Disbelieving looks were passed from table to table.

Bolt, mistaking the sudden protracted silence for a demonstration of respect, continued with roughly the same speech he had made minutes before: "I only ask you to take a look at this fine fellow standin' up here to my right . . ."

As he made a rather grand gesture indicating the claimant, one of his audience took more than a look; he took aim—and then let fly with a bit of crusty bread. It hit the claimant square in the face and brought forth laughter from the scholars and an oath from the claimant.

The first missile had been thrown. Others followed it. For near a minute, bread bits, oyster shells, and wads of paper rained upon them. The oyster shells truly did damage: One of them nicked Bolt on the forehead and sent blood spurting down his cheek. And as the air filled with debris directed at them, the multitude at the tables began a chant which soon echoed loudly through Mother Radford's. At first, I thought it Latin or perhaps even Greek. Then I made out the single word which, repeated over and over again, constituted their urgent demand: "Away! Away! Away! Away! Away!" They thumped and beat upon their tables just as they had before. At last, they succeeded in driving the two from their places. Shielding their faces with hand and arm, gathering up their belongings as hastily as possible, they started for the door. Only then did the chant cease, and a great cheer burst forth from the crowd.

And I? I laughed at them, along with the rest of that black-robed mob. I particularly reveled in Bolt's discomfiture. And hearing the jeers and taunts thrown out at them as they departed—"Never return!" "Blackbeard!" "Out with you, out with you, out! out! out!"—I added my insult to the rest: "Back to Kin-Tuh-Kee! Go 'cross the Cumberland!"

In response to that, I received a swift look of absolute fury from Eli Bolt. How strange it was, for he was a good thirty feet from me, perhaps more. Others were yelling. It was as Bedlam in the place. Yet Bolt turned and looked direct at me. There seemed not the slightest doubt in him from whom those words of mine had come. His eyes, cold and dark and penetrating as some wild animal's, held me for an instant and then released me. He had sent me a message, and I had received it.

It was only after that, after Bolt and the claimant had passed on, and I had heard them leave, that I realized I had done precisely what Sir John had warned me not to do: I had called attention to myself. What was it he had said? Observe them without being observed. Well, indeed I had been observed. The look given me by Bolt, the threat in his eyes, told me that he had certainly recognized me—whether from our encounter in Kingsmead Square, Bath, or from his appearance in the dining room of the Bear Tavern, I could not say, nor did it matter much. The important—nay, the disastrous—thing was that I had been recognized.

What was I to do? At first, I thought to drain my coffee cup, gather my books, and hie off to the Blue Boar Inn as quickly as possible. I set about to do just that, but then, taking a moment to consider the matter, I decided it might indeed be exactly the wrong course to take. After all, were I to go out too quickly, I might find Bolt just outside the door, awaiting my appearance. I summoned Mother Radford and requested a second cup of coffee. I had decided I would wait them out.

I know not how long I dawdled over my coffee. Probably it was not a great while. Lads of my age—which is to say, the age I was then—find it difficult to do nothing willfully, no matter how adept they may be otherwise at wasting time. In any case, after a delay of some length, I did as I'd earlier intended: finished the dregs of my coffee, left four pence on the bar beside my cup, took my books in hand, and made for the door. I noted, as I rounded the bar, that Lord Dickie and his chubby friend were no longer at the places assigned them by Mother Radford. I glanced back, looking for them among those at the tables, but saw them not.

Opening the door to the alley, I looked out and, seeing nothing, proceeded. Immediately the door shut behind me, I was plunged into absolute darkness. Night had fallen during the time I had spent inside. It was certainly a proper hour to return to the inn and seek out Sir John.

I sensed rather than saw some slight movement just ahead of me. For some reason, it came of a sudden into my head that it was Lord Dickie awaiting me. Feeling emboldened by the thought, for I had no fear of him, I strode forward ready to do battle. Yet I had barely taken two steps, when a cloth which bore a strong animal smell—that of a horse—was thrown over my head. Startled, I yelled loud and thrashed about with my fists, seeking to be rid of it—all to no avail.

There was a voice, a heavy voice—certainly not that of any scholar of Christ Church College. Was it Bolt?

And that, reader, is all that I remember, except for a pain in my head as I was dealt a stout blow with a club of some sort. I dropped swiftly into a state of complete unconsciousness.

I can in no wise vouch for the absolute accuracy of what follows, as I was present for none of it. Be assured, however, that I have the utmost faith in him from whom I heard it. My unease has more to do with the flattering nature of it all—flattering, that is, to me. I would not, reader, have you think that I sought to commend myself to you by putting words in the mouth of Sir John Fielding, or thoughts in his head. This is as I heard it from him.

He had had a most productive day. Though there had been some difficulty securing ingress to All Souls College— through an oversight, his name had not been left with the doorkeeper—all was right once his presence was made known to the Master of the College. He was accompanied by him to Professor Newcroft with whom Sir John was to meet. (As it happened, Lord Mansfield, who had made the appointment, was one of the college's most eminent old boys; the Master of the College wished to please him.)

Professor Newcroft, who lectured in natural history, remembered Lawrence Paltrow very well—so well, in fact, that he was utterly certain that the fellow who had called upon him and asked him to sign a statement, likable though he may have been, was certainly not the student he had known a decade before. The two men, magistrate and professor, talked at length about the true Lawrence Paltrow and his impostor. Sir John felt that at the end of their conversation he knew both much better than before. Once they had completed their business, Professor Newcroft accompanied Sir John to Merton College that he might introduce him to Professor Fowler, who was known throughout Europe for his knowledge in virtually every area of the natural sciences.

Professor Fowler was by nature more severe than any of the faculty members Sir John had met till then, and he proved to be less generous to Lawrence Paltrow and his counterfeit than all the rest. As Professor Fowler told it, immediately following young Paltrow's graduation, the professor had recommended him for an enterprise in the colonies. Paltrow, it seemed, had disappointed him—and his employer, as well. "A bright student," said the professor to the magistrate, "is sometimes simply unprepared for the demands of real life. In any case, he dropped out of sight shortly after this failure. Humiliation, perhaps, may have played some part." Sir John had been intrigued by this anecdote, alluded to rather than told; he asked to hear the details of the matter and was fascinated by what he heard. As for the visit paid to him by the claimant, the professor simply dismissed it as "a crude charade, not at all worth discussing."

Unable (or perhaps unwilling) to conduct him personally to the next and last on the list of the appointments made by Lord Mansfield for Sir John, Professor Fowler assigned the task to an eager undergraduate who was apparently there at his beck and call. The lad, hardly older than Jeremy by Sir John's estimate, knew precisely where and to whom he might convey the magistrate, for it was by chance that he had the same tutor, Mr. Inskip, that Lawrence Paltrow had had earlier. The lad gave it as his opinion, however, that it would do little good to ask Mr. Inskip about any student from a time so long past, for the tutor had considerable difficulty fixing names correctly even to his present charges.

As it proved, however, the lad's opinion was not worth much, for the tutor remembered Lawrence Paltrow perfectly—or, "as if he were here but yesterday," as he had put it. He remembered him as "altogether brilliant" and "as clever as ever a young man could be." He certainly did not concur with Professor Fowler's opinion that young Paltrow had in some way failed in the great world. Though he asked that what he said be kept confidential, he offered it as probable that his former student had been enlisted in some search for precious metals. He had, however, no idea whatever what had become of him after his last visit to Oxford in the early fall of 1763, near Michaelmas, it was. As to the claimant, the tutor had received no visit from him. "I doubt," said he, "that my judgment would have been thought of sufficient worth to be solicited. From what I heard from Professor Fowler, however, the man who recently visited Oxford could not possibly have been Lawrence Paltrow, as he sought to present himself. I understand he could not even identify nor explain the composition of iron pyrites."

Thus Sir John could look upon his day with some satisfaction. He had learned a great deal, and what he had learned gave him food for speculation. But food for his empty belly was what he craved! He could, he was sure, eat a whole middle joint of beef—and he would, by God, as soon as that lad returned. Where could Jeremy be?

Indeed, he did wonder at that, and he continued wondering for hours until he reluctantly found his way to the chop house and dined alone upon a small end chop, which was all that remained of that quarter of beef by the time he allowed himself to eat. The end chop, small as it was, caused him indigestion, for by the time he had eaten it, his stomach was all a-tumult from worry over Jeremy. He asked at the desk as he left the chop house and found no message had been left for him; no calamity, at least, had overcome the boy. Thinking it best to do so, he chose to sit in the parlor of the inn that he might be nearby should any word on Jeremy come to the inn. He could not wait in the room.

Where was that boy?

Sir John sat bowed, brooding upon Jeremy's absence, a blind man crumpled upon the parlor sofa. Those who passed through the room must indeed have supposed that he slept, so still was he. Yet his mind raced as he sought to consider every reason why the lad was so late in returning. There were really not so many possibilities.

The first was that he was the victim of villains of one sort or another; that he had been beaten and robbed and left for dead—or perhaps indeed he was dead. Who could tell?

There seemed a possibility, though certainly not a likelihood, that he had been recognized by the claimant and that brute, Eli Bolt, and been detained for some bizarre purpose which Sir John could not at that moment imagine. Yet that seemed unlikely, for Jeremy had been warned explicitly against presenting himself to them in such a way that he might be recognized, and Jeremy was a sensible lad.

He, of course, might simply have met with some accident—been run down by a coach or wagon, taken a fall from a considerable height, or quite suddenly fallen ill. All of these, of course, might have happened, as well as other events which could in no wise have been expected, or planned for. But the chances of such occurrences were so vague, so faint, that there seemed little need to consider them with the rest.

Finally, Sir John had to admit it as potentially possible that Jeremy had drunk himself insensible with gin, rum, or some other such substance and was presently asleep in some gutter in or near the heart of Oxford. And why potentially possible? Well, because Sir John was forced to confess (to himself, of course) that he had treated the lad rather shabbily that day. Their parting before All Souls College had been particularly unfortunate. "Do not make the mistake of thinking you are indispensable . . ." Had he really said that? Why, it sounded cruel, even now to him. Nor was it the only occasion at which he had lately brought the boy down with a harsh word, a cutting remark or two. What possessed him to treat him so?

He considered that at some length and decided at last that he both envied him his youth, and at the same time sought to deprive him of it. Sir John felt he had squandered his own youth on the navy—and lost his sight in the bargain. He had wandered in life rather aimlessly until his brother took him in hand, read law with him, and installed him as his successor at the Bow Street Court. Thus he had lost near a decade of his life before it had truly begun. Jeremy, on the other hand, seemed to know from the moment he stepped into the courtroom that he would be a lawyer—a barrister, no less—and he had not deviated from that goal during the past three years. How he envied him that single-minded resolve! The lad had even inveigled him into beginning his education in the law—reading Coke, et cetera. Certainly he was far too young for such an endeavor. Yet just as certainly he had shown a talent for it right from the beginning, so much that from time to time (and now more often) Sir John succumbed to the schoolmaster's temptation and sought to trip him up in various ways. As he grew more approving of Jeremy, he seemed, oddly, to be less. And so, by finding fault, by assigning him tasks too difficult for him (and for most others), and by refusing his help when it was offered in good spirit, he was robbing the boy of his youth, giving him the uncertainties and the frustrations of a premature adulthood. And that, thought Sir John, would be sufficient to drive any boy to drink.

He knew his Jeremy, however, and knowing him, he felt certain that this could not be the case. Yet it was, in most ways, the least drastic of the possibilities he had considered, was it not? Dear God, what if the lad *had* been killed by accident, or by evil purpose? The weight of such a thought seemed near to crushing him. Was this what it meant to be a father? All this worry? Then what a miserable state it must be.

Feeling a gentle touch upon his arm, Sir John sat up immediately, a look of expectation upon his face. He truly expected to hear Jeremy's voice.

"Sir John, would you like the night porter to take you upstairs to your room?"

But no, it was none other than the fellow at the desk to whom he had inquired sometime before if there was a message from Jeremy.

Disappointed, Sir John declined the offer, thinking it best to wait where he was. But then of a sudden, a thought struck him—a course of action which would at least permit him some part to play. He called after the fellow who, he sensed, had already turned away from him.

"I wonder if it is possible at this hour to summon a hackney coach?"

"Why, yes, sir, we have not so many as in London, but we have a few, and I shall send the porter to fetch one immediately. Where is it you wish to go?"

"I wish to go to the Magistrate of the City of Oxford."

And so it was that not long past eleven, Sir John Fielding, Magistrate of the cities of Westminster and London, paid a visit to Anthony Fowlkes, Magistrate of the City of Oxford. It was late by town custom (though in the colleges of the university, lights burned the night long); nevertheless, upon his arrival at the home of the magistrate, Sir John was informed by the driver of the hackney that there was a proper rout in progress at the Fowlkes residence.

"How can you tell?"

"Why, can't you hear the music, sir? There's a fiddler sawing away like he might never stop."

"Ah, so there is."

"And all the lights is lit."

"So much the better. I shall require your assistance in reaching the magistrate's door," said Sir John.

"As you wish, sir," said the driver, "though I must first tie up my team."

After attending to that, he helped Sir John down from the coach and took him by the arm.

"Would you mind," said Sir John, "letting go my arm so that I might take yours?"

"Any way you wants it, sir. I'm sure I don't mind."

In this way, they reached the door, whereon the driver knocked with no effect.

"I can do better than that," said Sir John.

"You're welcome to try."

With that, Sir John let loose a flurry of blows upon the door, which immediately silenced the voices and the music inside the house. There was a significant pause, footsteps beyond, and then through the door:

"Who is there who dares interrupt this social evening?"

"It is I, Sir John Fielding, Magistrate of the Bow Street Court."

"London?"

"That is correct, sir."

At that point, the door came open, and the magistrate within had his first glimpse of the magistrate without. "Why, I be damned," said he. "It is you, ain't it? I heard that you were blind."

"I daresay I am. And this silk band I wear over my eyes proves it, does it not?"

"Forgive me, sir. I meant no offense. What can I do for you?"

Sir John was now aware of others in the doorway crowding behind the master of the house. There was an undercurrent of whispered conversation. He cleared his throat and spoke loud above their voices as he responded; as he did, they fell silent.

"I am come," said he, "that I might report a missing person—in short, my assistant, Jeremy Proctor. First of all, I must ask, has any report been made to you today of one fallen victim to violence or accidental hurt?"

"No such report," said the Magistrate of Oxford.

"No corpus in the street? No report of one falling suddenly ill?"

"No, thank God. It has been a very quiet day, and may it conclude as such. But could you tell me, sir, what he—and, for that matter, you—have been doing in our corner of the realm?"

"I could," said Sir John, "but I may not."

"Oh, how is that?"

"To put it briefly, Jeremy and I have been taking part in an investigation, one which I am not at liberty to discuss."

"And why not? It seems to me that if your investigation takes you here, then I should have been told about it first. As one magistrate to another, does that not seem proper?"

Sir John had the notion that this had been intended by the Oxford magistrate as much for the benefit of those guests of his who looked on and listened as for him. An assertion of the local magistrate's importance had been made, and those who heard mumbled their approval. Sir John cautioned himself to proceed carefully: There would be no point in belittling the man whose help he hoped for.

"I quite agree," said he. "Had it been left to me, I would certainly have prepared the way by notifying you and asking your assistance, but unfortunately, when he sent me here, the Lord Chief Justice —"

There was a general intake of breath at the mention of such a grand personage. Yet their audience whispered not a word, but waited in expectant silence to learn what it was the Lord Chief Justice might have said or done. Sir John had no intention of telling them. He had simply used the office for effect. Having allowed them to wait, he placed hand to mouth as if suddenly stricken at his own temerity.

"Oh, dear," said he, "I fear I've said too much already. It was not my intention . . ."

"Nonsense! See here, I've left you out on the doorstep far too long, I fear. Do come in. I've some guests and I'm sure we would all like to know more about, well, whatever you can tell us of . . . you understand."

"Much as I would like to do so, I must decline your kind invitation. I shall hasten back to the Blue Boar Inn to be certain that Jeremy has not returned while we talked here. I had hoped, though, to enlist your help for a search tomorrow—*if* there is still no sign of him by then."

"You shall have it," said the Oxford magistrate. "My constables will be at your bidding. They are but two. I have not a whole group at my command, as you have."

"I'm sure they are most capable," said Sir John. And so saying, he bowed and thanked his way back to the coach, having grasped the arm of the coach driver for assistance on his way.

"Take me back through the city," he muttered to the driver. "I would be certain that there is naught and nobody to catch your attention along the way. Stop if there be anything in the least questionable."

And the driver helped him back up into the coach and, taking the reins, started them on their trip back to the inn. There were no stops along the way, though on one occasion the coach slowed so that the driver might look closer at what could have been a body crumpled in the shadow of a fence; it was no more or less than a sack, fallen, no doubt, from a farmer's wagon.

Sir John returned to the inn and found, as he had feared, that there was no word of Jeremy. He determined that they would start out in the morning and make a full search of it.

Dear God, please, he thought, where is that lad?

At that time, reader, I had no better idea where I might be than he had. Once, as I recall, I came to myself sufficiently to realize from the squeaks and groans and the sound of turning wheels that I was in a wagon of some sort. The bumps and shakes told me that the wagon moved along a country road. Yet I saw nothing, for my head was still covered by what I perceived to be a horse blanket, nor could I move in any proper manner, for I was trussed up at the wrists and ankles like a pig on the way to market. Unable to help myself, nor in any way alter my situation, I did what any sensible young fellow would have done, and slipped back into unconsciousness.

The next I knew, I found myself dragged across the wagonbed, then hefted up and thrown over a shoulder with an ease which I found quite intimidating. I had not been tossed about so since I was a young child. Of course, I could see nothing still, for the horse blanket was yet firmly in place, covering me from waist to head. Yet bounced about as I was, I could tell when I was brought through a door and into a house, then immediately below—down a narrow stairway to a dank, cold cellar. There I was dumped rudely upon the floor, against a sweating wall. All this time, not a word was spoken. I wondered at that, as well one might. Yet I had long before dismissed the possibility that my abductor could have been that puff-pigeon who had threatened me for failing to move away from his desired place at the bar; he might throw a blanket over me and beat me about the head, but he would not cart me off to some distant location for whatever dark purpose. Was I frightened? Oddly, I was not—at least not to a measure proper to my awkward position. I was certain that my captor was Eli Bolt—and perhaps the claimant, as well. They had been so careful to avoid my look that they had left me more or less blinded by the blanket over my head. They had even kept silent during the trip from town. Surely this meant that they intended eventually to release me.

Right above me I heard a door slam; no doubt it was the same one through which I had been carried only minutes before. Then did I hear the loud voice of Eli Bolt as he descended the stairs. I knew then that my theoretical safety was merely . . . theoretical. What I failed to understand was why I had been taken away. Eli Bolt might, in his anger at the crowd of undergraduates at Mother Radford's, be moved to hit out at one of the crowd—at me in particular, perhaps, because my unpropitious jeer had wounded him deepest.

"Where is that little whoreson?" It was Bolt, growling in anger, chewing his words, obviously drunk. He had come to the bottom of the stairs and was quite nearby. "No, I just wants to see him, maybe have a little talk, is all." There was a pause, and then the sounds of a scuffle, a few words grunted, pushing, shoving back and forth.

It could only be the claimant who blocked the way. He was as big as Bolt—and evidently as strong—and he was not drunk. A confused sound escaped from the older man, a kind of wail of dismay, followed an instant later by the sound of collapse as Bolt hit the floor of the cellar. The claimant had put him down.

All this, reader, I had heard—yet I had seen nothing, for the blanket covered my head still. Experiencing all this as I did, without benefit of sight, made me mindful of Sir John, for it was thus that he experienced all things and all events. What was it he had said so often? That when deprived of one sense, you must strengthen the rest. And only the night before he had told me that it was also just as important to heed the urgings of reason whilst reaching conclusions from information provided by the senses. I had been perhaps a bit indifferent when the lesson was offered; at this moment, however, I sought eagerly to apply it to my present predicament.

What was it my senses told me? Touch aided me little—except to assure me that I was so firmly tied that it was unlikely that I should alone be able to loosen the bonds that bound me. Anything else? Yes, for as I ran my fingers over them, I found they were of the sort described to me by Captain Harrison—ropes of braided leather—the sort with which Eli Bolt had played his tricks on the deck of the *Ocean Rover*.

Taste told me naught but that I was frightfully hungry: My churning stomach was sending up sour messages that it badly needed filling; my tongue seemed to have thickened, as well.

Smell? All that I could smell was horse sweat. The odor was both overwhelming and quite objectionable.

It was essentially, however, upon my sense of hearing that I depended. I have described the entry of Bolt into the cellar and the battle of push and shove which he lost—presumably (that is, according to the dictates of reason) to the claimant. Yet even as, in this manner, my mind raced, my ears provided me with further information: I heard a cork stopper removed from a bottle. And then there was something more—the gurgling sound of liquid being drained from that selfsame bottle. Bolt, it seemed, was drunk and bent upon getting drunker. Such sounds indicated that he sat upon the floor across from me, no more than ten feet away. As for the claimant, who had yet to speak a word, he stood nearly between us but to one side—or so my ears told me.

Then did I hear a distant door slam—upstairs in the house—and immediately afterward the sound of footsteps striding confidently across the floor above. It could be none but the one Sir John had designated the third party in the conspiracy. Or so my reason told me.

With some consternation, I heard the claimant leave; he hastened up the stairs to meet the third party. I felt unprotected, alone. There was little to deter Bolt should he wish to inflict bodily harm. Yet for the moment, he seemed far more interested in his bottle. Again, there was that gurgling sound. The bottle was upended, and, remarkable as it seemed, through the horse blanket which covered my head I caught a whiff of what it was that he drank—gin, pure gin. He emitted a sigh of deep satisfaction, then took another swig. From another place in the house, rooms away, came the sound of voices—one of them no doubt that of the claimant, and the other belonging, surely, to him who had just entered. I strained to hear them better, yet try as I might, I could make out neither the words spoken nor the true tone of the voices. All seemed no more than an indistinct hum.

"Where'd you get it?" No hum that, but a rough bark from just ten feet away. Bolt had addressed me at last.

For a moment, I considered feigning unconsciousness. Yet only a minute before, I had been twisting about attempting to find some position in which I might better listen to the conversation on the ground floor. I would not deceive Bolt, and I might very likely anger him.

"What is it you mean?" said I to him. "What am I supposed to have?"

With that there was some shuffling and a grunt or two—and Eli Bolt was up on his feet. In three lumbering steps, he covered the space between us. Then, with a sigh, he squatted down before me. I sensed his face only inches from my own. If I had before just managed to catch the strong scent of gin, it near overwhelmed me now.

"You know damn well what I mean," said Bolt. "It's that book he writ in and drew all them pitchers. You got it. I want it, and I want it now."

"Well, the truth is, sir, I don't have it with me—not here in Oxford, in any case."

He laughed out loud. "Listen to ye! If you ain't the little gentleman!" Then did he mock me: " 'The truth is, *sir,*' 'Not here in Oxford, *in any case.*' If you ain't somethin' to hear. What say we start all over again? First thing I asked was, where'd you get it? Now you answer me that one, and I'll not beat you 'bout the head."

This threat was followed by the sounds of gurgling and gulping as he took another swallow of gin. Drunk as he was, he was quite capable of delivering such physical abuse. I had no intention of testing his intentions in this matter. Why should he not know? It would in no wise compromise Sir John's investigation if I were to tell him.

Bolt banged his bottle on the floor. (I wondered, would he break it—yet he did not.) *"Answer!"*

"Very well," said I. "You refer to Lawrence Paltrow's 'Journal of Exploration and Discovery,' no doubt. That I found in the rooms of Margaret Paltrow in Kingsmead Square in the town of Bath. I searched her quarters at the direction of Sir John Fielding, following her death."

"So she had it! But Sir John Fielding, you say? Has he seen this book?"

"He cannot properly see anything, for he is blind."

"I knows that. Him and me, we go back a ways. But why is a London magistrate lookin' into such matters in Bath?"

"That you would have to ask of him yourself."

"Does he now have this book we're speakin' of?"

"That I would not know." I lied, of course, yet had not the slightest compunction in doing so.

"Does he know what's special about it? Do you?"

Obviously, something was. I knew not how to respond convincingly to his question, for I knew not myself what special power or importance there might be in an eight-year-old travel diary kept by one who had altogether disappeared. I preferred to lie, but to lie effectively one should know the truth.

As it happened, however, no answer was called for. For from above us (I would have put the location at the top of the stairs which led to the cellar) came a voice, one heavy with authority, which put an immediate end to the interrogation.

"That will be quite enough, Mr. Bolt."

"But, sir, I was just—"

"Come up here—*now*!"

Obediently, though with a sigh, Eli Bolt raised himself from where he sat, which was, as I reckoned, just before me, though slightly to my right. Just as he was about to depart, he muttered to me, "I'll be back. You better have the right answers for me." Then did he start up the stairs; his tread was heavy upon them.

I remained where I lay, listening—for I could do no more. There were footsteps above, but no sound of voices. I considered matters for a moment or more upon that voice which had summoned Mr. Bolt. It was doubtless that of the "third party." Yet what struck me as odd, even confusing, was the feeling that I had heard that voice before—and not so long ago. But whose was it? And where had I heard it?

I waited, expecting them to return, attempting to anticipate the questions they would bring with them. I was worried but not frightened. With Bolt brought under control, I felt I had naught to fear from the claimant or the "third party." Bolt, rude colonial that he was, had no experience at interrogation; even I, in his place, could have done better—of that I was certain. Why, with the questions he had asked, he had told me more about Lawrence Paltrow's "Journal of Exploration and Discovery" than I could ever have told him. He had made it plain, to begin with, that there was likely some ulterior purpose to the Journal. Perhaps it may have had something to do with the mysterious role that Paltrow was to play on the expedition—his scales, weights, and measures. Sir John himself guessed that the journey described by Paltrow may well have had something to do with the mining of precious metals. Gold? Silver? Men would kill for such, would they not?

Time passed. I waited, at first, expecting them to return at any moment; then, less sure of it, I wondered if they would return at all that night. I was hungry, thirsty, and by that time of night (whatever time that might happen to be) quite exhausted. My mind drifted back to the "third party," so-called, and to the familiar sound of his voice. If he had said just a bit more, I do believe I could have identified him sure and certain. But, alas, he had given me little to work with: "That will be quite enough, Mr. Bolt" and "Come up here—now." It was indeed not much, and I feared it would be not quite enough. Well, the "third party," who was obviously in charge, would probably have more to say to me tomorrow. But, repeating those two sentences in my mind, I fell asleep, still hoping to discover who it was spoke with that voice. My dreams revealed nothing.

I have no proper notion of how long it was that I slept. From later indications, I should say it was well over an hour but no more than three. In any case, my dreams were interrupted in deepest night by a repeated sound—a series of squeaks, I should call it—which informed me that someone was descending the stairs to the cellar. I was thus prepared when a touch was put to my shoulder, and I was given a light shake. In response, I twisted about to a new position. I was then pulled up to my feet by a pair of strong hands which I took to be the claimant's. When he began to work loose the leather rope which bound my ankles, I whispered, "I'm ever so grateful to you. It was so tight that I—"

"Shhh," he interrupted me; then did he put a hand on the blanket just at my mouth. "Shhh," he repeated, and then removed his hand.

Swiftly untying the rope round my ankles, he then undid that about my wrists, took me by the hand, and led me up the cellar stairs. The blanket covered my upper body still. I fought my desire to pull it off, sensing that he wished it just so. Thus I was led through the ground floor. Had there been so much as a lighted candle along the way, I am sure I would have seen it through the blanket, which was a bit threadbare to the touch. The darkened house was for me made even darker.

We reached the door: I was certain of that, having caught a draft of cold night air about my feet. Struggling quietly, he managed to get it open, and then he pushed me out. As he did so, he whispered, "Turn right at the road." With my back to him, he pulled the horse blanket from my head and sent me on my way. Knowing he would have it so, I did not turn immediately to discover my rescuer. By the time I did turn to look, all I could see was a good-sized house of the sort known well from two centuries past.

I reached the road without difficulty, turned in the direction I was told, and two hours later, more or less, I had reached Oxford and the Blue Boar Inn in High Street.

NINE

*In which Sir John
comes face-to-face
with the claimant*

I found Sir John awake and dressed still. He quite amazed me, for no sooner had I spoken, apologizing for my late arrival (it was six in the morning by the clock in our room), than he leapt upon me, hugging me to him and ruffling my hair, telling me how happy he was to have me safe.

"I have much to tell you," said I to him.

"Oh, no doubt, no doubt," said he to me. "But tell me, Jeremy, are you not hungry?"

"Sir, I am as one starved. I could eat an elephant, a whale, and then perhaps have a hippopotamus for dessert."

"And so you shall," said he. "If there be such beasts within a hundred miles of here, you shall have them on your plate." He sighed a great sigh. "You cannot know how happy I am to see you."

In the end, I was not called upon to make good my boast. I was most happy to settle for a grand breakfast of hens' eggs, rashers of bacon, bread, and good Oxfordshire butter. Never, I think, had I eaten so much of a morning. And never, I think, had I finished a meal and afterward felt so needful of sleep. I was utterly exhausted from my tramp down the dark road of near ten miles. In spite of all, however, I managed to tell my tale, or most of it, as I ate. I admitted that I had, for one brief moment, forgotten his instruction to me and called attention to myself and to Paltrow's Journal. Yet he took that in good stead, so happy was he to have me back. Sir John was eager to have a good description of the house wherein I was held prisoner, as well as its location; I did what I could. When I had finished my breakfast, I began nodding over my tea. It was then that Sir John ordered me up to the room that I might sleep the morning while he attended to some matters that required his attention. We would leave for London in the afternoon.

Thus it took place. Having slept, I was properly prepared for my return to Bow Street; Sir John, on the other hand, was so worn by his night of waiting that he fell asleep as soon as our stagecoach was under way.

Once we were back, Sir John assigned me the task of reading once more through the "Journal of Exploration and Discovery" that I might learn what there was about it that made it such a cause of concern to Mr. Eli Bolt. Well and good, said I to myself, for I had speculated upon the matter and thought perhaps the answer might lie in the drawings which decorated each page. One of them might indeed turn out to be a treasure map if viewed from one side, or even upside down. I was, in any case, quite eager to take another look at the book—so eager that, once I had done with dinner and the washing-up, I rushed up the stairs to my little room, atop the house, to fetch the book that I might begin to search out its secrets.

To my great consternation, I found it gone. I well remembered the space I had found for it on the second shelf; it was not there. In fact, it was nowhere to be seen on the second shelf—nor on the first nor the third. Carefully, I went back and examined each book, to be certain I had not carelessly misplaced it in my haste to join Sir John at our departure—yet I found nothing. Then did I look behind the other books in order to make sure it had not somehow slipped down, as it had when I found it in Margaret Paltrow's book-case (or had she hidden it so?).

It was simply not to be found anywhere—for I continued to search in all the corners and under my bed. I could con-clude only that someone had taken it from my room. But who? Surely not Eli Bolt! Could he have preceded me here as I slept through the morning? And even if he had, could he have managed to slip past Mr. Fuller and Mr. Marsden? Both possibilities seemed quite unlikely, the latter even less probable than the former. I allowed that it was passing strange that the "Journal of Exploration and Discovery" had disappeared at just the moment that the great villain, Bolt, had learned that it was likely to be found somewhere at Number 4 Bow Street. Could there be a spy somewhere?

Though I had no wish to do so, I knew that I must inform Sir John. With a heavy heart I descended the stairs, intend-ing to look for him in that little room—hardly large enough to contain more than a desk and two chairs—which he called his study.

I was about to walk into the study, so-called, close the door behind me, and tell him the bad tidings, when my eyes happened to stray down the hall. There, a shaft of light from a half-open door pierced the gloom of the hall. Something, I know not what, drew me forward to it. I leaned against the door as I knocked upon it, and it came full open. Annie sat at a small table, practicing her cursive script by candlelight. She looked up, smiled a vague, abstracted smile, and then returned to her writing lesson.

"Wherever did you find this?" It was Clarissa's voice. It came from the corner, where she lay abed, fully clothed though in her stocking feet. She had a book propped up before her—nor was it just any book. I recognized it imme-diately as the "Journal of Exploration and Discovery" in its brown leather binding and false spine.

I was altogether speechless, rendered dumb by feelings of surprise and indignation. Yet as I opened and shut my mouth, searching for words to express myself, she misinterpreted my silence and went indifferently on: "This fellow Paltrow writes well, Jeremy, but his romance lacks a proper plot, near as I can tell. It ends rather abruptly, of course—do advise him of that. Or is the manuscript completed?"

"No," said I, "no, it is not. And it is certainly no romance. But how dare you—"

"Not a romance? Ah, well, that explains a great deal—for instance, the absence of female characters. I could not suppose how he hoped to publish a romance without female characters. But do you mean to say that this man Paltrow actually experienced all this? How fascinating!"

"You find that fascinating?" said I, having recovered myself at last. "Let me tell you what *I* find fascinating. I am quite baffled—fascinated, I might say—that you feel free to go into my room and walk away with whatever takes your fancy. That is outrageous. It breaks all rules of decent human behavior. Why did you not ask me first?"

"Well, because you were in Oxford. You were not here to be asked. And as for taking whatever strikes my fancy, I have taken only books. And why do I take books from your room? Because that is where they are kept. Why you should have all the books in your keeping quite baffles me."

"Why . . . why . . ." I fumbled about, trying to think of a good reason. The truth was, most of them were in the room when I came to Number 4 Bow Street, the last remains of Henry Fielding's considerable library. "Well, let me tell you," said I, beginning again, "that the particular book which you filched from my room on this occasion has importance as evidence in a case which Sir John is presently investigating."

Then, from the other corner of the room, came Annie's voice: "Do please quieten down a bit, won't you? I'm working on my cursive, and that takes a bit of concentration."

I must admit that our ill-tempered wrangle had grown in intensity and volume as counteraccusation followed accusation. Though we had not quite started shouting, we might soon have begun had not Sir John put in an appearance. Thinking back upon it, I wonder that he did not come sooner, for we waged this verbal combat no more than a dozen feet from where he sat, with an open door between us. There, in any case, he stood, glowering at us most unkindly, as one might if he were rudely awakened from a deep sleep. I wondered if that perchance was the way of it.

"What, pray tell," said he, "is the cause of all this bickering? Or, perhaps more to the point, what is the need of it?"

Both Clarissa and I attempted to answer at once, and I fear that in doing so we became a bit unruly, each one trying to drown out the other as we made our bid for his attention.

"Enough!" he cried, and we both fell silent. He waited and, assured that we would keep the silence for a while, he said, "We shall proceed by alphabetical order. You, Jeremy, shall be the first, as P for Proctor precedes R for Roundtree."

Given such an opportunity, I gave forth the case for the prosecution. I drew a dark picture of one who would enter the room of another without permission, without respect for the privacy of another, and without conscience take from that room whatsoever might strike her fancy.

"*Her?*" repeated Sir John. "I take it, then, you are not speaking in some general fashion?"

"No, sir, I am not."

"You speak directly of Clarissa in your plaint?"

"I do, yes."

"So then," said he, turning in her general direction, "what have you to say to all that, Mistress Roundtree?"

"Well . . ." She was now up, standing beside the bed, leaning forward with her hands upon her hips; she appeared quite belligerent, though her voice seemed remarkably quiet and controlled. "I would say that if I entered *his* room without permission, so did he also enter mine just now."

"Indeed, I did not," I protested to Sir John. "Their door stood part open, and I knocked upon it before entering."

"Yet he waited not for an invitation to enter but came in straightaway. And it is well known," said she, "that a gentleman does not enter a lady's boudoir unless he be invited."

At that Sir John burst out laughing. "Child, wherever did you hear such nonsense?"

Somewhat taken aback, she answered with much less certainty, "Why . . . 'twas in a book, sir—a romance, it was." She hesitated, then: "I think it important to say in my defense that when I went into Jeremy's room and took the book, he was not about that I might ask. He was in Oxford with you."

"Where he was knocked over the head and abducted—and all for that book which you admit you removed from his room."

"I did not know that, sir," said she. "I am . . . well, very sorry for his trouble."

"As well you should be," said he. "Upon our return here to Bow Street, I instructed Jeremy to reread that same book, and all the entries therein, that we might have some notion of what it was interested those villains in it enough to harm him."

"Ah, I see," said she, frowning in thought. She remained thus, silent, for a moment. Then did she brighten a bit as she ventured on. "Perhaps it could be the map?" (It was definitely in the form of an interrogative.)

"The map?" Sir John repeated it—and I in chorus with him.

"Well, not a true map exactly—perhaps more in the nature of instructions as to how one might draw one."

"I don't . . . quite . . . understand."

"Well, I learned to read letters long before I could read a map. Even today I can't do it very well. Nevertheless, when I was but a young child, my mother used to send me on errands about our small city of Lichfield. And knowing it would do little good to draw a picture map for me, she would write out very explicit instructions as to how I might arrive at the destination. She called this her 'written map.' "

"Yes, well?"

"I was reminded of that as I read through this 'Journal of'—well, whatever it is. I believed it at first to be a romance, or a fiction of some sort, because of the manner in which it is written—vividly, with all manner of detail. But then I realized that there was perhaps *too much* detail for it to be successful as fiction."

"What do you mean?" Sir John asked.

"Well, detail of a peculiar sort. He would mention every sort of landmark along the way. Some of them, odd-shaped rocks and so on, he drew."

"She's right!" I interjected, for I remembered the many such drawings. "And he would always work in the number of miles traveled in a day."

"And the compass direction in which they went," said she.

"I believe you could draw a map by compiling all such details."

"Or," said she, "if there were a detailed map of the same parts, you could probably work out their route upon it."

I had quite forgotten my ill feeling toward Clarissa in the excitement of discovery. That occurred to me when I realized that as we exchanged information and speculation, she and I were smiling and all but laughing aloud. No less than I, she wished to play a part in the investigation.

Sir John seemed aware of this. The expression on his face had changed to one of amused indulgence. "It seems to me, Jeremy," said he, "that you purchased just such a detailed map from Bricker's in Grub Street. You said that with it you were able to follow the path of this mysterious expedition of Paltrow's up to a point. Perhaps with Clarissa's collaboration, you might be able now to go beyond that point. Why don't the two of you take the so-called 'Journal' and that map down to the kitchen table and see what you can accomplish working together? Perhaps two can do the job in half the time."

That, reader, is what we did. I know not whether in truth we accomplished our work in half the time, as Sir John suggested; I am convinced, however, that with Clarissa reading out to me the passages in question, and I tracing the way upon the map, we did indeed save a good deal of time. For some time afterward I was plagued by the suspicion that without her and her tale of the "written maps" which she had followed as a little girl, I might not have discovered the book's secret at all.

In any case, well before midnight we had done with the task he had assigned us. Together, though not without some disagreements, we had found the end of the long southward trail followed by Bolt, Paltrow, and company. It terminated much farther south than I had ever supposed. I had erred in my first attempt to mark their route, by believing it unlikely they could have maintained a fast pace following a rough path through the mountains. We found their destination to be far down in the northwestern corner of the colony of Georgia. What they had found there I could not then say—nor could I with any great certainty today. Nevertheless, Clarissa was sure as could be of the nature of our discovery.

"It's a treasure map, Jeremy. That's what it is, and you can be sure of it."

"Sure of it? Why?" I asked. With her, I seemed always to assume the role of the doubter, challenging her every assertion.

"Why? Well, simply because they went so far and had such difficulties. They lost one of their group along the way. There had to be a great prize for them to endure so much."

I hesitated, making a great show of examining the matter from every side. "I suppose you're right," I said at last.

"Of course I am," said she. Leaning back in her chair, she examined me a bit dubiously. "May I give you a bit of honest criticism?"

What good would it have done to say no? "Of course you may."

"You have many excellent qualities, Jeremy. You have good intelligence. You are brave and oftentimes generous. No doubt there are others, too, which do not immediately come to mind. But what you lack—the one quality which is made prominent by its absence—is imagination. You are simply deficient in that area. If I were you, I would attempt to develop my powers of imagination."

I was greatly annoyed at that. Who was she to give me such advice? It was apparent to me that she herself had too *much* imagination.

"What proof have you that I lack imagination? You've no notion what goes on within my head."

"Perhaps not. It is only the indications you've given me draw me to that conclusion." She paused but briefly. "Yet let us not part on such a sour note. We worked well together on this evening. Tell me, do you often have tasks of this sort for Sir John?"

"I do whatever he asks."

"Then you are lucky," said she.

And so, rising, she helped gather up the oddments we had scattered over the kitchen table in the course of our investigation. When she put her hand upon the "Journal of Exploration and Discovery," she hesitated, and then pushed it toward me. I pushed it back.

"I believe you had not read through to the end," said I.

"Oh, but I had. I was simply rereading a bit, thinking to discuss it with you. It's best that you keep it."

"Well . . . perhaps it is. I may need it for my meeting with Sir John in the morning. I shall give full credit to you."

"Oh, no, no," said she, insisting, "it has been an equal enterprise."

"Nevertheless," said I as I gathered up the items to be taken to my room. I started for the stairs and called back my goodnight to her.

(It is, by the bye, worth mentioning at this point that after giving the matter some thought, I moved the case containing the books out of my room and into the hall; only those I had chosen and bought for myself did I hold back and claim as my own.)

Next morning I carried the large map of the American colonies and Paltrow's Journal down to Sir John's chambers and acquainted him with what Clarissa and I had, with some certainty, established the night before.

"And where was it you said the trail ended?" asked Sir John.

"In the colony of Georgia, sir, just inside, in the northwest corner of it."

"That is perhaps somewhat farther south than you had first supposed, is it not?"

"It is, yes, but Clarissa showed me that even Paltrow believed they had crossed into Georgia."

"Well, pass along my thanks to her." He hesitated, giving some thought to the matter. "What do you make of this, Jeremy? What were they after?"

"Well, Clarissa is convinced this is a treasure map, and you, sir, said you thought the expedition had to do with the mining of precious metals."

"Yes, I did, didn't I?" Sir John rubbed his chin thoughtfully. He seemed about to add something to that, when a great bustle came from somewhere near the door to Bow Street. There were heavy footsteps all in a rush, a loud remark yelled out in such a way that it could not be understood—all in all, a great air of hurry and annoyance. It could be only the Lord Chief Justice.

As indeed it was. Lord Mansfield loomed large in the doorway. I jumped from my chair that he might seat himself, knowing full well that it was unlikely he would. He seldom did so on these flying visits; he preferred to pace about, adding urgency to whatever he had to say, or perhaps lean across Sir John's desk to whisper in secret.

"Come in, m'lord," said the magistrate. "What have you for me this morning?"

"Well, I was rather hoping you would have something for me," said he. "Or do you prefer to keep secret from me your activities in Oxford?"

"By no means. You shall have my report by the end of the day. We ran into a bit of unexpected trouble."

"Of what sort?"

"Jeremy here was abducted by one of the claimant's party."

Lord Mansfield gave me a surprised look. "Indeed? And I was depending upon him to see that no harm came to you."

"Well," said Sir John, "no harm did. And as for the rest of it, all in Oxford went about as you might expect."

There he let things rest. He must have been as sure as I was that the Lord Chief Justice had not come to get an early look. He had other matters to present, if not perhaps to discuss. I had noted that our guest had in hand a few papers. They no doubt had to do with the reason for his visit.

"I have here," he began, waving the papers aloft, "a letter from Mr. Thaddeus Bester, Magistrate of the City of Bath, which encloses the coroner's report upon the death of Margaret Mudge Paltrow by one Thomas Diggs, medical doctor and coroner for that city. I shall leave both with you that you may learn their contents."

"I'm sure I know them already," said Sir John with a wave of his hand.

"Oh? And what do you suppose them to say?"

"I would suppose that Dr. Diggs's report declares that the Widow Paltrow died by result of a misadventure and that Mr. Bester concurs with the finding and lodges a complaint against my conduct in the matter."

"Why, that is a fair summary, so far as it goes," said the Lord Chief Justice. "What did you do to earn such opprobrium?"

"What indeed? Well, I referred to them as boobies within their hearing. I am sure they did not like that—no, neither of them. But as to how I managed, specifically, to inflict the greater wound upon Mr. Bester—so great, in fact, that he complained to you of me—I confess I am somewhat in doubt. Yet, putting my mind to it, I do recall that at our second and last conversation, I'm afraid I shamed him somewhat and went so far as to suggest he had not pursued the inquiry into the death of the Widow Paltrow with quite the energy he ought. And, alas, it was true. He was, if anything, a bit underzealous in his efforts."

"And you called this to his attention?"

"I did."

"Ah! But you managed to satisfy yourself on the cause of her death?"

"Indeed. As I told you upon our return, it was murder, plain and simple."

"By the claimant?"

"More likely, I think, by his constant companion, one from the colonies named Eli Bolt. It was he, by the bye, who saw to the abduction of Jeremy."

"Have you enough to hold him for either crime? I can deal with Bester, should it come to that."

Sir John sighed and, with a shake of his head, dismissed that possibility.

"Well, what, then?" The Lord Chief Justice put the question to Sir John rather aggressively. "It would seem that the claimant keeps this fellow—what is his name?"

"Bolt."

"Yes, Bolt—that he keeps Bolt to do his crude work for him."

"Perhaps," said Sir John. "I'll not dismiss it as a possibility. Yet it seems to me that another is truly in charge. The claimant lacks the requisite ruthlessness. It seems to me that he is but a puppet. There is another, a third party, who is the puppet master. Remaining hidden, he pulls the strings for both the claimant and his brutish companion."

"That is most interesting," said the Lord Chief Justice. "I have myself had the notion for some time that there was at least one other involved in this matter, and that it was he who both planned and financed the enterprise."

"As you say, Lord Mansfield, it is most interesting."

"More perhaps than you realize, Sir John, for I have received a most tempting offer in this morning's post."

"Oh? And what is that?"

"Quite unbidden, a letter arrived from the claimant. In it he stated, bold as brass, that he had been gathering statements and had every intention of claiming the Laningham title and property. He had heard that a secret commission had been formed to thwart his action, and that I was heading it. In order to save both sides the time and expense of a trial, he was willing to meet with the members of the commission, that he might convince them that his intentions were good and honorable. To do this, he was willing to submit to questions by the members. If he might thus convince them, said he, then there would be no need to carry matters further. He then suggested the date when he would next be in London—it is but three days hence—and asked if it would be satisfactory for the commission to meet with him then."

"Well," said Sir John, "I call that a stroke of good fortune."

"Then you see it as I do," said the Lord Chief Justice. "There can be only advantage to us, for even if he astounds us all with his knowledge of the Laninghams and their history, his appearance before us should give us some idea of how we might treat him as a witness when the matter comes up in court."

"You feel, then, that it will go into Chancery no matter what the results of this meeting?"

"Oh, I daresay it will. And because I saw only gain for us, I wrote off to him in Oxfordshire and accepted the day for his visit suggested by him and asked that he come in the afternoon at three o'clock. Will that be convenient for you, Sir John?"

"Three days hence? I suppose so."

"Very good, then. I shall look for you along with the rest at about that time." At this point, the Lord Chief Justice paused significantly and looked my way. "I wonder how the claimant could have learned of the existence of the commission and the fact that I head it."

"You pose that question," said Sir John, "in such a way that you imply that you already know the answer."

"Perhaps I do," said the other rather slyly as he continued to stare at me. "Reason suggests that if this young man was abducted, he must have let them know all they wanted to know before they let him go. The fact is, after all, they *did* let him go."

My cheeks burned, and my heart beat faster. I longed to shout out the truth in my own defense, yet custom prevented me. The Lord Chief Justice had not directly addressed me, but had made his remarks against me to Sir John. I stood mute before my accuser.

Yet I was not to be disappointed. Sir John took up my defense and did so immediately. Rising from behind his desk, he addressed the Lord Chief Justice directly. "M'lord," said he, "Jeremy has given me a complete account of his abduction and brief imprisonment, including all that was said to him and by him. I accept his version of these matters completely and without reservation. Let me assure you that it does not include any disclosures regarding the commission."

The Lord Chief Justice was taken somewhat aback. He said nothing for a moment, taking time to consider the situation. Then did he finally offer this: "I wish I trusted any of my servants as you trust him."

To which Sir John replied: "Jeremy is not a servant."

"Oh? What, then? I thought . . ." Indeed, we never learned what he thought, for he never permitted himself to say.

Sir John gave him sufficient opportunity to finish the sentence. But having waited ample time, he said simply, "Jeremy is something more."

What that "something more" might have been he did not specify, yet my heart soared so high as he said it, I could not possibly have wished him to be more explicit.

"Ah, yes, well, mmm—hmm, I see," said the Lord Chief Justice, "well, then, Sir John, I shall see you in three days—Wednesday, that is—at three. I shall depend upon you to ask most of the questions of this fellow."

During that space of time, Sir John Fielding made special preparations for the coming of the claimant. Letters were written, and were delivered or posted. An invitation was extended. But for the most part, Sir John made ready by spending long periods of time alone. No sooner was he done with his court than he would set off pacing the long corridor which led from the Bow Street door as far back as the door to his chambers. As he walked, he muttered, and as he muttered, he moved his head this way and that, nodding it and shaking it, altering his expression according to the flow of his thoughts. Mr. Fuller, the gaoler, remarked upon it. Mr. Marsden, the clerk, ignored it. I, who knew something of what was passing through his mind, sought on a number of occasions to read Sir John's lips, or puzzle through the encrypted rumblings generated within his voice box. All I did ultimately gain from such efforts were a few words, particularly an oft-repeated "Who? who? who?" and a variety of names, such as Bolt, Mudge, Inskip, Fowlkes, some of which I was not then familiar with.

Nor was he more communicative during the evenings. He reserved himself from talk at table and then often failed to respond when he was spoken to. And afterward, during the three evenings preceding the meeting at the residence of the Lord Chief Justice, he sequestered himself in his study (which was not unusual) and closed the door (which was). Altogether, he was as near completely absent from us as I have ever known him to be.

On the appointed day, however, his mood seemed to change. With no apparent cause, he began speaking when spoken to, commenced smiling once again, and left off pacing and muttering to himself. Nevertheless, he did in no wise allow the matter of his coming interrogation of the claimant to be discussed with him. That I know quite certain, for I tried twice to bring the matter up to him. The first occasion occurred in midmorning. I encountered him discussing the day's docket with Mr. Marsden. When he had done, I stepped forward and asked, would he be dictating a memo in preparation for the interview at three. (This he often did on such weighty occasions in order to organize his thoughts.) Sir John declined, saying simply that he believed there would be no need. On the second occasion, I was surprised when he told me to be ready for an early departure: We would be leaving at two and allowing ourselves an hour to reach Bloomsbury Square by hackney coach.

"Is that not a great deal of time for a trip so short?" I asked him. "We can get there by foot in less than half that."

"As it happens," said he, "we will be traveling to the post

coach house to meet one who will be traveling here from Oxford."

"Oh? And who will that be, sir?"

"That will be revealed to you in due time."

In fact, the name of the mysterious traveler was given me when we arrived at the coach house. Richard Inskip it was, but at that time the name alone meant nothing to me. I vaguely recalled it as one of those he had conjured with as he paced the long corridor behind the courtroom at Number 4 Bow Street. Yet I knew not what part Mr. Inskip was to play in the day's proceedings, and so to have his name alone meant nothing to me.

"Just go and look for him," said Sir John to me. "If the Oxford coach is in, just call out his name and that should be sufficient to alert him. I shall wait for you to bring him here."

So it was done. An inquiry to the dispatcher made it clear that the Oxford stagecoach had arrived—or was indeed arriving as he spoke. He pointed it out to me as it entered the coach yard and showed me then where it would come to a halt.

I was thus waiting when the driver reined in his team, and a lad younger than myself leapt forward and threw open the coach door.

"Richard Inskip!" I repeated the name as the passengers descended from the coach. At first, it seemed that Mr. Inskip was not aboard. But then one, an old man he was, who had passed me by, returned and thrust his face at mine.

"What name did you call out?" he asked. "I fear I'm a bit hard of hearing."

I said the name once again, and he nodded, satisfied. "I am he."

"Sir John Fielding awaits you nearby," said I. "If you will just come this way . . ." I relieved him of his portmanteau, and with my free hand I took his elbow and guided him through the crowd toward the coach.

He was indeed quite an old man—well over seventy, he seemed to be. Yet others who were older might seem younger than he. His skin, wrinkled and spotted, seemed thin as paper. He moved somewhat falteringly, so that I judged it necessary to slow my steps to accommodate his own. Still, there was something youthful in the eager expression he wore as he looked about him. Clearly, he felt great excitement to be in London.

Having reached the hackney coach, I threw open the door, helped him inside, and handed up his portmanteau to the driver.

"Where to now?" the driver called down to me.

"Bloomsbury Square," said I.

Our destination was no great distance from the coach house, but it being the middle of the day, there were many coaches and dray wagons upon the streets and roads of the city, and as a result we made slow progress on our way to the meeting. As we went, my two fellow passengers discussed what lay ahead. It was soon apparent that Mr. Inskip, a rather humble individual, was distressed that he might in some manner disappoint the august gentlemen who made up the commission. Sir John would hear none of that.

"Absolutely not, Mr. Inskip," said he. "Why, let me assure you, sir, that you have more true knowledge at your command than all the rest of us together."

"But such personages as yourself, the Lord Chief Justice, the Solicitor-General—why, a man of my estate might never meet one such in his lifetime."

"Nonsense. I would wager you have taught your share of dukes and earls in the course of your career."

"In a way, I have, it's true, but they were mere lads—noblemen, as it were, in the potential. Not the same thing at all."

I had learned a bit more about Richard Inskip from that brief exchange. He was not only from Oxford, he was of the university. Yet he was much more modest in his demeanor than any of the professors there—or so I gathered from the tales of the faculty which I had heard. Were it not for his advanced years, I would have assumed Mr. Inskip to be in some junior position in the faculty.

They continued on a bit in just such a way. From further hints that were dropped, I learned that Mr. Inskip had been recruited by Sir John as an interrogator, that he was unknown to the claimant but had been well acquainted with Lawrence Paltrow at the time of the latter's attendance at the university. The two men discussed some of the details of the questions which Mr. Inskip proposed to put to the claimant—yet these were quite beyond me, for they dealt with matters of science which were then (as now) quite unknown to me.

In any case, in the manner that I have described, Sir John and Richard Inskip had prepared themselves well for the interrogation of the claimant by the time we arrived at the residence of the Lord Chief Justice. And in so doing, they had become as familiar as old friends.

As I remained behind to pay the coachman his fare and collect Mr. Inskip's portmanteau, the two gentlemen went directly to the door. Sir John, feeling about for the hand-shaped knocker, grasped it firmly when it was found and loudly made his presence known. Then, just as I arrived at the door, it came open, and there, of course, stood my old antagonist, the butler. Entering last, I took pleasure in presenting him with the portmanteau I had brought thus far. He took it with the ill grace I expected (and perhaps even hoped) he might show.

Perhaps we had arrived a bit tardy. I could in no wise be certain of that, for I had no pocket watch, yet all who were expected were already present—even one, I shall say, who was unexpected was present. The arrangement of the chairs was such that the claimant was placed in the center of the room, with the members of the commission ranged round him in a half-circle. Behind the rest and off to one side sat Sir Patrick Spenser, the Solicitor-General, who had been the moving force in the creation of the commission. My eyes went directly to him; why that was I could not say, though I then told myself it was only because I had been surprised to see him there. My gaze then shifted to the claimant, who sat at ease in the chair that had been provided him. He looked the very picture of self-assurance, as confident as any other in the room. In response to my stare, he gave me no response, not even the vaguest look of recognition.

A chair was found for Mr. Inskip; he was settled in it quickly. And I was assigned a place to the rear of Sir John's, quite apart from the secretaire, where I had sat in the past, taking notes of the previous meetings. I thought this odd, and leaned forward to inform Sir John of this circumstance. He in turn put the question to the Lord Chief Justice, who explained that the claimant wished no written record to be kept. At that, both men chuckled, as if a joke had been told. "I daresay," commented Sir John dryly, and the Lord Chief Justice left him to stand before the assembled group.

"This gentleman, whom you have never met, is known to you all. He has offered to answer our questions regarding his claim upon the Laningham title and holdings. Sir John Fielding and another gentleman, who shall for the moment remain nameless, will do most of the interrogating. It might be best if you held back your own questions until after they have done with him."

Then did he turn to the claimant. "Have you anything you wish to say before we begin?"

"Only that with my answers I hope to persuade all present of the justness of my claim." The voice was quiet but confident.

The Lord Chief Justice returned then to his place and seated himself. Sir John, altogether less formal, remained seated—in fact, arranged himself a bit more comfortably upon his chair before he began.

"What is your name, sir?" he asked.

"Why, Lawrence Paltrow, naturally," said he.

"But of course you would say that, would you not? Let me put the question to you differently: What is your full name?"

"Lawrence Mudge Paltrow."

"Whence came your middle name?"

"It was my mother's family name. She was especially proud of it in that hers were landed people in Oxfordshire, well known there when the Paltrows were still struggling to build a house with a proper roof on it—or so my mother used to say."

"Hmmm, interesting," said Sir John.

But was it, truly? I wondered how this discussion of his maternal forebears pertained to the matter at hand.

"You mention your mother," said Sir John. "I had occasion to meet her shortly before her death—uh, *very* shortly. I happen to know that there were a number of questions which troubled her with regard to your disappearance."

"My disappearance?" the claimant echoed. "I did not disappear."

"Well, then, your absence."

He hesitated briefly. "That is another matter," said he. "Yes, I was absent from England from the fall of 1763 until earlier this year."

"Could you account for your absence?"

"In what way?"

"Simply put, what did you do all that time? Where were you?"

"I was in the American colonies."

"Which of them?"

"A good many of them. As to what I did, I wandered a bit from one place to another, working at various enterprises and in the employ of others."

"Could you be more specific? What enterprises? What others did employ you?"

The claimant let loose a considerable sigh; it seemed to say that it was somewhat painful for him to look back upon that unsettled period in his life. Then he began his recitation:

"I worked for a time—over a year, perhaps not quite two, for a Mr. Custis in Virginia as secretary. It was not work for which I was particularly well suited. I worked in a number of colonies for a number of employers as a surveyor, as some of the great royal land grants were parceled into smaller farms and plantations. I invested in a coach line in Pennsylvania and helped in its operation until it failed. And then, having thus lost a good deal of money, I went back to surveying. In sum, sir, I did what I could do to earn my way. There is work aplenty in the colonies if a man be willing to dirty his hands, but if he be determined to live as a gentleman, he may quickly starve."

"Did one of those with whom you joined in enterprise go by the name of Eli Bolt?" asked Sir John.

"Yes, but that was very early in my stay in the colonies—my first employment in the colony of Virginia."

"You were employed and not a partner in the enterprise?"

"We were all, in some sense, employees of the colony."

"Oh? And how was that?"

"We were employed to explore what lay beyond the Cumberland River—that is, the western limit of the colony."

"You mean that no one had gone so far before?"

"Nothing of the kind," said the claimant. "Why, Mr. Bolt himself had been through that country many times. He knew it well. He led the expedition. Yet it had not been properly mapped and surveyed. This was why I had come along—to map and survey."

"And once this was finished, you were never again in contact with Eli Bolt?"

"Oh, I may have met him by chance once or twice. I recall one occasion five years past, when I was secretary to Mr. Custis. We drank whiskey together and talked of old times—the expedition and the like."

"What of Elijah Bolton?" Sir John pronounced the name with especial clarity, as if particularly desirous that he not be misunderstood.

"What of him?"

"Let me put it to you direct: Are not Eli Bolt and Elijah Bolton one and the same?"

With that, the claimant laughed in a most convincing manner; he seemed genuinely amused at Sir John's suggestion. "By no means," said he. "There is a certain similarity of the names, I grant, but they are two quite separate and different people."

"How, then, did you meet Elijah Bolton?"

"On shipboard. He was returning to England but had no employment awaiting him. He agreed to help me in my quest."

"Your quest?"

"For statements, affidavits, et cetera."

"Ah, yes, your proofs of identity. Why did you deem it necessary to collect them?"

"I was advised to assemble them by the family solicitor in Laningham."

"Why did he think it necessary, or even advisable?"

"Perhaps he would be the best one to answer that, but my understanding of it was that there were two reasons principally. First of all, my appearance had altered somewhat during my years in the North American colonies. I have become much stouter and stronger and even grown two inches since last I was in England. Such a phenomenon is unusual, I know, but I was, after all, barely twenty years of age when I sailed for North America. I can only suppose that the rigorous life that I led there played some part in this."

Sir John nodded and was respectfully silent for a brief time. "I am happy to hear of the improvement in your health," said Sir John. "But to bring you back to the matter at hand, I believe you said that there were two reasons for which you were advised to collect affidavits. So far we have heard of only one."

"What? Oh, yes, of course, the second reason. Mr. Bumbry, our solicitor, advised me that it would be in my interest to put together as many supporting proofs as possible because there would be those who would oppose my claim. He seemed quite certain that it would be so, and I must say that the existence of this commission demonstrates the sagacity of his opinion."

Quite unexpectedly and perhaps a bit inappropriately, Mr. Trezavant burst out laughing at that. "It does, rather, does it not?" he blurted out. But the scolding looks he then received silenced him quickly. Sir John had no choice but to bide his time through this interruption. At last, however, things did quieten down once again, and Sir John leaned forward to deliver his next question.

"Sir, each of these proofs you collected—with, by the bye, the help of your friend Mr. Bolton—each of them constitutes a separate recognition, and as such is quite important. But all are not equally significant. Most important to your cause was the affidavit given you by Margaret Paltrow, your putative mother. Am I correct in this?"

"Oh, most certainly."

"She not only signed an affidavit in your favor, but also let it be known to all who would listen that she indeed had regained her long-lost son. Tell me, sir, how did it happen that she regarded you as her long-lost son?"

The claimant, who had been quite forthcoming in his answers, hesitated a considerable time before attempting to respond. "We were not," said he, hesitating once again, "in communication."

"Not in communication?" echoed Sir John. "Have I heard you right? Am I to understand that during that entire period in which you were in the North American colonies, you failed to write your mother?"

"That . . . is correct."

"How do you account for that?"

Tears welled in the young man's eyes. I was altogether astounded: They seemed quite real. "You must understand my situation," said he. "It was my misfortune to be born the younger son. As it became apparent that Christopher Paltrow, Lord Laningham, would have no male heir, he lavished more and more attention upon my elder brother, to whom his title and wealth would fall. It's true he did also provide for my education, but upon my leaving Oxford, I knew that with my father dead, I could depend upon myself and no other to see me through this life. My mother was considerably reduced in her widowhood. She and I suffered most by these dreadful circumstances of primogeniture. I vowed to her when I set off for North America that I would make my fortune there and return to deliver her from her shameful state there in Bath. The pity was, I was never able to do so. I felt I had betrayed her by my inadequacy. In short, I felt ashamed that I was unable to keep my vow to her, so ashamed indeed that I could never bring myself to write her and confess my failure. I know that I should have. I am now even more greatly ashamed because of it. I can only take some solace in the fact that when at last we did meet after that long separation, she forgave me completely, and without reservation welcomed me back like the prodigal returned—all this before she had even heard tell of the improvement in my prospects."

"You tell that quite movingly," said Sir John. "It is a pity that she died shortly thereafter."

"A pity? Nay, sir, it is a great tragedy."

"As you say." Sir John nodded solemnly. "I have but a few more questions for you."

"And what are they?"

"Could you tell us how it was that you heard of your brother's death?"

"I learned of it first from a newspaper in the city of Philadelphia. The matter was much discussed in that city, which is quite dominated by the Society of Friends."

"The Quakers, as they are popularly known?"

"Just so. My brother's crimes were held as an example of the extreme corruption of the aristocracy."

"And what opinion had you of them?"

"His crimes? Why, something of the same sort, I suppose, in the beginning. You must understand that there was little between him and me in the way of love or even respect. Had he come to America, as I did, he would have perished, for he would have played the gentleman rather than attempt any real labor. That was how he lived his life—as one specially blessed, excused from all manner of earthly toil. He lived off the kindness of our uncle, then married and lived off his wife's fortune, and at last, with the death of our father, he naturally inherited all and lived off that. It was then, by the bye, that he turned our mother out and installed her in those squalid little rooms in Bath. Imagine! His own mother! I believe he was encouraged in this by that wife of his."

"Hmmm . . . well, yes," said Sir John mildly, "but, sir, you told us that in the beginning you felt as many did in that colonial city of Philadelphia regarding your brother, but by so saying, that indicated a later change of opinion. Could you describe that change?"

"It was a change of attitude, rather. I was so chagrined to see the name I bore linked to his that I found myself denying that he was any relation of mine. I told myself that this was the only proper attitude to take toward such monstrous behavior; I could make no excuse for it or for him. I thought at first I would make no effort to claim the title because of the shame that would accompany it. But then, as I thought upon it, I saw that I could do much to ease my mother's last years. I saw that if I were to come forward with my claim I might demonstrate to these colonials and, for that matter, to all true-born Englishmen, that it was possible for a nobleman to live a truly noble life."

"And therefore come forward you did. How long would you say that this change of heart required? You were a bit late in organizing your claim, after all."

"I suppose I have been," said he. "But when you consider the distance between here and North America, and the time required to cover such distance, I would say I have come along about as quickly as anyone might."

Sir John emitted a considerable sigh. "I suppose you are right. And I suppose, too, that I have now exhausted my store of questions. But as I believe Lord Mansfield mentioned, the gentleman who entered with me would now also like to put to you some questions. Will you consent to that?"

"Indeed I will," said the claimant, looking for the first time a bit uncomfortable, even perhaps slightly embarrassed. "But I confess," he continued, "I feel a call of nature. Could you direct me to the necessary?"

This question, addressed to Lord Mansfield, was answered by him as he pulled the sash located in a corner of the room: "I'll have one of the servants show you the way to the water closet."

Immediately, one of the footmen appeared, bowed at the order given him by his master, and led the claimant from the room. Their footsteps echoed in the great house. There was naught but silence in Lord Mansfield's study. I looked about me and noted the doleful expressions worn by those on the commission; only Sir Patrick Spenser remained unmoved by what he had witnessed.

"Well," said Lord Mansfield, his voice hardly rising above a whisper, "what did you think of him?"

His question fell like a stone down a deep well. There was a long wait until at last came the answering splash: "He was very good, wasn't he?" The response came from Mr. Hemmings, who seemed quite as glum as the rest.

"He seemed to account for everything, didn't he?" said Mr. Dalrymple. "I perceived no gaps in his story, and no hesitation in his telling of it."

"Did you see the tears in his eyes when he spoke of his mother?" said William Mansfield, the Lord Chief Justice of the King's Bench. "I should not like to see him before a jury. He would likely have them weeping along with him."

Then did he turn to the Solicitor-General. "Sir Patrick," said he, "do you have an opinion in this matter?"

To which Sir Patrick Spenser did shake his head in the negative. And with a wave of his hand, he indicated that the matter should not involve him, that it was entirely the affair of the commission. I recall reflecting at that moment how eloquently he managed to express himself by mere signs and gestures.

Silence once again. It was broken by Mr. Trezavant, who did no more than give expression to a thought which had occurred to others. "Could it be," said he, "that this fellow is telling no more than the truth? Perhaps he is who he says he is—Lawrence Paltrow, the true and legitimate heir to the Laningham title and fortune. You will surely admit that he is most convincing."

There were grunts of assent about the room.

But of a sudden Sir John Fielding leapt from his chair. "No, by God, *no!*" He wailed it forth, a strangled cry of frustration. "He is *not* Lawrence Paltrow. In the beginning, I might well have conceded the matter of his identity quite indifferently, but the closer I have got to him and the more I have learned of him and those about him, the more certain I am that he is an impostor."

"Yet, Sir John," said Mr. Trezavant, "you must know I put that forward only with the greatest reluctance. My inclination is to find against him, but how can one do that when his every word and his every emotion seem to argue in his favor?"

"I can only insist that no matter how convincing he is, no matter how pleasing his manner, he is *not* who he claims to be. And perhaps that will be revealed now with—" Sir John broke off in midsentence; his more sensitive ears had picked up the sound of the claimant's returning footsteps. "Soft, now," said he, "the fellow comes." And so saying, he seated himself once again and put upon his face that same impenetrable blind mask that he often hid behind; it took but a moment, and he appeared as one asleep.

The claimant reentered the room and nodded solemnly about him. He resumed his place, looking left and right, and said simply, "I am ready."

"I believe," said the Lord Chief Justice, "that the gentleman who entered with Sir John now has some questions." He looked hopefully in the direction of Mr. Inskip. "I do not know his name, so I cannot properly introduce him to you. Sir?"

The Mr. Inskip who came forward was hardly recognizable to me as the frail old gentleman who had come off the Oxford coach. Where that one moved with a halting step, this one walked with a bounce; where one seemed timid and fearful, the other was confident beyond measure; the former spoke in a high, fluting tenor, while the present Mr. Inskip's voice seemed mysteriously to have deepened.

"It is of no matter that you do not know my name," said

he, addressing the group, "but you, sir"—turning to the claimant—"you should certainly know me. Who am I?"

The claimant, taken aback, could for a moment do naught but stare at this curious old man who had assaulted him so rudely. But then, after a bit of silent sputtering, he did manage to say: "Why . . . why, I am not sure. Ought I to know you?"

"Oh, indeed you should. You and I met often—at least once a week for three years."

"Was it in the colonies? You must forgive me, but I have a lamentably poor memory for faces."

"Well, it was not always so. I can recall that a time there was when you would draw my face from memory and put it on a goat's body. What was it you wished to imply by that, eh?"

"I don't know that I wished to imply anything, sir."

The claimant had grown tense, his mood altogether altered in not much more than a minute. His audience, by contrast, had relaxed so considerably that two or three of the commission were now chuckling at his discomfiture.

"Not know what you wished to imply?" questioned Mr. Inskip. "I doubt that. Indeed, I doubt you completely, sir. You say that you are Lawrence Paltrow? Well, I say you are not. You must convince me."

"I believe I can," said the claimant. "I have well over a hundred statements and affidavits which I can—"

"Which you can what?"

The claimant sat, staring up at Mr. Inskip, his persecutor. His frustration and curiosity were plain upon his face. At last, he managed to form the question that now consumed him quite completely. "Sir, tell me, please—who are you?"

"I'll give you my name. It is Richard Inskip. Does that mean anything to you?"

The claimant closed his eyes and fixed his face in concentration. "You were . . . let me see . . . you were the tutor. At Oxford."

"Ah, so you do remember the name, no doubt from some

list that was passed on to you. During your recent visit to the university, you looked in on Professor Fowler and Professor Newcroft, but you failed to come to me. And so, given this opportunity, I took it eagerly that I might myself ask you the sort of questions that anyone who claims to be Lawrence Paltrow could certainly answer."

"I . . . well, it was not my intent to slight you, sir," spoke the claimant.

"Oh, pish-posh," Mr. Inskip replied. "To be quite frank with you, young man, I *do* have a good memory for faces. I can recall that of Lawrence Paltrow quite well, and yours is not his. I concede that there is a resemblance, one perhaps of a brother but not of a twin. Nevertheless, if you can answer my questions, I shall put all that aside and accept that you are who you say you are. And I shall advise these gentlemen to accept you, too." With that, the tutor gave him a flashing grin. "Shall we begin?" said he.

"Uh . . . well . . . I suppose."

At this point, reader, I fear I must apologize and offer an explanation of some sort. It has been my experience in writing these accounts and descriptions of certain of the cases of Sir John Fielding that it was only those matters which I myself understood that I have been able to render satisfactorily on the page. Even in medical matters which were not always entirely clear to me, I was able to consult with Gabriel Donnelly, physician and surgeon, that I might not err in their presentation. However, of what I heard from Mr. Richard Inskip during the time that followed, I understood very little (nothing, would be more accurate) and in preparing this narrative, I had none with whom I might consult and no one to question. So it is, reader, that I can give no true account of the questions put to the claimant by Mr. Inskip, for they dwelt upon matters of natural history and natural science which were simply incomprehensible to me. There were references to Sir Isaac Newton, of whom I had some knowledge, and Robert Boyle, of whom I had none. There was talk of a most peculiar table, one of "elements," as it were. Yet more: "Pliny," "igneous phenomena," "aqueous," "anthricitis," "hydrophane." On and on these strange terms, and many more such, passed from one to the other. There was a separate category of questions occasioned by the word (or name) "Linnaeus," and this included "mammalia," "molluscs," "hydroids," and such.

That last term, as I recall, occasioned this exchange between Mr. Inskip and the claimant:

Inskip: "Come now, sir. Hydroids? Surely that should be quite evident. Or have you forgotten all your Greek?"

Claimant: "Yes, forgotten it completely."

Inskip: "And your Latin?"

Claimant: "I've not retained a word of it."

Inskip: "Then, sir, I would say that your education was altogether wasted upon you."

Thus did the tutor bait his supposed student. He jeered and made sport of the claimant as he failed to answer one question after another. It seemed likely to me that this was the manner that he employed with most of his students. So was it also with many schoolmasters I had known: The cutting remark often made a greater impression than a ruler across the knuckles.

More important was the claimant's response to this cruel method. It seemed to hurt him deeply. In spite of myself, I could not but pity the poor fellow, so low was he brought by the tutor's jabs. I watched as he seemed to unravel like some ill-knit muffler: His eyes brimmed with tears and his chin trembled as he managed by force of will to keep from bursting into an unmanly fit of weeping. He kept control of himself until the end, when Mr. Inskip addressed the commission and inveighed against the claimant as a charlatan, a mountebank, and assured them that had the fellow been who he pretended to be, he would have answered not some but all the questions put to him.

"I remember Lawrence Paltrow very well," said he. "He was one of the best scholars it has been my pleasure to tutor in the last ten years, at least. Let me add that—"

Indeed, Mr. Inskip added nothing to that statement, for the claimant then rose to his feet and shouted to the room,

"M'lord, and you, gentlemen, I take my leave of you. I am neither charlatan nor mountebank. In truth, I am naught but a poor man tempted into affairs over which he had no control. I'll not trouble you further!"

And with that he ran from the room, the threatened tears now coursing down his cheeks. Those left behind were quite astonished. Some shouted after him to stop. Others recovered sufficiently to leap to the door in pursuit. But neither shouting nor leaping about did a bit of good. The claimant was truly gone and would not easily be brought back.

Nevertheless, as I looked about the room, I became aware that another of our number was missing. As they milled about, I attempted to ascertain the identity of him who had followed the claimant out the door. I realized with a start that it was none but Sir Patrick Spenser.

We were once more back at Number 4 Bow Street, in the kitchen, and about to sit down to our dinner. Though a good deal of time had passed since the claimant's departure, much of it had been spent in the residence of the Lord Chief Justice, where an argument raged for near an hour regarding whether or not the claimant had said he would no longer pursue his claim—and if not, what truly had been said. And there were other questions: Had he said he had been tempted into affairs over which he had no control? What had he meant by that? Should they prepare for a case in Chancery? Where had Sir Patrick Spenser gone? Why? And so on. Sir John had remarked sometime afterward that he had hoped that meeting with the claimant would clear up matters; instead, it had served only to complicate them further.

And then there was the matter of Mr. Inskip. It had been agreed that he should have no expenses to pay during this trip, and so he was given a lump sum out of court funds and then conveyed to the Globe and Anchor, the excellent hostelry on the Strand. Sir John had arranged with David Garrick for a seat at that evening's performance of *The Recruiting Officer*. Mr. Inskip was well pleased with his trip to London. Once again he was the timid old fellow I had met at the coach yard. Upon parting company with us at the hostelry, he said, "I hope I was of some help to you." Sir John assured him that he had been, and then remarked to me as our hackney pulled away, "I wonder what got into the fellow."

But all of that was now past. As Clarissa set the table properly and Annie served up the meal, Sir John seated himself beside Lady Fielding, and I made ready to take my place. Then came a knock upon the door which led to the stairs and the ground floor below. Sir John bade me open it, that he might know what prompted this interruption.

That I did and found Mr. Benjamin Bailey, captain of the Bow Street Runners, awaiting on the other side.

"Who is it?" called Sir John from the table. "Who is there?"

" 'Tis I, sir," said Mr. Bailey. "I've news I thought you ought to hear."

The magistrate sighed deeply. "Give it me, then."

"One of them from the Globe and Anchor just come by to tell us they got a corpus there in one of the rooms, looks like he killed himself."

"By what means?"

"Hanged himself, he did."

"Would he happen to be registered as Lawrence Paltrow?"

"That's the name the porter gave."

Sir John rose from the table. "Well, come along, Jeremy. We must see that Eli Bolt, or whatever his name be, does not play the same trick on us a second time."

TEN

*In which Sir John
is twice surprised
on a foggy night*

O ur arrival at the Globe and Anchor coincided precisely with the departure of Mr. Inskip from the
place. He seemed quite taken aback to find us there at the
entrance to the hostelry.

"Good God," said he. "Have you further need of me?"

"No, no, Mr. Inskip," said Sir John, "nothing of the kind.
We've some business inside to attend to." All this was spoken as I tried to push past him, with the magistrate trailing
close behind.

"But perhaps I could be of assistance?"

"No, no, go, sir, and enjoy the play. Visit Mr. Garrick
afterward."

"Oh, may I?"

"Yes, goodbye!"

Only then did the tutor give way and allow me to squeeze
by, with Sir John clasping my shoulder and Mr. Benjamin
Bailey bringing up the rear. I glanced back and saw him staring after us.

"Have we escaped him at last?" Sir John asked me once inside.

"It would appear so," said I.

"I thought I would have to set Mr. Bailey upon him to get us past. Imagine his dismay to see his victim of the afternoon a supposed suicide. It would quite crush him, I'm sure, for he seems a good man."

"But a hard master to his scholars."

"Indeed," he agreed. "Mr. Bailey?"

"Yes, sir?" The chief constable stepped forward and threw back his shoulders, all but saluting. "Come with us and search for the killer. Perhaps we may discover the room of this Bolt, or Bolton, or whatever his name be. It is, of course, quite unlikely he would still be about, having committed murder, but it would be worthwhile to search what had been his room. The next place to look, I suppose, would be the docks, any ships setting sail for the North American colonies, that sort of thing."

A well-dressed but distraught-looking young man had approached us meantime and, wringing his hands in a gesture of despair, he addressed us: "Ah, Sir John, thank God you've come. I must assure you that nothing of this sort has ever happened here before, sir. This is a most respectful hostelry."

"So I've been given to understand. But tell me, sir, who are you?"

"Oh. Oh, yes, of course, forgive me. My name is Templeton, and I am night manager here."

"Very good, Mr. Templeton, and was it you who found the body?"

"I . . . why, of course not. It was the porter called the situation to my attention."

"The porter, was it? Then I should like to speak with him."

"Uh . . . yes, of course. Right this way, please."

And so saying, he did lead us up a staircase which was not nearly so grand as one might expect in such a place. On the floor above, in a corner alcove somewhat removed from the rooms which opened to the hall, we encountered the porter, who sat, polishing shoes.

"Mr. Bailey," said Sir John, "is this the fellow who came to Bow Street to report the corpus which had been found here?"

"No, sir, it ain't."

"I sent the kitchen boy to you," said Mr. Templeton. "It was easiest to spare him. Uh, will you be needing me further? I ought really to return to my duties downstairs."

"We may wish to speak to you again, but as for now, you may go. I do ask, however, that you take Constable Bailey with you, that he may learn the room of Eli Bolt."

"Eli Bolt, sir? I know of no one by that name who—"

"Elijah Bolton? This fellow of whom I speak goes by a number of different names."

"I fear not, Sir John—unless one with such a name came to be registered during the day."

"Well, if that be the case, Mr. Bailey has a description of the man. Perhaps between the two of you, there can be some agreement on just who he is and what name he is using. He is suspect in a matter of homicide."

"Oh, dear me," said Mr. Templeton, "suicide and now this."

"Go with him, Mr. Bailey. Explain matters to him."

The two departed, leaving us alone with the porter, who continued to rub away at the shoe he held tight in one hand.

"What is your name, sir?" Sir John asked.

"Alfred Simmons," said the porter as he continued to buff the black leather; he barely raised his eyes to the magistrate. There was something insolent in his manner. "What will you from me?"

"Your full attention, for a start," said the magistrate. "Leave off that brushing, stand up, and address me respectfully, as you did in my court five years past."

"So you remembers me, do you? I'm surprised at that." He laid aside shoe and brush and rose to his feet.

"Yes, I remember you quite well, but I also recall that you went by the name of Simon then. Albert Simon, was it?"

"It was, but you brought ruination upon that one, and I had to alter it a bit."

"It was you ruined your name, and not I, sir. Lucky for you that you restrained yourself and stole no more than a pound. It was your respectful attitude and your convincing promise to make restitution and never again to steal that won you a light sentence."

"A light sentence served in Newgate is heavier than most men can bear."

"So I've heard."

"But should you wonder, sir, though I changed my name a bit, I kept my promise. I paid back the pound as soon as I was able, and I've not stole since."

"Glad I am to hear that, particularly since here you are in a situation in which you have ample opportunity for theft."

"I've no doubt you will change that."

The brow above the silken band which covered Sir John's eyes wrinkled in a frown. "What do you mean? I don't quite understand."

"Surely after you've heard what I can tell you, you will go to the night manager and tell him of our meeting five years past."

"Not necessarily," said Sir John. "Though I admit I shall have my ears set sharp for any reports of theft from this hostelry."

"Fair enough. You'll hear of none involving me."

It was then as if both men had stepped back and taken the other's measure. A slight space of time passed. When they resumed, the air between them seemed, metaphorically, to have cleared a bit. They were notably less guarded than before.

"Now, tell me, sir," said the magistrate, "how did it come about that you found the corpus?"

"Well, I had not much more than come on duty, which would put it a little past six, when this young fellow come up the stairs and past my station, and he stops and turns back to me, and he says, 'I'm checking out early. I wonder, would you give my coat a good brushing? Get to it when you can.

I'll be leaving in about an hour.' That's as near exact as I can make what he said to me. And right then and there he takes off his coat and hands it to me, then goes to the room at the end of the hall—the one to the right—lets himself in with his key. Now, that was, I daresay, a bit unusual, him takin' off his coat and handing it over in that way—but a long way from the most unusual I've seen since I've been working here."

"Had you seen the man before?"

"No, but remember, I said I'd just come on duty. It would not be at all the sort of thing I'd remark upon if half the rooms on my floor had changed tenants during the day."

"I see. Go on, please."

"There were a few other things for me to attend to, so I didn't get to brushing the coat for a time, and in the meantime, an old gent went on down the hall and lets himself into the room next to the first fella's, the young one. And he's not in there more than a minute or two, and he comes out, and says there is a great commotion in the room next to his. 'What sort?' I ask. 'Why, it sounds like there is a fight going on there,' says he. 'You mean, with a lot of yelling and cursing and such?' 'No,' says he, 'it sounds like a couple of big men are in there trying to kill each other—thumping and bumping about.' "

"What, then, did you do?"

"What could I do? I am certainly not a big man myself, and the old man who come to me with the complaint wouldn't have been any help, and so I ran for aid—downstairs, to the stable. On my way I told the night manager what was afoot. I returned with the ostler and the stable boy, and the ostler carried his pitchfork along with him. We numbered quite a party as we made our way back. We listened outside at the door—but there was naught to hear. At last we got up our courage and proceeded inside—the door was unlocked."

"Describe the scene as precisely as you can, please," said Sir John.

"Well, at first there wasn't anything to describe, for there was no light in the room at all." The porter thought again about that. "Now, that ain't quite true, for I remember a bit of dim light from a single candle burning off in one corner. The room was all tore apart, though—chairs overturned, one had the legs broke off, a table all flattened, dents in the wall. It looked just as the old man had said: Two men were trying to kill each other in that place—and one of them managed to do just that to the other one. We didn't find the body right off, for it was off on the other side of the bed."

"Could you be more specific?"

"It was between the bed and the windows."

"Go on, then. What was the condition of the body?"

"All battered and bloody, it was, but not like it had been cut with a knife, just beat hard with fists, a chair leg, anything that was handy."

"In your opinion, had he been beaten to death?"

"Oh, no," said the porter most emphatically, "not a bit of it. There was something like a rope round his neck, been pulled tight, it had."

"You say something *like* a rope. What did it look like? How was it not quite a rope?"

"I'd never seen one like it before. It wasn't out of hemp, or any such stuff. No, it was woven leather, so it was, just as tough and tight as it could be. There was no question in my mind but that he had been strangled with it. His tongue was sticking out in a manner most hideous, and his beard was all soaked with puke and blood, and—"

"*What?* Repeat that, please."

"Puke and blood."

"No, no, before that you said his *beard,* did you not?"

"Why, yes, I did, because he certainly does have one. He—"

"Then, sir, you must take us at once to the room. Jeremy?"

Together the three of us fairly flew to the door at the end of the hall. Sir John held fast to my arm, pushing me forward, urging me onward. We stopped before the room, and the porter felt hastily in his coat pockets for the key. He produced it and, explaining that he had thought it best to secure the room while waiting for Sir John's arrival, he unlocked the door.

The place smelled of death. There were the odors of sweat and bodily evacuation and there was a peculiar sour smell that I could not quite place. It was dark in the room. The single candle mentioned by the porter burned low in its holder and provided the only light. I grabbed it up and asked the fellow to light more candles. By the time I had located the body and knelt over it, there was appreciably more light by which to look.

There was, in any case, sufficient to see that the man upon the floor was Eli Bolt. But for his beard, I am not sure I would have recognized him. It was not only black and gray in the same pattern and proportions as Bolt's had been, but it was also long and braided. There could surely be only one such beard in two braids in all of London.

"It's Bolt, Sir John," said I to him.

"Are you sure?"

"The beard's the same, and the size of him is right. As for the rest . . ." I was reluctant to claim absolute certainty.

"Describe the body to me."

"The face is somewhat battered, the eyes protrudent—bulging nearly out of his head, they are—and his tongue is discolored, a sort of dark purple." I turned to the porter and asked if the body had been moved in any way.

"Well, we turned him over to see if he might still be alive," said he. "Though he surely looked dead, lying on the floor, it seemed only proper to make sure."

"You felt his pulse? His heartbeat?" asked Sir John.

"I didn't have to. I been up to Tyburn often enough I know how a hanged man looks." He hesitated, then added: "There was one of them with us—I think it was the old man from the room next door, he put his hand on this . . . this dead man's chest and said there was no heartbeat."

As the two discussed this matter, I discovered something that did pique my curiosity. The porter had mentioned the presence of vomit and blood in Bolt's beard. I had expected that the blood had been regurgitated with the vomit, and perhaps some of it was; but beneath that dark beard of black and gray I found a wound, a cut where the leather had dug so deep into Bolt's throat that it caused a wound and left some bleeding. I called this to the porter's attention and, holding his own candle close, he inspected the bloody wound in the throat.

"Aye," said he, "went deep, didn't it? Never seen that before, but then again, I never seen a rope of leather used before. You could damn near cut a man's head off with such as that, couldn' you?"

"Which reminds me," said Sir John, "the victim of that unfortunate hanging in 1763 had had his head nearly severed from his body by the leather rope from which he was suspended." He took a moment to ruminate upon that and then addressed the porter: "Mr. Simmons, or Simon, or however you would prefer to have it, could you suggest how it came about that the report carried to the Bow Street Court had it that Mr. Lawrence Paltrow had committed suicide? Now, it is evident to us that the dead man is not Mr. Paltrow, and should be evident also that he did not die a suicide. You did not cut him down, I assume?"

"Oh, no, sir, I did not. Except for the fact that he now lies on his back instead of his belly, he is just as we found him. But about your question on how the matter was confused when it come to you, I would say it was Mr. Templeton did the confusing."

"Mr. Templeton?"

"The night manager."

"Ah, yes, we met him, of course. Mr. Bailey is with him now, or may indeed have concluded his business with him. But how did it happen that the information I received was so confused?"

"Well, it was like this," said the porter, "Mr. Templeton is a squeamish sort, and so he had no wish to accompany us. When we'd had our look inside the room, found the dead man and all, we went back down to him, all four of us, and reported that there was a dead man in Room Twelve. 'Of what did he die?' asks Mr. Templeton. 'Of strangulation,' said the old gent from the room next to it. 'There is a rope round his neck.' Well, all that together must have meant suicide to Mr. Templeton, for that's how he told it to the kitchen boy he sent off to you. He probably looked into the register book and saw that Room Number Twelve was occupied by a Mr. Lawrence Paltrow, and so that was the name he sent along." Then did the porter add to what he had said: "Some of that I heard, and some of that is pure reckoning, for I returned right off to my place up above."

"But you knew that the dead man in Room Twelve was not Lawrence Paltrow," said Sir John, "didn't you?"

"Well, I knew that the dead man were not the young fellow gave me his coat and let himself into Room Twelve. Which of them was this Paltrow gent, I really don't know."

"Almost certainly neither one," said Sir John.

"What's that?"

"Never mind. You've been most helpful, sir, and you've made me regret the harsh things I said to you earlier. You may lock up this room again. A party will come here tomorrow morning to bring the body to the office of the medical examiner of the City of Westminster. You might pass that on to whoever it is relieves you."

"I shall do that, sir."

And having spoken, Sir John signaled to me that we might now leave.

"There was one more matter which I thought you should know," said the porter.

"Oh? And what is that?"

"The coat given me for a brushing by that—how was the name?—Mr. Paltrow."

"And what about it?"

"It was gone when I come back from making the report to Mr. Templeton."

"Was it hung in plain sight?"

"Well, you could see it, but it wasn't easy to get to."

"Do you believe it was stolen?"

"No, sir, I believe the owner of the coat come back for it

whilst I and the rest were in his room, or p'rhaps downstairs talking with Mr. Templeton."

Sir John rubbed his chin. It was evident that this opened possibilities which he had not considered. "Could he yet be here in this hostelry? Are there places he might sequester himself?"

"Oh, many," said the porter.

"Then as soon as you have done in here, lock the room up once again and return to your post, and I shall send a constable to you. Together with him, you must visit all the places Paltrow might hide, so that we may be absolutely certain that he is not here still. Will you do that?"

"You may count upon me."

With that, Sir John surprised him by offering his hand. The porter took it after a moment's hesitation and gave it a firm shake. We two departed then and made swiftly for the stairs.

Mr. Templeton, now situated behind the desk, seemed more composed than earlier. He held himself in tight control as Sir John corrected him on the identity of the dead man in Room 12, and went so far as to apologize for the confusion he had caused.

"You see, sir, this sort of trouble is simply unknown to us here at the Globe and Anchor. We've had no crime at all in this hostelry."

"Not even theft?"

"Not during my five years here—and certainly nothing like murder."

"Then, sir, you have indeed been fortunate. But let me ask you, what has happened to the constable who entered with me? Is he—"

"Is he still here?" asked Mr. Templeton, anticipating and interrupting. "Indeed he is. I admitted him to the room of—well, the *late* Mr. Bolton, which he proceeded to search. Ah, but look"—he pointed—"here he comes now."

I turned to look, and it was so. For one so large, Mr. Bailey moved with easy grace. His descent of the stairs was accomplished two or three at a time in a kind of loose, dancing style which brought him swiftly to us; he ended the dance before Sir John with a quick step and a bold salute. Ever the soldier.

"What have you to report, Mr. Bailey?" asked Sir John.

"Little that's good, sir," said he. "It seems that this fellow Elijah Bolton is ready to leave here at his earliest opportunity. I found his portmanteau packed and his greatcoat upon the bed."

"I fear he has already left us. He lies dead upstairs in Room Twelve, the victim of one whom he failed to surprise." Sir John went on to tell Mr. Bailey all we had learned from our trip upstairs, giving particular emphasis to the possibility that the claimant might yet be hiding somewhere within the Globe and Anchor.

"*Here?*" burst forth Mr. Templeton at that point. "But that . . . that is terrible indeed."

"Indeed it is," said Sir John. "Nevertheless, it is a possibility. Therefore, Mr. Bailey, I appoint you to go once more upstairs to the porter, Mr. Simmons, who will show you about the hostelry, that you might investigate together all the potential hiding places. Does that meet with your approval, Mr. Templeton?"

"Oh, yes, sir, of course it does."

"And are you armed, Mr. Bailey?"

"As you required, sir—a cutlass and a brace of pistols."

"Then, proceed. Jeremy and I shall return to Bow Street. We shall keep space in the strongroom for the claimant in the expectation that you will bring him in to us."

"That would be my pleasure, sir."

"It would also be mine." Then did Sir John turn to me. "Jeremy, let us be off."

And indeed we set forth together—out the door, then left up the Strand. Yet we had proceeded only a few steps in that direction, when before me there appeared a familiar figure quite unexpectedly out of a sudden fog. It was no less than Sir Patrick Spenser, Solicitor-General for the King, who had quite mysteriously disappeared when the claimant, shamed by his putative tutor, Mr. Inskip, ran from the residence of the Lord Chief Justice. I whispered hurriedly to Sir John the identity of him who approached.

When we were but a few feet away, Sir Patrick halted and, smiling broadly, greeted Sir John as one who had just come upon an old friend quite unexpectedly.

"Why, this is a pleasure I had not anticipated," said he. "What brings you to this end of the Strand, Sir John?"

"Ah, Sir Patrick, is it? What a surprise. You ask what brings me here, but it is no more than my usual round of business. But you, sir, you confused us all by your sudden departure from Lord Mansfield's residence. I hope it was no cause for alarm or distress that sent you forth."

"Ah, no, I, like you, had attended to gain some personal impression of the claimant. Having seen him reduced to stuttering foolishness, I had no need to see more. And so, when he left, blubbering like a child, I left also, for I had more pressing matters to attend to. Did I miss something of importance?"

"Oh, I daresay you did not. We discussed the interview that had taken place—that sort of thing—rather longer than was necessary, or so it seemed to me."

"The usual, eh? I'm happy to have been spared it. Ah, but tell me, did I not hear that it was your idea to bring that man Inskip down from Oxford?"

"Ah, yes, it was. I had met the fellow there not long ago and knew that the claimant had not visited him when he went through the university. He seemed singularly well equipped to put questions to him in areas about which I knew nothing."

"And so he proved to be! Why, he quite destroyed the fellow!" Sir Patrick seemed most enthusiastic. "In fact, I am come this way—should you wonder—that I might offer him my felicitations for his superb interrogation. I failed to do so, of course, because of my early departure."

"I'm sure he would be proud to receive them," said Sir John.

"I understand he is lodging at the Globe and Anchor."

"He is indeed."

Then, with a shaking of hands, a nodding of heads, smiles, and polite laughter, the two men parted company. We continued on our way up the Strand, Sir John and I, though we did not speak for some little while.

Frankly, I was trying to make sense of what I had heard. I have reported the conversation as I remembered it, thinking it rude to interpolate my feelings, as Sir John failed to say things which I would normally have expected him to tell the Solicitor-General.

First and most important, you must have thought it strange, as I did, reader, that when asked what it was brought us to that place where Sir Patrick encountered us, Sir John said only that it was his "usual round of business." Surely, he should have been more specific than that. What would not the Solicitor-General have given to know that the claimant had quite evidently committed homicide? (Whether it be murder or manslaughter could not then easily be said.) This indeed put a different complexion upon the entire affair, did it not?

Of lesser moment, though equally puzzling, was the question of why Sir John had allowed Sir Patrick to proceed to the Globe and Anchor with the expectation of seeing Richard Inskip, when he knew very well that Mr. Inskip had gone to the Drury Lane Theatre to see Mr. Garrick's revival of *The Recruiting Officer*. Of course, Sir Patrick could always leave a note for the tutor, yet that was not the point. The point, to my mind, was that Sir John sometimes acted in a secretive or indifferent manner toward others. I confess that what then came to mind was the comment made by Judge Benjamin Talley to his nephew Archibald to explain why Sir John was no more than a magistrate: "He has offended too many of the rich and powerful." Would not Sir Patrick Spenser be offended at Sir John's failure to communicate? I felt sure he would.

As I harbored such disloyal and critical thoughts, we walked on through the fog. It rose from the river and swirled on down the Strand in a way that it totally enveloped men, coaches, and horses in such an eerie manner that they seemed to be rendered altogether invisible. Full-sized hackney coaches would pass us by—that is, we *heard* them pass—yet they would remain quite invisible to me; at most I would see the indistinct glow of their top running light. The oil-burning street lamps, which normally lit the Strand so very well, were so muffled in fog that midway between them it seemed to darken so completely that we might well have been walking underwater.

Every now and again, the figure of a man would loom up suddenly before us. And often he would shy away, as fearful of us as I of him. But each time a figure appeared in that frightening way, my hand tightened about the butt of the pistol put into my pocket by Mr. Baker, our armorer and night gaoler. ("It will be foggy later tonight," he had said as he presented me with it. "Every footpad and villain in London will be out to try his luck.") And yet, miraculously perhaps, our walk back to Number 4 Bow Street was safe and without incident. Perhaps Sir John's presence, which intimidated many, frightened away all who might have detained us with criminal intent. Sir John himself was certain it was his reputation that kept us safe in dark and dangerous places. It may have been so, yet this firm belief of his did not prevent Mr. Baker from frequently offering me a pistol when he judged that the situation or the destination demanded it; nor did it prevent me from accepting it.

It was, as I suggested, a relatively silent journey. We were halfway to Bow Street, or so it seemed to me, before Sir John was inspired to comment. And when at last he did, it seemed to me merely mundane.

"Mmm," said he, "fog."

"Yes, sir," said I, "it is quite foggy. I can barely see my hand before me."

"Then are you reduced to my state, or close to it."

"What senses reveal the fog to you?" I was suddenly curious.

"Well, let me see. I can feel it upon my face as a slight dampness. And you might not credit this, nevertheless, it's true: Fog does have a smell."

"Oh, truly? What sort of smell, sir?"

"Not a very lovely one, I fear. I should say that the fog—the London fog, that is—smells of the Thames, for that is where it comes from for the most part, is it not? And we both know that the smell of the river is not an altogether pleasant one. Yet I can hear the fog, too, Jeremy."

"Surely not, sir."

"Yes, oh, yes, though not as a noise in itself, but rather as a condition which affects all other noise. It tends to dampen—or perhaps better put, to muffle all other sounds. And finally, my extra sense tells me something, too."

"Do you mean your common sense?"

"No, something a bit different. It's this way, Jeremy. Each time I hear muffled footsteps approaching through the fog, I sense you tensing with apprehension, and I perceive a small motion with your right hand to the pocket of your coat. You've a pistol in that pocket, haven't you?"

"Uh, well, yes, sir. I fear you've caught me again."

"You and Mr. Baker." He sighed. "Well, perhaps on a night such as this, it is not entirely unnecessary to carry along a pistol. Besides, you're older and wiser now than you were the first time I caught you out. How old were you then?"

"Thirteen, I believe."

"Good God! Well, you seemed older. And how old are you now?"

"Sixteen, sir."

"You still seem older—in most ways, though in some ways not."

I refrained from asking him to enumerate them, and he supplied no further information, so there the matter stood between us, and we lapsed into silence once more.

After a time, and a considerable time it was, he inclined his head toward me and, lowering his voice as if conversing in secret, he asked, "Have you made any progress toward placing that voice you heard in Oxfordshire?"

"What voice was that, sir?"

"Why, the voice of your captor, the voice of the puppet

master, the voice of him standing behind the claimant," said Sir John with some slight annoyance evident in the tone of his voice.

"He spoke but a few words within my hearing."

"Then I take it your response would be in the negative?"

I attempted to address the matter, realizing instantly that it could not be done so casually. "I suppose, sir, that it must be in the negative," said I quite regretfully. Yet what was it? Something there was, certainly, tugging at the back of my mind. "Let me give it some thought," I said at last.

"Could it, for instance, be one whose voice you have heard since our return from Oxford?"

I concentrated for a moment, seeking somehow to re-create the sound of the voice by repeating in my mind what had been said: "That will be quite enough, Mr. Bolt" and "Come up here—now." Little enough to go on. Still, it seemed that I had heard something like it not long before. I waited, but nothing seemed to come. Yet, finally, the only reply I could give him was "Perhaps."

Then did we pass another space of time in silence. I concentrated on the problem he had given me. And he? His thoughts were then a mystery to me—and, as I think back, they are still. Nevertheless, I should have taken some hint from his next remark, though it came some minutes later. We were, as I recall, just turning from Russell Street onto Bow Street, having nearly reached our destination.

"Lord Mansfield," he began, "told me something he thought rather amusing the other day."

"Oh?" This was something new. Though Sir John enjoyed laughing with his fellows as much as the next man, jokes and witticisms were not normally his line.

"Well, yes, he did. It seems that he was present when old Lord Chesterfield remarked to Sir Patrick Spenser that he had no sure notion of what might be the duties of the Solicitor-General. He suggested that perhaps Sir Patrick might make it plain to him. 'You ask what I do,' said Sir Patrick. 'Why, Lord Chesterfield, I do whatever I am asked and attempt to do so with a smile upon my face.' "

I sought to find the story humorous, yet it seemed rather pathetic to me. All I could manage in response was a rather weak chuckle.

"Then, you do not find it amusing?" Sir John pressed me with the question.

"Well, no, sir, I do not."

"Neither do I. Recall that I said that Lord Mansfield found it amusing—not I. And what he said he found particularly 'piquant'—his word and not my own, and I do dislike the Frenchification of the King's English—was the fact that almost in demonstration of that smile, Sir Patrick put one upon his face. It was ironic to the extreme, he said, quite cold enough to cause a shiver. Now, Jeremy, do you not suppose that a man who said he did whatever he was asked and could smile such a smile would look for the opportunity to bite the hand that fed him? To advance his own cause, even at the expense of others? That I find distinctly *un*amusing."

Such talk, then, tended only to confuse me, for the truth of it was I was then too naive and indeed knew too little of the world to understand truly what Sir John was getting at. Nor would I look in the direction he was pointing me; perhaps, reader, I was being willfully obtuse—a bit stubborn.

"Perhaps I would agree with all that you say, Sir John, but I must first think upon it." I felt frustrated and incapable. I wondered whether I might ever meet him on his own level.

"Well, then," said he, "do so. Think upon it, and we shall discuss these matters again soon."

Thus the conversation which led us to the door of Number 4 Bow Street—and to the surprise which awaited us there. I know not quite how to set the scene for this, and so I shall not even try. I shall simply say that as I opened the door on the right, which led to the area which Sir John referred to as backstage of the court, I heard the voices of two men in earnest discussion. The voices were familiar; one of them I identified immediately as that of Mr. Baker; the other I'd heard—and recently—though I could not immediately place it.

We advanced. I closed the door behind us. Sir John came

to a halt; he stood rooted for a moment as he listened, then did he whisper to me, "Good God, Jeremy, it's the claimant!"

I was quite as astonished as he. Since it was relatively certain that he had killed Eli Bolt, I wondered what could have persuaded him to seek out Sir John. Others in the same position would have left London quickly as ever they could, preferably for the colonies, possibly for the Continent and then to the colonies. Quite naturally, I had some affection for the fellow. After all, had he not rescued me from my captivity in Oxfordshire? Though he had whispered only his instruction to turn right at the gate, I had been certain even then that the fellow who had freed me was the claimant; once I had spent the better part of the afternoon listening to him at Lord Mansfield's residence, I was quite certain of it. Quite naturally, I felt in his debt. It disturbed me no end that he had not done the sensible (or at least predictable) thing and made a run for it.

"Sir John, is it you?" The claimant rose from his place opposite Mr. Baker, pulled himself to his full height, which was considerable, and advanced toward the magistrate with his hand extended in friendship; on his face he wore an expression that might have been described as a solemn smile. Solemn it certainly was, but there were hope enough and even confidence in it so that he seemed one about to ask a favor which he was reasonably certain would be granted.

For his part, Sir John stood flabbergasted into silence as the claimant came forward. I saw that he limped and, as he came close, I noted the bruises upon his face and the pained manner with which he bore his left shoulder and right hand. It was clear that though he had emerged the victor in a fight to the death, he had nevertheless sustained injuries.

He offered me a nod, and to Sir John he gave his hand—his left hand—grasping the other's right quite solemnly with it.

"You have surprised me, sir," said Sir John, pulling back slightly.

"I hope you will forgive my use of the left hand," said the claimant. "I fear my right hand is broke."

"I should not doubt that it is, having heard the use to which you put it. Mr. Baker? Did I hear you come forward?"

"Yes, sir," said the gaoler. "I am here." He had followed the claimant down the corridor and now stood directly behind him.

"When did this gentleman arrive?"

"Near an hour ago, sir."

"Not long after we left, then?"

"That would be about right."

"You must have come here direct," said Sir John to the claimant. "Were you so sure that escape was impossible that you dispensed with any such effort in order to save us all trouble?" There was a sharp edge of irony in his voice.

"Nothing of the kind. Escape did not occur to me as an option."

"And why was that?"

"Because escape would be tantamount to an admission of guilt."

"And you wish now to maintain your innocence? If you'll forgive me, sir, that strikes me as rather brazen. That was, after all, a corpus which you left behind in your room at the Globe and Anchor, was it not?"

"It was, though I wish it were not."

"No more than I," said the magistrate with a sigh. "Do you wish, then, to make a confession?"

"No, sir, I wish to make a statement."

"Ah, a statement, is it? That sounds ever so much more salubrious than a confession, does it not? Confessions are of their very nature untidy. They deal in guilt and hold nothing back. Statements, on the other hand, seem to say as little as possible and deal in distinctions. I am not sure I wish to hear your statement, sir, if by making it you suppose you can put aside the matter of the homicide without making a complete revelation of all that led up to it. Do you understand me, sir?"

"I understand you completely," said the claimant. "And I shall hold nothing back."

"In that case, Mr. Baker, prepare my chambers. Light every candle," said Sir John. "And you, Jeremy, come along and make sure you have a plenty of paper—take it from Mr. Marsden's desk if you must—for I shall want you to take down what is said in dictation."

ELEVEN

*In which the claimant
lays aside pretense
and tells all*

"What is your true name?" asked Sir John.

"Percival Mobley," replied the claimant.

"You have said that your true name is Percival Mobley. In so saying, do you give up all pretense that you are Lawrence Paltrow and renounce all claim to the Laningham title and fortune made in his name?"

An odd look passed across the face of him who had just claimed the name of Percival Mobley. "Indeed I do not claim now to be Lawrence Paltrow, but as for renouncing the Laningham title and fortune, I have never made the claim officially—that is, to the House of Lords. Though I admit, however, that I have presented myself to various individuals as Mr. Paltrow and registered as such in inns and hostelries. That, of course, I should no longer do."

(It may be pertinent here, reader, to reveal how I, as amanuensis, treated the material given above. Since Sir John wanted the statement made in Mr. Mobley's voice, I simply eliminated the questions and any discussion that passed between them and presented all in declarative sentences, as follows: "My true name is Percival Mobley. I hereby give up all pretense that I am Lawrence Paltrow and renounce all claim in his name to the Laningham title and fortune." But now to continue with the basic matter with which I worked.)

"Your age, sir?"

"Twenty-six."

"Where were you born, and where did you grow to maturity?"

"I was born in Southwark, and there did I grow up."

Sir John's brow wrinkled. "Southwark, you say? You mean just across the river? You do not sound in your speech as one from Southwark—and I am one who can usually place a man by his manner of speech."

"And so am I," said Mr. Mobley, formerly the claimant. "I was the youngest of six children and soon became the family mimic. And it was not long before I exercised my talent beyond the limits of our home. I was soon able to imitate speech and physical movements of all my teachers at school. Soon there was no one on either side of the river whom I did not consider fair game for my play."

"This, then, was a sort of game with you?"

"In the beginning, of course, but then, as a boy no older than this young fellow here"—indicating me, of course—"I discovered amateur theatrics."

"Ah, yes," said Sir John, "as many before you have. And did that lead to professional employment?"

"In the theater? Not in London's three companies, but one summer I went out with a troupe of strolling players and had a grand time. That did, however, move me to emigrate to the North American colonies. I told myself that things would be better there. At least there was no Licencing Act. I told myself that I might one day have my own company, my own theater, as Mr. Garrick has."

"You were ambitious."

"And am still. Yet I had to take employment where I could find it in the colonies. The history of work which I attributed to Lawrence Paltrow was my own."

"You speak as a gentleman, or at least as an educated man," noted Sir John.

"Mimicry—naught but a good ear, the actor's gift. Surveying, which saw me through when all else failed, was a skill I acquired quite casually along the way. As I said earlier today, there is work in the colonies for a man willing to dirty his hands. I might also say that I am reasonably intelligent, and as the youngest child of six, I was allowed to stay longest in school."

"You said that you were in the city of Philadelphia when you read of your brother's death and saw your claim to the title. Would you now like to correct that?"

"In truth, it happened quite different. I was in Georgetown in the colony of Maryland when I was approached by the man you seem to know as Eli Bolt. He has appeared with me as Elijah Bolton. As you perceived, they are one and the same."

"What did Eli Bolt have to say to you?"

"He had just attended a performance of *The Duchess of Malfi* in which I played a role. Though the drama pleased him greatly—no doubt because of its violence—it was not to discuss it that he invited me to a dram shop nearby, but to acquaint me with the facts of Arthur Paltrow's execution and its relation to the Laningham title and fortune. He told me that Arthur Paltrow had had a brother named Lawrence, who would now be in line as the next Lord Laningham, but that he, Mr. Bolt, knew as certain what no one else knew—that Lawrence Paltrow was dead. He had been with him on an expedition along the frontier seven or eight years past, and he had seen him drown during a river crossing. 'Let me tell you, young sir,' said he to me, 'you are the spit and image of Lawrence Paltrow, except a little taller and wider. You could fool his own dear mother, I'm sure.' Thus I began to understand the direction in which he was taking me, and I confess I did not resist him overmuch—perhaps not at all. Mr. Bolt flattered my abilities as an actor and hinted how much greater a role this would be for me to play—greater than any heretofore. My head was turned by him. I began to fantasize what life might be in the House of Lords."

"You consented, then, to impersonate Lawrence Paltrow?"

"In so many words, I did, yes," said Mobley. "He said there would be a man in London who would wish to meet me before the plan could be put into action. Would I be willing to sail to England to meet him? I said I would, and in less than a week we were on a ship bound for London. My fare was paid by Eli Bolt. I thought this most fortunate, for I was long overdue for a visit to my family in Southwark. I told myself that no matter how this adventure might turn out, I should at least have that out of it."

"What did you know of the Paltrow family and the last Lord Laningham at that time?"

"Nothing at all. Oh, I suppose I had heard the title bandied about some, yet I had no idea whether it was a dukedom, an earlship, or what it was. Nor did I know that Paltrow was the family name of the Laningham line. I have never taken interest in such matters. I had much to learn."

"And you learned it well," said Sir John with a respectful nod.

"I suppose I should thank you, yet if I had proved a little less conscientious as a scholar, I might not be in the position in which I find myself today. Mr. Bolt began my instruction on shipboard. He told me all he remembered of Lawrence Paltrow. I was especially interested in the Journal that he kept during their journey through the wilderness. It seemed to me that the man would have revealed himself through his writing. That might prove most beneficial. And so I asked Mr. Bolt if he knew what had become of it, and he became quite angry, though not at me—no, not quite. He would say only that the Journal had been lost when Mr. Paltrow drowned."

At this point, Percival Mobley fell into a thoughtful silence, as if he were seeking to remember something—or perhaps weighing its importance. After a hesitation of nearly a minute, through which Sir John waited most patiently, he resumed his telling of his long tale.

"I should probably add at this point, Sir John, that all during the voyage, as we talked about the man I was to become, Mr. Bolt played constantly with a rope of woven leather that he seemed to keep with him at all times. He had it fixed in a loop and would constantly throw it round objects on the deck, doing tricks with it for the amusement of others aboard. I mention this only because it will become important later in the story."

And to that, Sir John replied: "No doubt it does, and I have a good notion of just how. But tell me, how long after your arrival did you meet the man you were intended to see?"

"Oh, it was not long at all," said he. "It must have been the day after we docked that I met the man who would become the director and financer of this enterprise."

"And who was that man?"

"Why, it was the Solicitor-General—or, so that there be no confusion in the matter, it was Sir Patrick Spenser."

Sir John took this startling information with equanimity. I, on the other hand, was so disturbed by what I had just heard that the pen with which I had been writing dropped from my hand, fluttering down to the floor and landing just beyond my foot. In my effort to scoop it up quickly, I knocked down the pile of paper upon which I had been writing and came ever so close to tipping the inkwell where I had dipped my pen. Reader, I was at once surprised and chagrined. The first thought that passed through my mind was not really a thought at all, but the repetition of those words in my mind's ear, "That will be quite enough, Mr. Bolt" and "Come up here—now," which I had heard during the night of my abduction. Why, yes, of course, it had been Sir Patrick's voice, the same voice I had heard on that very night just outside the Globe and Anchor. *Why* had I not recognized it at that time, particularly after those hints dropped by Sir John? He, it was evident, had divined the answer by reason, by common sense, or by that extraordinary other sense which only he seemed to have. Yet now Sir John turned it all around and handed it back to Mobley.

"That is mere assertion," said he. "You must convince me."

"But how can I do that?"

"Let us begin with motive. What reason had he for backing you as claimant to the Laningham title and fortune? What was his plan?"

"That, at first, he was somewhat reluctant to reveal, but it gradually came forth that land was his object. Once my claim to the Laningham title had been recognized, it was his intention to strip the Laningham holdings one by one from the new Lord Laningham."

"And how did he intend to do this?" Sir John put the question quite directly. There was naught of skepticism or mockery in his tone.

"Oh, by legal means, you may be sure of it," said the other. "Sir Patrick is, after all, the Solicitor-General. As he had finally arranged it, the only laws broken would have been broken by me in gaining the title. The rest—the sale of lands and houses—was to be handled in full accordance with the law. Yet it was to be done at prices so low as to be legal theft."

"What were you to be left?"

"Very little, in fact. In money, no more than the proceeds of the sales, such as they were, and perhaps a house—though not the Laningham castle; that he intended to give as a gift to the King as a residence for the Prince of Wales when the son reached his majority."

"Ha! *He* would give the house, would he? How generous of him!" (I knew Sir John well enough to read the signs: He had begun to bristle.) "But tell me, Mr. Mobley, what would have happened if you had gained the title and simply refused to complete all or part of your side of the bargain? As it was, after all, the arrangement was not so favorable to you."

"It did not take me long to understand that. I have participated in a good many matters of business in the colonies, enough certainly to know that in an arrangement such as this, it was I who took all the risks—and very grave risks they were. I should be better rewarded. I called this to his attention in a rather joking manner by asking if it were not to his advantage if we, between us, negotiated a contract. Then said he to me, 'There is no need. We have a spoken contract between us.' And said I to him, 'What if I should break the contract?' 'You will not,' said he, 'for in coming to London you accepted the terms, and should you fail to execute them, I shall activate the enforcement clause.' I then asked him what was the enforcement clause, and he said to me, 'The enforcement clause is Mr. Bolt, and he will kill you.' "

"And did you then behave yourself? Or did you test the limits of that 'spoken contract'?"

"No, I was perhaps bolder than I ought to have been. If you will recall, sir, I welcomed the opportunity to visit London, for it would at least give me a chance to visit my family in Southwark. We had left Baltimore in a great rush, yet I did have time to write my mother and father to inform them that I was coming. They must have known that I was in London, yet I was not permitted to visit them."

"Not permitted?" echoed Sir John. "How, then, were you prevented?"

"I was near a prisoner in Sir Patrick Spenser's residence in Grosvenor Square. While it was not specifically said that I might not leave unaccompanied, each time I sought to do so, Mr. Bolt was there to insist on coming along with me wherever I wished to go. Since I had no intention of bringing this rough, bearded pirate of a man into my family circle, I simply kept quiet about my wish. Sir Patrick insisted, in any case, that there was much work to be done, much to be learned about Lawrence Paltrow—and of course there was, particularly in the area of natural science, which, I was assured, Mr. Paltrow had known very well. I was expected to teach myself during a few short weeks in London all he had learned in years at Oxford. It became at last a bit too much for me, and I insisted upon a holiday from my studies. It was to take the form of a visit to the Drury Lane and attendance at one of Mr. Garrick's productions of Shakespeare—*Antony and Cleopatra* it was."

"Ah, yes," said Sir John, ever the enthusiast of Shakespeare, "an excellent play and a good lesson in history."

"So it is," agreed the other quite as eagerly. "Would I could have seen it through to the end!"

"You left? But how could you?"

"It was only by escaping at intermission that I was able to elude Eli Bolt. He, indifferent to the tenderer passions of the play, had fallen asleep. I managed to get past him and into the crowd without waking him. I saw my chance and took it. Knowing my way well through the theater from earlier visits there, I was out and in a hackney in not much more than a minute. I surprised my parents at dinner. They were quite overjoyed to see me and sent word to my sisters and brothers, who came to welcome me back. We had a grand time of talking and eating and drinking, and I so forgot myself there that I stayed the night and slept in my old bed at home. When I returned next day to Grosvenor Square, I found I had been sorely missed. There would, I believe, have been more made of my absence had I not claimed to have gone off in pursuit of a courtesan and given the entire night to our amours. I do truly believe that Sir Patrick and Mr. Bolt were envious, for they fell to teasing me in a crude fashion. Nevertheless, next day Sir Patrick decided it would be best if I were to continue my studies at his country home in Oxfordshire."

"Let me stop you at that point," said Sir John, "so that I may ask if, while you were in the company of your family, you gave any hint of why you had come to London—that is to say, of the conspiracy to claim the Laningham title and fortune?"

"I told them nothing at all—or perhaps better said, next to nothing. I said I had come to London on business which I could not discuss, but that they were not to be surprised at anything which might occur in the future."

"Very good, continue."

"I continued my study of the model whom I knew to be dead. Upon Sir Patrick's instruction, I modulated my voice until I captured what was said to be Paltrow's tone. I practiced his halting manner of speech. Bolt recalled his walk, and I did all that I could to duplicate it. I did all that any actor could do to re-create him, and I later had reason to believe that I had done so quite successfully. Yet in one matter I failed and failed utterly, and that was in Lawrence Paltrow's learning. Had I the proper foundation perhaps, an informed teacher, or greater time, I might have mastered aspects of natural science sufficiently to have satisfied others. Nevertheless, I was judged by Sir Patrick as well prepared to go out and seek affidavits which would attest to the fact that I was who I said I was. We—Mr. Bolt and I—went first to Laningham town and found considerable success among those who had known Lawrence Paltrow from infancy to young manhood. Frankly, I was surprised at how easy it was for us to convince those who had had a long acquaintance with the true Lawrence Paltrow."

"How long did you stay there?"

"Perhaps a day or two less than a week."

"And then on to . . . ?"

"Bath," said the claimant. "There I faced what was the crucial test."

"Margaret Paltrow, the mother of Lawrence."

"Indeed, yes. If she were to reject me as her son, then there was no point in pursuing the matter further. I had, however, learned a great deal of Lawrence's childhood while in Laningham, for it seemed that every man or woman who said they remembered me had at least one story to tell about the boy they had watched romp through the town, and the youth who would ride bareback through the fields. Old family servants—and a number of them were still about—were a great source of such stories. In any case, I remembered them all, and putting them together, I was able to construct a sort of history of Paltrow's childhood in stories and anecdotes. This was extremely helpful in dealing with old Mother Paltrow, for when we met I was able to say 'Do you remember the time that I . . .' or 'I recall when you . . .' All of this was extremely helpful in bringing her round to our side."

"I suspect you may have used considerable charm upon her, as well," said Sir John.

"Not much was needed, in all truth. The poor woman was nearly blind. She could not properly see me."

"True enough, I concede. Yet when we visited her, she seemed healthy enough. She was greatly disturbed, however, that her son had left her so long without a letter, without a word. I fear I contributed to those fears."

"She said as much and threatened to withdraw her recognition and tear up the affidavit she had signed because of 'my' neglect during all those years. Bolt and I had visited her together the evening after you saw her, Sir John. You simply awakened the doubts she had managed till then to keep still. You asked her the same questions she had been asking herself for years. Yet as we left, she asked *me* a question, one that quite baffled me. Bolt and I had started down the stairs, and she called me back. I returned to her while he waited at the foot of the stairs. She whispered to me, 'Where is it? Where is the gold?' "

"And what do you suppose she meant by that?"

"I've no idea, sir. It was something between her and her son, I thought, but on the other hand, it made so little sense that I thought perhaps she was going mad. Other things she had said showed her grip on reality was not terribly firm."

"What did you reply to her?"

"I'm not sure, really. I mumbled something to her about waiting. I believe it was 'We'll speak of that later,' or something of the sort. In response, she gave me a rather fierce look and shut the door in my face. Bolt then wanted to know what she had said. I told him she had merely repeated her threat to withdraw recognition. 'We cannot trust her,' said he. I made no argument then. I wish that I had. Then did Bolt surprise me by parting company with me. He had said he would accompany me to the theater there in Bath—*Hamlet* was the play. But now he said he had no wish to go. He would return to the Bear Tavern, eat and drink, and leave me to my evening's entertainment. I was too happy to be rid of him to look deeply into this, and so I left him. I did not return to the hostelry until near midnight. By then Margaret Paltrow was dead at Bolt's hand."

"You're sure of that?"

"As sure as I could be without having witnessed the deed

or having heard him confess. Yes, I am certain of it in my own mind."

"So am I," said Sir John.

Though I knew this to be so, reader, I was nevertheless somewhat surprised to hear Sir John reveal it to Mr. Mobley. He had allowed himself to be more openly sympathetic to the man. It was, for him, a very good sign.

"You must continue," said he. "Was it then that you returned to Oxford?"

"Soon—but not immediately. First it fell to me next day to deal with the death of my supposed mother. I will say that the tears I shed for the poor woman were real enough. I arranged for her burial, promising I would return, which I never did. Bolt kept out of sight during all this. It was only for dinner that night that we came together again. That was when he spied you and another man he knew who was sitting at your table. He declared that it was time to leave Bath, and we rode out of the town about an hour later. He did not in the least like being recognized. After Bath, things went from bad to still worse. You know of my calamitous interview with the two professors, Fowler and Newcroft. I was in no wise capable of deceiving them as to the extent of my knowledge of natural science and natural history. Had I had a year to prepare for them, I might have done better—though I doubt it. After what had happened in Bath to Mrs. Paltrow—after her murder, to call it by its proper name—I had no wish to continue with this masquerade."

"Did you voice this to Sir Patrick?"

He sighed. "I did once, but only in part. I told him that I believed that Eli Bolt had killed Mrs. Paltrow. He simply dismissed my suspicions, saying something like, 'Oh, I think not. But still, with what you yourself told me about her sudden wavering, her threat to withdraw her recognition, and so on, she died at a most opportune moment, didn't she? There is but one way to be certain about whether Bolt killed her, and that would be to ask him yourself.' I had no intention of doing that."

"Quite understandable," said Sir John. "Since you were

nearly a prisoner, it would not have done to anger your guard."

"In fact, I was planning my escape. That was the point at which I had arrived, when Bolt took it upon himself to knock your young assistant here over the head and haul him back to Sir Patrick's. He had been angered by our treatment by the young scholars at a—"

Sir John raised a hand to silence Mr. Mobley. "I fear I know the circumstances all too well. Jeremy gave me a full report on his abduction. He went as far as to credit you with his rescue. For that I am greatly beholden to you. Nevertheless, the fact remains that you are here making a statement regarding a homicide. Let us get on to that, if you please."

"But, sir," said Mr. Mobley, "while you may know that it was I who set the lad free, you do not know what moved me to do it. Sir Patrick had sent the drunken Bolt to bed in disgrace, but then he had discussed with me just what was to be done with the lad. He gave it as his opinion that it might be necessary to 'remove' him. I pointed out that he was Sir John Fielding's boy. 'Yes,' said he, 'that makes it all the more necessary and all the more unfortunate.' "

Sir John turned in my direction. "Do you hear that, Jeremy? Your demise was at least considered 'unfortunate.' "

"Yet nevertheless 'necessary,' " said I.

"As you will. But now, Mr. Mobley, you must bring us to date."

"My appearance before the commission was, as all the rest of it, a scheme of Sir Patrick's devising. I had not even known that such a body existed; I learned from Sir Patrick that he had organized it himself purportedly in the King's service, hoping to use it so as to have a listening post in the enemy's camp. By the time I was instructed by him to write that letter, I believe he was quite despairing of the success of our entire enterprise. Bolt had become unreliable, and he must have perceived quite rightly that I was looking for an opportunity to get back to the colonies. For myself, an appearance before the commission would take me to London, where escape would be easier to accomplish.

"Well," he continued, "in the event, I believe I did well enough in the first part of the interrogation—"

"Oh, you did very well indeed," Sir John interrupted. "In fact, the commission was quite ready to disband when you left the room. The last thing they would have wished was to contest the claim in court so that you might have the opportunity to appear before a jury."

"But then was the second part," said Mr. Mobley, "and that fiend of an old fellow. What was his name? Ah, yes, Inskip. I remembered at last that I had been advised to avoid him at Oxford because of his merciless manner. He was evidently notorious about the university for just the sort of bullying he gave me. I was so destroyed by him that I wanted nothing more than to get away, so I made my little speech and left."

"Rather hurriedly," said Sir John.

"Yes, I wanted to leave my dreams of vainglory behind with Sir Patrick. I saw it as my chance to escape."

"Yet Sir Patrick went running after you, did he not?"

"He did, and he lectured me and threatened me. In reply, I did little more than repeat what I had said within, though with a few more colorful turns of phrase. I told him also that if he tried to stop me, I would tell all and name him as leader of our conspiracy. It seemed to me as I left him standing and looking after me in Bloomsbury Square that there was little he could do, yet I underestimated him."

"Get on with it," Sir John urged. "Get to Eli Bolt."

"Yes, indeed I shall," said the other. Yet he sighed deeply, unwilling to be pushed, before he resumed: "I walked about, attempting to organize myself, and decided that I must return to the Globe and Anchor, for there were certain personal items I did not wish to part with. And why should I leave London with no more than the clothes on my back? And so I returned to the hostelry."

"Did you expect trouble?"

"I was prepared for it. As I was about to enter the room, I

had a sudden vision of Bolt on shipboard, tossing that loop of rope again and again with great accuracy. And that, sir, was what saved me. The room was by then quite dark, near dark as pitch, when I kicked the door shut behind me. But as I did so, I put my right hand up before my face, and only an instant later I felt something light brush my ear and touch my cheek. My hand shot up and brushed that something away. Thus was I saved from strangulation. The noose was well tossed, but I managed to throw the rope off before Bolt could pull it tight. Yet I followed it back, pulled him to me—and we fought. Dear God, how we fought! With our fists, with our feet—we kicked and wrestled and scratched and rolled about on the floor and crashed against the walls. I could not have bested Bolt in his prime, but he was long past that. Drink and riotous living had weakened him. He lacked both strength and endurance. I was the younger, and I knew that I was fighting for my very life.

"The noose was still in my hand, or to tell it true, it was looped about my wrist. I had knocked Bolt to his knees and threw the noose round his neck. I warned him that if he offered further resistance, I would pull it tight. Yet Bolt attempted to throw me off his back, to turn and wrestle me down, and so I gave a good, sharp tug on that leather rope, but then I relaxed it when a horrible noise came from him down on the floor. He struggled to breathe, but finally lost the battle. I loosed the noose—but too late. I had cut his windpipe. The man was dead."

Percival Mobley had, in the telling, become so exercised in an emotional manner that with those last few solemn words, he collapsed beneath the great burden he bore and began to weep.

"So," he said to Sir John when he was able, "it was not my intention to kill him. I wished only to force him to quit trying to kill *me*."

"Then you would deny the charge of murder but are prepared to plead guilty to manslaughter?"

"If I must, I suppose I do."

TWELVE

In which Sir John
takes the
witness stand

I t took nearly a day, but by the end of it, word had circulated through London that a dead man, horribly beaten and strangled, had been discovered in a room in the Globe and Anchor hostelry, and that said room had been engaged by one Lawrence Paltrow. The dead man in the room was not Mr. Paltrow.

The city quite hummed with the news, for it was known to a few that this same Lawrence Paltrow was engaged in a claim upon the Laningham title and its great wealth. The few that knew this told only their most intimate friends, and soon thousands were informed.

What surprise when the drabs, layabouts, and such who were the regular attendants of Sir John Fielding's court at Number 4 Bow Street heard this same Mr. Paltrow summoned before the magistrate by the court clerk! The individual who came limping up in response was all bruises and plasters, one whose right eye was swollen shut, yet one still capable of speech, as he proved in a most interesting exchange with the magistrate. As the story was told, it went something like this:

"This is a case of homicide, sir, and a very serious matter," said Sir John. "How do you plead, Mr. Paltrow?"

"Why, how I plead is my own matter, sir, until you address me by my proper name."

"What's that you say? Are you being impertinent, sir?"

"That is not my intention. Nevertheless, Lawrence Paltrow is not my proper name."

"And what is it, then?"

"Percival Mobley."

At that, a great hubbub erupted in the courtroom. Though none there were acquainted with that name, nearly all knew the name Paltrow. It was that of the Laninghams, a family that had already provided the public with one murderer and two or three street ballads celebrating his deeds and death. Homicide seemed to run in the blood of the Paltrow clan. They had hoped to have their expectations satisfied by some dark revelation of a distant ancestor's pact with the Devil which exacted homicides from each successive generation. A rumor to that effect had raced through the city as soon as it became known that the dead man had been found in a room let to one bearing that surname. And so there was a definite air of disappointment to the comment of the crowd there in the courtroom, a sort of chorus of grumbling. It was easily silenced by Sir John; it took only three good whacks of his gavel to restore order.

"Mobley, is it?" said the magistrate. "Mr. Marsden, do you have record of any Percival Mobley?"

The court clerk made a great show of searching through the papers on the table before him. At last, prefacing his response with a sigh, he said, "No, sir, I daresay I do not."

"Why, there must be something." Then, addressing the man before him: "You made a confession last night, did you not?"

"No, sir, I made a statement."

"A nice distinction, yet hardly worthy of recognition. Did

you make it as Lawrence Paltrow, or as—what was the name?"

"Percival Mobley—and, yes, that was, of course, the name under which I made my statement, for that is my rightful name."

"Mr. Marsden, you say there is nothing there before you under that name?"

"Mobley? No, as I said, nothing under that name, Sir John."

"Nor Paltrow?"

"Nothing here, neither."

"Well, then, sir," said the magistrate to Mr. Mobley, "how do you account for that?"

"I know not. I have made my statement, and that is that."

"Not quite so quick. Were you or were you not marked down in the register of the Globe and Anchor as Lawrence Paltrow?"

"I have said as much."

"But . . ."

Round and round they went. It was all nonsense, of course. I had listened as they planned it all together the night before. Mr. Donnelly, doctor and surgeon and medical examiner for the Westminster coroner, bandaged and plastered Mr. Mobley and brought him to some semblance of good repair. By the time he had completed his ministrations, he, too, had joined in with a few suggestions of his own.

"What you must do," he urged, "is to mention the statement as often as possible, so that one cannot come away from the court ignorant of its existence, nor without wondering what riches it might contain."

"Just so," said Mr. Mobley.

"I shall acquaint Mr. Marsden with our little show," said Sir John, "and he will be eager to play a part. He dearly loves such mummery."

Pleased as they were with the planning, they were not thus occupied for their own entertainment. For as had been intended, I went out next morning to Fleet Street and Grub Street to offer Sir John's invitation to the editors of a number of newspapers, which promised intriguing revelations of interest to their readers if they were to send a representative to the Bow Street Court for that day's session. Since Sir John was not known to be one who puffed the sessions of his court, as indeed certain magistrates were known to do, three editors—those of *The Public Advertiser, The Morning Chronicle,* and *The Times*—sent representatives to the proceedings. I sat as close to them as possible (for, as journalists do, they huddled together) and was afterward pleased to tell Sir John that the response of the gentlemen of the press was exactly as hoped: At first confused, they became greatly interested when the existence of Mr. Mobley's statement became known. Why had he signed into the hostelry as Lawrence Paltrow? Was it true, as had been rumored, that the brother of Arthur Paltrow had been preparing a claim upon the Laningham title and fortune? In insisting that he be addressed as Percival Mobley, was he now admitting that he had been preparing a false claim? These and a number of other such questions were exchanged by them at the end of the little comedy played out between Sir John and Mr. Mobley. (Sir John ruled at last that the gentleman with two names might be charged under both of them.) The journalists were still talking heatedly among themselves as the courtroom emptied.

All this I reported to Sir John, and though he was greatly pleased, he set me to the next task, which was to make a fair copy of Mr. Mobley's statement of the night before and label it as such.

"For," said he, "you may be certain that Sir Patrick had one of his spies present, and it should not be long until we hear from the Solicitor-General direct or through an emissary."

As usual, he was correct in his assumption. Yet because I set to work upon it straightaway, I had finished the copy and had it ready by the time the young lawyer from the office of the Solicitor-General arrived with a formal written request for Mobley's statement. In his presence I read the request aloud to Sir John, who made a proper show of resistance.

He stormed and huffed a bit and declared that the Solicitor-General had no right, et cetera, but in the end he instructed me to fetch the statement from Mr. Marsden and deliver it to him. I made as if to do as he instructed, wandered about a bit, and then returned to hand it over to Sir John. (It had been folded and tucked away in the pocket of my coat all along.)

"I wish this to be sealed," said he to me in his most solemn manner. "I want no meddling done by this message-bearer nor anyone else."

"Sir," said the young lawyer, "I would do nothing of the kind."

"No doubt you would not, yet in this way I may also make plain to Sir Patrick that I surrender this to him only under duress."

Then I hastily melted the wax, allowed it to drip upon the paper, and pressed Sir John's signet ring firmly into the warm, wet seal. He ordered me to hand it over to the young man, and I did so with a face as solemn as his own.

The fellow was barely out of earshot—if that—when the magistrate pulled me close and said in a voice louder than need be that I had better bring the original to Lord Mansfield, lest I make a liar of him—that is, Sir John.

"How do you mean that, sir?" I was quite puzzled by what he had said.

"I mean that in an hour or, more likely, less than that, either the young man who just paid us a visit, or perhaps even the Solicitor-General himself, will return and demand the original. I shall be quite sympathetic but not, ultimately, very helpful, for I shall inform him that the original has been supplied to the Lord Chief Justice at his request."

"Did he request it?"

"Well . . . no. That is perhaps a bit of an exaggeration on my part. Perhaps I had better not add that." He grinned rather boyishly at having been caught out. "I shall assure Sir Patrick that the copy provided him is in every way the same as the original. It is, isn't it, Jeremy?"

"Oh, yes, sir—all except 'Fair Copy,' which was writ across the top."

"Well, then, you can see why it is important that we get the original to Lord Mansfield, for if we do not, then I am a liar—and that is not how I wish to look upon myself."

And so I made ready to go to the great house in Bloomsbury Square. Just before leaving, I was surprised when Sir John ordered me to wear a brace of pistols for my trip across the city. It was not near dark; nevertheless, he seemed to fear that I might be robbed on the way.

"I want no one to look upon that document you carry except Lord Mansfield. If you should be stopped, threaten to shoot dead him who stops you. But if one should move against you, or otherwise detain you, don't shoot him dead. You may, however, shoot to wound. The leg, I believe, is the best place."

This was indeed sobering. He had never, in my memory, described circumstances in which I might discharge a pistol at another human being.

Therefore, I made the journey to Bloomsbury Square in a most watchful state, always aware of the near weightless burden that I carried in my right coat pocket. The statement, read and signed by Percival Mobley, which filled near four pages of foolscap, was accompanied by a note from the magistrate dictated hastily as an afterthought. All were folded together letter-style, sealed, and stamped with the impression of Sir John's signet ring. The pistols were belted over the coat in such a way that the holsters in which they sat were fixed tight over the coat pockets; it would have been quite impossible for any pickpocket, no matter how light-fingered, to have thrust his hand inside and come away with the documents I carried.

I did not alter my route—though perhaps, upon reflection, I should have—but went north to my destination by the swiftest, most direct way I knew. Consequently, I arrived a bit earlier than I had expected. The Lord Chief Justice had not returned from his day at the Old Bailey Court—or so I

was informed by Lord Mansfield's butler. Fully expecting to
be barred from the house, I took a place a step down from
the door, folded my arms before me, and prepared to await
the arrival of his coach. Armed as I was, I thought I made a
rather imposing figure there. Yet the butler remained standing in the open door and looked critically upon me.

"Do you intend to remain there?" he asked.

"And why not?" said I.

He answered with another question: "Why not take a
walk round the square?"

"Because I wish to be here at the moment Lord Mansfield
arrives from Old Bailey."

"Why is it so important that you greet him at his
doorstep?"

"So that I may deliver a document."

"Is it of such importance?"

"Important enough so that Sir John instructed me to shoot
if anyone should try to take it from me by force."

"Oh, I see," said the butler. "Perhaps you'd better come
inside."

I accepted the invitation, even though it was reluctantly
given. He indicated that I was to sit on the bench there in the
vestibule. I was about to take a place there, when my curiosity demanded that I put a question to him: "Why did you
invite me in? I'm not dressed as you usually require for
entry."

"No," said he, "but you're wearing pistols."

"Had you thought I would shoot if I were not admitted?"

"Goodness, no! But it really wouldn't do to have one such
as yourself waiting at the door of the Lord Chief Justice dis-
playing a brace of pistols. It might be thought by the neighbors that you were an assassin."

"I shouldn't suppose that Lord Mansfield would care
what the neighbors thought."

"Oh, he wouldn't," said the butler, "but I do."

With that, he left me, and as I watched him go, I thought
what an odd sort of man he was. Were all butlers as he was?
No, I knew that was not so. Of all the butlers I had known, I

believed I liked best the one who served the last true Lord Laningham. His name had been Mr. Poole. I hoped that he and the rest of the servants who ran that great house had managed to find employment in other houses. I had passed by what had been the Laningham residence in St. James's Street and was astonished to find it boarded up, its hedges in need of trim, weeds growing in a wild swarm—all this in six months. In another six it would be well on its way to a truly ramshackled state. Who would occupy it? Would there ever be a true heir to the Laningham title? What a sad business it was.

Ruminating thusly, I do not believe I heard the butler's footsteps in the hall until he crossed the open space just beyond the vestibule. Yet the sudden clatter brought me from my reverie and to my feet.

"He comes," announced the butler in a manner most important. "Did you not hear the horses?"

"Well, yes, I suppose so," I mumbled. "I must've."

"Stand well behind me as I open the door," he instructed me. "I'll not have the master greeted by a man wearing pistols as he enters his own house."

For all the butler's concern, Lord Mansfield seemed to pay little attention of any sort to me as he strode through the open door. He growled something unintelligible to the butler and walked past me as if I had not been present. Not wishing to be rude, I nevertheless felt I had to do something to detain him. And so I boldly cleared my throat and coughed.

William Murray, Earl of Mansfield, Lord Chief Justice of the King's Bench, stopped in midstep, turned back, and looked at me distrustfully. "Well, what do *you* want?" said he with what seemed a sneer.

"I have a document and a note to deliver to you from Sir John," said I.

"Well, give it me."

That I did without greater preamble.

"Must he have an answer immediate?" the Lord Chief Justice demanded. "That is his way, more often than not."

"No, m'lord," said I. "Except that you recognize the nature and significance of the document, read the note, and agree or disagree to stop off at Number Four Bow Street tomorrow morning on your way to Old Bailey. Your response need not be written."

"All that, eh? Indeed? Well, let us see what he has given us."

Then did he rip open the document at the seal—and none too gently. "A statement, is it? Who is this fellow, Percival Mobley? Silly name, Percival."

"If you will but read on, m'lord. Who he is should be made clear in the first long paragraph."

He read on, and, of a sudden, burst out laughing. "Oh, dear!" he exclaimed. "Just see here! This fellow Mobley has quite dissolved our commission, has he not!"

"I would call your attention to the note, Lord Mansfield," said I. "Sir John warns you of an expected visitor."

"Oh? Let me see."

He found the note and perused it rather hastily, nodding, grunting, chuckling, though in a somewhat sinister manner.

"Ah, well," said he. "Just let him try. He shall discover that I have great powers of resistance. And yes, by all means, lad, tell Sir John that I shall be most happy to look in on him tomorrow morning."

As I walked out the door and into Bloomsbury Square a moment later, I happened to reflect that if I had done nothing more, I had succeeded in altering the mood of the Lord Chief Justice. He was positively jolly by the time I took my leave.

Upon my arrival at Number 4 Bow Street, Sir John took me aside and told me that in my absence he had been blessed by a visit from the Solicitor-General himself.

"As I predicted," said he, "he would have the original and accept no 'Fair Copy.' Indeed, he demanded all copies that had been made, along with the signed original. When I told him that there were no other copies, he made some remark expressing great doubt. When I said to him then, 'Sir, would you impugn my good word?' he said, 'Not your good word, only your good intentions.' And when I told him that the original was unavailable, for it was now with the Lord Chief Justice, he became altogether unreasonable and insisted that I send someone to fetch it back. I did then finally lose my temper. I told him that the statement made by Percival Mobley was material to his trial and belonged with the Lord Chief Justice. 'And,' said he, 'if I have anything to say about it, there will be no trial.' "

Then did Sir John ask me how Lord Mansfield responded to the package with which I represented him.

"He had only to read the beginning of the statement to become most eager to read the rest," said I. "And as for Sir Patrick, he seemed to look forward to a contest of the wills with the Solicitor-General."

"I'm sure he does. When Lord Mansfield digs in his heels, it seems none can budge him."

Yet I had been wondering a question, and I thought it only right to put it to him.

"Sir," said I, "if I may say so without being judged impertinent, you can be quite as stubborn as Lord Mansfield. Why did you feel it necessary to send the original to him in order to keep it out of Sir Patrick's hands?"

"A fair question," said he. "You will find when you grow to manhood, and particularly if you are a lawyer, that it is a good thing to know the limits of your own power—if only to test those limits now and again. Now, I, as a mere magistrate, am not afforded near so much power as, say, the Solicitor-General. If we consider that the Solicitor-General we have in mind is also well known at court and a friend of the King's, to the extent that the King has friends— consider all that, and you must concede that as an opponent he would be very powerful indeed. To tell the truth, I am not sure that I have power enough to resist him in this matter of Mr. Mobley's statement. In less dire circumstances, it might have been amusing to try, but this is too important a matter to turn into such a contest. And so, knowing that the office of the Lord Chief Justice is a much higher and more powerful one than my own, and knowing, too, that Lord Mansfield is specially capable in contests of this sort, I thought him in the best position and better suited than I to fight this out with Sir Patrick Spenser."

"If that is the case, Sir John, why were you so eager for him to see Mr. Mobley's statement that you had me copy it, and then sent it off with that young clerk to Sir Patrick?"

"Why, because, Jeremy, I wanted him to know the contents of the statement. In fact, I want the world to know, and that is why I sent you off with my invitations to the newspaper offices—but Sir Patrick I want most of all to know. I think it will tempt him to overreach himself."

Lord Mansfield did not wait till morning to confer with Sir John. He arrived quite unexpectedly with the usual flurry and shout, tramping up the long corridor to the magistrate's chambers, where Sir John and I were finishing an hour devoted to court correspondence. Thus we were not surprised by him as he made his entrance. I had time aplenty to shift my place to a chair in the corner. There I could hear all without being noticed.

"Well, Sir John," said Lord Mansfield, "he came, and he came earlier than expected. I'd scarce had the opportunity to read through what you had sent me."

"You're referring to Sir Patrick, of course. He must have gone to you directly from here."

"Oh, indeed! I'm sure he did, for he had many words of criticism for you, sir, and most of them decorated with most colorful curses."

"That sort of thing bothers me not in the least," said Sir John. "What disturbed me far more was his emphatic declaration that if he had anything to say about it, Percival Mobley would have no trial."

"I wonder what he could be planning," said Lord Mansfield with a frown. "He was quite conspiratorial," he continued, "at least in the beginning. When I made some reference to the false claim to the Laningham title and his part in it, he more or less dismissed it in that airy way of his."

"Did he deny it?" Sir John asked.

"No, he did not attempt that. What he said—" He hesitated. "If I may think a moment, I believe I can give you his very words . . ." He took that moment and then a moment more. "Ah, yes, Sir Patrick said, 'I see, then, you have been reading that bizarre confession by the claimant. I have seen it myself. He implicates me.' I asked him then if he confirmed or denied the accusation, and he refused to do either. He said, 'If you can show me that a crime has been committed by me, then I will do so. You know the law as well as I do. No formal claim has been made, and therefore no true effort at deception.' "

"Mobley said something of the sort in his own defense," said Sir John. "He must have heard it from him. But you may be certain that Sir Patrick is not as indifferent to his situation as all that."

"Oh, by no means! For in the next breath, he declared that this fellow who has been so free with his accusations is, after all, a murderer. He puts his faith in me that I am known for my short way with all who come before me accused of capital crimes. The facts are not in dispute, says he. Mobley killed this fellow Bolton by breaking his windpipe. That is murder. Make the jury aware of that in your summing-up. Direct them, as you often do, says he, and the jury will do the rest. 'There should be no need to go into these matters of the Laningham claim—neither his part in it, nor mine.' That last bit again is word for word from Sir Patrick's mouth."

"Then he expects you to hang Mobley and thereby rid him of any threat of exposure."

"Oh, yes, and all this was prefatory to his request at the end of our interview that I give to him this fellow Mobley's statement."

"And what was your reply?"

"I told him I could not possibly do that, for it was material to the trial."

"Precisely what I told him. What was his response to that?"

"It was more in the nature of a reaction than a true response. Of a sudden he went tight-lipped and cold and said something like 'Very well, then. I shall have no more to say.' "

"That is rather more sinister than a threat, don't you think?"

"From him, yes," said Lord Mansfield. "See here, we must make a plan. Is that lad of yours about?" He turned and looked round the room. "Yes, there he is behind me in the corner. Send him out of here, if you will, Sir John. What we shall be doing will no doubt bend, if not actually break, a few of the rules, and I prefer to have no witnesses to it."

"As you say, Lord Mansfield," Sir John agreed. "Do please depart, Jeremy," said he to me, "and while you are about it, tell Mr. Fuller to bring Mr. Mobley from the strong room to us here."

"Good God, what have you in mind?" asked Lord Mansfield.

"Something that will require the cooperation of the accused."

A most singular event occurred that night whilst I slept. Well past midnight it was when Mr. Baker was surprised by the entrance of a corporal and two private soldiers from a Guards Regiment stationed at the Tower. They were in full uniform, armed with muskets, and had the sort of serious faces that allowed no possibility of levity. Mr. Baker was quite alone, and it was probably a good thing, too. Had there been a prisoner in the strongroom, who knows what his fate might have been?

They had come, the corporal informed Mr. Baker, to convey a prisoner from the Bow Street Court to Newgate. He had an order for Mr. Baker to examine, should he wish to do so.

"It would do little good for me to look at it," said Mr. Baker, "for as you can see, there is no one here with me."

Nevertheless, the corporal took from his pocket the order he had mentioned and from it read to Mr. Baker: "Percival Mobley is the name of the prisoner, also known as Lawrence

Paltrow." He looked up from the slip of paper and fixed the night gaoler with cold blue eyes. "Where is he?"

"Why, I haven't the foggiest notion. He was here last night, right enough. I had a long talk with the fellow. But when I came on duty this evening, he was gone."

"Gone, was he? Well, we was warned there might be some trouble finding him here, so with your permission or without it, we'll do a search of this place. Private Pringle, Private Lockert, open all the doors and use your lantern in all the corners. I'll talk a bit more to this gent here."

As the two private soldiers went off to do as ordered, the corporal took a step closer and lowered his voice. "Where do *you* think he is?"

"Where I think he is don't matter much," said Mr. Baker, "for I don't *know* where he is. I will say this, howsomever. The last few years Sir John hasn't sent many to Newgate. He uses the Fleet, even though it's mostly a debtor's prison."

By this time, Pringle and Lockert had disappeared into the magistrate's chambers, dark and empty at this hour.

"What was behind that other door when we come in?" The corporal, as later described by Mr. Baker, had a rather insistent manner. It was as though he misunderstood or chose to ignore most of what was said to him.

"That would be the courtroom, magistrate's court. It's dark now, nothing going on this time of night."

"And those stairs? Where do they lead to?"

"Better forget about them. They lead to the residence of Sir John Fielding, Master of the Bow Street Court and Magistrate of the City of London and the City of Westminster. He is a fine gentleman, except when he is angry, and if your men was to rout him and his household out of bed, he would be very angry."

The corporal blinked. His resolve seemed considerably less than a moment before. Perhaps he had heard tell stories of Sir John excited to righteous anger. Or, more likely, he had glimpsed the new arrivals. For at that moment came Mr. Bailey and Mr. Perkins through the Bow Street door. They sensed most immediate that something was amiss. Both had pistols by their sides, and they drew them from their holsters. Mr. Bailey asked Mr. Baker what seemed to be the trouble.

"Why, no trouble at all, Constable," said Mr. Baker. "This corporal from the Tower and two of his men"—pointing down to the room at the end of the hall—"come by to assist in transporting a prisoner to Newgate, not knowing the prisoner was no longer here. They was just leaving. Isn't that so, Corporal?"

"That's as is," said the corporal, then called loud to the rest of his party: "Pringle! Lockert! We're ready to go!"

And in less than a minute they indeed were gone. The three constables watched them leave, frowning until they were out of sight. Then did Mr. Perkins speak up.

"Gents," said he, "we just won the Battle of Bow Street."

"And not a shot fired," said Mr. Baker.

All three did laugh then most merrily.

I had last seen Percival Mobley leaving Number 4 Bow Street under Mr. Fuller's guard and in the company of Lord Mansfield. He was to be taken by them in the coach and four to a secret destination, one that was judged by Sir John to be safer than the strongroom of the Bow Street Court. And so Mr. Baker told the corporal the exact truth when questioned by him; what he did not tell him, however, was that he had been forewarned by Sir John that he might expect such a visit during the night. Constables Bailey and Perkins had also been urged to look in from time to time on Mr. Baker, that they might be certain all went well for him.

When next I saw Mr. Mobley, he stood in the dock at the Old Bailey, defending himself against the charge of homicide. (I learned later that he had spent the night in one of the holding cells beneath the courthouse.) Directly he had concluded his business in Bow Street, Sir John had invited me to accompany him to the trial of Percival Mobley. Though I had no notion of what he, Lord Mansfield, and Mr. Mobley had planned during those hours of the afternoon—or indeed perhaps *because* I had no notion—I accepted his invitation eagerly, thinking perhaps I might even learn in the course of our short journey what I might expect during the trial. In that last I was quite disappointed, for he never breathed a word about what lay ahead; nevertheless, I should not have missed the experience of this trial for the world. Ultimately, it was one of the most instructive of my legal education.

As we arrived, Sir John was taken from me by a bailiff who conducted him through closed doors and thus out of sight. I sought a place in the section given to accommodate the public. There were not so many there, for the trial had been put on the docket at the last minute. Yet the gentlemen of the press were there in greater number than before. I recognized in the seats ahead of mine the three journalists who were at the Bow Street Court, and I saw that they had been joined by others of their kind. They were distinguished by their loud conversation and foolish laughter; I suspected that a few of them were drunk. Still, when the process began, all fell silent and began scribbling notes.

I was not entirely surprised when, just before the Lord Chief Justice made his entrance, Archibald Talley appeared, burbling at the pleasure of seeing me once again.

"I've missed you," said he. "Where've you been?"

"Away," said I, "out of the city—in Bath and Oxford."

"Bath, is it? What had you—"

Then came the command to rise and face Lord Mansfield as he took his place. Was it my imagination, or did he show a bit of spring in his step? I made room, and young Mr. Talley settled in beside me. Then: "Bring forth the prisoner!" Out came Mr. Mobley, clean-shaven and well kempt. He was an impressive figure. As he took his place in the dock, he commanded the attention of the jury in a way that I had not seen before during the trials I had witnessed at Old Bailey.

Young Mr. Talley leaned toward me. "This trial was not announced," he whispered. "Do you know anything about it?"

"Rather a lot, actually."

"He looks quite hale and strong. Who *is* he?"

"That would take too long to tell."

He gave me an annoyed look, but I put a finger to my lips in a plea for silence. The trial began.

It went reasonably swiftly. The counsel for the prosecution rose and did no more than state the facts of the case as sworn to by Alfred Simmons, the night porter at the Globe and Anchor. Though the condition of the corpus of "Elijah Bolton" was described, it was done dispassionately. There was room aplenty for the prosecution to improvise upon the lurid details, yet the opportunity went ignored. Quite frankly, I was surprised.

The Lord Chief Justice thanked the counsel for the prosecution for his presentation and turned to Mr. Mobley.

"Do you dispute the facts as offered?" he asked him.

"I have no quarrel with them," said the prisoner. "I do not dispute the facts as presented."

"Then what have you to say in your own defense?"

Mr. Mobley looked about to commence, when the Lord Chief Justice silenced him with an upraised hand.

"If I may make a suggestion," said the judge.

"Why, of course you may," said the prisoner with a barely suppressed smile. "It is your courtroom."

"So it is." He reached beneath his robe and pulled out a sheaf of foolscap. "You gave a signed statement to Sir John Fielding concerning this case before the court. It seemed an extraordinarily succinct account of a matter most complicated when it was given to me to examine it. We might all be well served, the members of the jury in particular, if you were to read it now to the court."

(I had never known Lord Mansfield to be so considerate, so polite, so *kind,* as he was at that moment with Mr. Mobley. Did this mark a change in his juridical behavior—or was he simply signaling to the jury that this fellow deserved a degree of respect? The latter, no doubt, though he seemed to be overplaying it a bit.)

Mr. Mobley agreed, of course, and the sheaf of papers

was conveyed to him by way of a clerk. He unfolded them and began to read.

The reading took a bit of time. He in no wise rushed through it, but applied his gifts as an actor to the recitation. It was most pleasurable to hear my words given such treatment; and indeed they were my words, though he was their source. His rendition held those in the courtroom quite in thrall for the length of the reading. Though unmoved, the journalists who sat in the row ahead were specially excited by the mention of Sir Patrick Spenser's name: Looks were exchanged, and their pencils fair flew across pages upon which they took their notes. When Mr. Mobley had done, bringing his audience to a pitch of keen arousal with his telling of the tale of his combat with Eli Bolt, he allowed himself to drop his head in a modest bow, a gesture somewhat out of place in the courtroom, yet one that seemed altogether fitting, considering the quality of his performance.

"Does that conclude your defense?" asked the Lord Chief Justice.

"No, my lord, I should like to call two witnesses."

"Call them, then."

"My first witness," said Mr. Mobley, "is Gabriel Donnelly, medical examiner for the coroner of the City of Westminster."

There was a delay of something over a minute as Mr. Donnelly, summoned from the witness room, made his way into the courtroom. Then, led by a bailiff, he took his place at the witness stand.

The prisoner put to him a number of questions which were meant to establish Mr. Donnelly's expertise on medical questions, how he came to view the body of Eli Bolt, and so on. But then the questioner and his respondent came to the heart of the matter, as the good doctor was asked to describe the condition of the body. Much was said in answer, but the key to it all was provided in this exchange between them:

Mr. Mobley: "You have read my statement to Sir John Fielding?"

Mr. Donnelly: "I have. Sir John gave it me to read without comment."

Mr. Mobley: "Would you say that the condition of the body was consistent with my description of our struggle in the room?"

Mr. Donnelly: "I would say it was completely consistent."

With that, Mr. Mobley thanked him and said he had no more questions. And the counsel for the prosecution declined the opportunity to cross-examine. However, as Mr. Donnelly was preparing to step down, the Lord Chief Justice asked him to remain, for he had a question or two for him.

"Mr. Donnelly," said the judge, "in your description of the corpus of Eli Bolt, if that be his name, you described his wounds and bruises, et cetera, quite well, but you did not tell us one thing that may loom as important in the minds of the jurors. Was the deceased a small man or a big man?"

"He was a very big man, my lord," said Mr. Donnelly. "It might be no exaggeration to say that he was huge."

"Larger than Mr. Mobley?"

Mr. Donnelly cast a look at Mobley. "Not quite so tall, but near two stone heavier—and quite muscular in his general physique."

The Lord Chief Justice then dismissed him with thanks and invited Mr. Mobley to call his second witness. That was done quickly enough, as the prisoner summoned Sir John Fielding. He appeared so quickly that I suspected he had been listening at the door to the courtroom. He was helped by a bailiff, who guided him to the witness stand by holding him at the elbow; Sir John disliked that manner of conveyance, as I well knew, yet he submitted to it with noble forbearance.

"Why, this is indeed a surprise, Sir John," said Lord Mansfield. "I cannot recall you ever before appearing as a witness. Do you do so willingly?"

"Most willingly, my lord. I believe I have something of some importance to contribute."

"Quite interesting. You may proceed with your defense, Mr. Mobley."

Sir John had come for one purpose and one purpose only:

to acquaint the jury with the supposed suicide eight years past of Herbert Mudge in the same hotel. He suggested it certainly might have been murder; in fact, he had felt at the time it must have been, yet he could neither prove murder from physical evidence, nor from his repeated interrogations of the man he held most suspect, Mr. Mudge's traveling companion, Elijah Elison. He invited all to note the similarity of that name to Elijah Bolton and Eli Bolt. "These are, as I have discovered," said Sir John, "but three names for the same man. I know not which indeed was the correct name. Perhaps none of them was. I have settled upon Eli Bolt because that is how he was identified to me by one who knew him years ago in the colonies. It was also how Mr. Mobley came to know him first in the colony of Maryland. The name Elijah Bolton, which he bore at the time of his death, was simply an invention to carry him safe, perhaps past my notice, in and around England."

Then, at some length, he compared the "suicide" of Herbert Mudge with what had evidently been planned for Percival Mobley. He noted that in both instances a woven leather rope was used; that on the more recent occasion Eli Bolt had entered the room illegally and secretly, as eight years before he must have done. On and on Sir John did go, drawing parallels, making comparisons, and concluding: "Finally, there is good reason to believe that eight years ago, Sir Patrick Spenser was involved with Eli Bolt in a manner similar to his recent relation. Ah, but there perhaps I go too far, for while I accept the role he played in the false claim for the Laningham title, I can only speculate on the part he may have played eight years earlier."

Mr. Mobley, who had aided Sir John in his testimony by prompting with questions each time the magistrate showed any signs of slowing down, said that he had but one more question to put to him.

"Oh? And what is that?" asked Sir John, seeming a bit surprised.

"Do you accept as truthful what I put forward in my statement?"

"By and large, I do, yes. Certainly, I accept your account of the death of the man we shall call Eli Bolt—and it is for that you have come to be tried in this court."

"Dare I ask what it is you reject?"

"I reject none of it, though I am less eager to accept your picture of yourself as a completely unwilling participant in the Laningham conspiracy. But as I say, it is not for that you are here today. No law was broken."

Percival Mobley stood awkwardly before the court, clearly wishing to justify himself, yet knowing he had not the opportunity to do so. For near a minute he seemed on the verge of saying something pertinent. But, at last, all that came out was this: "That is all, Sir John. You may step down. And, my lord, that concludes my testimony."

The final argument of the prosecution, indifferently stated as it was, is not worth noting here; nor, for that matter, is the last word from Mr. Mobley. Nevertheless, in his summing-up, Lord Mansfield took an approach which was for him eccentric—indeed, one might even say, unique—for he was, as every Londoner with criminal propensities knew, a "hanging judge"; he seemed almost to take pleasure in assigning the death penalty. On this occasion, however, the Lord Chief Justice put forth what amounted to a plea for mercy, yet it was framed in terms perfectly logical and perfectly legal.

He called the jury's attention to the last words of the statement presented in court by the prisoner. (I quoted them near verbatim from Mr. Mobley.) "It was not my intention to kill Mr. Bolt. I wished only to end *his* attempt to kill *me*." Thus he read it out to the jurors. Then did he comment upon it as follows:

"Such an assertion as this would ordinarily constitute a plea for a finding of manslaughter—that is, death unintended. Yet it strikes me, having read and now heard the prisoner's statement and heard the testimony of his distinguished witnesses, that we have the opportunity here to go even further. First of all, it cannot be murder, for Mr. Mobley was not the aggressor. Bolt, the deceased, lay in wait for him. He had no other reason to be in the room but to do harm to Mobley. When his first attempt failed, he did persist in his attempt not merely to do grievous bodily harm to the prisoner but to kill him. Yet he failed in that, too, because, though Mr. Mobley did not intend it so, he killed his adversary.

"It is very seldom that a true finding of 'killing, no murder, by reason of self-defense' can be justified. Alas, all too often the aggressor will press his advantage and kill his victim before the victim has a chance to defend himself. In this instance, that did not happen. Though the two, aggressor and victim, were fairly well matched in size, the victim fought back and saved himself. Perhaps it was that a man fights harder when he realizes, as Mr. Mobley did, that he was fighting for his life. And so he saved his life, though not without sustaining injuries of his own. You saw him limp to the dock. You see the bandage wrapped Mussulman-style about his head, the plaster on his ear and jaw. Eli Bolt, if that be his name, was a powerful adversary—yet he, and not the prisoner, died in the struggle. And what did Mr. Mobley do when he saw that he had killed the man who attacked him? He went straightaway to the Bow Street Court, seeking the magistrate, to surrender himself and make a statement, because in his mind and in his heart he knew that he had not committed murder but only defended himself. I tend to believe that this is one of those rare occasions when a finding of self-defense is justified. Yet I respect you, the members of the jury, far too much to direct you to find according to my belief. I send you off to your deliberations confident that you will find your way there on your own."

And so the jury went off to deliberate, and I turned to young Archibald Talley to discuss this singular case. I found him in the process of taking his leave of the court.

"What then?" said I to him. "Going so soon?" (Lord Mansfield had barely cleared the door.)

"I must," said he. "My uncle has to hear of this. My God! The Solicitor-General! There will be a terrible scandal!"

And with that, he rushed off. Nor was he the only one to make a swift departure. When I looked around me, I saw that the journalists who had sat in the row ahead of me were now all gone, unwilling to wait for the finding of the jury. For them, as with Mr. Talley, the true significance of these proceedings was not Mr. Mobley's fate, but, rather, the shadow of scandal that now fell upon one of power at court.

I thought to walk about a bit and loosen up, having sat in an attitude of strict attention for some time. But I had done no more than get to my feet, when all were bidden to rise the return of judge, prisoner, and jury. I had never known a jury to take so short a time to return with a verdict. One of them stood, and Lord Mansfield asked him how they had found.

"We find Percival Mobley, defendant, not guilty of 'no murder by reason of self-defense.' And no manslaughter, neither. And we hope we got the words right."

"The words are right enough. The jury is dismissed with our thanks." He turned to the dock. "Percival Mobley, you are free to go. My advice to you is to return to the North American colonies. There are those in England who would want to take revenge upon you for certain revelations made in your statement."

"I shall do that, my lord."

Then did the Lord Chief Justice slam down his gavel and end that day's session of the court. As soon as he himself had disappeared, a whole section of those seated in the rows nearest the front went quite mad with joy. They ran up to the dock and pulled him to them. They, I later learned, were friends and family from Southwark. Sir John had got word to them of the trial, and a goodly number had come across the river to give support. The courtroom, in fact, was in a fair transport of joy—except for one man whom I saw slipping out one of the back doors of the courtroom. He was none other than Sir Patrick Spenser. His face was set so dark, his expression so angry, that I believe that if he had been armed, he would have walked up to Mr. Mobley and shot him down on the spot, consequences be damned.

"Well, Jeremy, are you ready to return to Bow Street? I feel that a walk is in order, don't you?"

It was Sir John, of course. He was cheered by the outcome

of the trial, of course. Yet, most of all, he seemed relieved that this matter of the Laningham claimant was now over and done. All this I gathered in the course of our amble back to Number 4 Bow Street. I told him as we set out that I had many questions for him. He replied that he feared they would have to wait.

"Give me a day or two," said he, "that I may cleanse myself of this ugly business."

As it happened, it was near a week before he was ready to speak freely of the matter. After dinner one night, I managed to entice him into such a discussion with news I had just heard from Mr. Baker below. I found Sir John where I expected to find him—in that small room between the bedrooms which he called his study. He was settled there behind his desk, sitting in the dark, when I knocked upon the open door. He invited me in.

"I thought you would be interested to know," I said to him, "that I had just heard that Sir Patrick Spenser has been forcibly retired from his post as Solicitor-General."

"And who replaces him?"

"A Sir Thomas Dexter."

"Another courtier—no better, no worse."

"Sir John," said I, "you indicated after the trial that you might answer a question or two about the matter once you had had a few days' rest from it."

"Yes, I did."

"Well, a few days have passed."

"So they have. You may ask me what you like. I shall try to answer."

There was one question I had been saving for this occasion. I hoped that I might phrase it in such a way as to make it interesting to him. If he were interested, he gave interesting answers in return.

"You will recall, sir, that when you gave testimony in behalf of Mr. Mobley during his trial, all went well until the very end."

"You're right, indeed you are."

"Then he put a question to you—something on the order of 'Do you believe what I said in my statement?' "

"Yes, I recall."

"Then you told him that by and large you accepted it—for instance, you accepted all that had to do with the death of Eli Bolt. But then, because he asked, you said that you were less willing to accept him as an unwilling participant in the Laningham conspiracy. Now, during all that, something went wrong between you. He seemed quite shocked at what you had said. Could you explain that to me?"

"That I shall do gladly, for therein lies a good lawyerly lesson for you. You were sent away the day before the trial, when Lord Mansfield and I began to work with Mr. Mobley to help him prepare his defense."

"Oh, I remember. I felt quite like a child who had been sent out of the room so the adults might speak of adult matters."

"Well, I offered to testify," said Sir John. "My testimony and the statement he read out in court were the essence of his defense. He and I drilled his interrogation of me for two hours or more. You might say we prepared a script. I knew what he would ask and when he would ask it. Mobley was something of an actor. He played the role of a lawyer during the trial, reading the statement from the dock, and then questioning me according to the script we had worked out between us. An actor needs a script. But more often than not—or so I hear from Mr. Garrick—they like to stray from it, to improvise a little. Those questions that you noticed at the end of his interrogation were his improvisations, his deviations from the script we had prepared. When he did not get from me the answers that he expected or hoped he would get, then he was quite disappointed. But I could not lie for the fellow."

"Even crestfallen as he was."

"Yes, well, the lesson for you as a lawyer in all this is that you must drill your witnesses very well, so well that you know the answer to every question you ask. Or to put it as a principle of interrogation: Never ask a question to which you do not know in advance the answer you will receive."

"I shall remember that, sir."

"See that you do."

There was silence between us for a short time. Sir John liked the silence better than I did. I wished to coax more from him. Perhaps, I thought, this question might capture his interest: "Sir John, I understand well enough what happened involving Sir Patrick Spenser in the false claim for the Laningham title and estate, but it is not clear to me what happened eight years ago. I accept it that Bolt did then murder the man in the Globe and Anchor—but why? I accept it also that Sir Patrick financed the expedition described by Paltrow in his Journal, but what was the purpose of the expedition? The discovery of gold? If so, was gold discovered? I have heard of no such finding in our North American colonies."

"Nor are you likely to until Sir Patrick gains title to the land where the gold may be dug from the ground. I've made inquiries. He has made a discreet offer, yet perhaps not sufficiently discreet, for the proprietors have been set wondering what is in or on that mountainous land to interest one such as Sir Patrick."

"Gold was the cause of all this?"

"Oh, not all of it, I suppose. Greed for land and higher position also played a part in this later conspiracy. It is remarkable to me, Jeremy, how little content some men are with what they have been given—and by that I mean men who have been given a great deal. In truth, it seems that with some, the more they have, the less satisfied they are—indeed, the more they want."

I pondered upon that, thinking also of Lawrence Paltrow and the eagerness for more that he expressed to his mother in one of his letters: "We deserve better," said he to her.

"This may also have been the case with Lawrence Paltrow."

"Certainly it was."

"What do you suppose happened to him?" I wondered it aloud.

"I should think you would have guessed," said Sir John.

"Well, I don't think he drowned in a river crossing as Mr. Mobley was told. I believe it likely that he died somewhere out in the wilderness and probably at the hand of Eli Bolt."

"You have it partly right, in any case." He paused a moment to think how best he might present this. "Do you recall our discussion concerning aliases? I said that more often than not they are created from the name given at birth. Eli Bolt became Elijah Bolton, and, earlier, Elijah Elison. Well, there are some who do it differently. They dig back in their family history, not necessarily very far, to choose a name. Tell me, Jeremy, does the name Mudge mean anything to you?"

"Well, I recall from the 'Unresolved' file that it was the name of the man hanged in his room in the Globe and Anchor, almost certainly murdered by Bolt. Do you mean that he . . . ?"

"Mudge was also the family name of his mother. That information was on her death certificate from Bath and was given us by Lord Mansfield."

"I'm afraid I didn't notice."

"You must listen more carefully. Let nothing be lost on you."

"But why was Lawrence Paltrow murdered? Was it to keep secret the location of the site where gold might be dug?"

"No, as I have worked it out, young Mr. Paltrow hoped by deception to claim the gold for himself. This speculation of mine is based on information I acquired in Oxford when you were not present. But as I see it, he kept a written record of the journey in his Journal—a *written* record, by the bye, because Bolt was almost certainly illiterate but as a man of the frontier could read drawn maps with the best of them. That Journal he left with his mother.

"There was, and no doubt still is, gold to be mined at that site he described in his Journal. He was sent over to confirm this, gather samples, give an estimate of the yield, and so on—the sort of thing that one with a background in natural science such as he had could do very well. He had, as a matter of fact, been recommended for this work to Sir Patrick Spenser by Professor Fowler of Merton College, Oxford. Sir Patrick financed Paltrow's trip to America, as well as the expedition to the site discovered by Bolt the year previous. Paltrow was offered no partnership in the enterprise, I'll wager—simply hired to do the task. He began very early to devise a plan whereby he might eventually come away with all that Sir Patrick sought. In pursuit of this, he acquired samples of iron pyrites, popularly known as fool's gold. These he substituted for the gold ore samples they had mined in—where was it?—the colony of Georgia. With Sir Patrick he took them to Professor Fowler for confirmation of the discovery. Professor Fowler saw that what Paltrow offered him was nothing more or less than iron pyrites, of no value whatever, and he was quick to tell them so. Paltrow did not mind being disgraced in the eyes of his teacher if he might in some way gain control of this great prize.

"Sir Patrick must indeed have been furious, yet there was little he could do. It was simple ignorance that had led him to this end. Yet he must have become suspicious—perhaps when he heard from Bolt some word of the Journal. Perhaps he demanded to see it, and Paltrow could not produce it, for he had by that time deposited the Journal with his mother and told her something of his plan. Or perhaps Bolt had searched Paltrow's room at the Globe and Anchor and found the samples of true gold brought back from America. Whatever the circumstances leading up to it, Sir Patrick's suspicion was sufficient for him to order the murder of young Paltrow by Eli Bolt. I, knowing none of this, was called in to investigate the supposed suicide of Herbert Mudge. Where he found the name Herbert, I've no idea. Perhaps it was his maternal grandfather's name. In any case, I could prove nothing other than suicide. And because he had been traveling under an alias—part of the secrecy Sir Patrick demanded, no doubt—the Widow Paltrow never knew that her son was dead. That was why she proved such an easy prey to the claimant and asked him—her last words to him—where the gold was."

"And that," said I, "is what happened to Lawrence Paltrow."

"That is what I *think* happened to him—mere speculation which cannot be proven."

"A case could not be made against Sir Patrick Spenser?"

"Certainly not. He is the only survivor." A smile crept across Sir John's face. "But a man as greedy and unprincipled as he is sure to try another scheme soon. We shall keep an eye on him. In the meantime, I'd like you, Jeremy, to write an addendum to that case of Herbert Mudge's 'suicide,' setting things right and tying it to Bolt. Leave out my speculations. We will have enough then, that we may take it from the 'Unresolved' file and put it where it properly belongs."